As Cole looked do⌐ knew of a surety she wa⌐ in a place he'd thought l⌐

A younger man wearing a saucy grin approached Miss Palmer. "Evening, Lissie. Did you save me a dance?"

Cole's initial irritation for the man's cheekiness faded to puzzlement. He knew him from somewhere. A vague unease arose.

When the young man's gaze moved to Cole, he paled visibly. "You!"

Miss Palmer gasped. "Robert Palmer, where are your manners?"

Of course. Robert Palmer. From London. Cold dread trickled across his heart as he considered the ramifications.

Palmer took her arm. "We're leaving."

"Now see here—" Cole began, but Palmer pinned him with a dangerous glare.

"Stay away from my cousin."

"Your cousin?" Cole looked from him to Miss Palmer and understanding dawned. He cursed under his breath. He hadn't been aware Armand Palmer had a sister. Not that he'd bothered to find out. The ramifications he'd considered a moment ago took a more serious turn.

Miss Palmer sent Cole a look of apology and turned to her cousin. "Robert, explain yourself."

In a cold sweat, Cole waited for her condemning stare.

Palmer trembled in rage. He spoke quietly, but Cole heard every word. "He's the scoundrel who shot your twin."

The Stranger She Married

by

Donna Hatch

The Stranger She Married

COPYRIGHT © 2008 by Donna Hatch

Contact Information: info@thewildrosepress.com

Cover Art by *The Wild Rose Press*

The Wild Rose Press
PO Box 708
Adams Basin, NY 14410-0706
Visit us at www.thewildrosepress.com

Publishing History
First English Tea Rose Edition, 2008
Print ISBN 1-60154-334-4

Published in the United States of America

Dedication

To Cindy Hatch and Liz Roehr, and the rest of my family who have always been my best cheerleaders; Jennifer Griffith, for gentle suggestions, Rhonda Woodward for her tough love critique that forced me deeper into research, Jennifer Ashley for her patience, encouragement, and help, and all my Desert Rose RWA friends who mentored me along. Also to Joyce DiPastena, Anna Arnett and Lorna Hale, and all my sister writers at ANWA. A very special thank you to all the Beau Monders who continue to unselfishly impart all their knowledge of the magical and mysterious Regency Era. But most of all, to my husband, who is the inspiration for my heroes, and who continues to prove that there really is a happily ever after.

Acknowledgements

Thanks especially to my readers. I hope you enjoy The Stranger She Married. Please stop by www.donnahatch.net to enter my monthly contests, view deleted scenes and sneak peeks, and to join the private e-mail list to receive an announcement when my next books will be released.

CHAPTER 1

England, 1818

Alicia Palmer stepped down from the coach with
all the enthusiasm of a condemned prisoner about to
meet the executioner. She glanced up at the starry
summer sky, seeking courage. Liveried servants
lined the front steps like guards to the gallows. All
she needed was a crowd with an appetite for the
macabre; a role, no doubt that the other guests could
fill.

"Isn't this exciting?" Elizabeth squeezed Alicia's
arm as they mounted the front steps of the Sinclair's
country manor. Alicia's younger friend still retained
her debutante excitement from her first Season in
London, from which she'd just returned home, and
she shone in anticipation.

Alicia managed a smile for her friend's sake. "It
will be good to dance again."

"Of course it will, Alicia dear." Elizabeth's
mother, Mrs. Hancock, put a comforting arm around
her. "A young lady such as you should be enjoying
herself, not sequestered away at home." Mrs.
Hancock's perfume embraced her, a blend of roses
and sweet spices. The familiar fragrance buoyed
Alicia as much as the dear lady's touch.

Light spilled out of the open doorway guiding
them inside the manor as footmen hurried to assist
them. Alicia steeled her resolve and forced her feet
to keep moving forward when she wanted to flee.
She smoothed her gown. Shedding her mourning
attire for a ball gown had seemed irreverent, but

Uncle Willard had insisted she attend.

"I haven't set foot on a dance floor in over a year."

Mrs. Hancock gave her a motherly smile. "You always comport yourself beautifully, dear girl. You have nothing to fear."

Despite Mrs. Hancock's reassurances, Alicia's apprehension grew at the thought of subjecting herself to the further inspection of men who only viewed her as a piece of jewelry to be purchased.

Very expensive jewelry, without all the glitter.

Alicia paused in the great hall between her companions. Formal balls occurred less frequently during the summer than the London Season. Receiving the invitation from the Sinclairs had come as a surprise. Alicia was painfully aware that her Uncle Willard and Cousin Robert's behavior, and financial misfortunes, had become the subject of gossip all over the midlands. Knowing Catherine Sinclair, such gossip should have excluded Alicia from this social event. She wondered why she had been invited at all. Part of her apprehension sprang from the suspicion that Catherine Sinclair might use Alicia's misfortunes as a stone to whet her wit upon.

While an attendant took their wraps, Alicia's gaze traveled upward. Crystal chandeliers and sconces hung from the ceiling and tastefully papered walls of Lord Sinclair's residence. Flower garlands scented the room and adorned the wide marble hall where portraits of the current lord's proud ancestors hung between the carved columns.

A liveried footman led them into a nearby room where they could make final adjustments before entering the ballroom. Looking into a gilded mirror, Alicia smoothed her hair, wishing it were a prettier color. At least its length and thickness created a coil large enough to cover the back of her head, but next to Elizabeth's china doll beauty, Alicia felt dowdier than ever. She was neither tiny nor voluptuous. Brown eyes, regular features, and light brown hair created the perfect wallflower. Only the kindness of gentlemen had spared her such a fate during her one Season in London.

The mirror heartlessly assured her that her looks had not miraculously improved. The only thing to recommend her was her ball gown, which was without compare. Uncle Willard had apparently bullied the modiste into extending him the needed credit so Alicia could present herself well to any interested gentlemen in attendance. He would do anything to have her make an acceptable match. Acceptable, meaning wealthy. Her uncle seemed to have few other requirements for a worthy husband.

"We must gain an introduction to Mr. and Mrs. Fitzpatrick's nephew, Lord Amesbury," Mrs. Hancock said as she changed into her dancing slippers.

Elizabeth nodded, her blond curls bobbing. "I hear he's kept to himself since his arrival, but that he's terribly handsome."

Mrs. Hancock agreed. "He's a viscount of no small means and the eldest son of the highly respected Earl Tarrington. Lady Sinclair told me he is coming tonight, the first invitation he's accepted since he arrived here." She eyed them critically. "You both look lovely. Modest, neat and becoming. Come, ladies."

After donning her dancing slippers, Alicia squared her shoulders and left the safety of the room. They passed a three-story staircase with intricately carved railings, and continued to the end of the great hall. Ahead stood the grand stairway leading up to the ballroom. Music and laughter floated through the ballroom doors as they climbed the stairs. Yet to Alicia, the joyous notes of the music sounded like a death knell.

3

Forcing her hands to remain still, Alicia waited on the landing with head high until the major domo announced them. Then, with more grace and dignity than she felt, she glided down the stairs behind the Hancock ladies to the ballroom below.

Alicia thought it ostentatious of the Sinclairs to have their guests first climb, and then descend a stairway to reach the ballroom, but a few of the grander homes had been constructed in such a manner. However, she also knew how much the gentry and nobility loved a grand entrance, and descending a stairway provided a perfect opportunity to parade one's finery or beauty.

The evening's host and hostess stood below the staircase next to their daughter, Miss Catherine Sinclair.

"Mrs. Hancock, always a pleasure. Elizabeth, welcome. And Alicia, how well you look this evening," said Catherine in a practiced, contralto voice designed to weaken the knees of any male within earshot.

Alicia smiled woodenly. Catherine, of course, looked glorious. She'd been beautiful even as a child. Her meticulously arranged black hair shimmered in lustrous waves, and Alicia had no doubt that Catherine's gown epitomized the latest fashion. Rubies and diamonds sparkled at her throat and ears, emphasizing Alicia's obvious lack of adornment. The Palmer family jewels had been sold months ago to cover Uncle Willard's most pressing debts. Alicia's only remaining piece of jewelry was the simple gold locket she seldom removed.

Finding her voice, Alicia inclined her head. "Thank you, Catherine. What a beautiful gown." She hoped she sounded more gracious than she felt.

"How kind." Catherine feigned modesty with believable skill.

Her parents, Lord and Lady Sinclair, smiled and

greeted them with perfect civility. Yet, an instant before Lord Sinclair bowed over her hand, she caught the unmistakable glint of ridicule in his eyes. Alicia glanced at Lady Sinclair and saw the same mockery. Alicia faltered. Then she set her jaw.

She had lost everything; her parents, her twin brother, her fortune, but she would not lose her dignity. Raising her head as if completely unaware of their scorn, she dredged up a smile she hoped would not appear sickly.

"I must apologize on behalf of my Uncle Willard and my Cousin Robert. They were unable to attend due to business." Fortunately, her voice sounded steady.

Alicia entertained no delusions of her uncle's business involving anything more noble than gambling or other unscrupulous transactions. Her cousin Robert, no doubt, either lay in a drunken stupor or in the bed of some nobleman's wife. Though they had once been close, Armand's death had affected Robert deeply and Alicia hardly knew him anymore.

"Thank you for coming, Miss Palmer," Lady Sinclair said.

Alicia executed a curtsy that would have pleased *Maman* and swept into the ballroom with her head held high, leaving Elizabeth and Mrs. Hancock to converse with the Sinclairs.

Enormous murals, rivaling the works of Michelangelo, adorned the walls and the soaring ceiling. Tear drop crystals hung from the chandeliers, showering a rainbow of colors over the room.

Alicia skirted the edge of the dance floor, looking for a place to sit where she would remain unnoticed. Behind her, the dowagers disparaged everyone's gowns and behavior. She knew they would find something to criticize about her the moment she moved out of earshot.

More guests arrived steadily until the room grew quite crowded. To her relief, she did not see any of the men Uncle Willard demanded she consider as a husband. Most of them were far too old to attend such a function, but no doubt some would arrive later that evening.

It would be futile to resist them all; one of them would inevitably be her husband. Few gentlemen desired a plain orphan with only a small plot of land for a dowry. Alicia's only power in this predicament was to choose whom she thought she could bear to wed among the undesirable men interested enough to pay Uncle Willard's debts for her hand.

Elizabeth and Mrs. Hancock found her a moment later. "That must be him." Excitement laced Mrs. Hancock's voice. "The viscount. Cole Amesbury."

Cole. What an unusual name. It invoked an image of dark elegance.

A silver-haired gentleman and a lady wearing a turban adorned with feathers descended the stairs. Although Alicia did not know them well, over the years she had developed a fondness for the gregarious Mr. Fitzpatrick and his wife, the outspoken, but kind, Mrs. Fitzpatrick.

Behind the Fitzpatricks strode a man who captured her attention.

The immaculate and expertly tailored clothing he wore exuded wealth, tastefully elegant without appearing overly concerned with fashion. Tanned from the sun, he made the other men in the room appear pale and ailing. His commanding, arrogant air promised he could be nothing less than a peer of the realm. Combined with the strong, square planes of his patrician face, and rich dark hair, he created a devastatingly handsome image.

A calculating edge colored Catherine's voice.

"Welcome, Mr. and Mrs. Fitzpatrick."

"Thank you," replied Mr. Fitzpatrick. "Please allow me to introduce you to my nephew, Lord Amesbury."

In his black superfine, Lord Amesbury's tall, broad-shouldered frame mocked the physiques of every other gentleman present. He inclined his head politely, but with an air of detachment that extended beyond the fashionable, urbane boredom so many pinks of the *ton* attempted to emulate.

"I am delighted to make your acquaintance, Lord Amesbury," Catherine purred.

Before Alicia heard the viscount's reply, another voice drew her attention. "Miss Palmer, I hoped you would be here." That thin, nasally voice always set her teeth on edge.

In dismay, she turned from the paragon of masculinity to his perfect opposite. "Colonel Westin."

She was wrong; at least one of her unwanted suitors had indeed come tonight. The colonel always stood too close and she felt smothered in his presence. Alicia took a step back and opened her fan in a futile attempt to form a protective barrier between herself and the colonel.

"I enjoyed our visit last week, Miss Palmer. I look forward to another very soon." Colonel Westin eyed Alicia much as a man might evaluate horseflesh at an auction.

She had no intention of spending another moment with the colonel, a sour, disagreeable old man. She couldn't imagine him as a heroic cavalry leader. But then, forty years ago, he might have been a formidable officer. He certainly bullied his servants with the authority of a general.

Alicia's gaze strayed back to the staircase. She started. Lord Amesbury stared directly at her with an intensity that sent a tremor through her stomach. His masculine beauty was almost painful, like looking at a handful of diamonds in the bright sunlight. Even at this distance, she could see the sharp brilliance of his blue eyes. As he moved through the crush, others gave away. His predatory grace mimicked that of a great cat, each movement deliberate, powerful, athletic, as if he held a vast reservoir of strength that lurked, coiled, ready to strike. Those piercing sapphire eyes remained fixed upon her with unnerving intensity.

Colonel Westin's voice interrupted her thoughts. "I don't dance, but I hope you'll honor me with a walk in the gardens later this evening." His condescending tone suggested that she should be the one honored by his request, rather than he.

The Viscount Amesbury drew her gaze again. He now stood in a circle of guests as his aunt and uncle introduced him. His mouth twitched as if he suppressed a wry smile during the introductions. A dark eyebrow lifted slightly, suggesting that he found them mildly entertaining, but secretly laughed at them all.

"Miss Palmer. You are not attending me." The colonel's tone grew irritated.

And Uncle Willard certainly would not approve of Alicia irritating any of her suitors, regardless of her feelings for them. Her entire family counted on her to marry well. And soon, or they all faced debtor's prison.

Oh, how had she become so trapped? The room became too warm, the crowd too close. She cast about for an avenue of escape and only then realized that Elizabeth and Mrs. Hancock were no longer with her.

Biting back an impolite response, Alicia offered what she hoped would be an apologetic smile. "Forgive me, Colonel." She nearly choked on the words. "I would be pleased to take a turn about the garden with you. Appropriately chaperoned, of course. Would you excuse me, please? I believe Mrs. Hancock wants me."

The Colonel glared at her through his monocle.

Forcing herself to not run, Alicia curtseyed and wound her way through the revelers in search of Mrs. Hancock and Elizabeth. She had to remind herself to breathe. She had no desire to marry for money. She wanted to marry for love. Her parents had been in love; shouldn't she be granted the same privilege?

But, no. One well-placed bullet ripped from her everything she held dear.

Since the day Uncle Willard inherited her family estate, he stumbled through one business loss after another, gambled away what he didn't lose in unprofitable investments, and continued to spend as if he had the wealth of Midas, until they were nearly destitute. And worse, she had to face it without her best friend, her twin brother, the other half of her soul.

Alicia found Elizabeth and Mrs. Hancock speaking with Mr. and Mrs. Fitzpatrick. Their stunning nephew, Lord Amesbury, stood with them. The light rippled across his rich, sable brown hair every time he turned his head. The chiseled planes of his face would be hard if he ever frowned, she decided, but his half-smile softened them. He seemed to view the evening's festivities as an amusing inconvenience, but made every attempt to be polite, if cool.

Mrs. Hancock beamed as Alicia reached her side. She put an arm around Alicia and brought her into their circle. "Miss Alicia Palmer, allow me to introduce Lord Amesbury."

Even more devastating up close, Lord Amesbury turned to her. His piercing blue eyes threatened the strength in her knees. Though taller than most ladies, Alicia still had to look up to meet his gaze. No other color existed in those eyes; no green or gray, only deep, dark blue, like the fathomless depths of the sea.

All the other men she had met lately, namely those her uncle insisted she consider for a husband, had taken careful note of her figure. But this gentleman only looked into her eyes. Very deeply.

Lord Amesbury inclined his head. "Miss Palmer." His resonant, bass voice touched her very soul.

Alicia met his frank gaze and felt a stirring she did not quite understand. Breathing became a conscious effort. Mrs. Hancock discreetly coughed, and Alicia realized she'd been locked in eye contact with the Viscount much longer than appropriate.

Unable to pull her eyes away, Alicia sank into a curtsey. "My Lord."

No longer merely polite, his smile broadened, warmed, transforming an already handsome face into a perfectly stunning visage. Sensuality radiated off him, not in a manner that left her feeling threatened, but in a way that left her breathless for more. More of what, she did not know. But she wanted to find out.

"Miss Palmer, may I have the next dance?"

Alicia blinked. She looked back at Elizabeth who smiled encouragingly. Mrs. Hancock also smiled and nodded, but a touch of disappointment tainted her approval, reminding Alicia the dear lady had hoped her daughter would attract the attention of the very eligible Lord Amesbury. That he'd singled out Alicia seemed a dream.

She squelched all hope that she might hold his interest. Surely only politeness motivated him to dance with the plainest girl first. He'd soon turn his attention to the beautiful ladies.

Finding her voice, Alicia replied, "Thank you, Lord Amesbury. I would be honored."

As the final notes of the current dance ended and the next began, Lord Amesbury offered his arm. She took it, an unfamiliar quiver beginning in her stomach. The art of dancing, she found as the set began, had not abandoned her as completely as her wits. The handsome viscount danced with athletic grace, his attention focused upon her. The warmth of his hand seeped through their kidskin gloves. He held her gently, firmly.

A playful glint touched his sapphire eyes. "I must warn you. Now that we've danced, my aunt will take it upon herself to ask you your opinion of me. She will most certainly interrogate me regarding you."

She met those probing eyes and felt her mouth curve. "Oh? Is she your self-proclaimed matchmaker?"

A wry smile touched his lips. "Of course. I'm thirty and not yet married. She feels it her duty to ensure I produce an heir before I'm too old. Despite my efforts, she persists."

Alicia nodded, her smile deepening at his indelicate statement. "That is a dilemma."

"Since you and I have only just met, it will be difficult to offer a fair assessment of your character. And if I say anything positive about you, she'll plan the wedding." His smile brightened, lighting up his stunning face.

Alicia missed her step. Even while dancing with the very handsome Duke of Suttenberg two Seasons ago, she had never felt such a keen attraction for a man. She was nearly twenty, for heaven's sake, not a missish debutante!

"Your aunt is a strong woman and a kind lady, my lord."

"I suppose she possesses a good heart deep, deep down inside, but be truthful; she's sharp-tongued and outspoken."

11

She laughed and then clapped her hand over her mouth. "My Lord! She might hear you."

He chuckled. "Fear not. We needle each other as frequently as possible. I say worse things to her face. I enjoy watching her squirm and plot a counter-attack."

That reminded her of the playful banter she shared with her cousin Robert. "I don't recall her ever mentioning you, my lord."

His smile turned self-deprecating. "I'm one of those relations no one mentions."

She laughed softly. "You're teasing me."

"No, but I dare not shock you with all of my misadventures."

"She has mentioned a nephew named Christian."

"My youngest brother. Everyone loves him." A touch of rancor colored his voice.

As the dance pattern repeated, Alicia saw Elizabeth dancing with a young gentleman, who smiled at her with an adoring gaze. "Will you honor my friend Elizabeth Hancock with a dance this evening, Lord Amesbury?"

He raised an eyebrow and his lips pulled in a sardonic smile. "On the rare occasion that I invite a lady to dance, she doesn't normally ask me to seek out another."

"I didn't mean it that way. I only meant that there are a number of ladies in attendance who love to dance, and there is a shortage of men. I hope you will seek out others. Especially those who do not have many partners."

Alicia always felt sorry for the wallflowers, herself having been one more frequently than she cared to admit. And the brief flash of envy in Mrs. Hancock's eyes when Lord Amesbury asked her instead of Elizabeth to dance tugged at her conscience.

He glanced briefly at Elizabeth before returning his focus to Alicia. "Miss Hancock does not appear to be at a loss at the moment."

His eyes fixed upon Alicia so intently that she saw images of him becoming her fairy-tale prince charming, battling her unwanted suitors, rescuing her family, and then carrying her off to his castle. Under his unusually direct gaze, she had the impression he knew her hopes and fears.

She swallowed. "Yes, Elizabeth is so lovely, she's seldom without admirers." A wistful tone crept into her voice.

His mouth twitched in amusement. She wondered if he found her truly diverting or if he merely thought her silly. But there did not appear to be anything scornful or mocking in his eyes.

"And you want me to have a look at your friend since I'm so eligible?"

"Ah ..." Those vivid eyes made thinking difficult.

"Do you find me more suitable for her than for you, Miss Palmer?"

Sickened that the handsome and charming viscount would see her for what she was, Alicia resigned herself to the truth and met his gaze fully. "She is more suitable for a man of your station than I, my lord."

His dark brows raised. "Why is that?"

She fortified her courage. "She's lovely and has a substantial dowry. I have little to offer a husband."

There. She had confessed. Now her dream of this handsome gentleman rescuing her from all the undesirable men she must consider would come to an end.

A playful smile hovered at the corners of his mouth. "You are a fortune hunter?"

How quickly he cut to the truth! She could almost hear the crashing noises her sweet fantasy made as it fell. Biting her lip, she controlled the moisture that threatened her eyes.

"I am."

CHAPTER 2

Lord Amesbury's expression became guarded. "And why would you reveal that to a man with a fortune instead of merely pursuing him to attain your goal?"

Alicia looked away. "Because I don't want any misunderstanding. And I would never stand in the way of Elizabeth's happiness."

"If I told you I were a reprobate, would you still wish me to consider your friend?"

Her eyes flew to his. Was he needling her again? "No. If you were anything less than a perfect gentleman, then I certainly would not wish you anywhere near her."

He chuckled. "Then I promise to not only dance with your friend, but to conduct myself as a perfect gentleman at all times in her presence."

Alicia eyed him sharply, but his carefully honed façade revealed nothing about him that he did not wish to show. "Are you laughing at me, my lord?"

"No, Miss Palmer." His smile grew gentle.

Gentleness? How many men possessed such a trait? Again, she had to fight tears of disappointment. She had found the man of her dreams, but he was as unattainable as a sunrise.

The dance set ended far too soon. As the viscount escorted her back toward Mrs. Hancock, Alicia heard Mrs. Hancock say as she leaned toward Elizabeth, "Don't worry, dearest. If you fail to secure Lord Amesbury, perhaps we can garner an introduction to one of his brothers. I hear the younger three are equally handsome. You could do worse than the younger son of one of the wealthiest and most respected earls in England."

Alicia's stomach twisted. She glanced up at Lord Amesbury beside her as they wormed their way through the crowd, but he showed no sign that he had overheard the conversation. She determined to draw Elizabeth and Mrs. Hancock aside and explain that she had no designs on Lord Amesbury. Or at least, no right to have any. Not only was he too far above her, she did not want to damage her friendship with Elizabeth.

Among the crowd, she spotted a thin man with silver hair and a widow's peak. The sight drove away all thoughts of Elizabeth. Her stomach dropped to her feet.

"Oh, no. Please excuse me, my lord."

"What is it, Miss Palmer?"

"I must not let him see me."

She fled through the throng toward the opened doors to the gardens. Outside, moonlight and Chinese lanterns illuminated the foliage. Couples strolled along the paths, their feet crunching on the gravel. She took a deep breath, the scent of roses and jasmine filling her senses, calming her fear. The stillness of the garden promised a welcome reprieve from the noise and crush in the ballroom.

Alicia crossed the balcony and descended the garden stairs to a wrought iron bench shadowed by an arbor. A nearby fountain trickled and splashed soothingly. A cool breeze stirred the tendrils around her face and neck. She took a calming breath. When she turned to glance back toward the doors, a broad, masculine chest blocked her view.

"Oh!" Surprised and alarmed, she took several steps back.

The dark form neared and the Chinese lantern overhead illuminated Lord Amesbury's face. "My apologies, Miss Palmer. I did not mean to startle you. From whom are you running?"

"Mr. Braxton."

Lord Amesbury glanced back. "No one is coming out, so you must have lost this Mr. Braxton. Why do you hide from him?"

She clasped her hands to still them. "My uncle would have me consider him as a suitor."

"One you do not wish to consider? Not wealthy enough?" A condemning tone entered his voice.

He must think her shallow and grasping. She was. That her uncle had forced her to such measures did not change who she had become. "He's very wealthy. That's the problem."

Lord Amesbury fixed a searching gaze upon her face as if he did not believe her.

"No one is coming outside?"

He looked toward the doors again. "Only a couple."

She released her nervous tension in a long exhale, still knowing her time in the garden only offered a brief escape from the men she wished to avoid. When had she become such a coward?

"I would be happy to act as your lookout, Miss Palmer, but I think you owe me an explanation."

She fingered the locket around her neck. "Something about him frightens me. He looks at me as if... as if he has impure thoughts about me."

"You must be afraid of every man alive," he replied dryly.

"Don't tease me, my lord. No honorable men have those thoughts. And no honorable men are interested in me. I'm merely a fortune hunter, remember?"

His expression thoughtful, he took a step closer. "I'm sorry to disillusion you, but even a saint would have impure thoughts about a beautiful woman."

With the light softly illuminating his handsome

face, she again became acutely aware of him on an elemental level. The breadth of his chest and the bulk of his arms stirred images of physical strength and virility. His gaze intensified as he studied her. At that moment, she would have traded anything to have a man such as he consider her beautiful.

"Then, it's fortunate for me that I am not a beautiful woman," she whispered breathlessly.

One of his brows twitched and he angled his head as he continued his penetrating gaze. She should step back. For that matter, she should not be out here with him alone, but the thought of risking a meeting with Mr. Braxton frightened her into remaining still. Or perhaps her motives centered around her present companion.

A lady and gentleman, their heads close together, laughed softly as they walked by without giving either Alicia or Lord Amesbury a glance.

That predatory image she'd first had when she saw him enter the ballroom returned. He seemed poised to pounce. Her heartbeat quickened, but not in fear. His hand reached toward her. Stepping back, she drew in a quick breath, alarmed at how alive she felt in his presence, and how badly she wanted to step closer to him, instead of safely, properly away.

His mouth twitched in amusement, and he seemed to consider. He withdrew his hand and merely indicated the locket she worried in her hand.

"Forgive me for alarming you. Your locket caught my eye. Someone special, I presume?"

She nodded.

"May I?"

She nodded again, releasing the locket, and tried to breathe as his dark head neared. She was a respectable young lady; she should not let him get so close. But somehow, she lacked the strength to resist his very forward, intimate action. He reached toward her as he had a moment ago. His fingers lightly touched her skin as he pick up the locket. She shivered at the touch, her senses reeling. He examined the tiny painting of *Maman* inside.

"My mother," she explained.

"She's lovely. I see the resemblance." He released the locket and it fell back into place.

A flash of memory assaulted her. She blinked, astonished at the intensity of emotion that swept over her. Time hadn't healed those wounds yet.

His hushed voice was almost a whisper. "Is she departed?"

"There was a...carriage accident..." Her voice cracked. Alicia put a hand over her mouth and squeezed her eyes closed. She should have died with them. An image burst into her mind of an overturned carriage, the thrashing legs of horses, and the bodies...

"Miss Palmer?" His voice sounded so concerned that it nearly undid her again.

His glove felt warm on her arm. Alicia firmly clamped down on her emotions and opened her eyes. Lord Amesbury stood only a heartbeat away, gentleness in his face.

"I recently lost my mother, too. Her loss is killing my father." For one brief moment, sorrow shadowed his eyes. Then he looked away and all expression closed over.

She wanted to step nearer and put her arms around him, comfort him, tell him she understood. Her grief faded and a new, more foreign, more adult desire slipped into its place.

She swallowed. "I should return, my lord. Mrs. Hancock will wonder where I have gone. Thank you for your assistance."

He fixed her with an unreadable stare. "Why do I have the feeling I'm being dismissed?"

Uncertain what to make of his comment, she searched his face for clues but only got lost in its chiseled angles and curves. "I only meant that there are probably others with whom you wish to dance."

"Because you are not eligible for a man like me?"

If only she were. If only he wanted her. She glanced in the direction of the doors, but a rosebush obscured her view. "Is a man there looking as if he seeks someone?"

Lord Amesbury's gaze moved to the open doors again. "No. You're safe for the moment."

Alicia took his offered arm, and they went up the garden steps toward the ballroom while music wafted through the open doors. She missed her step but hardly had time to cry out before his free arm encircled her waist, steadying her. Their eyes met. With his face so near hers, she saw his eyes focus on her lips. Her heart began thumping against her chest so hard, she wondered if he could hear it.

Acutely aware of his presence and the danger of behaving unseemly, she put her hand against him and pressed lightly. His chest felt hard under her hand. She drew in a deep breath but it failed to steady her. Instead, it filled her with the scent of soap, linen and citrus, a curious combination of raw masculinity and civilized gentleman. Underneath it all, another scent lingered, something uniquely *him*.

"Thank you." She laughed nervously but it sounded more like a hysterical giggle. She wanted to clap a hand over her face. "You appear to be making a habit of coming to my rescue. First my lookout, and now this."

A crooked grin quirked his mouth. "I hope I'm always present when you need rescuing."

Handsome, wealthy, and kind? This had to be a dream. Alicia had never believed in love at first sight, but she now understood what gave birth to the idea. If only she could transform into someone beautiful and poised, he might be interested in her.

What was she thinking? She came from the

impoverished gentry, without a respectable dowry, and her family was quickly losing acceptance in society. A man of Lord Amesbury's ilk would never wed someone like her.

And yet, his eyes held a gleam suggesting he might be interested in her at some level. That gleam should have frightened her, but instead only quickened her pulse. She pushed harder, and he released her. Slowly.

"We should go in separately so people will not think my behavior unseemly, my lord."

The curves of his mouth softened and the gleam deepened. "Fear not, my lady, I shall declare my honorable intentions as your protector to your vigilant chaperone."

"It's not only Mrs. Hancock that concerns me."

"Then I shall call out anyone who dares to question your purity."

Startled, she stared at him, but his features revealed nothing of his true thoughts. She hoped he merely jested about calling anyone out. Dueling, while illegal, happened far too frequently. It had been the cause of her brother's maiming which led to his untimely demise.

She missed her twin, Armand, with a pain that eclipsed even the loss of her parents. Some days, she might never have gotten out of bed were it not for her younger sister, Hannah.

Her troubles lay squarely upon the shoulders of that dueling fiend. If not for him, her twin brother would still be alive. Her parents might even still live. Then she would not be in this dilemma of needing to marry for money. Even when her father lived, they were not considered wealthy, but she had never been tempted to seek out a husband merely because of his riches. She had always despised fortune hunters, and to be forced into their class seemed a fate too humiliating to bear.

Donna Hatch

Aware of his probing stare, she moistened her lips. "Still, I must guard my reputation."

"In this crush, we will not be seen entering together, I assure you."

She glanced up at him, curious at his insistence. Could he be so chivalrous that he now saw himself as her protector? She smiled to herself. Her silly romantic notions had little to do with real people. Lord Amesbury, however kind he seemed, had no reason to protect a plain, penniless orphan. Still, walking on his arm gave her the absurd urge to preen. He escorted her to Mrs. Hancock who sat gossiping with the dowagers.

"There you are my dear, I nearly sent someone in search of you." When she noticed Lord Amesbury standing next to Alicia, her eyes narrowed in concern.

"Forgive us for alarming you, Mrs. Hancock," Lord Amesbury said smoothly. "Miss Palmer felt the need for some air and I insisted upon escorting her to protect her from any unsavory characters that may be about." The disarming smile he turned upon Mrs. Hancock would have transformed stone to mush.

Mrs. Hancock actually blushed. "Oh, of course. How kind, Lord Amesbury."

Alicia smothered a smile. Who would have thought this sensible lady would fall for the charms of a gentleman? But as she let her eyes rest upon him, she wondered how long she would retain a hold over her own sensibilities if he actually tempted her to discard them.

A young man with serious dark eyes approached and bowed, preventing further conversation with Lord Amesbury. "Miss Palmer."

She curtsied instinctively and then as she recognized him, a smile crept over her face. "Mr. Hawthorne? Is that you?"

He nodded. "It is. Only it's Captain Hawthorne, now."

"Oh, yes, I had heard. You have grown taller. How many years has it been?"

A faint grin curved his mouth. "I left for the peninsula eight years ago. You've grown up as well, and become quite lovely. May I have the honor of the next dance?"

Alicia accepted, knowing his flattery as only a polite gesture. She introduced him to Lord Amesbury, and then smiled back up at Mr. Hawthorne. He had grown broader and more handsome, but he'd always had those heavily-lashed, dark eyes. Something about him made her think of her father. Memories of her family, and the longing for them, dimmed her pleasure.

With a will, she pushed them aside and looked back up at Captain Hawthorne. "How is your father?"

His face closed. "Not well, I am afraid."

"I'm sorry to hear that. He and my father were friends years ago I believe, although I never knew him well. Please give him my best."

A strange light entered his dark eyes that gave her the insane desire to rub her arms.

"Yes," he replied slowly. "I shall."

Elizabeth hurried to her on Mr. Wallace's arm. "Alicia, Lord Sinclair has offered to take a group of us on a tour of his gallery. Will you come with us? Captain Hawthorne and Lord Amesbury, you of course, are invited as well."

"I've seen it, and I'm afraid I don't have much of an eye for art." Captain Hawthorne bowed to Alicia. "I shall await your return, Miss Palmer."

Alicia nodded. "Of course, Captain Hawthorne." She turned to Lord Amesbury. "Lord Sinclair's gallery is rather extensive, I hear."

Lord Amesbury smiled again. Alicia had never

23

met anyone who smiled so easily, or with such warmth. Odd, but moments ago, she'd had the distinct impression he secretly laughed at everyone. Now he seemed genuinely warm. Perhaps her first impression had been wrong.

"Then I would be remiss if I failed to view it," Lord Amesbury replied graciously.

On his arm again, and trying to smother the unreasonable joy that honor elicited, Alicia followed Elizabeth and Mr. Wallace to a group forming at the edge of the ballroom. She caught sight of Colonel Westin, but fortunately, he did not appear to notice her. She maneuvered herself so that Lord Amesbury shielded her from the Colonel's view.

Her uncle hoped she would choose either Colonel Westin or Mr. Braxton for a husband. In return for marriage to Alicia, both had agreed to pay off Willard's debts and provide a fresh start for the Palmers. Of the two, the whining retired Colonel Westin seemed a better choice than Mr. Braxton, a man who simply terrified her. She looked up at Lord Amesbury. If only...

She sighed. Such wishing would lead nowhere but disappointment.

"I believe everyone who is interested in seeing the gallery is present," Lord Sinclair announced. "If you will all follow me."

Their host led the group into the gallery. A marble floor mirrored expansive ceilings. The walls were painted a deep red to showcase the art. Gilded, carved molding lined the soaring ceilings. Gas lamplight revealed the most breathtaking works of art Alicia had ever seen.

"Oh, Ali, look, isn't this exquisite?" Elizabeth pointed out the nearest statue and pulled on Alicia's hand until she was obliged to release her hold on her escort.

As Lord Sinclair informed the crowd about some

of the more impressive pieces, Alicia spotted Mr. Braxton near the front of the group. Her heart sank. Would she spend the entire evening evading undesirable men?

Catherine Sinclair appeared next to them and smiled up at the viscount. "Lord Amesbury. How delightful that you've joined us. I understand your brother is something of an artist, so you must have a great eye for art as well. I'd appreciate your opinion on our latest acquisition." With a seductive smile, she urged him forward. "It's this one, my lord."

Out of the corner of her eye, Alicia saw Lord Amesbury glance back at her, but she pretended to be engrossed in a nearby painting.

It was inevitable. No man would ever look at her for long with Elizabeth and Catherine nearby. She linked her arm through Elizabeth's and hoped her disappointment did not reveal itself.

"I'll return shortly, Miss Palmer," he whispered.

Nodding dismissively without looking at him, she hushed the cry in her heart as Lord Amesbury left with the radiant Catherine.

She could not see Mr. Braxton at the moment, but did not dare remain and risk an encounter. She needed to escape. Alicia remained standing in place while the crowd trickled past her toward the next display. Perhaps she could go back out the door they came in. No, it was too far. She could be spotted. Another door just on the other side of the nearest marble column might be a better choice. She glanced back to the art enthusiasts, but only saw Catherine with her arm through Lord Amesbury's. Curse the man, he appeared to be enjoying her company.

As Lord Sinclair continued his steady stream of history and explanation, Alicia looked back at the door. Each time the crowd moved forward to admire another piece of art, Alicia held back a bit more until she stood at the far edge of the group.

When she was certain no one would notice her missing, she stepped toward the column. The door to freedom lay just beyond.

"Miss Palmer, how considerate of you to leave the others." Mr. Braxton stepped out from behind the column, leering at her.

Alarm rose within her. How had he left the main body and made his way to her without her seeing him?

She spoke curtly. "I find that art no longer holds any appeal. I am returning to my chaperone. Good evening."

He stepped into her path. "How interesting. Art holds little appeal for me at the moment, as well."

With a pounding heart, Alicia backed away. Over Mr. Braxton's shoulder she saw the group leaving the room through a far door.

"Excuse me, Mr. Braxton."

Abandoning thoughts of fleeing through the nearest exit, she stepped around him to catch up to the others. He caught her arm and pulled her behind the column out of view.

Her heart leaped into her throat. "Let go of me. How dare you!"

He clamped a hand over her mouth and dragged her through the door she had hoped to use as an escape. Inside she found a small sitting room, poorly lit, and empty. Terror nearly choking her, she struggled against him and bit his hand.

Instead of becoming angry, he grinned wickedly, his eyes glittering underneath his bushy eyebrows. "How un-ladylike of you, Miss Palmer."

He kicked the door closed and pushed her against the wall, pinning her with his body and seizing her wrists. Though more than twice her age, he proved to be anything but weak and feeble.

"Release me at once or I shall scream." Her voice rose to a hysterical pitch.

"That would be a poor choice. What would people think of you if they caught you in such a compromising position?" He pushed her hands up over her head and held them both in one hand with surprising strength.

Alicia struggled against him, her terror growing. Mrs. Hancock thought she was with Elizabeth and Lord Amesbury. Elizabeth only had eyes for the art and Mr. Wallace. Viscount Amesbury had fallen for Catherine's charm and beauty.

She had no hope for rescue.

Mr. Braxton was right; if anyone saw her now, she'd be regarded as compromised. She would be forced to marry him or face complete ruin.

"I am considering paying a great deal of money for you. I merely wish to sample the goods first. Your uncle wouldn't blame me, I am sure."

"No—!"

His mouth came down hard upon hers, roughly silencing her scream. He tasted of stale cigars and wine. He tried to force her mouth open with his tongue while a free hand groped her body. Horrified and humiliated, she bucked and kicked him in the shin.

His mouth came away. "I expect a meek and submissive wife. But I don't mind taming you first."

"I'll never marry you. Let go of me." She tried to wrench her hands free but his hand shackling her wrists tightened until she cried out.

His free hand fisted in her skirts, and then he began to draw up her hem, exposing her legs.

No!

Desperate, she thrashed. In a moment of clear thought, she remembered something her twin brother Armand told her years ago about male anatomy when she had accidentally hurt him during play. Hoping the same were true for all males, she brought her knee upward in a sharp, hard motion.

Mr. Braxton's hold on her broke. He collapsed, coughing, onto the floor. Alicia wrenched open the door and flew out of the room into the gallery, right into another man.

She let out a cry and staggered back.

A pair of arms came around her. "Miss Palmer?"

She looked up and sobbed in relief. "Lord Amesbury."

CHAPTER 3

Cole Amesbury put a comforting arm around the distraught girl as she collapsed against him. Her hair smelled faintly of lavender, and her slender body felt warm and soft. He looked back into the open door from whence she had fled. An older man lay curled up and groaning on the floor. Alicia Palmer trembled in his arms wearing a look of wild terror, her lips swollen and showing signs of bruising. Her crushed gown and disheveled hair completed the picture.

It didn't take a genius to figure out what had happened.

White-hot fury shot through Cole. He had been justly accused of many scandalous things, but assaulting a woman had never been one of them. Though tempted to beat the old man senseless, clear reason broke through the rage; he could not leave Miss Palmer alone. At the moment, she required care. From the looks of him, her attacker would be going nowhere soon. There would be time to confront the man later. And confront him, he would. Tonight.

Struggling against the violent urges that raced through his veins, he asked, "Who is that?" His voice sounded harsh and angry even to his own ears.

"Mr. Braxton," she choked.

Of course. The man she had been avoiding when she fled to the garden. Still shaking, she visibly tried to control her tears. An uncharacteristic surge of tenderness crept over Cole, nudging aside his anger. Most women used tears as a form of manipulation.

29

Few wept out of true emotion. He doubted Miss Palmer was even capable of deception. All evening, she'd proved herself genuine, without guile. He wanted to protect her from all the ugliness of the world that would shatter her innocence and teach her to be cynical.

Cole cursed himself. He had known a man she feared pursued her that night. If he had not released Miss Palmer's arm when her friend pulled on her, Catherine Sinclair would not have been so bold as to take him away from Miss Palmer. He had meant only to be polite to the host's daughter, not to abandon the girl he escorted, thus leaving her open to danger.

He pulled her closer against his chest and wrapped his arms around her, whispering words of consolation. She tensed and pushed him away. Reluctantly, he released her. He should have known that the touch of another man would not be welcome at the moment.

She appeared to search for something. "I don't have a handkerchief. I must have dropped my reticule." She accepted the handkerchief Cole offered. "Thank you." She heaved a tremulous breath as she dried her tears. "Forgive me for falling apart."

He clenched his fist to avoid touching her cheek. "Think nothing of it."

"You must think badly of me." She gasped and worry leapt into her face. "You won't tell anyone, will you? My reputation will be sullied and then I will never be able—Oh! Uncle Willard will be angry when he hears I rejected Mr. Braxton in such a manner."

"I should think he'd be angry that the man tried to force himself on his niece," he replied grimly.

She shook her head and looked as if she would say more, but closed her mouth instead. A moment later, she looked up at him. "Thank you for your assistance, my lord."

"I will escort you to the withdrawing room where you may splash your face and straighten your hair. Then we'll find...ah, Mrs. Hancock, was it? Your chaperone for the evening?"

She nodded. "That's very kind, my lord."

Again the girl's large eyes drew him. They were the color of coffee and cream, flecked with gold. Unusually long, dark lashes clung together with the dampness of her tears. They were the loveliest eyes he had ever seen, and they had captured his all evening. *She* had captured him all evening. What it was about her that had so completely entranced him, he could not say. But he wanted to find out what it was about this girl that was so, well, different.

He glanced back into the smaller room, but the groaning body on the floor had disappeared. Mr. Braxton must have gone out through another door while Cole's focus lay upon Miss Palmer.

"I shall deal with Mr. Braxton later."

"Please, I know you must think ill of me now, but I beg you to say nothing of my shame."

"Your shame?" Incredulous, he stared. "He should be ashamed. And punished. What he did— what he tried to do—is reprehensible."

"Please. I will be ruined."

Her frightened, desperate plea tugged at his heart as much as her terror a moment ago. He stilled. His heart? He wasn't aware that he still possessed one.

"Very well, Miss Palmer, I will say nothing. But I assure you, you are clearly blameless. I'd like nothing better than to shoot that man." After he'd beaten him with his bare hands.

She gasped as if he'd just said something dreadful. "No dueling, I beg you."

Cole dredged up a lazy grin despite the righteous anger still coiled in his stomach. "Duel?

31

What makes you think I want to hand him a gun and let him shoot back at me?"

She shuddered. "I don't wish that either. But please, don't challenge him to a duel. I couldn't bear it."

"Even a man such as he?"

She shook her head. "I do not wish anyone to suffer from a gunshot wound. Even him."

Her reaction puzzled Cole. A year ago, another woman in a similar situation had been adamant that her honor be satisfied. She had later proven not worth the effort, more's the pity.

He froze. Alicia Palmer? As in…?

No, surely not. Palmer was too common a name to suggest any relationship.

"I beg you, Lord Amesbury, do nothing."

All night, expressions passed over her face, easily readable, even if he did not fully understand her reasons. He found her refreshing. "You are remarkably forgiving."

"Please, my lord. The scandal would ruin me." She fixed those beautiful, heavily-lashed eyes upon him. Only a heartless cad could refuse those eyes. And Cole knew that the social back-lash, if others ever suspected she had been deflowered or even caught engaging in any unseemly behavior, would destroy any hope of a good match.

"Very well, Miss Palmer. You may trust me to keep your secret."

As he looked down into Alicia Palmer's face, he had no doubt she would be worth any risk. Her sweet, unspoiled temperament touched him in a place he thought long dead.

He held out his hand. "Shall we?"

After she retrieved her reticule, he escorted her through the crowd to the retiring room. Cole waited outside the door, his tension building. He kept a tight rein on his anger, but it mounted like a raging river trapped behind a dam; rising, building, threatening to shatter the barrier. It took all his self control to remain there instead of seeking out Mr. Braxton and thrashing him. He would place Miss Palmer in the care of others and then go have a nice little *tête à tête* with Mr. Braxton.

When Miss Palmer emerged, she had perfectly composed herself. Her hair was smoothed back into place and her freshly washed face showed no trace of tears. Careful scrutiny revealed that her gown still showed signs of being crushed, but a casual glance might not discover it. However, a tiny bruise formed around her full, rosebud lips. Worse, her expressive eyes still revealed her terror.

The volcano of rage threatened to erupt, demanding action. Cole offered her his arm and patted her hand, hoping to give her some measure of comfort. He struggled to keep his touch gentle when a lust for enforcing his own code of justice left him shaking.

They found Mrs. Hancock gossiping in a circle of older ladies. "Back already, dear?"

Miss Palmer looked poised to flee. "Ah, we left a bit early."

"Captain Hawthorne decided to dance a few sets in your absence but he asked me to tell you he will return shortly to claim his dance."

Elizabeth joined them at that moment. "Alicia, Robert is here looking for you."

Miss Palmer noticeably brightened. "He's here?"

At that moment, a younger gentleman wearing an insolent grin approached Miss Palmer. "Evening, Lissie. Did you save me a dance?"

Cole's frown of disapproval for the man's cheekiness became one of puzzlement. He knew that young man from somewhere. A vague unease arose.

When the newcomer's gaze moved to Cole next to her, he paled visibly. "You!"

Miss Palmer gasped. "Robert Palmer, where are your manners?"

Of course. Robert Palmer. From London. Cold dread trickled across his heart as he considered the ramifications.

Maintaining his cool demeanor, Cole inclined his head. "Mr. Palmer."

"What are you doing here?" Palmer demanded.

Cole raised a brow. "Dancing. And you?"

Palmer took Alicia's arm. "Come with me, Lissie. We are leaving."

"Now see here—" Cole began, but Palmer pinned him with a dangerous glare.

"Stay away from my cousin. Haven't you done enough?"

"Your cousin?" Cole looked from him to Miss Palmer and understanding dawned. He cursed under his breath. He hadn't been aware Armand Palmer had a sister. Not that he'd bothered to find out. He glanced at Alicia Palmer. The ramifications he'd considered a moment ago took a more serious turn.

Palmer shot Cole a venomous glare and took the girl by the arm. Anger rolled off his body as he led her out of the ballroom. Wanting desperately to explain, Cole followed them out into the foyer, away from the others.

After sending Cole a look of apology, Miss Palmer dug in her heels. "Robert, explain yourself."

Cole remained rooted to the floor and waited for the condemning stare she would surely turn upon him.

Palmer trembled in rage. "That's Cole Amesbury."

"Yes, I know." She looked back at Cole again, clearly puzzled.

Palmer spoke quietly, but Cole heard every word. "He's the scoundrel who shot your twin."

The disbelief and horror that crossed Alicia Palmer's face seared right through to his very soul.

She blinked as she struggled with the news. Her eyes locked with Palmer's. She shook her head. Then she turned her golden-brown eyes to Cole. Mute and stunned, she stared at him while her face drained of all color.

Cole felt his façade slip. Sweat trickled down his back. He could not explain why her opinion mattered to him so much, this girl he'd only met tonight, but watching her estimation of him shift from shy admiration to utter revulsion left him cold.

Without any defense for his actions, he waited. He wished she would fly into a rage and scream at him. Anything would be better than that stare.

Somewhere in the back of his mind, he wondered if there were more to this story than he knew. Had Armand's injury been more serious than he'd been led to believe? Her reaction declared that Cole's actions had significantly altered her life. The knowledge that he'd hurt this girl for whom he'd grown to care in so short a time twisted in his gut like a knife.

Robert tugged on her arm and threw Cole a murderous glare. "Come, Lissie. I'll take you home."

The strength seemed to leave her. Her shoulders slumped in defeat. Without another word, she turned and left with Palmer, almost leaning on his arm.

Cole had the sinking sensation that he had just lost something irreplaceable.

He remained standing in the empty foyer like a lost child until he heard their carriage leave. Cole collected himself and retreated to the library. Ignoring the others present, he downed two glasses of cherry brandy before his courage returned. He cursed his weakness for letting Aunt Livy bully him into coming to this ball. He had come expecting to be perfectly bored, just the same as every other ball and soiree he'd attended since his return to civilization two years ago. What he found had been far more horrifying; himself at his worst.

What had he done?

After another bracing drink, he composed himself and left the library. He had an appointment with Mr. Braxton. Not that Braxton knew, of course, but it existed, nonetheless.

Cole sought out the host and found Lord Sinclair's wife instead. "Lady Sinclair."

She turned to him with the same calculating smile her daughter Catherine wore. "Lord Amesbury. I do hope you are enjoying yourself. May I be of assistance?"

"I wonder if you'd be kind enough to introduce me to one of your guests. Mr. Braxton."

Her practiced smile never altered. "Of course." Her gaze focused on someone off to the side. "Why, here he comes now."

Cole watched a man in his late forties approach with a slight limp. Cole inwardly saluted Miss Palmer. She surprised him; he would not have suspected such a sweet-mannered girl to know how to inflict such a personal and effective attack upon a man. Mr. Braxton wore an expensive suit and a family crested ring on his finger. He looked harmless, respectable, incapable of the violence Cole knew the man had committed against Alicia Palmer.

While Lady Sinclair made the introductions, Mr. Braxton studied him shrewdly. "If I remember correctly, your father is the Earl Tarrington."

"You remember correctly." Cole clenched his fists.

A light of recognition entered his eyes. "Ah, yes, I see the family resemblance. I have had occasion to meet him over the years. I understand his health has not been good of late."

"He is convalescing in Bath," Cole replied tightly. "Sir, I wonder if I might have a word with you in private."

"As it is, I am not feeling well. I have come to make my apologies to our lovely hostess." He turned to Lady Sinclair. "With regret, my lady."

"Then please allow me to escort you to your carriage," Cole interjected before the hostess could reply. "I insist."

A brief flash of alarm crossed Mr. Braxton's face as he no doubt saw the murderous look that must have been visible in Cole's eyes. He glanced at the hostess, who raptly watched their interchange.

His gaze returned to Cole and he nodded stiffly. "Of course, my lord."

They stepped outside. The cool night air did nothing to cool Cole's temper. Too bad he couldn't just pull the man into a dark corner and stick a knife in his ribs. Perhaps that year on Jared's pirate ship had affected Cole more deeply than he realized.

Mr. Braxton watched him warily. "What can I do for you, Lord Amesbury?"

Fully aware of his intimidating stature, Cole faced him and folded his arms. The longer the silence lasted, the more uncomfortable Mr. Braxton became.

"I understand you are considering making an offer for Miss Alicia Palmer," Cole said at last, letting his voice convey his disapproval.

Mr. Braxton flinched. "I have not yet decided. She seemed quite proper at first, but flew into a temper and behaved in a manner most unbecoming of a lady."

With effort, Cole held on to his rising rage. "Perhaps because you behaved in a manner most unbecoming of a gentleman."

"How dare you, sir." Braxton tried to appear affronted but only managed to look afraid.

37

"I saw her running from a room a few moments ago as if the devil were chasing her. You were lying on the floor looking most uncomfortable."

In a defensive maneuver, Braxton attempted to collect his courage. "Earl's son or no, I don't know who you think you are that you can accuse me of—"

Cole grabbed him by the collar and pulled him in until their noses almost touched. "I think I am a very dangerous man to cross. I should call you out, but I do not wish to further humiliate Miss Palmer. Know this; if you ever go near her again, or frighten her in any way, I will come back and take great pleasure in whipping you like the cur that you are." He shook the man a little, just for good measure, his temper straining against its restraints. Sweat beaded on Braxton's face.

Cole continued, "And if one breath of scandal ever arises in association with her name, regardless of the source, I will rip out your heart with my bare hands. No one will ever find your body."

Braxton made a strangling noise that had nothing to do with Cole's grip.

"Have I made myself clear?"

"Perfectly," the other man gasped.

After a slow, dangerous perusal that always left opponents begging for mercy, Cole released him, thinking his year as a pirate had not been entirely in vain.

Still bristling with unreleased fury, he stalked back into the house to tell his aunt and uncle he'd had enough of tonight's festivities.

Just inside the ballroom, standing in a circle of debutantes, Elizabeth Hancock smiled at him. Then her smile faltered. He realized his expression must be thunderous. He pulled on his practiced mask and called up a polite smile. Seeing her reminded him of his promise to Alicia Palmer. With perfect civility, he asked Miss Hancock for a dance and she accepted demurely. The girls nearby all either giggled or shot her looks of envy.

As lovely as a doll, Miss Hancock executed the dance moves perfectly, and said everything expected and proper, but only served to remind him why he avoided missish debutantes. Despite the aura of grief that surrounded her, Alicia Palmer possessed poise and dignity that remained notably absent in Elizabeth.

Cole nearly cursed out loud before he caught himself. When did he begin comparing women? The only ones who interested him were lonely young widows who no longer cared about propriety. He still couldn't explain what had drawn him to Miss Palmer's side in the first place.

Or why losing her good opinion was so crushing.

Where the devil were his aunt and uncle? He needed to retreat before he cracked. After returning Miss Hancock to her mother, Cole downed another cherry brandy, fighting to regain his normal bored, amused expression. He failed miserably.

Uncle Andrew found him then. "Care to have a go at billiards?"

"I'd rather leave now."

Uncle Andrew held his hands up in a gesture of helplessness. "You'll have to take that up with your Aunt. In the meantime, you can do what I do and enjoy a tactical retreat into the billiards room until it's safe to come out. Your aunt is dancing and I daren't interrupt."

"Fine." Cole set his glass on a passing tray.

"I'm surprised at you, nephew."

"Oh?"

"You actually danced."

Cole uttered something between a snort and a laugh. "I did. Twice."

Uncle Andrew smirked. "Truly? Twice? Both with the same lady?"

"No. Two different ladies."

"Widows?"

Did Uncle know him that well? "No, I thought I'd live dangerously and dance with young ladies actively seeking a husband."

Andrew chuckled. "You do thrive on danger."

"The second was because I promised the first that I'd dance with her friend."

Andrew opened the door to the billiards room. Decorated in dark paneling and rich reds, and smelling faintly of cigar smoke, the billiards room had a decidedly masculine feel. For the moment, they were the only gentlemen using it as a refuge from the ball and its feminine snares.

Uncle Andrew set up the billiards balls. "Since when do you make such promises?"

"As you say, I miss the danger of my former life and decided to stir up some." Cole carefully lined up his shot, took a practice stroke, and neatly sank two balls.

Alicia Palmer's face appeared in his mind's eye. He'd never met a woman with such an unspoiled temperament. She did not possess the studied, flirtatious mannerisms of so many ladies of the *beau monde*, nor did she seem capable of any deceit. Each emotion, each thought, crossed her face unconcealed. Shame-faced, she had declared herself a fortune-hunter. But she did not fit the type; she lacked the calculating edge.

He remembered her in the garden, her mantle of quiet, dignified sorrow, the tears she tried so valiantly to suppress, her sweet concern for her friend. Normally, Cole avoided wide-eyed innocents, but something about her drew him the way no one ever had. It touched him deep inside where he thought he no longer had any feeling. It excited him. It frightened him.

It didn't matter. When Robert Palmer had told

her Cole had shot her twin brother, the horror that overcame her features was more gut-wrenching than the fright she suffered at the hands of Mr. Braxton.

He banked the next shot and missed.

He cursed and Uncle Andrew chuckled. "Something has you a bit rattled tonight, Cole."

"Yes. Interfering busybodies who drag hapless relations to marriage marts," Cole snarled.

Andrew chuckled again and positioned his cue stick.

Cole didn't care what Alicia Palmer thought of him. She was a self-proclaimed fortune hunter desperate for a husband, and he only liked experienced women seeking a nice, uncomplicated affair. Clearly, they did not belong together.

The pronouncement did nothing to sweeten his mood.

The door opened and Aunt Livy's turbaned head appeared. "Oh, there you are, my love," she said to Uncle Andrew. She frowned at Cole. "Cole, dear, you should be out among the guests, not in here out of circulation."

"I danced, Aunt. Twice. With two different young ladies."

"I know dear, and you did me proud, but there's someone to whom I must introduce you."

Cole scowled and heaved a sigh. "Another one? Haven't you done enough?"

She smiled, unimpressed by his dark mood. "Oh, no."

Cole indicated the billiards table. "We just started the game. I'll be out when we've finished."

She turned an imploring look upon him and smiled. "Please, dear? This is the last one tonight, I promise."

Cole rolled his eyes. If this was the last one tonight, then heaven help him tomorrow night. How could he be such a weakling when it came to Aunt

41

Livy? No one else could manipulate him as she did.

Uncle Andrew chuckled. "I'll rescue you later, Cole."

Cole groaned loudly but offered his arm to his aunt. "If I marry, your purpose in living will vanish. I must resist for the sake of your life."

"Fear not. You have three younger brothers. Christian will be easy. He may not even need my help. Jared and Grant will be difficult, but then, you know me; I love a good challenge."

"Challenge? Hopeless, if you ask me."

"I'm a very determined woman."

"Utterly ruthless," he agreed.

Though he refused to look at her, he knew Aunt Livy watched him as they strolled down the hallway toward the ballroom. "It was kind of you to dance with Miss Palmer, Cole."

Instead of his usual quip, Cole found himself asking, "What do you know of her family?"

She glanced at him. "The present-day Palmers or the former gentleman and his lady?"

"Either. Both."

"The former were lovely people, respectable. She was French and had a sort of gentleness about her. Very beautiful. After their deaths, his younger brother inherited the estate." She tsked. "Willard Palmer is not the gentleman his brother was. Gambler, drinker. He's made terribly risky business ventures. His debts are mountainous, and he might be forced to sell the family estate soon or risk having it seized. Unless he can arrange a good match for his niece."

Cole glanced at her. "Oh?"

"The family is counting upon her to marry well in the hopes that her husband will rescue the family from their straits. I believe her uncle is exerting considerable pressure upon her."

The thought of that pure, unspoiled girl at the

mercy of unscrupulous old men like Mr. Braxton rekindled his anger. It also explained why she needed to marry a wealthy man without fitting the profile of a true fortune-hunter. Her uncle was the fortune-hunter, using his niece to solve problems of his own making.

"She has refused to wed any of them so far," Aunt Livy added.

"Smart girl."

"Sooner or later, Willard Palmer will force her to accept one of them, he's getting that desperate. Such a shame. She's a delightful young lady, not the great beauty her mother was, but still pleasing, nonetheless. Well-mannered and sweet. Such a tragedy to endure so young. She took their deaths very hard. Understandable. First her parents and then her twin brother, all in a matter of months."

Cole blanched. Armand Palmer was *dead*?

He opened his mouth but nothing came out. Standing rooted in the hallway, he pressed the heel of his hands over his eyes. Had he...?

No, it couldn't be. He had not killed Armand Palmer. He'd only shot him in the arm. A few days later, guilt had driven him to visit the town home the Palmers had let for the Season. The servants had assured him that his former dueling opponent had only suffered very minor injuries.

Then what the devil happened to Armand? A slow, sinking dread crept over him.

Aunt Livy took his arm and drew him into the ballroom. "Stop being theatrical, Cole, and come meet her. She's lovely. I promise this would be the last girl tonight. Ah, there she is."

Cole fought to gather his scattered wits. Armand Palmer could have died from anything. A hunting accident. Disease. Anything.

He drew a steadying breath and painted on a smile as Aunt Livy introduced him to a blond debutante dressed appropriately in white. The girl offered a blatantly hopeful smile which somehow restored order to his world. Cole caught himself before he rolled his eyes. If he survived this night, he would have to forge a stronger resistance against his aunt and her machinations.

Perhaps he should return to piracy. It was less hazardous.

CHAPTER 4

"Did you meet anyone interesting at the Sinclair's ball last night?" Uncle Willard asked as he entered the parlor.

Alicia realized she'd only been staring at the book in her hands instead of reading it. "I danced a set. And I have decided that I will never marry Mr. Braxton. He was horrible."

She shivered as she remembered the repulsive feeling of his hands upon her body, his foul mouth on hers, the way he trapped her, and made her feel so dirty. She pulled her sleeves lower over her wrists to cover the bruises and wished for a way to feel clean again.

He frowned. "He'd be willing to pay all my debts if you please him."

"No, Uncle. Nothing you say will make me marry him."

He stared at her in surprise.

"Surely you can't expect me to marry a man who will make me miserable. I can't believe you are forcing this upon me."

"If you don't marry soon, I will lose everything."

Alicia knew he only spoke the truth. She bowed her head. "I need a little more time."

"One of my creditors has given me until the end of the month or he will seize the estate."

Alicia pressed a hand over her eyes. She knew that threat truly existed. Someone in the line had forgotten to renew the entailment which protected the property from just such a situation. By the time the lapse was discovered, it was too late to remedy it.

"And another creditor threatened to throw me in debtor's prison. I have five weeks to repay the loan in full before he acts. If you fail to find a husband before then we will all go to debtor's prison." He looked ill. "I hear the guards have special treatment for young ladies. You and Hannah would be at their mercy."

Alicia turned cold at the thought of Hannah being subjected to the same treatment she'd nearly suffered from Mr. Braxton.

"Choose a husband. We are counting on you to marry before the month's end."

Alicia closed her eyes and prayed for a miracle.

****

Cole Amesbury took careful aim and squeezed the trigger. A fat, healthy pheasant dropped without a twitch.

"Nice shooting, Nephew," Uncle Andrew praised from behind him. "I see a life of ease and lechery hasn't softened you yet."

Cole grinned. He had earned his reputation as a dead shot in his youth and still took pride in his skill.

"The population is so large that it's hardly sporting," Uncle Andrew added. "Don't have to step two paces before we find game now."

Cole shouldered his gun and watched the dog run out to retrieve the bird. "Oh? Was hunting less than ideal before?"

"Poachers nearly decimated the game. Ten years ago, we'd hunt a whole day and see nothing worth shooting." Andrew patted his dog's head and handed the kill to a waiting servant.

"What happened? Caught them and sent them to Newgate?"

Andrew chuckled. "No, of course not. I found out

46

my worst poacher was the twelve-year-old son of one of my tenants, a widow with five children. I took him two dozen chickens and offered him a reward to keep the poachers off my property." He winked at Cole.

Cole laughed. "You're a soft touch, Uncle."

Uncle Andrew shook his head. "No, lad, not really. Putting that boy in gaol would not have helped the matter. Giving them chickens provided them with needed food, and I won not only his undying loyalty, but that of all the tenants." He winked again. "Word spreads."

Cole remembered aloud an old proverb his childhood nurse used to say; "Give a man a fish and you've fed him for a day; teach a man to fish..."

"Exactly. They raise the chickens, sell some, sell the eggs they don't eat, and eat the chickens too old to lay. That boy has a family of his own now. He still watches out for my land. And he's the first to pay his rents. Nary a poacher has stepped foot onto my land since. I may have a hunting party to keep them under control. The deer are becoming pests. The gardener complains that they trample the gardens."

Cole walked in companionable silence next to his uncle, who limped with an old wound. Cole's favorite horse, a white Lipizzaner stallion named André, grazed near Uncle Andrew's roan in a stand of trees where they left them. At Cole's whistle, the stallion came to him. It had taken a great deal of time and trouble to acquire the beast, but Cole's determination, some creativity, not to mention a considerable expense, had won him this beautiful animal. Cole stroked André's neck, admiring the horse's graceful lines before mounting.

Andrew glanced sideways at him. "Want to go swimming?"

Cole returned the grin. "Not going to let me forget that, are you?"

The waters of the pond lapped at the edges,

bringing memories of childish games and dares with his brothers and sisters. Cole's family had visited this estate every few years for as long as he could remember. He and Jared, his younger brother by fourteen months, had combined more mischief than Cole cared to admit. His sisters had no use for younger brothers. Grant had always been a solitary creature. Christian usually had a sketchbook or an easel in hand or was torturing the pianoforte. That left Cole and Jared to terrorize the country. He was always surprised when Aunt Livy and Uncle Andrew invited them back.

He loved the country, and this tiny town in the Midlands provided a welcome reprieve from his travels. On the surface, his life seemed complete. Yet, a wistful whisper suggested his life lacked...what? Purpose? Meaning?

Inexplicably, Alicia Palmer's face crept into Cole's thoughts. He cursed his stupidity. Calling out that Palmer boy over a woman who later proved unworthy of the trouble had been one of his more brainless acts. But tempers had flared and Cole had seen himself as the lady's defender. Later, when they met to duel, Cole had nearly called it off. He'd been wrong to challenge a mere boy who lacked his skill with arms. And as an officer in the Royal Navy during the war, and his subsequent acts as a pirate with his brother Jared, he'd developed a definite dislike for bloodshed, which eventually overshadowed even his insatiable need for danger. But Vivian had demanded he defend her honor, and foolishly, he had obliged. He later realized how wrong he'd been about her.

He had absolutely no doubt Alicia Palmer would be worth any risk. He wondered again what had happened to her brother Armand. He knew the answer to that question mattered a great deal.

Lost in thought, their arrival in front of the

stables surprised Cole. After overseeing André's care, Cole parted with his uncle and strode into the house, stripping off his riding gloves. He handed them along with his hat and coat to a servant.

"Is that you, Cole?" His aunt's voice echoed through the foyer. "In here, dear."

Normally, she preferred to sit in her parlor, a room that made him feel like a clumsy oaf among her frills and dainty furniture, but today her voice led him upstairs to the drawing room.

He found her frowning in concentration over her needlepoint. Cole liked this room. It was full of light and filled with sturdy furniture. He poured himself a port before he took a seat beside her. Stretching out his legs, he sipped absently at the drink, staring at the squares of light on the floor cast by the window panes.

"Good day hunting, Cole?" she asked after several minutes of silence.

"Landed a pair of pheasants." He closed his eyes and rested his head against the chair.

"What is it, dear? You've been so quiet today. You hardly said a word at breakfast. And now...it's not like you."

This threatened to grow too serious. He preferred their usual banter. He dredged up a grin. "You often tell me I need to be more sober. I'm accommodating you for a change."

"I only want you to sober enough to find a wife. Not lose your good nature."

"Now my nature is bad?" he quipped.

She refused to take his bait. "You are not yourself. Are you troubled about something?"

He sighed. "No, just facing one of my many demons."

"Anything I can help you with?"

For a moment, he wished for his childhood days when he could tell her anything. But that was no longer possible. If she truly knew him now, she'd be shocked and disappointed.

He shook his head in reply to her question. "What did you do this afternoon, Aunt?"

"I called upon Miss Palmer." Aunt Livy's face clouded.

Cole glanced at her, pleased at the unexpected opportunity. He'd been tempted to ply her for information, but he knew the moment he brought up any girl, Aunt Livy would never quit until she saw him happily wed to the poor chit. Now he could satisfy his curiosity without Aunt Livy being aware of his interest.

With the correct amount of polite boredom, he asked. "Have a pleasant visit?"

"Their situation is most desperate. Some of their servants have had to take other posts. She seemed subdued today. Perhaps her grief still weighs upon her."

"You mentioned her parents died recently?"

Aunt Livy leaned in as if to divulge a great secret, and Cole suppressed a smile. Even if the servants hovered nearby, he doubted she knew something they didn't; servants had their own web of gossip. Often, if he needed information, his valet, Stephens, knew all Cole required.

"They were in a carriage accident. Only the girl survived. Even the coachman perished."

"All in a single accident?"

"Tragic, isn't it?"

"Odd."

"Their youngest daughter, Hannah, had remained home due to an illness, so she was spared the accident, thankfully. I called upon Alicia Palmer once she had mended enough from her injuries to receive visitors, but she was so wrapped up in her own grief that I failed to provide any consolation. I believe she blames herself for surviving the accident that claimed her parents."

Cole nodded pensively as a kinship for the young lady awakened. It prodded an uncharacteristic surge of protectiveness. Strange, he couldn't seem to rid himself of that annoying flaw with regard to that girl.

But at least now he knew how Armand had died. He paused. Armand *had* been in the carriage accident, had he not? Aunt Livy had not mentioned his name.

He opened his mouth to ask about Armand's death, but Aunt Livy cut in. "Would you care to spend more time with the very available Miss Palmer, Cole?"

Cole frowned and almost waved farewell to the opportunity to learn more. "I humored you the other night at the ball. Give me a reprieve, Aunt."

She snorted in a decidedly un-ladylike manner and grinned. Finally. "Since when do I take advice from you? Perhaps if you weren't so wicked, I'd stop pestering you."

Wicked? If she only knew half of his sins. "Perhaps if you'd stop pestering me, I'd stop being so wicked."

She patted his hand. "Yes, yes, and if I didn't care, I wouldn't pester."

"Then I shall endeavor to remove myself from your good graces."

"Cole." A rare look of tenderness crept into her eye and she banished the momentary lightheartedness. "You survived the war. Does marriage seem that much more terrifying?"

"Any sane bachelor would answer with an emphatic 'yes' to that question."

She chuckled. "Your brother Grant and I had a similar discussion last Season. It will be even more difficult to find him a wife than you."

"Impossible." He heaved a dramatic sigh. "I will

marry someday, Aunt, if only to put an end to your meddling."

His attempt to draw her back into their comfortable banter failed, and worse, her voice quieted. "You've been home from the sea almost two years. I think you've punished yourself enough."

He shifted, not meeting her eyes. "You speak nonsense."

"This life you've lead since your return from the Peninsular war. The risks, the women—"

Cole summoned a practiced, lazy grin and looked directly into her eyes. "Punished? Don't you know that a life of debauchery is the perfect reward for a returning war hero?"

Aunt Livy fixed her penetrating gaze upon him, but he ensured that his practiced façade remained firmly in place. She pursed her lips and shook her head, her attention turned back to her needlepoint. "Perhaps I shall invite Miss Palmer for tea. For a time when you will be home."

"I don't think she likes me, Aunt Relentless."

"I'm not relentless, I'm determined. But if she doesn't like you, then she must already know you too well," Aunt Livy said mournfully, slipping back into their familiar banter and safer ground. "We shall have to find you a wife who will be less discerning."

Relaxing, Cole grinned. "Quite right."

Aunt Livy glanced up at him. "The Hancock's dinner party is tomorrow. And we've already accepted. All three of us."

He made a face. "Why must you insist I attend all of these pointless exercises?"

"To find you a wife, of course. How else are you going to do it?"

"Perhaps I don't wish to do it yet."

"Good. It will take time to cajole some poor girl to take you."

Cole chuckled. "You are the sharpest-tongued

old woman who's ever lived."

"Thank you, dear. Now, go be useful and tell the cook I wish to have lobster bisque for dinner tonight."

"No one else gets away with ordering me about, you know."

"You ought to visit more often. It's good for your humility."

Cole kissed her cheek. All the way out the door he muttered about bossy women loudly enough for her to hear. Her laughter followed him into the hall.

Alicia's brave, grief-stricken face flashed into his mind. Intrigued at how truly genuine he found Alicia Palmer, Cole anticipated their next meeting with mingled excitement and dismay. Against his better judgment, he knew that there would be a next meeting. Even if he had to arrange it.

CHAPTER 5

Alicia paraded about the sitting room adjoining her boudoir wearing a pale amber moiré.

"Oh, dearest, this one is your color. It makes the gold flecks in your eyes dance, and oh, your skin simply glows. And how slender and graceful you look. I fear I shall be quite dowdy next to you." Elizabeth affected a pretty pout.

"Ha! The day you look dowdy is the day I sprout wings." Or become beautiful. She turned to Hannah who wore a creamy white that complemented her fair skin. "Lovely, Hannah."

Hannah smiled shyly.

They spent the afternoon trying on dresses Elizabeth brought them while Elizabeth's maid measured both Alicia and Hannah. They enjoyed tea and scones, chatting happily while Witherspoon made the alterations. When the gowns were completed, Alicia swallowed her pride, thanked Elizabeth for the gowns, and bid her goodbye.

That evening, feeling like a princess in a green silk creation, Alicia came downstairs with Hannah, but when they came across Uncle Willard's path, her joy dimmed.

Willard eyed their gowns. "Where did you get those?"

"Elizabeth let us borrow them, Uncle."

He nodded in approval. "Where are you going?"

"The dinner party at the Hancock's, remember? We've already sent our acceptance."

"I'd forgotten. I'm sorry but I cannot attend with

you. I have an appointment."

Robert miraculously arrived downstairs looking neat and clean, and even had managed to sober up enough to drive Alicia and Hannah to Elizabeth's dinner party. Male cousins could only loosely be considered an appropriate escort for young ladies, but they had no one else. And Robert had tried to take on the role of her protector whenever he was not too foxed. Uncle Willard had lost his own phaeton in a card game and the family coach had been sold. They bid good night to Uncle Willard.

The one horse that remained of the enviable horse flesh that once filled the stables pulled Robert's carriage. They rode in comfortable silence.

Robert cast a sideways glance at them. "How pretty you both look tonight."

Alicia smiled. "You look dashing, Cousin. I hope you will exercise restraint tonight. We depend on you to drive us home."

"Yes, Mother," he mocked.

She sighed. Since Armand's death, Robert's drinking had become alarming. She feared he would kill himself with it.

They passed through the darkened countryside under a clear, starlit sky. Robert turned the carriage down the Hancock's drive. Light poured from every window of the Hancock's home. As the carriage rolled to a stop, footmen hurried to assist.

Inside, Elizabeth and her parents greeted them warmly. "The other guests are gathering in the drawing room."

Charles, Elizabeth's brother, clapped Robert on the shoulder. "Come join me at billiards?"

"Really, Charles, you ought to stay with the rest of the guests," Elizabeth scolded.

"We'll be out later, Lizzy."

Robert followed Charles down the hall while Elizabeth and Alicia exchanged looks of disapproval.

Hannah nervously smoothed her dress. Elizabeth linked her arms through theirs and drew them both into the drawing room. The guests had divided into smaller, similar age groups. Catherine, in all her glory, sat next to her friend Marie, holding court with the young Mr. de Champs and the dark-eyed Captain Hawthorne.

"Sorry," Elizabeth whispered. "Mother insisted we invite the Sinclairs."

Catherine waved to her, a false smile pasted upon her face. "Alicia, Hannah, come join us." She perused Alicia's gown, but her composure seldom revealed any emotion except contempt.

Hannah looked frightened. Poor Hannah. She always became dreadfully shy in the company of others. She would be terrified in London, if she made it there. Alicia drew her sister with her and glided over to them with all of the grace of a queen.

The gentlemen quickly jumped to their feet and made room for them, Mr. de Champs fetching a nearby chair. Next to the raven-haired beauty of Catherine, Alicia felt plain and drab, but at least she was impeccably dressed, thanks to Elizabeth.

Alicia greeted each in turn. Catherine's friend, Marie, smiled kindly. Alicia often suspected that Catherine had befriended Marie because of the girl's plainness; next to her, Catherine's beauty shone. Or perhaps Catherine liked Marie because she did not view her as a threat. But Alicia clearly posed no threat, either. Catherine, the beautiful daughter of a wealthy baron, was clearly Alicia's superior in many ways. So why did Catherine dislike her so much?

"Marie is telling us her system of finding the perfect husband." Catherine wore a sly smile.

Marie beamed, basking in the center of attention for a change instead of simply shadowing Catherine, unaware that her friend mocked her. "Yes. I have written down my desired qualities in a husband. Then when I speak with a gentleman, I find out as much as I can about him. I have a code that I use based on what I learn of him and how many of his qualities meet those on my list."

The gentlemen present seemed undecided whether or not they approved of this so-called system.

Feeling the need to rescue the poor girl, Alicia turned to Marie. "What are these desirable qualities, Marie?"

"He must be a learned man and appreciate poetry, and art."

"Are these of interest to you?" Alicia asked.

Marie smiled hesitantly. "Yes. I'm not beautiful, nor am I a great conversationalist, so I have little to offer most men. Perhaps if we share the same interests..." She shrugged.

"Nonsense, you are a delightful conversationalist and you are quite comely," Mr. de Champs protested gallantly. Alicia's opinion of the young man rose even higher.

Marie giggled. "You are kind, sir, but I know what I say is true. However, I can discuss these interests and I want someone who appreciates them as I do."

"Isn't she clever?" Catherine interjected, purposely drawing attention back to herself.

Catherine glanced at something behind Alicia, as if contemplating her next move in a game she played, but Alicia resisted the urge to see what had drawn her attention.

The raven-haired beauty lifted her chin. "I shall marry for love, of course, but my family honor is a consideration. Our interests need not be similar. In fact, I would encourage my husband to pursue his own hobbies and pleasures. And unlike some, I will not marry simply for title or great riches. I only wish to be kept comfortable."

Alicia had no doubt that Catherine's definition of comfortable living would require much more than many other people's definition of wealth.

Catherine affected a demure posture. "I would consider any gentleman of good breeding." She smiled, falsely sweet. "What about you, Alicia? If you had a choice, what kind of husband would you choose?"

As all of Catherine's words sank in, Alicia stared, wondering if her uncle's intentions were common knowledge. Likely.

Alicia realized joining a group that included Catherine had been a grave mistake. Her pride would have been better spared if she had simply declined their invitation. Yet to move to another group now would only confirm Catherine's veiled insinuations.

Alicia moistened her lips. "I would choose a gentleman who is honest and kind. One who values the opinions and feelings of others. And who is mild-tempered."

Catherine appeared too satisfied, as again, her eyes moved upward to something behind Alicia. Alicia paused, wondering if she had said too much, but the handsome Mr. de Champs' encouraging nod gave her courage to continue. Next to her, Hannah stared at her in rapt admiration.

"What else, Lissie?" Hannah asked, her voice just above a whisper.

Alicia drew from her heart. "I have no interest in men who gamble or drink excessively. And most of all, I desire a husband who would be capable of fidelity." She stared out of the blackened windows, forgetting the others, forgetting her discomfort. "I wish, more than anything, to marry a man I love, and who truly loves me in return."

Surprised at herself for speaking her desires so boldly, Alicia felt her face grow hot. She twisted her hands in her lap.

Hannah offered a timid smile. "Like *Maman* and Papa."

Mr. de Champs gave her his full attention, admiration clear on his face. Captain Hawthorne's thoughts could not be discerned, but then he smiled. Again, his dark eyes drew her.

Marie sighed dreamily. "Ohhh, me too."

Catherine's lips curled into a mocking smile "How... sweet." Insult dripped from her words as if she found Alicia a romantic fool. Catherine's glance swept over all the gentlemen. "Oh, excuse us. We are chattering away and not letting you say a word. Tell me, what qualities do you desire in your ideal lady?"

A brief, uncomfortable silence followed. That was the first tactical error Alicia had ever seen Catherine make.

Someone directly behind Alicia spoke. "I'm sure our preferences are as varied as we are, Miss Sinclair."

She knew that rich, resonant voice. With dread, Alicia turned to a broad chest in a black superfine suit with a dark blue waistcoat. Her gaze moved upward to a snow-white cravat and a diamond stick pin, then further up to his beautiful, masculine face. She fell into his glittering sapphire eyes. She caught her breath. She had almost forgotten how deadly handsome Lord Amesbury was.

Deadly being the key word.

His eyes met hers and something akin to gentleness showed in his. She stilled. Gentleness? In the eyes of a killer? She turned away, clutched by dismay.

Alicia felt the walls closing in on her. She needed to escape. Now. She did not wish to hurt Elizabeth's feelings or drag Hannah away, who appeared, despite her shyness, to be enjoying herself. But Alicia could not bear to endure a dinner party in the presence of the man who had destroyed Armand. How could she leave without causing a scene?

Hannah touched her hand, her brows raised in concern and inquiry.

Elizabeth's father, Mr. Hancock, cleared his throat. In response, the talking died down. Mr. Hancock greeted his guests and invited them to enter the dining room. As the guests began to file into the dining room according to precedence, a footman hurried in and whispered urgently into Mr. Hancock's ear.

Mr. Hancock listened, nodded, and beckoned to Alicia. "Miss Palmer. Will you come with me, please?"

Alicia turned to Hannah. "I'll join you in a moment."

Hannah looked petrified at the prospect of dining without her, but Mr. de Champs gallantly offered his arm. "If I may?"

Alicia smiled in gratitude at Mr. de Champs before following Mr. Hancock out of the room.

In the hallway, Mr. Hancock turned to her. "Robert has fallen and hit his head." Before she uttered a word, Mr. Hancock held up a hand. "It does not appear to be serious, but we've sent for the doctor. I assume you'd wish to see him."

"Thank you, sir."

She followed him down a paneled hallway to an open door. Cigar smoke hung heavy over the billiards room. Robert lay sprawled on a sofa pressing a cloth to his forehead. Alicia sprang forward and picked up his limp hand.

"Robert?"

He opened his eye and grinned crookedly at her.

"You're foxed," she accused.

"Good thing. Prob'ly would've 'urt much worsh if I weren't."

She dropped his hand with a frown. "You wouldn't have fallen if you weren't."

"Ah, Lishie, you'll make shome man a perfect wife one day. You've got the nagging down jusht right."

She let out her breath. He wouldn't be needling her if he'd been truly hurt. He removed the cloth from his head, but the bleeding resumed with a vengeance. Alarmed by the sight of so much blood, Alicia grabbed his hand and pressed it and the cloth back over the wound.

"You've ruined everything, Robbie."

"Alwaysh manage to."

"I want to go home. Lord Amesbury is here."

Robert cursed and tried to sit up.

Alicia pushed him back down. "You're in no condition to go anywhere now, you idiot."

He closed his eyes and slurred, "Shorry, Lisshie. Should've talked Armand out of accepting that challenge to duel. But I was so hot to shee him humiliate that arrogant viscount. Should've shtopped 'em."

"Hush, Robbie, it's not your fault. Lord Amesbury should never have issued the challenge."

When the doctor arrived, he ushered Alicia out. While she paced the floor outside the room, a footman motioned to her. "Dinner is still being served, Miss."

Alicia nodded. She might as well eat as it would be some time before Robert would be in any condition to move. Shyness had probably paralyzed Hannah without Alicia beside her.

She halted. Lord Amesbury was in there.

"This way, Miss," the footman urged.

She gathered her courage. Dinner. She could face dinner with him. And she would do it without falling apart. Hannah counted on her. Alicia found her courage and entered the dining room with her head high.

Instead of one long table, smaller round tables dotted the dining room. Hannah looked up when Alicia came in, worry touching her face.

Alicia leaned down and spoke into her ear. "It's all right. Robbie fell, but it's just a little bump. The doctor is looking in on him as a precaution."

Hannah nodded and Alicia took the empty seat between Mr. de Champs and Mr. Hawthorne. To her dismay, Lord Amesbury had been seated between Marie and Catherine, which put him directly across from her. She tried to keep her eyes off him, but they seemed drawn to him.

How deceived she had been by his pleasing face and form, his charming manners, his dry wit. She had failed to see the heartless monster that lurked beneath. The kindness he displayed must have been an act. She had little experience with men, and Lord Amesbury hid his thoughts so effectively that she could be sure of nothing. Yet, he had seemed not only gallant, but compassionate and understanding instead of condemning when he aided her after she fled Mr. Braxton.

She shivered. Every time she remembered that horrible, humiliating experience, her stomach lurched.

Feeling his gaze, she glanced Lord Amesbury's way. A smile touched the corner of his mouth. How easily he smiled. How lightly he must take life.

And the lives of others.

She looked away. With his eyes upon her repeatedly, discomfort heated her face, and she found it difficult to enjoy the wonderful repast before her, or maintain a polite conversation with the kind and charming Mr. de Champs beside her.

Catherine turned her charm upon Lord Amesbury with a vengeance. "Tell me, my Lord Amesbury, do you enjoy the fox hunt?"

"Yes, very much." He wore an unreadable expression.

Alicia dragged her eyes away from him again, but Catherine demanded that she be the center of attention.

"I have no doubt you are a great shot," Catherine cooed.

An image of Lord Amesbury shooting her twin brother forced its way into Alicia's mind. She choked.

"I have that reputation," the viscount replied.

Alicia pressed a napkin over her mouth.

"I understand you are new to this area?" Catherine eyed him as if she suspected he was made of sweet cream.

The viscount appeared distracted as he swirled his drink in his hand, but he met her gaze politely. "I came often as a child, but this is my first visit here in years."

"Do you travel much?"

"During the war, I served aboard a Navy ship, so my travels were limited to duty. Since then, I have enjoyed a bit of travel to more desirable locations."

"You must be rather bored with dreary old England after your life abroad, my lord."

Alicia looked away.

"Not at all. England offers a number of interesting diversions," Lord Amesbury's voice rumbled.

"Do you consider horse racing an interesting diversion, Lord Amesbury?" asked Captain Hawthorne. "We have a very informal race here each year. There's some nice horseflesh here, not racers, mind you, but good for a hunt. The Baron Von Der Au has a beautiful Arabian, and he has a private race course on his land that we use."

"When is the next race?" asked Lord Amesbury, sounding genuinely interested.

"Thursday next."

"Excellent."

"You enjoy the races, Lord Amesbury?" Catherine interjected. "Do you own racehorses?"

"A few, and a new colt who's untried as of yet, but I believe he will be a winner. His pedigree is impressive."

"I can see that you are a man of varied interests." She smiled, and then lowered her eyes in a perfect imitation of a demure lady.

Only Alicia's self-control kept her from rolling her eyes. She wondered how gentlemen could be so easily deceived by her obvious charade. But then, Catherine was also beautiful and wealthy, and the daughter of a peer. She had much to offer. Except a heart. But that probably would fail to deter most men.

Alicia turned her attention away from Catherine and her prey. She focused instead on the truly wonderful meal in front of her, but with the man who destroyed Armand sitting so near, she could hardly eat more than a bite.

"Who do you favor for the race, Hawthorne?" asked Mr. de Champs.

"The marquis has a new stallion he claims will sweep the others," the dark-eyed captain replied.

Mr. de Champs smiled. "Ah, but the baron's Arabian won the derby the last two years in a row. My bets are on his horse."

Lord Amesbury leaned back, something forbidden glittering in his blue eyes, a hint of a smile on his full, sensitive lips. It awakened that undesirable awareness of him.

Alicia felt ill. Dueling fiend. Killer! She realized, belatedly, how foolish she was to have deliberately put herself in company with Lord Amesbury. She should have asked to eat in the kitchen with the servants. Or feigned a headache and taken a tray in a bedroom. Stifling the rising emotions his nearness brought, she battled her frayed nerves.

Those searching eyes pierced her, stirring a cyclone of anger and sorrow. With a smile, he raised his glass to her.

She turned away and tried to think of something intelligent to say to Mr. de Champs, who, while charming and handsome, seemed almost effeminate compared to Lord Amesbury.

Footmen cleared away the dishes from the table and placed them on trays. A gasp behind her caught Alicia's attention, but before she could turn around, a crash echoed through the dining hall, and something warm and wet landed on the back of her neck and shoulder. Stunned silence followed the noise.

"Oh, no," the footman wailed from behind Alicia.

Alicia looked down to see gravy on her neck and shoulders, sliding down her arm.

Horrified, the footman rushed forward with a cloth to try to mop up the gravy mess. "I'm so sorry, Miss," he stammered.

Mortified to have so many eyes focused on her, Alicia wished she could disappear. "It's all right."

"Good heavens, Alicia," Elizabeth cried. "Are you burned?"

"No, it's only warm." To the footman she said, "At least it isn't hot. No harm done."

By now, the footman's ears and neck were as red as his face as he frantically attempted to clean up Alicia's gown. His eyes repeatedly moved to Mr. and Mrs. Hancock in fear of their reaction. Other servants abandoned their duties to clear away the broken dishes and the ruined food on the floor. The footman's well-meaning ministrations only spread the mess on Alicia's gown.

Alicia held up her hand, halting his efforts. "Please don't be distressed. I'm not angry. I will simply retire to another room and clean up."

Elizabeth rose. "I'll help you, dearest."

"No. Don't trouble yourself, Lizzie, please. You have guests. I can manage."

Alicia turned to Hannah whose eyes shimmered in tears of sympathy. "It's all right, Hannah. Enjoy your dessert. I'll return in a moment."

Alicia refused to meet Lord Amesbury's eyes, though she felt them on her. She made the mistake of glancing Catherine's way but instantly regretted it. Catherine's condescending slant to her mouth revealed no sympathy for Alicia's plight, but rather glee at seeing her thusly embarrassed. Other guests observed the incident with various expressions of pity and amusement. Both were equally humiliating. Elizabeth's mother, Mrs. Hancock, came to her feet at the same time as Mrs. Fitzpatrick.

"Here, my dear, I'll accompany you." Mrs. Fitzpatrick came to her.

Alicia blinked. She hadn't even noticed the older lady in attendance. Mrs. Hancock sank back down in her seat with a grateful smile at Mrs. Fitzpatrick.

"That's very kind of you," murmured Alicia still fighting tears of humiliation.

"Sybil, go with Miss Palmer and help her," Mrs. Hancock said to a nearby maid.

The maid came forward and led them to an empty room. The footman followed, still apologizing.

Alicia took command over her tears and turned her attention to the distraught footman. "It's all right. It was a simple mistake. And only a very few dishes were lost. Do not be so distressed."

Mrs. Fitzpatrick nodded. "Quite right. No one is angry, lad. If I sacked every servant who dropped a dish, I would be doing my own serving."

"Thank you for being so forgiving," the footman said.

"You may go on with your duties, lad," Mrs.

Fitzpatrick said.

With a sigh of gratitude, the footman bowed and departed. Inside the empty room, the maid poured water into a basin and moistened a nearby towel. She rubbed a bar of milled soap over the towel until it produced suds and used it to carefully wipe the back of Alicia's neck, shoulder, and arm, before turning her attention to the sleeve.

Mrs. Fitzpatrick smiled benevolently. "You handled yourself beautifully out there, Miss Palmer. I know you were terribly embarrassed to be the center of such unwanted attention. And you were, indeed, most understanding about it."

"I've dropped my fair share of things," Alicia admitted.

"The other day my nephew asked about your family."

Alicia paused. "Your nephew? Lord Amesbury?"

"Yes. I am so pleased he finally came to visit. He does not often attend the London Season and I do not have as many opportunities to see him as I would like." She smiled proudly.

"You seem quite fond of him," Alicia said in undisguised surprise.

"I sense in him a kindred spirit." Mrs. Fitzpatrick looked directly into Alicia's eyes. "Did you enjoy your dance with him at the Sinclair ball?"

With a start, she wondered what he had told her. She dropped her gaze. "Of course. You said he asked about my family?"

"Indeed. He has never expressed any interest in the family of a young lady before."

Alicia felt her face heat, remembering his nearness as he looked at her mother's picture in her locket, the intensity of his gaze, his arm around her waist when she had stumbled. He was nothing like she'd imagined of the man who shot Armand. But then, he had been eager to duel Mr. Braxton when

67

he discovered her fleeing the man. At the time, she'd thought he was being chivalrous. Now she knew he enjoyed bloodshed.

"I hope he behaved as a gentleman," Mrs. Fitzpatrick said.

"Of course he did. Why wouldn't he?"

"He plays the role of a scoundrel with relish. In his defense, underneath it all, he is a surprisingly decent man. He came home from the war dramatically changed. But I think the right lady can uncover his true self buried deep inside under all those protective layers." She pinned Alicia with a stare. "He's quite wealthy in his own right."

Alicia could think of nothing to say in reply. Even if her nephew wanted her—an unlikely possibility—she would never marry the man who had killed her brother as surely as if he had put a bullet through Armand's heart instead of his arm.

"Now, there, all is well, Miss," the maid said triumphantly. "It should dry perfectly clean."

Alicia lifted her arm and craned her neck to examine the sleeve. Only a damp spot remained of the gravy spill. "Thank you. That was most expertly done."

The maid bobbed a curtsey.

Mrs. Fitzpatrick patted her arm. "Will you and your sister come have tea? We will be attending a house party next week, but I would love to receive you the following week."

Alicia returned the smile. "Thank you."

They returned together to the others. In their absence, a game of whist had begun. Alicia watched with mingled disgust and amusement as Catherine set her wily sights on her prey; the viscount and his bank account. Although to be fair to Catherine, any young lady would be interested in a young, handsome, wealthy, titled lord. But Catherine did not look starry eyed, as if she found him charming and handsome. She looked scheming.

Naturally Lord Amesbury appeared to be enjoying the beautiful lady's company. Not that Alicia cared. Catherine could have that dueling fiend! Clearly they deserved one another.

Elizabeth came to her. "The doctor said Robert will recover nicely but recommends he stay and rest tonight. He's sleeping. Will you and Hannah stay here? We can send word to your uncle."

Alicia involuntarily glanced at Lord Amesbury. She was loath to remain under the same roof with that man a moment longer than she must. She returned her focus to Elizabeth. "I had hoped to return home soon."

Elizabeth's face fell. "Oh. Well, then Mother and I could accompany you home."

"And leave your guests?"

A slight frown touched her brow. "I suppose that would not be appropriate."

Alicia sighed. "No."

Elizabeth took her hand. "What troubles you, Alicia? You have not enjoyed yourself all evening."

"Forgive me, dearest. Your party is lovely. I'm just a bit out of sorts."

Elizabeth studied her face. "Something else is wrong. You were unhappy even before Robert fell. Before the gravy accident. Oh, dear. This has not been a good evening for you, has it?"

Alicia put her arm around her. "You are not to blame for any of it."

Captain Hawthorne appeared, his dark eyes probing. "I just heard about your cousin."

"He had a fall, but he will be fine," Alicia said.

"That's a relief." He smiled, his dark eyes intense upon her face. Alicia realized that his smiles never seemed to touch his eyes. He seemed troubled. His father's poor health? Was soldiering still difficult even though the war had ended?

69

The game ended among cries of victory and defeat, drawing their attention.

Mr. de Champs joined them. "I am relieved you did not suffer any ill effect from the mishap at dinner, Miss Palmer. And your sleeve is even dry now."

What a shame her uncle would not consider men such as Mr. de Champs or Captain Hawthorne as suitable husbands. True, they were not outrageously wealthy, but they seemed decent men, much more so than her current would-be suitors. But, no, Uncle needed more money than they could, or would, give him for her.

Lord Amesbury entered the circle, his disturbing nearness making the room too warm. She deliberately averted her eyes. How could she have been attracted to that man?

Mr. de Champs touched her arm briefly. "Miss Palmer, are you unwell?"

"I'm...just tired, I think."

Mrs. Fitzpatrick edged closer, concern in her face. "I have called my carriage. May we offer you a ride home?"

And ride in the carriage with her nephew? "No! Ah, I mean, no thank you. I don't wish to impose."

Mr. Fitzpatrick appeared. "No trouble at all, young Miss Palmer. Not out of the way at all. We insist."

Alicia drew a fortifying breath. The Fitzpatrick house lay off the same highway as Alicia's home, but hers was several miles beyond. It would most certainly be out of the way.

"You're very kind, sir, but—"

"Not at all, not at all." Mr. Fitzpatrick cut in. "Don your wraps, there's a good girl. Where's your sister?"

Hannah arrived then, watching Alicia curiously, while the footmen brought their wraps.

Mrs. Fitzpatrick smiled as if she enjoyed a great joke. "Come, ladies, your cousin will be well cared for here. I'm sure they'll send him home right as rain in the morning."

"You're very kind," Hannah said softly.

Alicia found herself ushered to the coach but she hung back and waited for the nobility to enter first. She glanced up expectantly at the viscount, since he clearly outranked her poor, untitled self, but he motioned her in ahead of him. As she stepped in, his hand appeared under her elbow, steadying her.

Holding her tongue out of respect for Mr. and Mrs. Fitzpatrick, she swallowed and uttered a breathless "thank you" instead of the scathing words that entered her mind. She seated herself inside the comfortable coach. Hannah settled beside her furthest from the door. A lantern hanging from the ceiling illuminated the dark velvet trappings of the luxurious coach. The Fitzpatricks seated across from them. The viscount eased himself down next to Alicia, his thigh casually brushing against hers.

Alicia shrank back from him and edged closer to Hannah. "This is too kind of you, Mr. and Mrs. Fitzpatrick," she managed.

"Nonsense, my dear child, we are happy to do it." Mrs. Fitzpatrick happily leaned back against the cushioned seats. "This gives us further opportunity to speak with you."

Fortunately, they did not require much from her in the way of conversation, and Mr. Fitzpatrick kept them entertained with his dry sense of humor. Despite the hateful Lord Amesbury's magnetic and disturbing presence, Mr. Fitzpatrick and his charming wife's easy banter and unbelievable tales soothed her nerves and she actually began to relax as she listened to them.

"You're home." The viscount's voice sounded very near.

Disoriented, she rubbed her eyes. The coach had stopped. As she realized that she had fallen asleep in their company, a flood of mortification swept over her.

"Oh, no. Oh, please forgive me." Then, to further her shame, she became aware that her head had fallen onto Lord Amesbury's shoulder.

Amusement danced on his mouth. "I hope I provided some comfort to you, Miss Palmer."

There seemed no end to the embarrassments she must suffer in front of them. Or him.

Appalled at herself, she stammered, "Thank you. I mean, I'm so sorry. How rude of me."

"Think nothing of it, my dear," soothed Mrs. Fitzpatrick. "The hour is late and the evening eventful. I'm fatigued, myself."

In the lamplight, the viscount's face appeared deceptively soft and gentle. As she beheld his masculine beauty, the compassion and gentleness in his eyes, she had to remind herself that his face concealed a black soul. For a moment, she was sorry she had discovered it. The fantasy had been so sweet.

He smiled. "Aunt Livy is right. There is nothing to be concerned about."

Mr. Fitzpatrick agreed. "Quite right. We are all confident in our own ability to entertain guests. You were merely tired. Good evening, Miss Palmer. Miss Hannah."

"Good night, sir. Madam. And thank you very much. We're both in your debt."

"Any time, my dear."

Lord Amesbury handed her out of the coach but Alicia snatched her hand out of his. "Thank you, my lord," she said coldly.

His mouth curved upward as if he found her ire amusing. "You are quite welcome, Miss Palmer."

She battled a sudden heaviness and waited with

her back to the carriage for Hannah to alight. Lord Amesbury's heavy footsteps started toward her, but Alicia hurried up the front steps of her home as quickly as she dared.

"Miss Palmer."

No. Contempt flooded her until she thought she would drown. Only a man with no conscience could smile as he did after taking an innocent boy's life. Had he known before he pulled the trigger that the young man he dueled would loose his arm and die? Had he cared?

She wanted to hurl these questions at him, but knew she would burst into tears and make a scene. She had already been the center of unpleasant attention once tonight and did not care to do so again. Or upset Hannah, who did not know Lord Amesbury as the man who shot Armand.

"I have nothing to say to you, Lord Amesbury," she threw over her shoulder.

He caught up to her. "Miss Palmer, please wait."

She turned. "Please, you've done enough."

"Alicia, listen to me."

Shaking in anger, she turned in the middle of the steps. "I have not given you leave to call me by my Christian name."

"You're right, I apologize, but Miss Palmer, allow me to—"

"You've done enough. Leave me alone!"

Alicia bolted up the stairs and continued running until she reached her room. Before she could shut the door, Hannah wormed through. With the door closed, Alicia leaned against it and drew a steadying breath.

"What has gotten in to you tonight, Lissie?"

Alicia shook her head. "I'm sorry, Hannah. I'm very tired. And my head hurts."

"What was that all about with Lord Amesbury?"

Alicia sighed. "Nothing I wish to discuss at the

moment."

Hurt, Hannah sat down on the bed. "Why does no one ever tell me anything?"

"Forgive me, Hannah. I am a bit concerned for Robert. And the matter with Lord Amesbury is...not something that I wish to discuss in my present mood." She went to Hannah and put an arm around her. "Let's wash and change and retire. Things will look brighter tomorrow, you'll see."

What a disaster the last few days had been! Instead of attracting a husband, she had only run from every man who showed any interest in her. She pressed a hand over her mouth. Heaven help her, but the only man who ever truly interested her, had killed her twin.

CHAPTER 6

Alicia swept downstairs wearing her borrowed gown of pale amber moiré. Robert had just arisen. She shook her head at him but he grinned lazily back at her. For a moment, he appeared as he had before Armand's death.

"Where are you going, Cousin? How pretty you look."

"Elizabeth and her mother have invited me to attend the horserace at the Van Der Au's."

"Oh. Yes. Hmm. Planned on attending. Hannah not going?"

"She has a headache."

He looked down ruefully at his dressing robe. "I suppose I ought to bathe and change. Or at least change."

With mingled affection and disapproval, Alicia frowned. "You need a shave, too. I don't think there's enough time before the race begins for you to pull yourself together, Robbie."

"Probably right. I believe I'll have a brandy instead."

"Leave it alone, Robert," she pled.

"Have a nice time at the race." He waved over his shoulder as he headed to the library.

Uncle Willard appeared as the Hancock's carriage pulled up to the front steps.

"Elizabeth is here, Uncle. Good day," Alicia said.

"Tomorrow we are invited to the home of Colonel Westin for tea," Uncle Willard informed her.

Alicia gulped and fought the urge to burst into

tears. "Yes, Uncle," she replied meekly.

Heavy of heart, she climbed aboard the Hancock's coach, but Elizabeth's contagious excitement broke through Alicia's melancholy. Despite Mrs. Hancock's calming influence, they were exuberant when they arrived at the Van Der Au's estate for the race. The whole countryside appeared to have come.

"Miss Palmer. How lovely you look."

Evoking first pleasure, then dismay, that richly resonant voice set her nerves on edge. Steeling herself, she looked up at Lord Amesbury's smiling face. "My lord," she said shortly.

"Mrs. Hancock. Miss Hancock." The viscount smiled at the other two ladies, but when his gaze returned to Alicia, his eyes softened with true warmth.

Alicia faltered. She had been nothing but rude to him every time they met, and yet he always treated her with kindness. If only he had been kind to Armand.

"May I escort you lovely ladies?"

Before Alicia could open her mouth to refuse, Mrs. Hancock accepted. Lord Amesbury offered his arm to the lady.

She glanced at Alicia with a motherly smile. "Thank you, my lord, but I can walk with my daughter. Miss Palmer needs an escort."

Alicia pressed her lips together while Elizabeth and Mrs. Hancock fell in step together, leaving Alicia to walk with Lord Amesbury. He smiled and held out his arm.

She wanted to reject him. She truly did. Then why did her hand move to his arm?

Only to avoid a scene in front of the Hancocks, of course. His gaze held hers and for a moment, she thought she saw sorrow and gentleness there. She looked away.

"Mrs. Hancock!" Catherine's carefully schooled contralto voice called out. "Please, come join us. And Elizabeth, lovely to see you again. Good day, Alicia. Lord Amesbury." Her eyes locked on Lord Amesbury, though she greeted the ladies. "Come, join us. We've more food than we could possibly eat." She already sat between Captain Hawthorne and Mr. Walters, both very handsome young men, but needed Lord Amesbury to have the complete ensemble.

The viscount glanced at Alicia and then turned a gracious, if aloof, smile upon the raven-haired beauty. "How kind of you, Miss Sinclair, but we have a picnic spot already prepared. Good day. Come, ladies, shall we?"

Surprised, Alicia looked up at him. Perhaps she'd misjudged him. If the viscount saw through Catherine's beauty to the false, title- and fortune-hunter that lurked underneath, perhaps he was less shallow than she assumed. Other gentlemen stumbled all over themselves to gain her favor.

Catherine's face fell at the viscount's rejection, but she rallied and turned a venomous gaze to Alicia. Under Catherine's stare, Alicia raised her chin a fraction and tightened her grip on her handsome escort's arm, just to spite Catherine. Certainly not because she wanted to be in the viscount's presence.

Sitting next to Catherine, Captain Hawthorne's eyes rested upon her, his dark eyes holding her gaze a moment longer than seemed polite. Awkwardly, Alicia smiled, which he returned, but something in the coolness of his gaze gave her pause.

Lord Amesbury led them through the emerald lawn spread with chairs and blankets. Unfurled parasols dotted the sun-drenched landscape like colorful clouds floating above the ground. Fragrances of honeysuckle and lilac wafted across the breeze. Other couples and families walked or sat in groups as they enjoyed the clear summer day, reveling in the anticipation of the race, or the hunt of the two-legged kind. Ladies fluttered their eyes and flirted with gentlemen, who in turn joined the game with their own agendas.

Mr. de Champs' wide smile flashed as he nodded at them in greeting. When Mr. de Champs met her eyes, his guileless smile broadened. After he introduced them to the lovely redhead on his arm, they chatted for a moment before parting.

"Miss Palmer!"

Oh, no. That nasally whine could only belong to Colonel Westin. She halted and turned, wishing she could ignore manners for a change.

Colonel Westin frowned at her. "You never took a turn about the garden at the ball with me. Then I called upon you yesterday and was told you were not at home." He glowered in disapproval. "If I agree to marry you, I will expect you to report to me your whereabouts at all times."

Stunned at such an outrageous statement, Alicia took at step back. Horrible, hateful man. She would rather marry a disfigured cripple than him. She made a mental note to tell Uncle to send their regrets for the tea tomorrow. She paused. She couldn't. Regardless of her feelings for the man, he remained her best prospect for saving her family from prison.

Lord Amesbury broke in smoothly. "You are not wed, nor are you even affianced. Therefore it is not her duty to report to you at all, sir. Come, ladies, our picnic awaits."

Alicia found herself drawn into Lord Amesbury's eyes. He had come to her rescue, instantly and incisively protecting her, and putting Colonel Westin in his place. She could not deny his action had been nothing short of gallant. As he looked down at her, a lazy smile appeared on one side of his mouth.

She severed their eye contact. She would rather be indebted to anyone but Armand's slayer. And now, she might have just lost her family's one hope of rescue.

"The nerve of that man!" Mrs. Hancock cried. "You can be sure I'll never put Colonel Westin on any of my guest lists."

"That was most chivalrous of you to come to her defense, Lord Amesbury," Elizabeth said.

"Quite right, sir. Glad you cut him. I shall be sure Mr. Hancock cuts him dead the next time that odious man has the nerve to address one of us," sniffed Mrs. Hancock.

Elizabeth turned to her. "Surely that wasn't a prospect."

Alicia shot a warning look at her friend and then risked a glance at the viscount. He wore an impassive expression, but his jaw had hardened. She did not wish to discuss her situation within hearing of anyone else. Least of all, Lord Amesbury.

She realized her hand clenched his arm, and she purposely relaxed her fingers. "He has not yet made a formal offer," she replied quietly, hoping her friend would drop the subject.

Lord Amesbury placed his free hand over hers. She was appalled at how comforting the gesture felt. "Shall we take a turn about the grounds first, or shall we fall upon the picnic?"

"You really do have a picnic?"

A rakish grin lit up his handsome face. "A gentleman is always prepared in the hopes that he might be graced with the presence of desirable company."

Elizabeth looked up at him adoringly. "How lovely. And how considerate of you to invite us to join you. I have never been to a race and I confess I did not know what to expect." She looked searchingly at Alicia, confused at her reluctance.

Alicia did not enlighten her.

The viscount had indeed come prepared. His tiger, a rosy-cheeked lad who appeared to not have quite grown into his new legs, turned away from the matched team he tended and helped the viscount retrieve blankets and enough food to feed several grown men. Lord Amesbury grinned and ruffled the tiger's hair. The boy beamed before he returned to the horses.

Lord Amesbury leaned on one elbow on the blanket with his legs stretched out, and regaled them with wild tales from the sea. Alicia suspected they were two parts fabrication and one part truth, but his rich voice wrapped around them and held them spell-bound. His eyes sparkled mischievously, as if he mocked himself each time he mocked the manners and mores of English culture and compared it to life at sea. She could not resist his infectious laughter.

When the conversation reached a lull, Mrs. Hancock primly wiped her mouth with a napkin. "How are your aunt and uncle?"

"Very well. My aunt is busily organizing some sort of charity. Uncle Andrew had planned on attending the race, but his leg sometimes bothers him due to an old injury. I'm grateful to you all for not letting my picnic go to waste. Cook would have been most put out if it had returned uneaten."

"Your uncle's cook is legendary," Mrs. Hancock agreed.

The viscount's eyes twinkled. "Indeed. I tease my aunt that the only reason I visit her is so that I might partake of Cook's remarkable meals."

Alicia smiled in spite of herself.

Elizabeth giggled. "That's wicked of you." Then she looked alarmed as if she had just realized what she had said. "Ah, I mean, my lord ... "

The viscount waved away her concern. "Quite

right. I am wicked and not ashamed of it, Miss Hancock. My aunt makes a habit of reminding me of that flaw continuously."

"Your aunt is a bit outspoken, but I have never known a kinder woman than Mrs. Fitzpatrick," Mrs. Hancock interjected.

His face softened. "That she is, Mrs. Hancock."

A cry went up and Alicia craned her neck, trying to find the source.

"The race is about to begin." Excitement colored the viscount's voice. As they approached the racecourse, Lord Amesbury eyed the racers lining up. "If I were to bet, I would choose the chestnut."

"Would you? Why?" Alicia asked, interested in spite of herself. "The Arabian is the chosen favorite, I hear."

"The Arabian will be a good contender. They typically have great endurance, so they're ideal for a long race, but this isn't a long race."

Elizabeth peered at the horses. "Which one is the Arabian?"

"The black coming on. He's a beauty. But the chestnut has powerful hind quarters so he's probably a good jumper. And this race is shorter which will be the advantage for a sprinter like him. The bay, however, is taller and would have a longer stride. Of course, appearances are not everything. The one with the heart of a winner will cross the finish line first."

Alicia turned to him. "You don't consider the others contenders?"

The viscount scanned the horses as they lined up to begin, his blue eyes thoughtful. "No, I wouldn't say so, but I haven't seen any of them run, so it's hard to tell."

A signal began the race. Though Alicia had never before taken an interest in horse-racing, her pulse quickened in excitement as the horses and riders vied for the lead. The chestnut horse pulled out in front but soon the Arabian caught up to him as they passed the spot where Alicia stood. The racers ran past a second time in the same position, but by the third, the Arabian had passed them. With only one more lap to go, a gray from behind the group darted in front, taking the lead by a nose as they crossed the finish line.

Lord Amesbury wore a self-deprecating smile.

"And you did not even see that one as a contender," Elizabeth mused, clearly surprised.

Alicia looked back at the gray stallion slowing to a trot under a rainfall of flowers. "The one with the heart of the winner."

"Indeed. Appearances truly are often deceiving," Lord Amesbury mused.

Smiling, Alicia rode home that afternoon with Elizabeth and Mrs. Hancock, grateful for a few hours to forget about her impending marriage to the unknown man of her uncle's choosing. She'd enjoyed herself despite Lord Amesbury's presence. Or perhaps because of it.

However, notwithstanding his winning smile or charming conversation, a picnic and a pleasant afternoon certainly did not buy forgiveness for her brother's death.

CHAPTER 7

"I believe I shall offer for Alicia Palmer."

Cole stared at young Mr. de Champs, shocked at his bold statement.

The senior Mr. de Champs, a thin, elegant gentleman, removed the cigar from his mouth.

Before he could speak, the younger man held up his hand. "I am aware that she has only a small piece of land for a dowry, and that her uncle is counting on her husband to pay his debts, but she has won my affection. She comes from a good family; her parents were exemplary. I also understand that potential husbands are already in negotiation. If we had more time, I would court her first, but we do not have that luxury. I have no doubt that my esteem for her will only grow after we marry."

Having delivered his announcement, young Mr. de Champs, wearing a determined expression, left the fireplace mantle and took a seat in the de Champs' study.

Overall, de Champs seemed a good man. Not good enough for Alicia Palmer, but certainly more fitting than any of the other prospects Cole knew her uncle asked her to consider. At least this man's affection seemed genuine.

"I shall call upon her, and ask her feelings upon the matter before I speak with her uncle," the younger man continued, his voice growing steadily more confident.

The de Champs family, close friends of Uncle Andrew and Aunt Livy, had invited them and Cole for dinner, after which the men gathered for their habitual male-only companionship, leaving the women to discuss what they would. Cole suspected that their topics often included the men, and not in flattering tones. Rightly so, perhaps.

The senior Mr. de Champs said, "Do you know what kind of debt her uncle has amassed?"

The younger man faltered. "I understand it's a great deal."

When Mr. de Champs named the sum, considerable coughing followed.

The would-be suitor looked crestfallen. "I don't know how I can part with that sum and still be able to offer her a comfortable life."

"Nor do I wish you to spend it more or less buying a wife, however desirable," added his father.

Uncle Andrew frowned slightly. "Both Colonel Westin and Mr. Braxton have shown interest. What's odd, is Mr. Braxton suddenly closed up his house and left England. Said something about wanting to see Africa for an extended holiday."

Cole almost laughed out loud. Apparently, their little *tête á tête* had been a success. Now he didn't have to be concerned Braxton would spread a vicious rumor about her.

The elder Mr. de Champs put his cigar back in his mouth and drew a long drag before speaking again. "She's not even what I'd call beautiful. Pretty, perhaps, but not uncommonly so."

"Oh, but she is, Father," young de Champs protested. "If only you would speak with her. She has the prettiest eyes. And she's the most sincere and truly kind lady I've ever known."

Cole had to agree, but he refrained from commenting. He watched young de Champs narrowly, seeing flaws he had not noticed before, with a growing sense of dislike. Young, flighty, and impulsive. Rather foppish. Bordering on effeminate.

Foolish. He should not think of de Champs as a competitor. What did he care? He did not even wish to marry in the immediate future. And he certainly had no designs on Miss Palmer.

But with the exception of the very young and naïve Mr. de Champs, the other men interested in marrying her gave Cole the shivers. He had no wish to see such an innocent creature wed to the likes of Colonel Westin, the devil who publicly dressed her down at the races as if she were an errant child. Alicia Palmer's fate with the colonel would be no better than with that brute Mr. Braxton who'd assaulted her at the ball. Under the colonel's thumb, she would either shrivel up and die, or become embittered like his sister Margaret with her disastrous marriage.

"Few could compete with Colonel Westin's fortune." Uncle Andrew said.

"Do you know the man?" Cole asked.

"Recluse. Has buried two wives already. Stingy curmudgeon. I'm surprised he's willing to part with his money at all. He employs far too few servants because he's too miserly to hire more. Has had to close off both wings and live in the main house. He seems harmless, but I've seen him fly into a rage I found truly terrifying." Uncle Andrew virtually shuddered. "I wouldn't marry *my* niece to him."

Mr. de Champs looked crestfallen. "I wish I could save her from such a fate."

Cole did, too. He stilled. No. Stupid idea. He did not have the desire to marry. Not yet. Not even out of pity. Especially not out of pity.

He had the means, though. It could be done. And he did admire the girl. She had revealed herself a delightful, witty young lady with a smile that rivaled the sun after a storm. He'd grown aware of her in a keenly male way and had caught himself plotting when he could arrange their next meeting. Marrying a lady such as she did not seem an unpleasant prospect.

He almost cursed out loud.

Absolutely not. Sympathy, or its equally stupid brother, Chivalry, both presented ridiculous notions that should not be followed. Ever. Especially when they involved a permanent arrangement such as marriage.

Besides, she clearly hated him for shooting her brother. Her *twin* brother, no less.

Cole remained silent while the senior Mr. de Champs stripped his son of any hope that he might ever marry Miss Alicia Palmer. All the while, Cole swallowed the urge to rise to her defense and declare her many fine qualities which made her a desirable wife, well worth the exorbitant fee her uncle required. For someone else. Not himself, of course.

When they finally said good night, Cole stared unseeing out the dark windows of the coach.

"Cole."

He blinked and then realized that Aunt Livy had been addressing him. "What, Aunt?"

"Miss Hermione de Champs. How did you find her?"

"Painfully shy."

"Yes, poor dear, but pretty, was she not?"

Cole pressed his fingers to the bridge of his nose in an attempt to ward off a looming headache brought on by an over-use of his patience. "Is that why we were invited to dinner, so you and Mrs. de Champs could determine our suitability?"

Aunt Livy waved her hand impatiently. "Of course, dear."

Cole lowered his hand. "Perhaps I should find Jared. The sea is looking more appealing."

"Don't you dare run away and play pirate again with your brother. I haven't forgiven you for the last time. It's taken you too long to remember your genteel upbringing."

Cole turned a baleful frown upon her. "The time I served as an officer in the Royal Navy was far bloodier than the year I sailed with Jared."

"We were at war. Your service in the Navy was honorable. Piracy is disgraceful, and if it were ever common knowledge, you'd both—" She stopped herself from pronouncing a fate he knew all too well. "I wish your brother would just come home."

He barked a sharp laugh. "Not likely. That would thrust him back into 'polite' society where determining one's foes becomes more difficult, and the battles more vicious."

"You are the firstborn son of an earl and have a duty to marry to further the line."

"You take great delight in reminding me of that."

Uncle Andrew chuckled. "You may have better luck finding Grant a wife, my love."

Aunt Livy snorted. "That might take the rest of my days."

Cole choked at the thought of his brother Grant marrying. "What daft female would take him? He's the most cynical, hardened man I've ever known. Hence his disreputable pastime."

"Bow Street Runners are doing much for the safety of London." Uncle Andrew protested.

Cole nodded. "Because they're as ruthless as the criminals they fight."

Aunt Livy fanned herself. "Certainly not a fitting occupation for the son of an earl."

Uncle Andrew would not be deterred. "Besides, he's not actually a Runner; he only assists them when they have a particularly interesting case. And the Runners are honorable men dedicated to protecting the public. I can understand why Grant likes them."

"I suppose there's a shred of honor in Grant's

black heart," Cole conceded. "In his own twisted way, he's trying to contribute. However, I still think he should have been a Magistrate if he wanted to uphold the law."

"Every family needs a black sheep, I suppose. Only yours has two. A thief-taker and a pirate." Aunt Livy made a tsking sound. "Why is it that Christian is the only member of the family willing to do as he ought?"

"The perfectly perfect Christian," Cole said in the same sing song voice with which they'd taunted the youngest Amesbury brother all his life.

Aunt Livy waggled her closed fan at Cole. "Don't think you can get away with changing the subject, you naughty boy."

"Not me. Uncle Andrew brought up Grant." How did Aunt Livy always manage to make him feel like a six-year old?

Uncle Andrew smirked. "Perhaps I should go buy Miss Palmer for you, Cole. You could get the whole marrying business over with, produce an heir and then set her up in the country where you can ignore her if you wish. It would save her from all those other unsavory characters. And better yet, it would silence your aunt. I've been trying for thirty-seven years and am starting to believe it cannot be done."

Aunt Livy whacked his arm smartly with her fan.

"I don't need your money, Uncle. I certainly have the means to pay off her family myself, if I were so inclined." Cole realized that they both watched him too carefully. He quickly arranged an uninterested expression on his face and brushed an imaginary spec off his sleeve.

"Ahh." Uncle Andrew exchanged meaningful looks with Aunt Livy whose triumphant smile grew in direct proportion to Cole's attempt at appearing bored.

"It's not what you think." He knew with growing alarm that nothing he could say now would dissuade them from believing what they wished. "Stay out of this," he snapped.

Uncle Andrew cleared his throat. "Cole, there's nothing wrong with developing feelings for a young lady."

"I have no feelings. Not for her. Not for anyone. And I'll thank you to not bring it up again." He felt like a petulant child trying to profess his innocence. "Perhaps I've stayed too long. I hear Italy is nice this time of year."

Aunt Livy leaned across to pat his arm and he had to force himself to not yank back out of her reach. "Don't go yet, dear. I vow I will respect your privacy."

"Why start now?" he snarled.

"Because I can see that you are quite vexed by it. You both may consider me silenced." She pressed her fingers over her mouth and glanced at Uncle Andrew. "In *this* matter, at least."

Andrew grinned and kissed her gloved fingers. Their expressions for one another betrayed their obvious affection, despite their banter. They loved each other, despite the years and accompanying illnesses and injuries, and their strong personalities. Or perhaps because of them.

That he might have such a comfortable relationship with another seemed a tantalizing dream.

CHAPTER 8

"Touché."

Grinning, Cole lowered his rapier and held out a hand to his opponent. The duke shook it before they removed their protective coverings and handed their rapiers and gear to the servants.

"Well done, Amesbury," the other man praised.

Beads of perspiration ran down Cole's face and back. "And to you, my lord duke. You execute your moves flawlessly."

Fencing always proved an interesting diversion. Submersing himself in technique and strategy restored a sense of balance to his world.

"Next time you have the urge to fence, send me word. I enjoy a challenging opponent. So many are unable to offer any real sport," the duke said.

"I shall, my lord duke. Thank you." Cole toweled off his face.

Over the course of the week-long house party, the duke had proven himself remarkably gracious. A dignified gentleman, the duke was an attentive and generous host.

Too bad Miss Sinclair and her family were also invited to the same house party. Cole had grown weary of her scheming.

"Your Grace." A servant ran into the room.

The Duke gave a wry smile. "Duties, it appears, Amesbury."

Cole grinned. "Thank you again for the excellent match." They shook hands again and Cole went back to his room to bathe and change.

"Are you enjoying yourself, sir?" His valet, Stephens, asked as he assisted.

Stephens was far too outspoken and opinionated, but Cole viewed him as a friend first and a servant second. A former comrade-at-arms, they had saved each other's lives many times. And Stephens proved his loyalty repeatedly when Cole found himself dodging eager debutantes or their overzealous mothers. Or when he wished to arrange a discreet liaison.

Cole grimaced. "Outside of the hunting and fencing matches, the only things I truly enjoyed, the week has been filled with games of all kinds and women with matrimony on their minds. Aunt Livy probably helped plan the menu, commonly known as the guest list. I'm surprised they didn't serve me to the ladies on a platter sautéed in butter."

Stephens chuckled. "Miss Catherine Sinclair would have been the first to take a serving."

"No doubt. Although she did prove herself a worthy partner in whist. Her ability to bluff won us many rounds last evening." Few women had perfected the art of keeping her face as perfectly impassive as Miss Sinclair. He wondered if the woman was even capable of emotion. "Overall, however, the whole party has been an adventure in escapes from feminine wiles."

He'd briefly considered accepting the lovely young widow Norrington's offer for a liaison last night. Lately, however, even the most skilled and passionate women failed to fill the emptiness that seemed to be devouring him, one bite at a time.

"Thank heavens tomorrow the party will come to a close and we can escape back to the relative safety of Uncle Andrew's estate," Cole added.

After bathing and changing, and receiving a fortifying grin from Stephens, Cole went downstairs for the next round. Dinner passed as smoothly as could be hoped, but he still welcomed the after-dinner ritual to enjoy port or brandy and manly conversation, *sans* the ladies.

Cole nursed his brandy outside the circle of men. He had his own opinions but kept them to himself tonight. Anytime Members of Parliament or of the House of Lords began discussing politics, Cole usually kept his ears open and his mouth closed. His father, the fifth Earl Tarrington, always took his responsibility as a member of the House of Lords seriously and never missed a session until his health began to decline.

When Cole assumed the title of Sixth Earl Tarrington, he would do his duty faithfully, and be a man of whom his father would be proud. It was the least he could do considering how he'd disappointed his father in his youth.

The conversation became bawdy as the glasses drained and refilled and drained. Cole only half-listened without comment, staring into his glass, absently watching the liquid swirl. Then the name Palmer jerked his attention back to the men.

"Willard Palmer can't make a business deal to save his life these days," the marquis said.

The duke frowned. "I met him years ago. He seemed a decent sort then."

"Ever since he inherited his brother's estate, it's been bad luck. One loss after another."

"Too bad. Decent sort," the duke repeated.

Alicia's face swam before Cole's eyes. He had never obsessed over a woman in this manner. And Alicia Palmer failed to fit the type that normally piqued his interest—unremarkable in many counts and far too innocent.

But she was different. Perhaps there lay the key. He had met so many Catherines that he grew weary of their pretenses.

Alicia's compassion had been refreshing. Her

concern for people. Her desire to include and attend everyone with whom she came in contact, not in a calculating way like Catherine Sinclair, but in a way that made them feel important, as if she truly believed they were. Cole had witnessed Mr. de Champs' chest swell his pleasure in her attentive company at Lord and Lady Sinclair's ball. She had done the same with every man she spoke with, looking at them as if they were the only person in the room, asking in her soft tones about their families and their lives, as if she truly cared. After only moments in her presence, each man, young or old, all walked taller.

Her expressions revealed her true feelings when she thought no one watched; her hurt when Catherine and her parents scorned her, her amused disapproval at Catherine's flirtatiousness, her alarm when she could not remember a name right away, her sweet pleasure when others remembered her. Seeing her thoughts cross her face so plainly had been so entertaining, he wanted to sit down and watch her. Her genuine kindness continued to amaze him. She'd been compassionate to Catherine Sinclair's friend. Her reaction to the footman dropping a tray of food at the dinner party revealed no anger, no vindication, only concern for the footman's distress and embarrassment for being the focus of attention.

Cole scowled. Kindness. Bah! When did that become anything but blasé? So she was uncomplicated and wore her heart on display. So what? He did not want to marry for several more years, despite his aunt's machinations. Surely it would take another decade or so to find a suitable girl. That settled, he squared his shoulders and left the study to find Stephens.

"Oh, Cole, there you are, dear."

Cole arranged his mouth into a smile. Then

when he turned and saw his aunt, his smile turned into a grin. Her turban sat crookedly upon her head.

"We were just discussing you, dear. Come into my room, I need to speak with you."

Cole grimaced. That never boded well. Perhaps someone convinced her that he'd developed an interest in their daughter. His hopes of escaping faded as he followed her to her room.

She sat at a chair near the fireplace and turned toward him. "May I offer you a drink, dear?"

Cole waved it away. "I already had a brandy downstairs."

"Now, dear, tell me. What do you think of the duke?"

"I wish I'd met him sooner."

She leaned back, pleased. "And his sister?"

Cole blinked. His sister? Oh, the redhead who giggled too much. "She's not someone I had thought of at all, Aunt."

"Cole! She is our host's sister. She likes you. Be honest, what do you think of her?"

Since this would surely be a long night, Cole found a comfortable chair. "She is unremarkable."

Aunt Livy's face fell. "Oh, that's too bad. She would be an excellent match, you know. And the duke thinks highly of you. He would probably give his consent."

He raised his brows. "Are you saying other fathers would not give their consent?"

"One never knows. And you have developed a bit of a reputation, you know."

"Good. It will scare off any promising matches."

She pulled her turban off and waved it at him. Her hair stuck out in all directions, making her appear as if she'd suffered a terrible fright. "You are heartless, you know that?"

Cole fought to keep his face straight at the comical sight. "If I ever make the mistake of forgetting, I am sure you will remind me soon enough."

"Cole, be a good boy and find someone soon. I won't live forever and I wish to meet your son before I die."

Cole frowned. "You are only sixty and in excellent health."

"Then think of your father."

"Yes. He had the misfortune of having a son like me. And Jared. Then Grant. I wouldn't wish children such as us on any respectable girl." Cole leaned back with his hands folded behind his head and stretched his legs out, crossing them at the ankles.

"Perhaps your heir will be respectable. Not like you. Nor Jared."

"No, I think Jared makes even me seem a gentleman."

"Your poor mother," she lamented.

"Have you ever considered that it might be your influence upon us, Aunt?"

She wagged her finger at him. "Come, now, Cole. My own children turned out all right. And perhaps your children will be more like Christian."

Cole grinned. The perfectly perfect Christian should have been the heir to the earldom. He was good, and responsible, and everything Mother longed for in a son. At times, Cole almost hated him, except no one could muster up a disliking for the youngest Amesbury boy.

"I doubt such goodness is likely to be produced from me."

"Cooperate with me. Your father asked me to help guide you. Isn't there anyone here who piques your interest? Catherine Sinclair comes from a good family. She's quite beautiful."

"She harbors a stone in her breast she calls a heart."

Aunt Livy nodded pensively. "She is a bit

manipulative, I suppose, but it will take cunning to win you." She proceeded to list the names and virtues of every girl in attendance at the house party, and everyone who had been at the Sinclair's ball. Cole's ears perked when she mentioned Alicia Palmer.

"Now, she is truly a delightful girl. Very closed-mouthed about your first meeting. I think she has mixed feelings about you. Perhaps you could correct whatever went wrong then. I have already asked her to come to tea sometime after our return home."

However tempting, now would be the worst possible time to ask Aunt Livy about Alicia Palmer; she might mistake his questions for genuine interest and then there would be no stopping her.

He stood up. "I am through discussing this boorish subject. Good night, Aunt."

"Cole, please, sit down." Her face and voice both sobered.

Cole complied, but he folded his arms and glared at her. The fire popped and crackled in the grate in the stillness of the night.

"What is wrong with you, dear? If it isn't a lady, what is it?"

He let his arms slid down to the arms of the chair. Perhaps it was the brandy. Perhaps he was tired of wondering. "Someone mentioned a Palmer boy who had been shot."

"Yes."

"Do you know the details?"

"No. I am not close to the family. Why? What's disturbing you?"

He stood and pressed a kiss to her cheek. "Nothing, Aunt, just curious. Good night."

CHAPTER 9

"Oh, look at this one." Hannah inhaled deeply before she carefully snipped a flower. Beaming, she handed it to Alicia. "We'll have a lovely table arrangement for dinner tonight."

Sunlight slanted through Hannah's hair, making it shimmer gold. She had all the fragile beauty of *Maman* and the same thoughtful, careful ways of Papa. Alicia dredged up a smile, trying to cover her concerns.

The head cook said if she didn't receive her pay by the end of the month, she'd be forced to give notice, as well. The cook's assistant had already left. How could they hope to cope without a cook? Of course, Uncle Willard's creditors had only given them until the end of the month, too. If she didn't marry by then, a cook would be the least of their concerns.

Mr. Braxton had left the country without making an offer, and Alicia's relief overshadowed any curiosity of the reason. But Colonel Westin, despite the set-down Lord Amesbury gave him at the races, had agreed to pay Uncle Willard's debts and provide a respectable dowry for Hannah in exchange for marriage to Alicia and her dowered plot of land bordering his own. No one else could afford her. Or had the desire.

Alicia made a vow to stop running away from her troubles. She would encourage Colonel Westin, and when his offer came, tell him she'd be honored to be his bride. And hope the sick feeling in her stomach would fade in time.

Hoof beats reached her ears. A stunning white horse cantered into view and rode up to the house. Alicia could not clearly see the rider from this distance, but knew Colonel Westin never rode horseback. Perhaps the visitor sought Robert or Uncle. She turned her attention to Hannah, accepted the next flower, and laid it in her basket with the others.

They spoke of inconsequential matters, enjoying each other's company while Alicia tried to shake off her melancholy. A chill breeze began, blowing in a large, dark cloud. Alicia looked up to determine if the cloud looked dark enough to threaten rain.

Hannah began humming. She seemed so content that Alicia did not wish to spoil the afternoon by suggesting they return inside merely because of a few clouds. She said nothing.

"Miss Palmer," a male voice called.

She looked up. At that moment, the clouds parted and shone down on the most devastatingly handsome man that ever lived. She gaped at him, undone by the sheer power and masculinity of that man. His long, muscular legs brought his marvelous form toward her in space-devouring strides. Again, the graceful, predatory way he moved reminded her of a great cat. His immaculately tailored clothing included a creamy cravat, rich green frockcoat, striped waistcoat, fawn breeches, and black Hessians. He casually carried his top coat over his arm and his hat in his hand, but there was nothing casual about his purposeful stride. Sunlight shimmered off his sable hair. How could such a heartless man be encased in such beauty!

"Lord Amesbury," she all but stammered.

She and Hannah both sank into curtseys while Alicia's heart pounded so noisily she expected Hannah to stare. The clouds darkened, covering the sun.

"Forgive me for interrupting. May we walk?" He bestowed that familiar, heart-thumping smile. Clearly, any conscience he might have possessed at birth no longer resided within him.

Alicia glanced at Hannah who could have lit up a large room with the intensity of her blush. Alicia wanted to run, to escape the unrelenting power of his magnetism. Her mouth dried and her palms grew moist, but she could hardly refuse. Fiend!

She reminded herself of her vow to stop running and drew herself up. "Of course."

The coolness of her voice brought Hannah's head up in surprise. Lord Amesbury sobered and glanced back the direction he'd come, as if second-guessing his mission. Alicia wondered if it were the first time any lady had been less than enthusiastic at the honor of spending time in his presence. Perhaps this would be good for his humility.

He solemnly offered them each an arm. He slowed his pace to match their smaller strides, and they strolled down the garden paths, commenting on the gardens, the weather, and everyone's health. He smiled down at her, his eyes almost a tangible caress. Again, gentleness shone there. Alicia wished heartily he would leave and take her swirling, chaotic emotions with him.

Finally, realizing that he would never mention the reason for his visit with Hannah next to them, she turned to her sister. "Hannah, dearest, I see O'Leary up ahead. Would you ask him when he plans to dig up the bulbs?"

Hannah blinked at the odd request, glanced at Lord Amesbury and murmured an assent. She curtsied prettily to the viscount, before trotting to the gardener out of hearing.

The look of gratitude he gave her might have softened her heart if it had come from anyone but

99

Lord Amesbury.

"Is there something you wished to discuss, Lord Amesbury, or is this merely a social call?" Alicia could not decipher his sideways glance.

"I know it's bold of me to pry, but I must ask, whom are you considering for a husband?"

She pressed her lips together. "You're correct. You are both bold and prying."

"Please oblige me."

Alicia looked over the horizon. "Colonel Westin."

"The cretin who spoke so rudely to you at the race?"

She stared down at the ground. "I have no choice."

"Everyone has a choice."

She shook her head, trying to steady her voice. "I don't. This will save us all from debtor's prison. It's the only way."

He nodded. "I understand."

Alicia stared at him. How dare he think he understood her! A surge of anger loosened her tongue as she jerked her hand from his arm and whirled on him. "It's all your fault. If you hadn't shot my twin in that ridiculous duel in London, he would be alive and I would not be subjected to my uncle's problems."

A brief pause followed her outburst and his features settled into a puzzled frown. "I only shot him in the arm."

"He developed an infection from the wound and the surgeon had to amputate his arm at the shoulder. They gave him opium for the pain. It became an addiction. He faded further and further away. One night..." her voice caught and she tried to swallow. "One night he took too much. Whether he could no longer face life without an arm, or it was accidental, I will never know. I found him late that night..." A sob tore through the lump in her throat.

"You killed him just as surely as if you had put a bullet through his heart!" Her whole body shook, and her fingernails dug into her palms.

Though she could not see him clearly through her tears, he remained motionless, without a word of defense.

"After my parents died, Armand would have inherited and I would be safe with him. But he died three months after they did and now I am at the mercy of my uncle who has ruined us!"

His voice hushed. "I'm so sorry. I truly did not know."

Alicia turned away. She began walking faster and faster until she was running back to her home. Drowning in grief, she stumbled to her room and collapsed upon her bed.

What was Lord Amesbury's game? Why did he act with kindness toward her when he was so clearly a man of depravity?

It did not matter. His handsome face harbored her brother's killer and no amount of wishing would change that truth.

CHAPTER 10

Cole heard Alicia's retreating footsteps. He felt nothing but emptiness as he stumbled to a stone bench and sank his face into his hands.

He had killed that boy.

He had killed him over a lightskirt in lady's guise who demanded he defend her honor. After all the carnage of the war, the last thing Cole wanted was more blood on his hands. For that reason, he hadn't lasted more than a year as a pirate. It was bad enough to kill in war; fighting over a bit of treasure seemed shallow, even for a hard-hearted cad like him. But like the fool he was, he'd challenge the duel and had watched, recoiling, as Armand groaned in pain, clutching a bleeding arm.

Cole went to the Palmers townhouse to inquire about his opponent. The servants told Cole that the bleeding had stopped and Armand would make a recovery. Instead, he had lost his arm. And then he had died. Alicia had watched him suffer.

And now, one of the few truly genuine ladies he had ever met was alone, doomed to marry a man who would look upon her as an object and mistreat her.

It was his fault.

Rain began to fall, gently at first, but gradually increasing in ferocity. Alone in the garden now, Cole raised up and stared into the gloom and blinked as water hit his eyes.

She hated him. He couldn't blame her.

Cole stumbled toward André, mounted, and

urged the horse to a reckless gallop along the dark highway.

Alicia would marry another. He should not care. She was nothing to him.

But his actions directly affected her fate. Because of him she was alone, and that made her his responsibility. He had to act. The shame in her eyes as Colonel Westin publicly humiliated her angered him. The terror as she fled from Mr. Braxton at the ball enraged him. He had to do something to protect her. His honor, annoying thing that it was, demanded action. His heart had nothing to do with it.

He was also turning into a liar.

The only way he could save her would be to marry her himself. But she would never marry him, not even to escape a worse fate at another man's hands. If only he could find another to marry her, someone who would treat her well and protect her from harm.

He ground his teeth. The thought of another man touching her made him ill.

The rain had progressed to a howling storm by the time he got back to Uncle Andrew's house.

"Cole! Good heavens, what has happened to you?" Uncle Andrew said as Cole burst through the doors. "Go and change at once. Here, you need this." He thrust a brandy into Cole's hand.

Cole downed it in one gulp and handed the empty glass back. He strode up stairs to endure Stephens' ministrations.

Stephens held his tongue longer than usual as he peeled off the wet clothing and helped him dry. "Met with the devil today?"

"Yes. His name is Cole Amesbury."

"Ah. Skeletons out of the closet?"

"One I didn't know I had." Fearing Stephens would suffer a breakdown owing to his curiosity,

Cole sighed. "Remember Armand Palmer from London?"

"The insolent boy who needed a lesson in manners?"

"The same. He died."

Stephens whistled slowly. "And you just found out?"

Cole nodded glumly.

"Why wasn't there an inquiry?"

"He died from an opium addiction. After they amputated his arm. The arm I shot."

Stephens shook his head and swore like a sailor. "Incompetent English doctors. They probably just bled him and then puzzled over why his wound sickened." He helped him into dry clothing. "Any relation to the Palmers here?"

"Alicia Palmer's twin brother."

Stephens paused. "Ooooh. The scuttlebutt among the servants' circle is that she needs a rich husband."

"Don't they all!" Her fate wasn't his problem. Dozens of young ladies shared her predicament and he had never been tempted to rescue any of them. Thank heavens.

And yet, he killed her brother, however unwittingly, which made him responsible for her.

Cole clenched his jaw. He thought he had silenced his conscience years ago. If the war hadn't done it, his year as a pirate with his brother Jared should have. A conscience had proved a bothersome thing, and honor, even worse.

"She's an orphan, isn't she?" Stephens asked.

"Yes. So what? Another sad tale. Women love them."

Stephens remained silent, but on days like today, Cole wished his valet would give him an excuse to thrash him. Or maybe he did not need one. "Let's go box."

Stephens looked appropriately horrified. "In the mood you are in? Do you think I've suddenly gone barking mad?"

"Drop the valet guise for a few hours and fight with me like the prize pugilist you were meant to be."

Stephens considered. "Does your uncle have any gear?"

"Do we need any?"

Stephens grinned. "Don't hit me in the face. One of the cook's assistants is pretty, and she thinks I'm a handsome fellow." With his striking Romany looks, Cole knew Stephens seldom lacked for feminine company when he desired it.

Cole snorted. "She must be near-sighted. And if I hit your face, it will be because you were too slow to block me."

They found an empty room and cleared away the furniture. After stripping down to their breeches, they began. If they were in a civilized club in London, they would have sparred in their shirt sleeves, but today they fought pirate-style in a way that tapped into the beast inside.

It soon became obvious that his former comrade-at-arms did not have his heart in it; he did not exploit obvious openings and remained mostly defensive to let Cole work through his self-recrimination. The pity tactic only fueled Cole's anger.

"Come on, don't go soft. My sister fights better than you."

Stephens humored him. His valet excelled in fisticuffs, but tonight Cole's frustration made him reckless, which made them evenly matched. By the time they were both too tired to stand, Cole felt like he'd been beaten with a tree trunk. Hurting in places he forgot he owned, he lay gasping on the floor and turned his head toward Stephens. The other man lay with his eyes closed and dabbed at his lip, not looking any better than Cole felt. Their breath sounded harsh in the quiet room.

A servant cautiously opened the door. "My Lord?"

Cole raised his head.

The footman moistened his lips nervously as he eyed them. "If you're finished, the missus would have a word with you."

Perfect. Aunt Livy's tongue lashing would hurt as bad as Stephens's fists. He should hand her a horsewhip and let her do her worst. He deserved it. He rolled over on the floor.

Stephens opened his eyes and grinned at him. "I haven't had that much fun since we left your brother's ship. It isn't everyday a valet gets to hit his master."

"Don't become too comfortable doing it."

"Shall I draw you a bath, sir?" Stephens asked in his formal, valet voice.

"Indeed."

CHAPTER 11

Alicia took the familiar path through the gardens on her favorite circuit. She stopped in the formal garden to chat with the head gardener, who likely couldn't remember whether or not he'd been paid, as he talked to and nurtured his 'lovelies.'

Alicia wondered how peaceful the wizened man's simple life must be who gave no thought for anything other than caring for things that grew. Did he have hopes, fears, regrets? Did anyone alive not have those?

He turned back to his 'lovelies' and promptly forgot her. She moved on to the herb garden laid out in an order only cook would understand. Its smells of rosemary, sage, thyme, onions and other herbs made her think of savory dinners. She passed the stables which now only housed one horse, but still carried the sweet, musty smell of a full stable of horses.

Maman had loved to ride, but Alicia never became an accomplished rider. Only weeks before her death in the carriage accident, *Maman* had been in a riding accident, but, undaunted, she'd gotten right back on the horse without fear. She'd always been a woman to be admired.

Alicia tightened her shawl against a chill breeze that still accompanied the early morning hours. The goose girl called to her gaggle of geese as she herded them along a path, and the milk maid sang as she carried her pails to the kitchen. There was an order to her life in these moments as everyone carried out their routine duties. Taking her customary walk

107

after dawn may not be fashionable, but it restored her sense of balance.

The gravel walkway gave way to smooth, spongy earth, still damp from yesterday's rain. The shaded grove was cooler, chilly. Bracken grew thick along the path. Birds sang in a cacophony of sound. Courage returned, and with it, a renewed determination to save her family, regardless of the cost to herself. She realized then if they were condemned to debtor's prison, all the remaining servants would lose their homes and employment. So many people depended upon her. She refused to fail them. Conviction brought peace.

She stumbled over a bit of soft, uneven ground and glanced down at the sunlight dappled path. She let out a cry. There, in her path, lay a snake, hissing and poised to strike. She realized that she'd stepped on the snake when she'd stumbled on what she thought was a raised bit of earth. Before she could react, the snake struck and bit her. She cried out again and staggered backward. The snake moved its sinuous body in an S-shaped form as it recoiled, poised to strike again. Pain worked its way up her leg.

She turned and ran back the way she had come. The snake remained in the path. Nausea and dizziness closed in around her as she lurched toward the house.

"Miss Palmer?"

Someone, she was never sure who, came to help her. The pain in her leg grew outward. She found herself in the kitchen, surrounded by concerned voices.

"My leg," she gasped, when someone posed the question. "A snake."

Her shoe and stocking were removed. A feminine voice uttered a cry of dismay.

The gamekeeper appeared. "What did the snake

look like?"

Alicia fought waves of nausea. "Dark, with a zigzag pattern down its body."

He exchanged a concerned look with someone outside her line of vision. "Did it have a distinctive dark V or X on its back?"

She nodded. "I think so."

"An adder," the gamekeeper pronounced. "They aren't usually found so near people. Bring cleavers and mistletoe."

Moments later, a slender plant with tiny white flowers appeared in someone's hand.

"Here's some cleavers. I can't find mistletoe." Alicia recognized Cook's voice.

"That will do."

The gamekeeper applied a sticky paste to the snake bite on her rapidly swelling leg. Alicia mentally blessed the elderly gamekeeper for not abandoning them when so many other servants had. The man had been with the Palmer family since before Father was born. Perhaps the venerable man had nowhere else to go. Alicia liked to think that he remained out of loyalty.

Cook pressed a cup of tea in her hand. Alicia breathed in the scent of chamomile and honey, and sipped the warm tea. Her stomach settled.

Robert leaned over her face. She wondered when he'd arrived. "I've got you, Lissie." Surprisingly sober, he picked her up. He carried her as carefully as a bowl of milk up the stairs to her room.

Hannah fluttered in ahead of them, pulling back the sheets, fluffing pillows. Robert laid Alicia on the bed. Someone helped her out of her dress and stays. Wearing only her shift, Alicia curled up. Her leg throbbed. She pushed at the blankets, numbly wondering how she could be both hot and cold. Sweet oblivion enveloped her.

****

Alicia blinked at the late afternoon sun streaming in through the windows. A window stood open and a cool breeze stirred the curtains. Hannah lay fully dressed next to her on the bed. Alicia shifted, and the pain her leg reminded her about the events of...was it earlier today? Yesterday? She remembered vague images of pain and fever and Hannah leaning over her, pressing tea or water against her lips.

Hannah stirred and opened her eyes. When she saw Alicia awake, she smiled in tentative relief. "How do you feel?"

"Better, I think. My leg hardly hurts at all."

Hannah released her breath. "I was so worried. The gamekeeper said adder bites could be either mild or," she choked, "or fatal. You ran a fever for two days."

Alicia took her hand. "Thank you for taking care of me."

Hannah smiled, relaxing a little more. "Cook helped. Robbie came in often to inquire about you. Uncle seemed anxious."

"It's nice to be loved."

Hannah wrapped her arms around her. "Oh, Lissie, what would I have done if I'd lost you, too?"

Alicia hugged her back. "I'm all right, Hannah."

"I couldn't bear it if you'd died," sniffled Hannah. "Some days I feel God is taking every single member of our family until we are all gone."

"There, there. All is well."

But Alicia knew that if she had died, Hannah would be left to either marry quickly, or go with Willard and Robert to debtor's prison. She doubted her sister possessed the stamina to survive either. If she did nothing else in her life, she'd make sure Hannah remained safe. Marriage to the colonel seemed a small price to pay to ensure Hannah's well-being.

CHAPTER 12

Cole took a bracing breath and knocked on the door of the Palmer residence. The footman solemnly took his card and bid him wait in the front parlor. Once inside, Cole understood how desperate Willard Palmer had made his family. Large, bright rectangular shapes on the wallpaper revealed missing paintings. Furniture in the parlor had become scarce, as if missing several key pieces. Footsteps drew him from his observations and he turned to face Robert Palmer.

"You!"

Cole removed his hat. "Mr. Palmer."

Young Palmer continued to stare at him. "You," he repeated, his voice hushing.

"Mr. Palmer. I ... regret the matter that transpired in London, and the subsequent events." Cole swallowed. "I never meant to cause serious harm to Armand."

The young man stared at him as if he were the very devil. "He was my closest friend."

Cole felt as if the other man had punched him in the stomach. "I'm sorry. I truly am. I did not know until recently that he developed an infection and lost his arm. That the opium..." He looked down at his hat becoming crushed in suddenly nervous hands. With effort, he loosened his grip. "I didn't know he had died."

Robert sagged against the door frame. "I was his second. I should have talked him out of it. But I wanted to see him humiliate you. You were always

111

so confident. Arrogant. All the ladies wanted you, you could have had any of them. Instead, you wanted the one who showed interest in Armand."

"She used us both."

Young Palmer nodded numbly and let his breath out slowly. "She was poison. I told him so." He looked up. "He didn't ravish her. She seduced him."

"I know. That became painfully obvious later." The raw pain in Robert Palmer's face made Cole want to beat a retreat, but he still had a task to complete. Even knowing he would certainly fail, he had to at least try. "Mr. Palmer, I need to speak to your father."

He became wary. "What about?"

"I am trying to save your cousin from a forced marriage."

Mr. Palmer looked affronted. "My father is not forcing her. She's refused several already. No one will put a gun to her head and drag her to the altar."

"She seems concerned about the looming deadline of marrying anyone who will have her by the end of the month. To save all of you."

Robert's ire melted. "We've tried everything. Father's never had such a rash of wretched luck. Every investment—even the most conservative one—has soured. He used to be famous at cards, but lately every game he played has cost him."

"I have a solution that can benefit you all."

Robert studied him coldly. "Force her to marry you?"

Cole stiffened at the use of the word 'force.' "No. By *asking* her to marry me. I have doubts that she will accept the man who killed her brother, but I must try. I owe her that. I owe Armand that."

"I should kill you myself."

"Would that help your family out of their current straits?"

The younger Palmer considered. "Very well.

Come with me."

Cole followed him into a dark, dust-covered study where he found Willard Palmer standing by a fireplace with a glass of port in his hand.

"Father. Lord Amesbury would like a moment."

The look of pure hatred on the elder Palmer's face as he recognized the name nearly unnerved Cole. He steadied himself. "I have come with a business proposal for you."

Beside Cole, young Palmer shifted.

Willard Palmer's eyes narrowed. "I should throw you out."

"It would be to your benefit to listen, sir."

The elder Palmer shifted his gaze to his son. "I can't believe you let that blackguard into our home. Have you no backbone?"

"My proposal is this, Mr. Palmer," Cole cut in, "I will settle every debt you owe, finance Hannah's debut in London next Season, and pay ·you an additional sum to help you form a new start, if Alicia agrees—willingly—to marry me."

Willard considered, and the hope in his eyes nearly softened Cole's distaste for the way he insisted on using his niece. Then the hope faded and his face hardened.

"You shot my nephew in a duel, inflicting wounds which ultimately killed him. The feelings my niece undoubtedly harbors for you will preclude a marriage to you. She may feel as if she must accept you for our sake, but I am not a heartless monster. I will not ask her to marry a man such as you."

Cutting as Palmer's words were, they actually earned Cole's admiration for Palmer for protecting his niece from a perceived villain. Cole had been so ready to believe him to be callous and grasping enough to use her for his own agenda. It was possible the man simply had no judgment of character, based on the men he asked Alicia to

113

consider as suitors.

"Then you believe Colonel Westin to be a better choice."

Mr. Palmer pinned him with an accusing stare. "To my knowledge, he does not engage in dueling."

Inwardly wincing, Cole raised his head. "Then allow me to ask her feelings on the matter. Let her decide if she'd rather have me or Colonel Westin."

"No. I saw how upset she was after your last meeting. I will not subject her to another. Good day."

Not an unexpected response, but a foolish, senseless one, nonetheless. Cole ground his teeth and forced his voice to remain steady. "Sir, I urge you to reconsider."

"She will marry the Colonel. We have only to formalize the agreement. Remove yourself from my house."

Conceding the battle, but not the war, Cole bowed to the father and turned to the son. "Will you see me out, Mr. Palmer?" he asked the younger Palmer quietly. He was almost surprised when the young man complied. In the foyer, he turned. "Can you arrange a meeting with her?"

"She's not receiving callers. She's recovering from a snake bite."

Alarm jolted Cole. "A snake bite?"

Palmer looked very grave. "An adder, apparently."

"Is she seriously ill?"

"She gave us a good scare, but she's much improved now."

Cole rubbed his hand over his face, dismayed at how the news frightened him. He'd heard of people dying from adder bites. He held out a note to Palmer.

"Give this to her. Please."

Palmer stared at him for a long moment. Slowly, he reached out and took the note, staring at it as if it were a poisonous serpent. Or an adder.

Keeping his voice barely above a whisper, Cole urged, "At least give her the choice."

Palmer nodded slowly. The note was only folded, not sealed, and Cole had no doubt Palmer would read it before deciding whether or not to give it to his cousin.

A light rain began as Cole rode, but he passed through it with little notice. He would have to resort to more desperate means. Cole had the plan formulated by the time he reached his uncle's house.

When he explained it to Aunt Livy, she pierced him with her gaze. "Cole, I fear no good will come of this."

"I admit it's not a perfect plan. I could simply abduct her. That would save her from anyone who might harm her."

"And bring that kind of scandal upon her? You can't be serious."

It would also fuel her already strong hatred toward him. Cole fixed a baleful stare upon her. "Do you have a better suggestion?"

"Give me time and I'm sure ..."

"There is no time. I must act now."

She heaved a sigh. "Why won't Mr. Palmer consider you? You could help them."

"Because she hates me and so does he."

A faint smile touched her mouth. "You do seem to have that effect on their family."

He couldn't blame them. "I have that effect on many."

"Care to explain why?"

"No, ma'am."

Her shrewd gaze left him with the urge to squirm. "Very well. I will help you with the arrangements, but I want you to know that I do not approve of this scheme."

"I know. But I don't know what else to do."

Her gaze nearly pierced his shields. "Do you love her?"

Cole forced himself to look her in the eye. "Of course not. I'm just trying to save her."

"You are the man she should be marrying."

"That's no longer a viable alternative."

"So you would have Nicholas marry her? He's a stranger to her. It would be an arranged marriage. She'll be terrified."

"I know." His voice sounded as hollow as the place in his heart. "It's the only way to save her."

"Then who will save you?" she asked quietly, with tears shimmering in her eyes.

More frightened than he cared to admit, Cole left to see to another detail. The light rain had turned into a drenching downpour when Cole went outside and remounted. André's hooves slogged over the seldom traveled road to Colonel Westin's manor house. Soaked and grimly determined, Cole pressed on. Trees leaned mournfully under the rainfall against a darkened sky.

At the Westin's manor house, an elderly footman opened the door and eyed Cole with disdain.

As if completely unaware of his clothes dripping on the doorstep, Cole solemnly handed him his card. "I would like a moment of Colonel Westin's time, if he would be so kind."

The footman read the card and eyed Cole suspiciously, convinced any man with such a shocking appearance could not possibly be a viscount. "A moment, if you please, my lord." He disappeared without taking Cole's hat or coat.

Cole waited in the foyer and dripped on the floor. No candles burned, leaving only the faint light from outside the windows to illuminate the room. Not only the temperature, but the ambiance of this house felt cold. Though the décor whispered of money of an era long gone, gloom drowned out the opulence of the room.

The spreading puddle at Cole's feet reached the first doorway when a balding man approached. Though customary for a servant to lead a guest to the host, the master probably came to him because he did not wish to have his carpets sodden by an unseemly visitor.

The Colonel perused Cole with disdain. "Lord Amesbury, I presume."

"Yes, sir. We met briefly at the race."

"To what do I owe the honor of this unprecedented visit?" His tone suggested he felt anything but honored by Cole's call.

Cole kept his voice deferential. He clearly outranked the Colonel in social standing, but the man was still Cole's elder, and that, at least, required respect. "It is my understanding that you have been courting Miss Palmer."

"I fail to understand why this is your concern."

"Her brother Armand and I were old friends." The lie rolled glibly off his tongue. "Now that he is departed, I feel it my duty to look after her welfare. I do not believe either he or her father would approve of a match between you."

The colonel stiffened. "I have much to offer her."

"She's the age of your granddaughter."

The colonel's mouth tightened. "Our age difference may not be as much a hindrance as you suppose."

"You are on a different maturity and intellectual level."

The colonel's bluster faded. "She...she needs a husband quickly. She has few choices. And I am weary of being alone."

Cole hated stripping the man of his dignity, even if he was an overbearing cad who publicly degraded Alicia. His purpose was to convince the man to lose interest in Alicia, not question his

117

manhood. He poured a soothing tone into his voice.

"She still has other options, do not be concerned for her. You, however, are a respected war hero. You deserve a mature wife who shares your interests. You don't want a wife who marries you because she has no other choice, do you? That's a bit insulting."

The Colonel deliberated. "I had considered going to London next Season in the hopes of meeting a more mature widow."

"Splendid! My aunt Olivia is one of the most well-respected ladies of the *ton*. She may be able to garner a few introductions for you to ladies of your station. I will speak to her immediately. I understand you've hunted in Africa?"

The colonel's chest puffed out. "Yes. A number of times. Capital game there."

"The ladies adore tales of travel, especially Africa. I'm confident you'll have no trouble finding someone who appreciates you. All you need are a few introductions."

The colonel considered. Cole curbed his impatience.

"Very well, my lord, I accept."

"Excellent. My aunt loves to play matchmaker. She'll have an impressive list of suitable prospects for you to consider."

The colonel stood a little taller and shook Cole's hand. "Thank you, my lord. Forgive me, may I offer you a drink?"

"Thank you, Colonel, but I am expected at another engagement shortly. But I appreciate you taking time to see me."

Cole affected a bow and departed. Now that the competition had been eliminated, he could implement the final stage in Alicia's rescue. If only he could just carry her off and marry her himself. Abduction sounded more appealing every moment.

CHAPTER 13

Alicia awoke to a knock at the door and a terse whisper calling her name. The sun had set hours ago. She threw on a robe and opened the door, pushing her hair away from her face.

"What is it, Robbie?"

"Colonel Westin has withdrawn his offer."

Alicia's mouth fell open. She shrank from the prospect of marrying the overbearing colonel, but without him, and his money, she had no hope of saving her family. Panic edged in.

"What are we going to do?"

"There's a new suitor, some baron from Northumberland. A distant relation to Viscount Amesbury, I believe. I hear he's badly scarred and wears a mask."

Alicia's heart dropped to her stomach. She'd been spared the man who had tried to force himself upon her, as well as the complaining stuffed-shirt who publicly humiliated her. Now she faced a scarred, masked stranger. She pressed her hand over her eyes.

"The baron's agent is here with his offer. He and father have been speaking for hours." He paused. "Alicia, there is a way to save yourself."

She lowered her hand.

"Lord Amesbury has offered for you, but Father wouldn't consider it. Amesbury asked me to give you this." He held out a folded paper. "He wants you to elope with him. He promises you an honorable marriage and to be generous with the family."

Aghast, she stared. "You wish me to wed Armand's killer?"

Looking anguished, Robert dragged a hand through his hair. "I think he'll treat you better than the others would have. And I don't hold Amesbury entirely responsible for the duel. I should have stopped them, but Armand was so eager for it. And that woman was there, egging them both on, demanding her honor be defended. Amesbury only shot Armand in the arm. He didn't intend to kill him."

Bitterness welled up inside her. "His intent does not change the outcome. You may be able to forgive him, but I cannot." She crumpled up the note and threw it down. "I'll take the scarred stranger over Cole Amesbury." Chill spread through her limbs and her words choked her.

The following morning at breakfast, Uncle Willard announced that their transaction had been agreed upon, and all they lacked was Alicia's cooperation.

"The baron will meet you this afternoon. Unless you object, he will wed you after he obtains a special license."

Alicia sat with her head bowed, absorbing the news that her marriage to a stranger had already been arranged. "Have you any notion of his character?"

"His agent was most loyal to him and assured me that the baron lacked any vices that normally plague the aristocracy. He doesn't gamble or drink excessively, and has never kept a mistress. He said his lord is most generous and is viewed as a kind and tolerant man by his servants and peers."

Alicia was frankly surprised that Uncle had taken such care as to inquire about the baron. None of the other men he insisted she consider had appeared to have undergone any sort of scrutiny.

With Hannah's aid, she dressed with care to prepare to meet her future husband. Hannah and Alicia waited nervously in the parlor. Uncle promised to be present, but Robert had already drunk himself into oblivion.

"A grand coach is here," Hannah said from the window.

Alicia listened with pounding heart as the footmen spoke. The other voice was too low to carry to her, but footsteps neared.

"Lord Amesbury to see you, Miss."

Alicia shot up out of her seat. "Lord Amesbury!"

Uncle Willard strode in. "Ah, excellent. Show the baron in."

Then she realized her error. Not Cole Amesbury, but rather that distant relation, the baron, had come as promised. Her mingled relief and disappointment left her reeling, but she did not have time to examine her feelings.

A large man stood in the doorway, his face covered by a loose, cloth mask. A billowing, dark green cloak concealed all but his legs and head. An ominous sight, he executed a stiff bow and limped into the room, leaning heavily on a cane. Her imagination conjured images of a monstrous, twisted face. The dark form stopped too close. Gulping down her fear, she refrained from stepping away. Hannah's hand felt icy in hers.

As Uncle Willard made the introductions, Alicia and Hannah sank into curtseys.

"Miss Palmer. Miss Hannah." He spoke in a gruff, gravely voice muffled by the mask.

Alicia stammered a reply with no more eloquence than poor Hannah, whom she feared would swoon. When they sat, the baron took an armchair nearest the divan where Alicia was seated with Hannah. Alicia consciously refrained from squirming or fidgeting as they made customary small talk. The baron faced her but the mask was so featureless, he could have been looking behind her. Even his eyes were covered. He spoke carefully, quietly as they exchanged dutiful pleasantries.

When there was a pause in the conversation, the baron turned to her. "Miss Palmer, I know you must believe yourself without any say in the matter, considering the circumstances, but if you favor another, I will be a gentleman and step aside."

Alicia twisted her handkerchief in her hands. "There's no one else, my lord."

"I realize I'm not exactly every young girl's dream of a husband. But I wish for the companionship of a wife and I desire to have an heir eventually. I live quietly, out of busy social circles, and cannot offer you a life of glamour, but I have enough wealth that I can promise you that you will lack for nothing."

Alicia forced herself to look at the expressionless mask. "I appreciate your gesture, my lord." She almost added that she was not motivated by money, but that would make her seem a liar, since she clearly only considered him because of his wealth, of what an alliance with him would do for her family. In the settlement to which he and Uncle Willard had agreed, he'd offered a staggering sum to Uncle Willard. To Alicia, he'd given generous pin money, dress allowance, and jointure if she outlived him. No other suitor came close to his settlement. He spoke the truth; she'd never live in poverty. And he would save her family from debtor's prison.

She directed her attention to the baron who was speaking.

"I'm not temperamental, and I would never raise my hand against you. I give you my word that I will be a good husband to you, Miss Palmer."

Unable to look at that expressionless mask, she looked down at her wet, crushed handkerchief.

"Will you have me?" he asked softly.

Already he seemed a better man than either Mr. Braxton or Colonel Westin. But her fear nearly overwhelmed her. He waited expectantly. Her imagination conjured horrifying images of his face, his body, the demands he as her husband would make upon her. It was him, or prison. She had no other options.

She forced herself to look at the blank mask. "Yes, my lord. I will have you."

Hannah fainted.

CHAPTER 14

The day of the wedding dawned bright and clear. Hannah had stayed in her bed with her, weeping so much that Alicia feared she'd have to give her laudanum to make her sleep. Hannah had been ill at the thought of Alicia marrying such a frightening-looking man, and worse, that she did it to save them all from ruin. For Hannah's sake, Alicia attempted to show a brave face and tried to speak anything positive that entered her mind.

Alicia rose quietly so as not to disturb her sister who finally had gone to sleep. A beautiful wedding gown from one of the finest dressmakers in Paris lay draped over a chair surrounded by flowers. A veil and silken undergarments lay nearby; gifts that had arrived from her future husband, delivered by the newly arrived maid, also courtesy of her betrothed.

Monique, a ladies' maid four or five years Alicia's junior with dark hair and eyes, came in quietly with a tray of fruit and hot chocolate. Alicia had forgotten how wonderful it had been having a maid to care for her. Monique's arrival also brought a noticeable improvement in the quality and variety of food, and Alicia suspected that the baron must have provided some sort of advance to her uncle.

As Alicia tried to swallow some fruit down a very dry throat, Hannah stirred and woke. "Oh, Lissie, what am I to do without you?"

Alicia hugged her. "It isn't as if we'll never see each other again. I'm sure he'll allow us to visit." They'd taken to calling her future husband "he" rather than by any name.

Hannah nodded soberly. "I hope so." Tears swam in her eyes and her mouth worked.

"Hannah, don't weep so. I need you with me on my wedding day."

Rallying, Hannah heaved a shuddering sigh and got up. After they'd bathed, washed and dried their hair, and got dressed, they attempted to eat breakfast downstairs. Robert and Uncle Willard were still abed. Alicia and Hannah picked at their food, alternating between strained conversation and subdued silence. The thought of this being Alicia's last meal at home lingered between them. Even the servants seemed agitated. At least they'd been paid all their back wages, thanks to the baron's generosity.

"Let's go for a walk," Hannah suggested.

Alicia agreed. As they donned bonnets and gloves, the butler arrived.

"Lord Amesbury, Miss. The other one, the viscount."

Cole Amesbury.

The butler's face clouded. "Your uncle gave orders that I not admit him all the other times he's called, but he says he refuses to leave until he speaks with you."

At that moment, Cole Amesbury pushed his way into the room, his stunningly handsome face giving no clues as to the dark soul lurking beneath the pleasing exterior. How could such a contradictory nature exist inside one man?

"Please speak with me." He looked determined.

She tied her bonnet under her chin and pulled on her wrap. "Very well, Lord Amesbury."

"Walk with me? Alone?"

She drew herself up. "I am to wed another today, my lord. Speaking with you alone will surely not please my intended."

"I can handle him. Walk with me. Please." The desperation in his expression tugged at her heart.

Hannah squeezed her hand and nodded with a shy smile. Alicia hadn't had the heart to tell her of Cole Amesbury's involvement in Armand's death. No doubt, she hoped this handsome Adonis would save her from the masked man she felt compelled to marry.

Alicia consented and allowed him to lead her out to the gardens.

He reached for her hand, but then stopped himself. His arm dropped. "It's not too late. Leave with me now. We'll go to Gretna Green and marry. I'll give your uncle all the money promised him. And I'll provide a trust for Hannah's dowry. My Aunt Livy has agreed to sponsor her the next Season. She has connections and can ensure Hannah is invited to Almack's, and is presented to the queen." The intensity and desperation in his eyes chipped at her resolve.

She stared in amazement. "Why would you do this, Lord Amesbury?"

"Because I ..." he paused. "I desire you for a wife."

His words rang of sincerity and Alicia blinked at the admission. "I can't imagine why."

He hesitated. "I do admire you. And I want to help you and your family, and—"

"Don't." She held up a hand. "I would never wish to mislead you, so I will speak plainly. I will not marry you. Not now. Not ever."

He looked stricken. "Because of Armand."

She made no reply. None was necessary.

He nodded, his face hardening. After a stiff bow, he turned away. She watched his broad back and shoulders as he left. Some of the usual grace in his walk had faded. He mounted his stunning white stallion and cantered away. A white stallion. Like her dream knight. All he lacked was the armor.

And honor.

Alicia smothered the tiny voice whispering she'd made a terrible mistake. She sank down on a stone bench. How could she marry the man who had destroyed Armand?

She couldn't. She would marry a man whose face she may never see. A man who frightened her.

Hannah joined her. "I thought he'd come to propose." Disappointment laced her voice.

Alicia forced a laugh. "Whatever gave you that idea?"

"He seems the gallant type who would rescue a lady from marrying someone she does not wish to wed. He rose to your defense at the races and—"

"Hannah, marriage is a much greater commitment than merely giving the cut direct to a rude man!" Alicia spoke more sharply than she'd intended. "Sorry, dearest." She put her arm around Hannah. "I'm just nervous about my wedding day."

"I don't blame you. The man was simply terrifying." Hannah pulled her shawl more closely around herself, her face thoughtful. "He did speak like a gentleman, though, didn't he?"

"Yes, he did. I'm sure I will fare better with him than some ladies do with the men they marry. Think of all those arranged marriages that happened for centuries. At least I had the opportunity to say no."

"But you didn't really have a choice, did you?"

Alicia did not reply.

They went back to the house and began preparing for the wedding. Her new French maid, Monique, helped her change out of her clothes. Monique dressed her in new silk undergarments and stockings, all trimmed with delicate lace. Alicia had never seen such fine things.

After months of caring for herself, with only Hannah to help with her stays, being waited upon

seemed a strange luxury, but her hands had begun
to shake so badly, having help today was necessary.
Just the companionship and touch of another human
was comforting.

As Alicia sat at a dressing table, Monique
dressed her hair, deftly piled it on top of her head,
and pinned it in place, allowing a few tendrils to
hang down against her neck. White roses nestled
among the curls in a more beautiful arrangement
than she had ever seen.

After the maid had finished with her hair, she
carefully lowered the wedding gown over Alicia's
head and fastened tiny pearl buttons down her back.
Monique had altered it after she arrived until the
gown fit Alicia perfectly. Monique stepped back to
allow Alicia to admire it in the mirror. Despite the
gloom hanging over her, her solicitous maid had
raised her spirits. A little.

Alicia eyed her reflection. The dress was silk
satin, set with pearls and tiny ribbon rosebuds.
Matching slippers completed the ensemble. Alicia
remained still while Monique arranged every fold of
her dress. She had to admit, she had never looked so
well. The veil added the finishing touch.

Hannah gazed at her in breathless adoration.
"Oh, Lissie, I've never seen its equal."

"*Voilà.*" Monique wore a pleased smile.
"*Magnifique.*"

If only she felt 'magnifique.' Instead, she felt
only empty. Frightened. There was nothing to do
now but wait. To marry a stranger. A scarred
cripple. A man who would soon have the right to
demand anything of her.

Alicia feared she might become ill. She
interlaced her fingers in an attempt to stop her
hands from shaking.

The footman scratched at the door. "The
bridegroom is waiting, Miss Palmer."

Alicia rose on unsteady legs. "Tell his lordship I am coming."

Hannah hugged her, her lower lip trembling.

Alicia summoned courage for Hannah's sake. "All will be well," she said, her voice choking on her tears. "*Maman* used to say, 'there is good in everything if you look hard enough.' Good will come of this, you'll see."

Hanna visibly tried to brighten. Voices led them to the study. Alicia paused at the threshold. Robert stood at the sideboard table wearing a black superfine. He glowered at her soon-to-be-husband, whose masked face allowed him perfect neutrality regarding his thoughts. Robert tossed back what appeared to be the latest of many drinks and shot another red-eyed glare at Lord Amesbury.

"I assure you, young Mr. Palmer," her betrothed said in measured, muffled tones, "I have no intention of mistreating her in any way. I was raised with the belief that a man should treat his wife with dignity, respect, and kindness. It is a philosophy I embrace."

Robert poured another drink and gulped it down.

Uncle Willard intervened. "We don't mean to be ungrateful. And thank you for your advance, my lord. Things have been much more comfortable."

The masked head inclined. "I'm happy to have been of assistance."

"Those were all the papers to sign, then?" Willard asked. "Everything is settled?"

"All but the wedding, Mr. Palmer." A hint of humor laced the baron's voice.

Uncle Willard noticed Alicia and Hannah then. "Ah! Well, you turned out all right after all, eh?"

Robert looked up and offered a sickly smile, his eyes bloodshot and tortured. "I have never seen a more beautiful bride." He leaned in to kiss her cheek, his breath so strong with drink that Alicia's eyes watered.

Poor Robert, who would take care of him now? At least now they could afford to have a full staff of servants again. She hoped one of them would look after her cousin, who seemed bent on drinking himself to death.

The baron limped to her, leaning on his cane. Alicia stood unflinching before him. "Stunning, my dear. The gown suits you well. May it be the first of many."

He was dressed in the same manner as before with a large billowing cloak, loose mask, and kidskin gloves.

He took her hand and pressed it to his mouth, protected by his mask. "Any man would be pleased to have a beauty such as you by his side."

Alicia could not look at that featureless black head. "Thank you, my lord," she whispered, unable to find her voice.

He tucked her hand into his arm and led them outside. The waiting coach appeared new, embellished with carvings and a family crest. Four perfectly match black horses stood as if at attention. An immaculately liveried footman waited at the door.

They all climbed in and seated themselves wordlessly. Inside the carriage, the cushions were red velvet, matching the curtains at the windows. She had never ridden in a more luxurious coach in her life. It traveled smoothly over the rain-rutted road and through the cobblestone streets of town.

Outside the church, they stopped. The baron helped her out and led her to the stairs of the church. At the bottom step, she stopped, her heart pounding like a wild bird flinging against the bars of its cage.

Who was this man? What if he proved to be a man like Mr. Braxton, who had tried to force his advances upon her? She would have to allow it. As her husband, he would have the right.

Seized by panic, she cast about for avenues of escape, all thoughts of cooperation fleeing.

"This way." The baron placed his hand under her elbow. She stumbled along next to him up the steps to the front door strung with flower garlands.

Alicia glanced back outside toward her only hope for freedom, but the baron, coachman, and footman all remained nearby, preventing an escape. Alicia gulped.

Inside, the vicar and his wife greeted them. "Lord Amesbury," they said in turn, their voices hushed.

Alicia started. Could she ever speak to, or even think of, her husband without images of Cole coming to mind?

The vicar's wife turned to her. "I'll show you where you may touch up first, Miss Palmer."

"A moment." The baron held out his hand to Alicia and waited.

Alicia reluctantly placed her hand in his gloved hand. The others drew back to a respectful distance. Hannah looked pale with fear.

"Alicia." He spoke in a gruff, gravely voice muffled by the mask. "You still have a choice in this. It's not too late. Do you wish to go through with this marriage? I know that there are others who—"

"I agree to this marriage." Her voice sounded thin in her own ears. She prayed that he would have gentler hands than the last man who touched her.

The cowled head nodded and he stepped back. The vicar's wife led Alicia, Hannah and Monique to a small room down a hallway until they reached a dressing room. Monique and Hannah fussed over her, touching up her hair and smoothing her wedding gown.

They made a small procession as they went into

the chapel. Two witnesses stood nearby to legalize the hasty wedding. Dully, Alicia mused that the baron must have important connections to secure a special license so quickly. A few others had come as well, but Alicia suddenly had difficulty seeing. With her hand on Uncle Willard's arm, she mustered up what she hoped would be an adequate amount of dignity and walked down the aisle.

The baron's masked head nodded once and he held out his arm to her. She placed her trembling hand on his glove.

She heard little of the ceremony except the pounding of her heart. As she battled tears from forming, she barely found enough voice to repeat her vows. The black monstrosity at her side slipped a wedding band on her icy, shaking fingers. They were pronounced man and wife.

A condemnation akin to death.

Somewhere in the back of her mind, she found it ironic that, although she had rejected Cole Amesbury, she would take the same name when she married his kin.

The vicar blessed them and read several verses and they had communion. Then it was over. They signed the papers, her hand trembling so badly that she could barely hold the pen.

The wedding breakfast took place about noon on the church lawn in the shade of a grove of trees, and though the meal looked wonderful, Alicia could not swallow anything. There were toasts, but the guests were subdued, as if unsure how to act around the masked groom. Elizabeth smiled, trying to appear supportive and encouraging, but only managed to look as though she were about to burst into tears. Robert drank grimly until he passed out. Then the baron rose, thanked their guests in his soft, slightly gravelly voice and bid them farewell.

Elizabeth hugged her and wished her well.

"You're a titled lady now, you know." Alicia knew Elizabeth was trying to be positive for her sake. "I'll write to you every week."

Alicia nodded and hugged her. Elizabeth's mother, Mrs. Hancock, drew her into an embrace, whispering words of encouragement and affection. Then Hannah was there, weeping and clinging so desperately that Elizabeth had to take Hannah into her arms. Alicia's new husband led her away.

The coach that had brought her here still waited in front of a second, smaller one. Her husband handed Monique into the smaller coach before escorting Alicia to the larger coach and then climbed in after her. He sat with his right leg extended, as if bending it caused him pain. Alicia glanced at the man in the seat across from her, but quickly looked away, feeling his steady gaze on her, even if she couldn't see it. She kept her eyes fixed outside the window, afraid to look at the hulking form in front of her.

"We're going to Northumbria. My home lies northeast of Hadrian's Wall. Have you ever been there?"

She shook her head, unable to find her voice and realized that she had not even thought to ask of their destination. She found it difficult to think at all.

"I hope you like it. It's a bit isolated, I'm afraid, but it's beautiful country with rivers and a lake. The gardens are expansive. A number of renowned artists have painted them."

"It sounds lovely." Her voice sounded dull.

"Have you any desire to travel?"

She drew a breath, and forced herself to look at him. He was her husband. He deserved her courtesy. "I'd like to go to France. My mother was French."

"I've spent time there. It's worth seeing. If you wish to go there, we shall."

She attempted a smile. "You're very kind, my lord."

The carriage went over a bump and Alicia had to shift in her seat. The silence grew uncomfortable.

"Tell me about your family, Alicia."

"What do you wish to know, my lord?"

"Whatever you wish to tell me."

She glanced at the masked face, but its featureless appearance unnerved her too greatly and she looked back out the window. "It is my understanding that most men wish for a silent, obedient wife."

"We are going to spend the rest of our lives together, Alicia. Perhaps we should learn a little of each other?" There was a chuckle in his voice.

She gulped. *The rest of our lives* sounded ominous. She dropped her eyes and tried to think of something to say.

He came to her rescue. "What was your mother like?"

She paused.

"I saw the portrait in your home the day we met in person. You bear a strong resemblance. Were you close?"

"Yes. Very."

He waited.

She took a breath but continued looking out of the window. "*Maman* had a gentle quality about her that made everyone love her. *Papá* would do anything for her. We all would. I even learned to play the pianoforte because it pleased her, although I have no talent for it. Later I learned to enjoy it. She was also an excellent horsewoman."

They left town and headed down the highway. The trees lining the road had grown so large, that in places, they met overhead like a great canopy.

"My parents are both gone," he said, "but I have two elder sisters. Perhaps you will meet them some day."

Somehow, the thought of the inhuman shape across from her having sisters seemed too absurd to be true.

A headache pounded between her eyes and she felt a bit faint.

The coach turned off the highway and followed a smaller road. They fell silent as the coach rode smoothly over the rutted road. Visions of living with a monster swam before her eyes and she had to call upon all her courage to prevent herself from opening the door and throwing herself out of the moving carriage.

Before nightfall, they stopped in front of a quaint inn. Her husband slowly and cautiously exited the carriage. Once outside, he held a gloved hand out to her. She barely touched it as she climbed down. Once on her feet, she swayed in dizziness, but when he put a steadying arm around her, she shrank away from him.

The innkeeper ushered them inside to a snug parlor where a meal waited for them. Even though the smells were tempting, the knot in her stomach forbad food. After only a few bites, she feared she would not be able to keep it down. She noticed that her husband was not eating either. Though tempted to ask him, she remained silent. Perhaps he did not eat in front of her because of the mask. Perhaps he was anxious for the wedding night.

She choked. The wedding night. The horror of being trapped by Mr. Braxton's attack at the ball burst into her mind.

A tremor began deep in the pit of her stomach.

As if sensing her rising terror, he took her hand. "Alicia. You need not fear me. I will never force you to do anything that would seem frightening or distasteful. I don't believe a man should be his wife's absolute master."

She glanced at him sharply. Was the baron speaking in general terms, or did he mean specifically that intimate act between man and woman? She wondered if he would show her his face in private, or remain masked. A slow horror built as she realized only moments from now, she would have to allow the kind of humiliating experience Mr. Braxton had tried to wrench from her.

The innkeeper appeared and cleared away the table. "I'll show ye to yer room, milady, if yer ready."

Alicia rose on unsteady legs. She stumbled on the stairs and had to keep a white-knuckled grip on the banister. Spots danced before her eyes and the pounding in her head became torturous. To her surprise, the baron stopped outside the door to her room.

"I'll be with you after you've had a few moments to change." He bowed and left.

Inside the room, Monique stared at her in concern. "Are you unwell, *madame*?"

"My head."

"Have you eaten today?"

"Not much."

Monique mixed a small amount of something in a glass and handed it to her. "This will help."

Alicia gulped it down and coughed at the strong flavor. "What is that?"

"A little laudanum and brandy."

Alicia sat on the edge of the bed while Monique busied about the room. Gradually, the throbbing pain numbed and her shoulder muscles unclenched. Monique dug through an enormous chest sitting in the middle of the room and pulled out toilette items. Gowns and underclothes of every description lay inside.

Monique pulled out a nightgown of gossamer white silk with the same tiny white ribbon roses that had been on her wedding gown and helped her change into it. The nightgown clung sensuously to Alicia's body and showed just enough cleavage to be tantalizing. She wanted to be anything but tantalizing.

Monique handed her a toothbrush, already sprinkled with powder. After she finished brushing her teeth, Alicia sat while Monique brushed her hair. It fell in soft waves down her back past her waist.

"You are beautiful, *madame*." Monique blew out several candles and lamps so that the lighting was soft.

Alicia stared unseeing back at her own reflection. Would he be rough and brutal? Would he hurt her? Tears stung her eyes. She realized Monique had left and her husband was entering the room.

Her husband. What kind of man was he really? She dried her cheeks and turned slowly to face him.

He locked the door and leaned against it without making a move toward her. "Alicia. You are lovely." He sounded as if he truly meant it.

With such effort fighting back the tears, she had no voice to reply. He came closer, leaning heavily on his cane. She sucked in her breath. One giant gloved hand reached for her. She closed her eyes and bit her trembling lower lip.

"Alicia," he whispered. "I won't hurt you." He touched her shoulder with his gloved hand.

She flinched at the touch and took a tremulous breath, her whole body shaking. A tear ran down her cheek.

His hand dropped and he regarded her silently. "Alicia. I'm not a savage beast that would force myself upon any woman, least of all my wife. I will not demand you to consummate our marriage before you are ready. I only ask that you give me a chance to earn your trust."

She nodded, hardly daring to believe her ears, and eyed him warily. He leaned in. She braced herself, but he only kissed her cheek through the mask and left the room, closing the door firmly behind him.

Her husband. A crippled, scarred man who never showed his face. There might never be enough time to learn to become accustomed to such a frightening-looking man.

Or the act he would one day demand when his patience ran out.

CHAPTER 15

As Cole walked, his thoughts skittered chaotically out of reach. Doubts teased, taunted.

Had he done the right thing?

At the top of a rise, he paused to look out over the valley bathed in moonlight. He continued down the other side, stepping carefully over the rocky ground. At the time, having his cousin Nicholas marry Alicia seemed the best possible alternative. Now he wasn't so sure.

He came upon a stream and followed it until it pooled, mirroring the moonlight. He picked up a flat stone, and with a quick flick of his wrist, sent one skipping across the stream where it fell with a clunk among the rocks at the far bank.

Uncle Andrew and Aunt Livy had been attentive hosts, but a vague anticipation settled on him at the thought of going home and escaping the weary parade of hopeful ladies and their overzealous mothers. He hadn't been home for more than a handful of days since the war, but now he had interests there.

Horses, for one. He had searched all over Ireland and found a promising new thoroughbred he hoped to enter in the next derby. Since then, he had only visited home long enough to check on the stallion's progress and consult with the trainer and jockey. The emptiness of his childhood home, once so full of joy and love, mocked him, and he always quickly left again, preferring London, or the homes of his numerous relatives. But this time, home beckoned to him.

If only Alicia had agreed to marry him.

The future lurked, uncertain. He had watched Alicia, unbeknownst to her, as she married a masked stranger. She stood white-faced and trembling in fear, trying so hard to be brave. How he longed to comfort her, to reassure her!

But she had rejected him on every level.

He left the pool and followed the stream through a thickening stand of trees, wondering if he would ever rid himself of this mad, burning desire for the girl with soft, gold-brown eyes who hated him no matter how hard he tried to win her affection. The night he found her fleeing Mr. Braxton, she had cried in his arms and snuggled against his chest before she remembered herself and pushed away. Having her in his arms, however briefly, stirred an unfamiliar sense of belonging. He ached to hold her again.

A taunting dream.

But there were moments when she seemed to have forgiven him, or at least forgotten her abhorrence. At the race course, she chatted with him amiably and laughed with abandon. There were other times that she looked at him with shy, innocent desire. At first, he thought he had merely imagined those moments, but they continued to happen with some regularity.

Although there had been no question of her feelings when she'd soundly refused his proposal. He did not entertain any delusions that Alicia's rejection stemmed from a fear of social ramifications a scandalous elopement would bring. No. It came from her hatred of her brother's killer. When faced with a masked, scarred cripple as her only alternative, still, she had rejected Cole.

He wasn't surprised. But it hurt. Deeply. Much more than he had expected.

He didn't blame her. He couldn't. Anyone astute enough to see beneath his pleasing façade would see the monster lurking below and shrink in fear. Shooting Armand had only been one in a long list of sins.

Her new husband would never hurt her, and even if she didn't know it, she was safe.

But was Cole safe?

He desperately hoped that this would not prove to be the gravest mistake of his life.

CHAPTER 16

Alicia and her husband traveled slowly, stopping to eat and stay at inns along the way. They spoke occasionally, and though their conversation was forced and awkward, he treated her with courtesy, his voice soft and muffled by the mask. Each night, the baron escorted her to her room, kissed her cheek and left her alone.

As they traveled through the heart of Northumbria, the baron straightened in the seat across from her. "We're home."

They pulled off the main road onto a long driveway lined with towering trees. The trees parted, revealing an enormous castle, situated upon a slight rise, commanding an impressive view. They drove across a bridge spanning a murmuring creek and pulled up in front of the castle.

As they alit from the carriage, Alicia caught herself staring at the castle that graced the countryside. This would be her home?

The baron tucked her hand into the crook of his arm and led her slowly up the stairs. She looked down at his feet and his cane, wondered if walking up stairs hurt him.

They paused inside. The baron's estate was a far grander place than even Catherine's home. The wide, main hallway boasted marble columns and floors that had been scrubbed to a mirror-like luster. Crystal chandeliers hung from the ceiling and crystal sconces lined the room. Tapestries and paintings hung from the walls, and a mural of angels and cherubs frolicking among the clouds adorned the ceiling. Two grand, sweeping staircases led upstairs on either side of the curved entry way. Elegant, intricately carved and richly upholstered furniture promised comfort. The splendor took her breath away.

"It's magnificent," she breathed.

"I'd hoped you would be pleased."

Servants lined the entryway, and her husband introduced her to the head housekeeper, Mrs. Hodges.

After Alicia had met all the other servants, Mrs. Hodges beckoned to her. "Come, my lady, I will show you to your room. You must be most fatigued by your long journey."

The baron bowed to Alicia. "I will leave you to become settled."

Alicia followed Mrs. Hodges up the staircase as it curved around to the second floor, stepping on lush, thick carpet, and holding on to a banister as intricately carved as the pillars and molding. All the tall, sparkling clean windows had their draperies firmly pulled back to let in the bright afternoon sunlight. Magnificent portraits lined the hallways.

Mrs. Hodges showed her to a room near the end of the hall and motioned to the door next to it. "That room belongs to the baron. Here is yours."

She opened the door, revealing an enormous boudoir with an adjoining sitting room. Through another door Alicia found the dressing room. The furniture and wallpaper had a subtle French flavor in soft greens. It felt serene and restful. Everything had been scrupulously cleaned and polished. Even the wood shone like glass.

"It's beautiful," she said in awe.

Mrs. Hodges looked pleased. "We will be happy to redecorate it or refurnish it to suit your taste. Lord Amesbury ordered me to spare no expense making you feel at home. I'll send in your abigail to help you change."

Two footmen lugged in her chest and set it near an enormous clothes press in her dressing room. They bowed to her and retreated. Mrs. Hodges left Alicia to look over her new surroundings. A beautiful watercolor painting of a landscape hung from one wall signed 'Christian Amesbury.' A relative, perhaps? On the opposite wall, tall windows framed a view of breathtaking gardens extending to the horizon.

"*Madame*? Are you ready to change?" asked Monique in French as she stepped inside the open doorway. Because Alicia had grown up speaking French with her mother, she and Monique often conversed in that language.

"*Oui*, Monique, *merci.*"

Monique opened the clothes press. Inside were several gowns.

"For you, *madame*," Monique beamed. "A whole new wardrobe. And look." She opened a jewelry case lined in black velvet. Several pieces of fine jewelry lay inside, clearly precious family heirlooms. Alicia lifted a diamond and ruby brooch, admired it, and then on a whim, turned it over. On the back was an inscription, *"To my beloved Anne. Bound forever by love."*

Overwhelmed, Alicia folded both hands over the brooch and hugged it to her chest. She'd dreamed of one day finding a love such as this. That dream had faded.

"Ah! *Magnifique!*" Monique exclaimed, admiring the jewels still lying inside the case. "You are most fortunate, *madame*, that your husband is so generous."

"Yes, he certainly is generous."

Her husband had already proved to be more kind and thoughtful than she ever anticipated. In many ways. She hung her head. And she had repaid him with fear and rejection.

"Come, we must prepare you for dinner."

Alicia bathed, changed and sat at a dressing table while Monique arranged her hair. Mrs. Hodges announced that dinner was ready and that Lord Amesbury would be with her shortly thereafter. The tightness in Alicia's chest, which had eased as she explored her new boudoir, returned at the mention of her husband. She fidgeted with her wedding ring.

Mrs. Hodges gave her a sympathetic smile. "I know he must seem overwhelming, even frightening, but your husband is a good and kind man. As a youth, he was mischievous and energetic, but he always had a good heart. He has suffered many losses, but the time that I have spent with him since his return from the war has assured me that he isn't all that different."

"Then you have been with the family long?"

"Oh, my goodness, yes. Why, I knew his mother as a new bride. Saw her through the birth of her children and watched them grow. A delightful family. I loved them like my own."

Timidly, Alicia eyed her. "Is he that badly scarred?"

Mrs. Hodges smiled sadly. "He won't allow any of the servants to see his face, but don't let that frighten you." She patted her arm. "I think if you give him a chance, you will discover that the man behind the mask is everything a woman could wish for in a husband."

He might give her everything money would buy, but she doubted he could give her anything else.

They went into a breakfast room off of the kitchen. "This is where the family usually dined when they weren't entertaining. The grand dining room is on the next floor."

Mrs. Hodges served her in the warm and

friendly room. It was a place where children would feel welcome. "Lord Amesbury takes his meals in privacy so that he can remove the mask. He sends his apologies at requiring you to dine alone but he will join you shortly."

Alicia was unsurprised. He'd done the same during their trip. Despite her apprehensions, she found that her appetite had returned and she devoured the delicious food. There was such a tremendous variety, and all so beautifully prepared, that she wanted to sample everything.

After she had finished, she sat sipping her tea, comfortably full. She heard the soft thumping of a cane and heavy footfalls outside the room. As the sounds approached, Alicia set down her teacup and sat up straight, her heart beginning a low thud. Despite traveling with him over these past few days, his presence never failed to instill fear. His large form appeared in the doorway and he thumped his way toward her.

"I hope you enjoyed your dinner," his soft voice rasped.

Alicia swallowed and found her voice. "Yes, very much, thank you." She nervously fingered the locket around her neck.

"I brought my cook with me from Versailles. I told him I was in love with his cooking and that I should pine away and grow thin if he didn't come cook for me."

In spite of herself, Alicia felt her mouth curve. "I can see why you wanted to keep him."

"I thought you might enjoy a brief walk in the garden before you retire?"

"I would, thank you, my lord."

A clear, moonlit night greeted them as they strolled along the walkway in the garden. Insects sang and a light breeze brought the mingled scent of flowers.

"In my youth, the gardens became forests that hid wild beasts, and ferocious dragons that deserved to be slain. That tree," he indicated a cypress, "served as my castle where I looked out for approaching enemy soldiers. I often played a black knight and attacked my sisters, much to their dismay."

Alicia offered a polite smile.

They stopped at the edge of a small lake, its shimmering surface reflecting, with barely a ripple, the silver and white moon. A night bird cried, soaring overhead, and insects sang.

"That lake became Loch Ness where I battled its fearsome beast repeatedly. I always defeated it, but somehow, it returned another day to terrorize our fair kingdom again. Even after I went away to school, I loved coming back here to challenge the beast again."

When he began walking, Alicia matched his unsteady pace.

"Tomorrow, if you wish, I will give you a tour of the gardens. My great, great, grandfather designed it based on Greek mythology, and each generation has added to it. There's even a maze in the middle, my grandfather's addition. He was a second son and had no hope of inheriting, but when his oldest brother failed to marry and produce an heir, the title fell to him. He determined to make his mark in the family history."

A nightingale sang in the distance and a light breeze stirred her skirts. The lake mirrored the star-dotted sky. She remained silent.

"I understand your family is quite old as well. If I recall correctly, your great uncle was a marquis?" he asked.

"Great, great uncle," she corrected. With growing courage, she added; "My father's father was a third son. He had our manor constructed. The one

147

that belongs to my Uncle Willard now." A faint resentment flared, but she quieted it.

He gestured off to the right. "The stables are beyond those trees. Do you ride?"

"Not well. My mother was an excellent horsewoman, but I never became competent."

After concluding their walk, he led her inside to a comfortable study decorated with deep greens and rich browns. It smelled of leather and wood polish. Though the fireplace stood black in the warm summer night, several lamps had been lit, giving the room a cheerful illumination.

Her eyes fell upon a chessboard set up at a small teakwood table. "Do you play chess, my lord?"

His breath expelled slightly and she imagined a smile underneath the mask. "My father tried to teach me, but there were fish to catch, lakes to swim in, fencing, riding, shooting, boyish mischief that I shall not disclose...well, I am sure you understand. I never developed the skills to be truly competitive at chess."

"I occasionally played with Papa on winter evenings."

"Then will you accept my challenge?"

"Very well." Anything to prevent their first night in his home where he would no doubt insist upon becoming her husband in every way.

She sank weakly into a chair. They began politely, but as the match progressed, Alicia forgot her fears and played with more vigor, and he proved a worthy opponent. While he clearly had not played often, he still had a fine eye for strategy. Growing confident, she played without mercy. Perhaps beating one's husband their first night in their new home may be bad form, but Alicia suspected if she threw the game, he would be offended.

She glanced up at him with a mixture of timidity and triumph. "Checkmate."

He leaned back. "Yes. You were kind. I am sure you could have taken me several times, but did not." He did not sound angry, but he always spoke so softly, it was hard to know for sure.

Growing bolder, she said, "You tease me, my lord. You play much better than you led me to believe."

"I hope to be full of pleasant surprises."

The mantle clock chimed. Alicia twisted the ring around her finger.

He rose. "It grows late. Perhaps we should retire."

Her eyes flew to his face, but the mask revealed nothing of his meaning or intentions. With a slight quiver, she allowed him to escort her to her room. Along the way, his gloved hand indicated a painting of a sharp-eyed woman in scarlet who looked back with bold disdain.

They paused in front of her. "That was my great aunt Millicent. She ran away from home and traveled all over Africa dressed as a man."

In surprise, Alicia gasped and then laughed softly. Further down the hall, he pointed out another portrait of a gentleman wearing a ruffled collar and a large ruby ring.

"That was my grandfather. He scandalized the *ton* by marrying his mistress. They never had children. Later, when she died, he married a proper lady, who bore him three sons, but he never loved her as he loved his first wife."

"What an unconventional family you have, my lord."

"We do seem to take delight in thumbing our noses at society." His hand moved to the small of her back.

She froze.

He noticed. "Shall I never earn your trust, Alicia?"

149

A chill settled in her stomach at the thought of this dark, hidden creature touching her in the same manner as Mr. Braxton. She wondered how she could ever willingly submit to such advances. She couldn't bring herself to look at the hulking figure before her while images of scarred, twisted skin flashed before her eyes. Would his skin be cold and lifeless? Would he be rough? Did he even have any feeling in his limbs?

"As I said, I shall wait until you are ready. I..." he paused as if trying to form his thoughts into words. "Despite my appearance, I am a whole man and have the needs of any man."

Guilt wormed through her fear. "I thank you for your understanding, my lord."

He remained motionless for several minutes, his gaze tangible underneath his mask. When he moved, it was only to brush a smothered kiss against her cheek and then turn and walk away with his cane thumping slightly.

Alicia threw herself into her pillow and sobbed her relief. And her dread of things to come.

****

"This garden was patterned after the stories of Athena, the goddess of war, but I saw only a forest peopled by gnomes and dark caves where dragons guarded their treasure."

Sparkling streams graced the lush gardens filled with flowers of every description. The baron led her through an arch to a new garden. Marble statues adorned the pathways, and stone benches carved with winged cherubs dotted the path.

"This is the garden of Aphrodite, the goddess of love. I stole my first kiss under this tree." Embarrassment colored his voice.

Alicia tried to picture a young Lord Amesbury, but only created a smaller masked figure.

In the garden of Poseidon filled with

meandering streams, waterfalls, and fountains, a picnic luncheon awaited them. A small cascade fell into a pond filled with colorful fish. As servants laid out the meal, he held a chair for her at the small wrought iron table under a spreading tree.

"I thought this would be a good place to have our luncheon."

"It is indeed a beautiful place," she breathed. "Each garden you've shown me has been more wondrous than the last."

"I'm glad you like it."

Emboldened by the pleasant morning, she asked, "Do you have a favorite Greek hero or story?"

He paused a moment. "I've always been partial to Perseus."

"Why?"

"He had many enemies who conspired against him, but he was resourceful. He always managed to do what he felt he must despite the seemingly insurmountable obstacles he faced."

Alicia knew little about mythology, but this name seemed familiar. "Isn't he the one who killed the creature with snakes for hair and whose gaze would turn a person to stone?"

"Medusa. Yes. He also defeated other fearsome foes."

"Is there a garden for him, yet?"

"No."

"Perhaps that will be yours to build."

He paused. "Perhaps. That remains to be seen."

She enjoyed a delicious meal and afterward sat enjoying a gentle breeze as water splashed happily nearby. With a twinge of guilt, she realized since he only ate alone when he could remove the mask, he must be growing hungry watching her consume all the food.

"Do you wish to go eat, my lord?"

He shook his head. "I'll dine later."

151

Alicia tossed a tiny piece of bread into the water and watched as colorful fish swallowed it whole. She brushed a few crumbs off her bronze silk gown and looked up to find her husband's masked face directed toward her.

He cleared his voice softly. "Are you tired or do you wish to continue touring the gardens?"

"I would love to see more of the gardens."

They spent all day exploring while he regaled her with stories of the mythological heroes and heroines. His own childhood exploits often surfaced among the tales. As they followed a path leading back to the house, they passed an arch over a path leading to a garden they had not yet explored.

She paused before the arch. "What's in there?"

"That's Zeus's garden. I never go in there anymore." The tone of his voice became flat, unemotional.

"Why?"

"My brother died there."

She turned to him in shock and then dropped her eyes, unable to look at the mask. "I'm sorry."

"He fell from a tree. I was up there with him, and powerless to help him. The fall broke his neck."

Though his voice sounded detached, she felt his bleak loss. "How terrible for you."

"It was a long time ago," he said gruffly. Cloaked in his own memories, he led her silently to the house.

She ate dinner alone in the breakfast room, well attended by servants. Before she'd finished, the baron joined her. "Thank you for allowing me to show you around. I hope I did not weary you with my tales."

"Not at all, my lord. I enjoyed it enormously."

"I had hoped you would like it. And that you would like my home."

"It's beyond compare," she replied truthfully,

amazed that a mere baron had amassed such wealth. But then, titles did not often equal affluence.

"You mentioned that you play the pianoforte," he said as she finished her dessert.

She put down her napkin. "Not well."

"Ah, yes, the conventional answer. Will you play for me?"

"I assure you, my lord, it is not false modesty. I really do not play well. Our pianoforte was sold months ago, and I have not touched the keys since."

"Then you are long past due. Please." He led her into a music room where a Louis XIV pianoforte with gilded carvings stood in one corner. A harp stood in another.

He gestured to the pianoforte. "I know it's a bit ostentatious, but it has a lovely tone. Will you?"

With some misgivings, Alicia played the first thing that came into her mind; a sonata that *Maman* had loved. Despite the age of the instrument, or perhaps because of it, the sounds it issued were rich and resonant. She stumbled a few times, her fingers awkward from disuse, and unnerved by the dark presence nearby. She breathed a sigh of relief when she finished.

"Technically, that was very good. But I could see that you did not have your heart in it."

Alicia smiled faintly. "My governess scolded me often for not playing with passion." Her fingers itched to play more now that she had begun, but she did not wish to do so while her husband loomed over her. Perhaps she would come back and play in private another time.

Evenings became more comfortable after that, sometimes playing chess, or billiards, or backgammon. Sometimes he requested she read aloud to him. He asked her opinion on a great many matters men usually assumed were not the concern of ladies, and she found their conversation both enriching and stimulating.

The baron always spoke carefully, thoughtfully, as if contemplating the higher meaning to life. He proved to be unlike either Colonel Westin or Mr. Braxton in every way.

When she found herself alone, she devoted more time to playing the pianoforte and felt her soul soothed by the sounds she created with the instrument. Her skill even improved through her diligent playing, but she never played in the presence of others.

Alicia wrote to Hannah, assuring her that she was happy and that her husband was treating her well. She also said that *Maman*'s saying had proved wise. Then she wrote to Elizabeth, saying much the same.

Each day that she spent time with her husband, she grew less afraid of him. The ominous cloak and mask no longer intimidated her so much. As her fear dimmed, she saw his gentle spirit and a quick wit.

But each evening, after he escorted her to her room, he placed his hand on her waist, drew her to him gently, and pressed a kiss to her cheek or brow. She shivered and steeled herself against the night his patience ran thin and he would force himself upon her. He always left without pressing her, and she would go to bed in relief, yet feeling, despite her contentment, something precious had passed her by.

CHAPTER 17

Cole's rapier clanged against his opponent's as he poured all of his concentration into each parry, each thrust. It wasn't until the match was called that Cole lowered his rapier and re-sheathed it. Sweat soaked his clothes and dripped off his hair. His muscles ached but he felt a satisfaction at having passed a few hours without thinking about Alicia. He bowed to his opponent, complemented him on his form and thanked him for an excellent match before he moved to mop his face with a towel. Fencing had always proved an effective diversion when he might be tempted to sink deep into his cups.

After changing, Cole went out to the stables and took his Lipizzaner, André, out on a long run. He had not been home much since the night he'd quarreled with his father and left for the sea. He'd been young and idealistic with a thirst for adventure and a misguided desire to rebel against his father. How foolish he'd been.

Cole looked out over the landscape. He had almost forgotten how beautiful it was here, but his heavy heart prevented him from fully receiving pleasure from his home. He galloped André across the fields, through the woods, to the far borders of his land where the trainer and jockey were running his latest acquisition, a thoroughbred with an impressive lineage.

His trainer waved and Cole guided André to meet with him.

The trainer leaned over the fence. "He has all the makings of a winner."

"He does," Cole agreed.

"We should consider transferring him to the heath land to further his training. He'll be ready to enter his first race next spring."

Cole nodded. "Make the arrangements."

The jockey had a soft, firm touch and an intuitive sense of the horse's abilities. The thoroughbred had the heart of a winner. They were a perfect match.

They discussed details of the thoroughbred's training and then Cole left, wishing he could share it all with Alicia.

He had hoped her marriage to the baron would be the next-best solution to eloping with her. Instead, things had worsened. She filled his thoughts, his desires and yet, she was completely untouchable. Cole cursed.

He should go bang his head against a tree.

He rode to the lake, stripped off his clothes and dove in. The cold water slipped over his skin, cooling his frustration. Fish darted from his path as he forged through the dark, greenish world filled with waving plants and scaly creatures.

His head burst through the surface only long enough to take another breath. He swam the length of the lake and back before he climbed out among the reeds and cattails to throw himself on the grassy bank. After drying in the sun, he dressed and rode into town. Darkness had fallen when he reached a small tavern.

The barkeep nodded but said nothing as Cole took a seat in the corner. The barmaid ambled toward him smiling broadly.

"What's yer pleasure, yer lordship?"

"Just bring me an ale, Ann."

She smiled and flipped her hair. "That'll do fer

now." She turned and cast a come-hither look over her shoulder as she moved away with swaying hips.

Other regulars drifted in, nodded to him, but left him alone. The locals had grown accustomed to the earl's son occasionally coming into their territory during his infrequent and brief stays nearby, but seldom approached him.

Ann brought him his drink and took a seat nearby. "And me, later?"

"Not this time, Ann."

She pouted prettily. " 'Not this time' is all I 'ear from ye now since ye returned, milord. 'ave ye forgotten how I make ye feel?" Her voice took on a throaty tone.

"Things have changed."

"Nothing changes that much. I'll bathe for ye first, just like ye like."

Cole drank from his cup deeply, stamping down temptation. The barmaid was young and pretty and had always proven an enthusiastic diversion, but he could touch no one else when he craved Alicia so badly.

Ann reached over and brushed back a stray lock of hair that had fallen over his forehead. She giggled. "I don't think I ever saw you with you hair mussed. At least not until after."

Cole dragged his fingers through his hair to push the errant strands away from his face, knowing his swim had left him in a state that would give his valet, Stephens, the shivers.

"Yer always so gentle, milord. Ye make a girl long fer the next time."

Cole stood. "I'm sorry, Ann. There won't be a next time." He handed her more money than he'd ever paid for her services and left payment for his drink on the table.

Outside, someone approached from the shadows. Cole dropped into a defensive stance with his knife in his hand.

"My lord?"

Cole relaxed as he recognized the local constable. "What is it, Conner?"

"I thought you'd want t' know someone's been asking about Lord and Lady Amesbury."

Cole frowned.

"He seemed rather shady, if ye know what I mean. Do ye want me t' nab 'im?"

"No, Conner. Thank you for letting me know. She has an uncle that might be concerned for her. I'm sure it's nothing to worry about." But Willard Palmer knew where Alicia's husband had taken her to live. Why send someone to ask about them?

His instincts whispered danger.

****

One evening, Alicia sat with her husband in the darkened garden. Completely enigmatic, he sat with his head lifted upward to gaze up at the starry heavens made glorious by a cloudless sky.

"Did you ever study astronomy?" he asked softly.

"No. I know a little about mythology, so some of the stories you told me of the gardens are familiar, but all I can find in the sky are the North Star and the Big Dipper."

"See that cluster of stars?" His leaned near, his chest brushing against her shoulder, his arm reaching across her, as he traced a group of stars with his gloved finger in the far northern sky. "That is Andromeda. There are her arms, this is her belt, and her legs. Pegasus is here nearby."

A light, masculine scent permeated his cloak and she breathed it deeply, invoking an awareness of him on a new and elemental level. To her surprise, she did not recoil.

"When did you become interested in the stars?" she asked.

"At Cambridge. I was good at mathematics but I

loved astronomy, probably because of my professor." His soft chuckle rumbled. "He was a bit unconventional, and quite eccentric, but he instilled a great love of astronomy in his students."

"Tell me about Andromeda."

"Her name is Greek for 'Ruler over Men.' She is also referred to as 'The Chained Maiden.' She was the daughter of Cepheus and Cassiopeia, king and queen of Aethiopia. Cassiopeia made the mistake of boasting that her beauty equaled the beautiful Nereids of the sea."

Her husband's soft, muffled voice, as he painted the characters, swept Alicia away. "Of course, such a claim drew down the vengeance of the gods. Poseidon, king of the sea, sent a sea-monster to destroy man and beast. The only way to save the kingdom was for the king to sacrifice his daughter, Andromeda, to the monster, so they chained her to a rock on the shore. She was saved by Perseus who slew the monster and freed her. Though she was promised to another, Perseus married her and they had many children. They are supposedly the parents of the Persians. After Andromeda died, the goddess Athena placed her in the constellations near Perseus and Cassiopeia."

When he had finished the story, Alicia realized her neck was straining as she gazed upward. She rubbed her neck. "The Greeks had a rather dim view of their gods."

"They were pagans who saw God, or rather, gods, as selfish, vain creatures who were the cause of human misery. What they failed to recognize is that humanity causes its own misery."

"You are quite a philosopher. And a scholar. An astronomer. What else do you do?"

His shapeless face turned toward her. "Less than I once did." His tone was flat, betraying his despair.

Was she the cause of it? She hung her head. She had the power to offer him comfort, companionship, acceptance; things that he surely did not receive elsewhere. Others no doubt saw only his mask without seeing the intelligent, gentle man underneath.

The servants treated him with respect, even affection. The head housekeeper, Mrs. Hodges, loved him as a member of the family. But then, she had known him as a child.

Her eyes strayed to him, but she could distinguish nothing of his thoughts or mood. She tried again to imagine him as he had been before his injuries; whole, complete, but she failed utterly. "Are there any portraits of you as a younger man? You know, before...?"

His cowled head turned toward her. "Not here."

"I try to imagine your face, but I have nothing upon which to base it. Are you dark or fair?"

"Dark. I assure you, you don't want to see my face. Would you care to see the maze in the morning?"

His obvious desire to redirect her inspired pity for this gentle man who'd lost so much. How would it be to no longer desire to show—or see—one's own face?

"A maze?" She imagined becoming hopelessly lost within a labyrinth of green.

As if reading her thoughts, he put his hand over hers. "I will guide you in and out safely, rest assured. And I will show you the secret so that you will never become lost inside it."

"Very well." She withdrew her hand.

The following morning, he kept his promise. The maze proved more interesting than she expected. With a bright morning sun shining down on them, he led her confidently through it. Inside the wall of hedges, it was a world of quiet stillness, peaceful rather than suffocating. When they emerged in the center, she found a marble fountain falling into a perfectly round raised pool filled with water lilies. Frogs croaked in a rough chorus. Mist from the falling water dampened her face.

He leaned his cane against a stone bench and took her hand. He tugged gently on her hand as he stepped closer, and slowly pulled her into his arms. The contact sent waves of alarm racing through her veins. She tensed, but he did not demand anything beyond holding her. He stood silently, his arms around her, lightly pressing her against him. She had expected the soft body of a near invalid. Instead, he felt solid. When he made no further move, her fear faded—just a little—and she let him pull her in tighter. After her initial fear abated, she rested her head lightly against him and listened to the beating of his heart. It somehow reassured her that he was human and not a beast.

"Alicia, is it me you fear, or men in general?" His voice rumbled his chest against her head.

She moistened her lips and tried to organize her feelings into coherent words. "I fear the act men desire. And husbands require."

Wordlessly, he held her. The water fell merrily into the pool, and birds sang and flirted among the hedges.

"Did someone force himself upon you?"

With startling clarity, the humiliation and terror she suffered at Mr. Braxton's hands flooded over her. She realized she was trembling when his arms tightened around her.

"One of my suitors tried to, but I fought him off. He did not rob me of my virtue, but I learned enough about it that I...am reluctant to do that. I know it's your right, but—"

"Shhh. I will never do anything that you will wish to fight off."

161

"But someday you will—"

"It's a completely different thing when a woman is with a man who cares about her, and who desires to please her. There is no place in it for fear or hurt."

His words, though gently spoken, did not reassure her. Instead, they dredged up his emotionless mask in place of Mr. Braxton's face and the sick terror she had experienced. They were completely alone. There would be no way of escaping him if he should try to take her here in the middle of the maze.

A quiver ran through her body and she pushed herself away from him. "May we go back, now? Please?"

He released her and stepped back but his hands fisted at his sides. He drew a breath, exhaling slowly and then spoke with controlled softness. "Yes. The secret is to turn left at the first junction, pass the next entrance, and then turn right. The pattern repeats. If you do that, you will come back out where we began outside the maze." He retrieved his cane and indicated that she proceed in front of him.

She led the way, with his reassurances at each intersection, until they stepped out into the gardens. Once they were on a familiar path, he made a slight bow.

"I need to attend to business, Alicia, but I will join you after dinner."

"Of course, my lord."

He started to speak, but turned and left without speaking another word. She drew a breath and sat on a cool bench.

That night, after she undressed, she stood in her boudoir looking up at the stars. A shooting star burst across the eastern sky and faded quickly.

Like many of her dreams.

CHAPTER 18

Cole read through the columns of figures that sat on his desk. Several of his investments had paid off handsomely and his solicitor had sent him the latest set of figures and proposals.

His steward had brought a stack of papers including a request for the cooper to attend one of his tenant's houses, and a suggestion to raise the rents to help cover a rash of repairs many of the houses needed lately. Cole approved the use of the cooper and rejected the rent increase. Then he wrote a letter to a man purported to be a genius at improving crop yield, and asked him to come tour the estate.

He sat back and rubbed his bleary eyes, glancing at the clock on the mantle. It was not yet dinnertime, but already it felt like midnight. Alicia Palmer, now the Lady Amesbury, had robbed him of sleep many nights. If he didn't work so hard at wearing himself out riding, fencing, and boxing, he might never sleep.

A letter sat to one side of the desk, fluttering gently in the breeze from the opened window. Aunt Livy had written, asking how he fared and expressing a desire to visit. As much as he enjoyed their company, he did not wish to entertain them at present.

Restlessness tugged at him and he had to remind himself that he needed to stay here. Always before, he fled back to London or other haunts after the briefest of stays here in the country house, but this time, he needed to remain and take care of long overdue duties. In an attempt to restore his health, his father now resided with the youngest Amesbury son, Christian, at the house in Bath. As the heir, it was time Cole assumed responsibility of caring for the family estate.

He wrote back to Aunt Livy, inventing wonderful lies about his happiness and told her he would see her in London this Season if he decided to go. After he finished his correspondence, he leaned back in his chair, wondering again if he had made a colossal mistake in arranging Alicia's marriage to Nicholas.

How badly he wanted her!

Stephens poked his head in the door and grinned. Cole scowled at him, which only broadened the offensively happy expression.

"Wipe off that idiotic grin, you half-wit," Cole grumbled.

His valet tsked, sounding annoyingly like Aunt Livy. "The heat makes you irritable. Perhaps you need to go enjoy the fresh air. Cool off."

"Perhaps I need to thrash a cheeky valet."

Stephens chuckled.

Cole rose and thrust several missives into Stephens' hands. "See that these are posted."

Stephens eyed Cole's clothes with a frown. "I just pressed that and already it's rumpled."

"I don't need a nursemaid."

Cole went outside and rode André to the fields where the thoroughbred trained. He listened with interest to everything the trainer said to him, and admired his new thoroughbred. Cole watched the fine lines of his newest acquisition as he and his jockey flew past them in graceful strides.

Without any warning, the horse stumbled and went down in a spray of dirt and turf. The horse rolled over, screaming, with the jockey underneath him.

Stunned, Cole stood frozen for an instant before he snapped into action. He called for a doctor as he sprinted to the scene of the disaster and fell to his knees in front of the motionless young jockey.

He touched the jockey. "Adair? Can you hear me?"

The young man breathed, but his face was pale and his forehead bled. His eyes remained closed. Cole began running his hand over the lad's limbs, checking for other injuries.

The trainer arrived breathlessly. "Adair?"

"He's breathing," Cole said. "See to the horse."

The head groom dashed to the thoroughbred. The horse rolled over and struggled to his feet. He walked with a limp. Cole returned his attention to the jockey. He found at least one broken bone in Adair's arm and, he couldn't be sure, but possibly a few ribs. Cole shaded the boy, and tried to assuage his fears when he awoke. It seemed an eternity before the doctors both arrived.

The jockey would make a full recovery. The bones had been reset and he would require a long rest.

However, the thoroughbred was so badly injured that he may never race again. He'd have to be put out to pasture for an indeterminate amount of time.

Cole took the news in stoic silence, nodded, and went back out to the course. The trainer squatted near the scene of the fall examining the ground.

"What caused it?" Cole asked.

The trainer looked grief-stricken. "A mere divot."

Heartsick, Cole nodded, arose and went for a long walk. He suddenly desperately needed to be with female companionship.

****

Alicia sat reading in Poseidon's garden, enjoying

the air and the bright sunshine. As she looked up, she nearly dropped her book.

Wearing an impeccable suit, a self-mocking smile tugging his mobile lips, Cole Amesbury approached. Her memory had failed to duplicate this devastatingly handsome man. His long-legged stride brought his lean, muscular frame to her before she was ready to face him.

She jumped to her feet, sending her book tumbling to the ground, and clutched at her heart in a vain effort to still its traitorous thumping.

His smile broadened, turned smug. "Could it be that you are happy to see me?"

"Absolutely not!" she replied with as much venom as she could muster. "I was simply surprised."

She picked up her book, dusted it off and carefully closed it. When she felt composed enough, she looked up at him and tried to resist admiring his perfect, patrician features, or the way the sunlight glinted on his sable hair, or the broad, strong lines of his body. She found the task difficult.

She moistened her lips. "To what do I owe the pleasure of your company, my lord?"

His grin widened. "Since we are cousins, I believe it would be quite appropriate for you to call me Cole."

Sitting quickly before her knees gave out, she pressed her lips together and lifted her chin. "I pity my husband for having you as a cousin."

He laughed, which only intensified her heart's fluttering. "Well, you know what they say, 'you can pick your friends but not your relations.' However, we are a bit of both." Exuding latent sensuality, he sat down on the bench next to her and looked her over with a languorous smile. "You're looking well. There's color to your cheeks and you have filled out. Very nicely." His gaze traveled over her figure while her cheeks heated under his openly appreciative assessment. "I see marriage agrees with you."

"He...is good to me." She wished that the bench was longer so that he would not be seated so near.

He tilted his head to one side. " 'Good' to you. He doesn't make you blissfully happy, though. Less than satisfying as a man, is he?"

She looked at him sharply. "That's a terrible thing to say!"

"It's true, isn't it?"

She opened her mouth and then closed it. Did his eyes have to be so blue? She rose and took a few steps away to put some distance between them and tried to calm her ridiculous heart. It was maddening the way her senses throbbed when he was near.

"It is not appropriate for us to discuss this," she said primly.

"Oh, I think it is. Actually, it is the reason I came see you." He arose and followed her.

Incredulous, she stared. "You're joking."

"I have come to ask if you're ready to leave that scarred cripple for a real man who can satisfy all your needs."

Her mouth dropped open. "How dare you!"

Those blue eyes bored into hers with intensity that contradicted the lazy grin on his face. He prowled nearer like a dangerous feline stalking its prey, filling her with his presence, his scent. "You don't want him. You probably haven't even consummated the marriage."

"How dare you!"

"Am I wrong?"

She spluttered. "It's no concern of yours."

"It does concern me. I have come to rescue you from this farce of a marriage. We could leave the country. Go to the continent. No one would ever know of your first mistake."

Her eyes blazed. "You *are* conceited! You assume

that I would ever want to be with you, but you are very wrong. I wouldn't have you if you were the last man alive!"

A slow smile spread over his lips. "So, you do not claim any loyalty to him, just a healthy hatred of me. That's all right. The opposite of love is apathy, not hate. Your passion could be channeled into a more useful activity." He lightly traced his fingers along her cheek.

Stunned at how delicious his touch felt, she stepped back. "Your lifestyle of debauchery has no place here."

His eyes darkened with desire, his lazy grin turning sultry. "He isn't even a whole man, is he?"

"I don't know if he's whole or—" she broke off, mortified. She had said too much. She put her hands over her burning cheeks.

His smile broadened gleefully and he pounced on her words. "It's not him, it's you! You have rejected him and locked him out of your chambers. If I know Nicholas, he isn't the type of man who would force his advances." Determination smoldered beneath his lazy, unconcerned exterior. "If he's so repulsive that you won't let him into your bed, then leave with me. I'll make you forget all about your first so-called marriage, sham that it is."

"Of all the aggravating...underhanded...disloyal... immoral...."

His knowing laughter snapped her mouth closed. The dratted man had perfect knowledge of his effect on her. He neared, his handsome face, his strong body, his masculinity all stirred her awareness in an alarming manner. Like a predator, he advanced, his meaning clear. She backed away until she found herself stopped against the unforgiving trunk of a tree.

A slight smile touched his sensitive mouth as he rested one arm on the trunk beside her shoulder and leaned toward her. "Come away with me, Alicia."

Her senses filled with his potency, his scent, the desire burning in his eyes. He was wholly male and he desired her. She drew in a ragged breath as trepidation and something else she could not name shot through her. Frightened and ashamed at his power over her, but more at her response to him, she cast about for a lifeline and then channeled her emotions toward something else entirely.

Sudden anger flared. "I'd die before I'd have a heartless murderer like you!"

****

The baron appeared in the doorway of the dining room before Alicia had finished her dinner.

"I have come too soon, I see. May I sit with you as you finish?"

She nodded and returned her focus to her plate but ate with little appetite. Cole Amesbury was without a doubt the most aggravating man she'd ever known. He was without conscience. Without scruples. How dare he expect that she'd have anything to do with him, after all he did to her family!

"You seem distracted tonight," her husband observed.

Alicia realized that she had been stabbing her food with her fork without even tasting her dinner. Looking up, she also became aware that he had been speaking and she hadn't heard a word he had said.

She set down her fork and picked up her napkin. "Forgive me, my lord."

"Is something on your mind?"

She shook her head wordlessly.

He leaned back in his chair. For several moments, he watched her. "I understand my cousin Cole paid a visit today."

She started, her eyes flying to his face, but, as usual, found no answers there. Had the servants seen and reported to him? She tried to keep her voice uninterested. "He did. Are you close?"

"We've been friends since childhood. He used to spend the summers with us. We even went to Cambridge together." He cocked his head to the side. "Did you talk about anything in particular?"

She picked up her glass and kept her eyes fixed on it. "Nothing worth mentioning." She wasn't sure if she was angrier that Cole had the nerve to try to tempt her to leave her husband who had shown nothing but kindness, or that he would so quickly betray a family member who was also a close personal friend. He truly was despicable. The more she learned about him, the less she liked him. What a fool she was for letting his beautiful face affect her.

"Did I mention the Duke of Northumbria is having a ball now that his daughter is of age?" Lord Amesbury asked.

She gathered her skittering thoughts and focused on his question. "No, I don't remember you mentioning that."

"Would you like to go?"

"Of course."

"I thought so. I already sent our acceptance. If I remember the process correctly, it requires you to have a new ball gown?"

Alicia always felt uneasy when he made purchases for her when she clearly did not deserve his money or gifts. "I don't believe there's time to have one made. I can wear something I already have. I have so many pretty new things, thanks to you."

In the last few weeks, such a vast array of lovely gowns had arrived from both London and Paris that she hadn't even worn most of them yet. Her wardrobe bulged with gowns, hats, gloves, shoes, stockings and all the appropriate undergarments of the finest silk and trimmed with yards of delicate lace.

"I have already taken the liberty of arranging for one to be made. Monique saw to the details. It should arrive any day."

Guiltily, she dropped her eyes and forced cheer into her voice she did not feel. "Thank you. You are most thoughtful."

She could feel his smile under the mask. "I have two sisters. I would be unforgivably unobservant if I didn't know at least part of the requirements of a social gathering."

Casting about for an appropriate response, she said; "Tell me about your sisters."

He paused. "Twins, two years older than I."

"Twins," she whispered. "I was a twin."

"I'm so sorry you lost him." Softly spoken, the sincerity in his voice could not be mistaken.

She looked sharply at him, but, of course, saw nothing in the expressionless mask. "You know?"

"Cole told me everything. He lives nearby, so we have occasion to speak often. In fact, I have him to thank for our marriage. He wrote to me, described you, and told me of your circumstances. He wanted very badly to help you. And when I knew, I did, too."

She stared at him. "Why would he wish to help me?"

"He feels responsible for your predicament."

Alicia studied the glass in her hand. "In a way, he is."

"Perhaps someday you will find it in your heart to forgive him."

Alicia clenched her teeth and she carefully set down her glass. "Armand was my better self. I was braver, kinder, smarter when he was with me. Watching him die slowly..." She struggled for composure but continued without finding it. "It's probably not fair, but I also blame Cole for my parents' death." Tears blurred her vision, and he became a shapeless mass. "Robert had sent a message that Armand had been wounded, and was gravely ill. We were rushing to London when the carriage overturned and killed them. If Armand had not been shot, we would not even have been in that carriage on that road that day." A sob broke through. She put her hand over her mouth.

After a long silence, he stirred. "I can't tell you how sorry I am."

She pulled her hand away, dried her eyes with her handkerchief. "Thank you. Fear not, I do not hold any malice toward you. After all, I can hardly hold you responsible for the actions of your cousin."

Lord Amesbury remained silent throughout the evening, sitting more hunched than usual. After she had finished dinner, he excused himself and she did not see him for the remainder of the night, but the next day after breakfast, he came into the kitchen where she sat with Mrs. Hodges going through the linens.

"Would you like to walk down by the lake?"

"Yes, I would." She hesitated. "Does it hurt you to walk?"

"A bit, but I think it's good for me."

They strolled silently, the trees whispering in a gentle breeze. Their feet and his cane crunched on the walkway. She glanced several times at him, unnerved by his expressionless mask and the difficultly with which he stepped. She wondered if she would ever grow accustomed to it all. To him.

"Are you...." She stopped, unsure of how receptive he would be to her questions.

"You may ask me anything. Even if you fear it improper."

She drew a breath. "Are you in any pain?"

"Not more than I can bear."

"How did it happen?"

There was a long pause. "I served as an officer

172

on a ship in the Royal Navy. During a battle, I noticed a young gunner had forgotten to pour seawater on the cannon to cool it before he prepared to fire it again. He couldn't hear me shouting at him over the noise. I rushed to him and tried to stop him from firing it while it was too hot. I didn't reach him in time. He lit the fuse. The cannon exploded. I threw myself to the deck, but I was burned. The boy was...there was not much left of him." His voice took on a flat, unemotional tone as if he tried to protect himself from the emotions that must have sprung up at the memories. He remained silent for several minutes. "He was only thirteen. I failed to save him. Or the others around him."

"Surely you did all you could."

"Not enough. Watching countless young men die all around me while I lived...it haunts me. I wasn't a better officer than those who died. I lived because I was lucky. I was burned, but at least I live. I'm undeserving." The last came out in a whisper.

Alicia's own memories washed over her and she struggled against the feelings of loss. She should have died with her parents in the carriage that day. She, too, was undeserving. They walked in silence until they reached the lake where they found a place to sit on a carved stone bench.

"Are you sorry you married me?"

She turned to him. "No, of course not. I'm safe and I have everything I desire."

"Except the man of your dreams."

She bowed her head in shame, acutely aware that she was not fulfilling her duty as a wife. Cole's face flashed into her mind. Guiltily, she shoved away the image. "You must be sorry you married me."

"No. You are a delightful companion and I am growing quite fond of you. This is more than I had ever hoped. Not many women would agree to marry a monster such as me." His shoulders sagged.

"You are not a monster," she assured him quickly. "You are a kind, warm man. A true gentleman. The others would not have treated me with such courtesy."

They sat in companionable silence.

"Do you still wish to go to France?"

She brightened. "Yes. Some day.

"Next spring."

"Truly? I'd like that very much."

"Then we shall plan on it."

She smiled and managed to look at the masked face for a moment longer than normal before letting her eyes drop.

"Alicia, I know it makes you uncomfortable when I escort you to your room. You feel as if I'm pressing you to let me in. I desire you. And I have developed feelings for you. But I will not come to you. When you are ready, come to me." His muffled voice hushed. "I hope you decide to come to me soon."

Alicia stared at her hands twisting in her lap and wondered if she would ever find the courage to willingly go to him and subject herself to his touch.

After preparing for bed that night, she picked up a book, knowing sleep would not easily come.

She must have fallen asleep reading, for rough hands shook her awake. Groggy, she blinked through a fog and tried to focus on the insistent voice.

"Alicia! Wake up!"

A pair of arms scooped her up and carried her through a haze. Alicia coughed. Her room seemed terribly warm. Was that smoke? She pushed weakly against the steely arms that held her. She was set on her feet but she sank weakly to the floor. Voices shouted. She tried to speak, but could only cough. Wondering why she found it so hard to draw a deep breath, she did not resist when another pair of arms led her to a chair. She heard the sound of a window being opened. She continued to cough and had to fight to keep her eyes open. A cold breeze blew across her face, helping clear her head. A blanket wrapped around her body. Her coughing abated, and her eyesight cleared.

"That's done it, my lord," a male voice called.

"Here, *madame*, drink this." Monique pressed a cup into hands.

"What happened?" she asked the maid.

"The candle by your bed must have fallen over, *madame*. My lord smelled smoke and discovered a fire in your room."

"Fire? How awful. Was anyone harmed?"

"No, my lady. But you would have perished if my lord had not awakened."

The baron appeared then.

"I can't understand how the candle fell over," mused Monique. "It was resting in a candleholder with a wide base. And how did it fall against the bed curtains?"

Her husband paused at Monique's words, then came to Alicia. "Are you all right?"

Alicia nodded. "I owe you my thanks."

He reached out as if to touch her and then drew back. "I'm only grateful you are unharmed."

She wished she could see the expression on his face. Tentatively, she reached out a hand to him. He took it and squeezed her hand briefly. Oddly disappointed he hadn't held her, and surprised that she'd wanted him to, she watched him leave. She wondered if he would ever trust her with his face.

Did she really want to see it, or would it only repulse her?

CHAPTER 19

Alicia's comfortable life was disrupted by Cole Amesbury again. Wearing that maddeningly self-assured smile, he strolled languidly into the library, a great, hungry predator on the prowl.

She leapt to her feet.

"Dearest cousin." He planted a kiss on her cheek.

She glared at him.

His smile faded. "Fear not, I have not come to harass you. Is Nicholas at home?"

She blinked. She never thought of her husband as Nicholas. She always called him 'husband' or 'my lord,' even in her thoughts. "I haven't seen him all morning. I'll send a servant to look for him."

"Never mind. I'll wait for him. Please, sit with me. I'd also hoped to speak with you."

Alicia hesitated but sank to a chair.

Cole paced the floor, going to the window, to the fireplace and then to the sofa. Then he went to the bookcase and leaned upon it.

"Shall I ring for tea?" she offered.

He shook his head. His careless façade slipped away and he appeared so distraught that Alicia actually felt sympathy for him.

He turned to her. "I know I don't deserve your forgiveness."

"Which of the many wrongs are you begging forgiveness for, now? Trying to tempt me to abandon my husband, or something else?" She expected his wry grin.

Instead, his brilliant blue eyes fixed upon her face, gravely serious. "For shooting Armand."

She gripped the arms of her chair.

"All I ask is that you allow me to tell you what happened."

She did not want to hear this. "My cousin Robert told me what happened. He was there, remember?" she managed through clenched teeth.

"I need to explain what led up to it."

Alicia leaned back, folded her arms, and forced herself to look at him. Why must he reopen this wound now? "Nothing you say will change what you did."

"No. And I'm not asking for forgiveness. I only hope if you hear the whole story, you will find some measure of peace."

Fighting tears, Alicia made no comment.

Cole began pacing again. "There was a girl named Vivian. She was the Season's sensation. More than beautiful, she was intoxicating. The *ton* obsessed over her."

Alicia nodded. She remembered seeing the beautiful, elegant Vivian from afar, and noticed how the gentlemen stumbled all over themselves in their desire to catch her eye. Her beauty had outshone even Catherine's. Armand, like every other gentleman in London, was smitten with Vivian, but Papa had said there was something about her he didn't trust.

"She had a way of making men forget all reason. Something about her drove a man wild with desire and yet she always stayed just out of reach, leaving men desperate for one more smile, one more dance, one more kiss. She seemed to prefer Armand and me over the others. I liked Armand well enough, but he seemed to dislike me. Told me once that he found me insufferably arrogant. I suppose I was." His voice hushed. He rested his arm on the mantel and hung

177

his head for a moment. "She pitted us against each other. Played us both for the ridiculous fools we were. She said she favored me and that she might choose me, except for Armand. Apparently, she told Armand the same thing. His actions can be excused as the folly of youth. I'm not a green young buck. I should have seen through her."

Alicia marveled that she had never seen the charismatic Cole Amesbury in London, especially since he knew her brother. Perhaps he was one of those men who avoided balls and musicales. Armand attended places Alicia did not, such as a gentleman's club.

Cole moved to the window and stood staring out before he spoke again. "I went to meet Vivian in the park and came upon them in their coach. Their clothing and hair were mussed and I knew he'd compromised her. Armand grinned at me and told me I had lost. Vivian insisted that I defend her honor. We had words. Vivian demanded justice. I challenged him and we chose our seconds. Robert was his."

Alicia's heart turned to ice.

"By the time we met, my temper had cooled. After all I witnessed during the war, the last thing I wanted was the blood of an innocent man on my hands. I should have backed down."

"Why didn't you?" she gasped.

Cole's body sagged against the window, his head bowed, eyes squeezed shut, pain rippling through him and permeating the room. "I felt I must defend Vivian's honor. And I'd issued the challenge. It would have followed me if I'd rescinded it. So I aimed carefully for his arm—the left, so there would be no chance that his fencing and shooting arm would be maimed." He sighed heavily. "I went to check on him a few days later and they told me he was only grazed and the bleeding had stopped. He seemed to have a strong constitution. They thought he would recover without complication. I had no idea he'd grown ill."

Silence weighed heavily. Alicia stirred herself and realized her face was streaming with tears. Without bothering to search for a handkerchief, she used her hands to dry her cheeks.

Cole faced her, anguish lancing his features. "I would do anything to go back and change what I did. Pay any price." His voice broke. "I'm sorry. I truly am." He stood, clenching and unclenching his fists, looking utterly lost. He did not wear the mien of a cold-blooded murderer. With startling clarity, she realized he never had.

He turned and strode out of the room, leaving Alicia alone with her grief. After sobbing until her tears were spent, she lay weakly against the sofa.

She remembered Armand's easy smile, his contagious laugh, his willingness to listen even late at night when she wanted to talk. He could always cheer her when she felt sad. He teased her mercilessly, but could always chase away the monsters under her bed.

She thought of her parents; *Maman,* gracious, gentle, always with a story and a soft caress, Papa, quiet, solemn, kind. All snatched from her by the whims of fate. Or the whims of a vain and lecherous woman who did not deserve the men who fought for her.

Robert blamed himself for not stopping that foolish duel. And Cole clearly suffered. Somehow, seeing him thus as he relayed the events had a healing affect on her. He was not the monster she thought he was. He had been rash, charmed by a deceitful woman. And now he lived with a grief and guilt that she would never understand. But she was beginning to.

Forgiveness chipped away at the ice in her heart

179

and she wept again, this time for a man with tortured blue eyes.

****

Slowly enough for her husband to keep up, Alicia walked in the gardens. All around them, the gardeners worked quietly. In Andromeda's gardens nearest the house, water tripped over the edge of their fountains and into the pools below with soft tinkling sounds like tiny silver bells. Alicia walked in silence next to her husband, each lost in thought.

"Alicia," he began in his low muffled voice. "Are you happy here?"

"Yes."

"Do not answer too quickly. I need to know the truth. Do you feel comfortable here? Do you feel that this is your home?"

"Yes, I do. It's beautiful here and I have everything I could possibly want."

There was another moment of silence. Finally, he turned to her. "Do you still fear me?"

She considered. He seemed less intimidating than he had at first. He had been a perfect gentleman in every way since she had met him. She realized that she had grown fond of him, of his gentle mannerisms, his wit.

But the thought of allowing him to touch her, the humiliation, the fear and degradation that accompanied such touches, turned her cold.

Knowing he awaited an answer, she moistened her lips. "Not as much, my lord."

He nodded but said nothing more and remained quiet all evening. Since that day he showed her the maze, he made no further attempt to touch her except to press chaste kisses to her cheek.

Late that night, Alicia sat up to finish a novel. As she read the last page and set the book down, hunger niggled at her. She donned a robe and slippers, picked up a taper to light her way, and slipped out of her room down the darkened hallway toward the kitchen. Lord Amesbury's bedroom door stood ajar, revealing a dying fire in the darkened room. He sat in a large arm chair drawn up to the fire, hunched over with his head in his hands as if desperately sad.

A pang of remorse shot through her. They had been married for weeks, yet she still failed to welcome him into her bed. Alicia knew she was being terribly selfish, that she should submit herself to him as was his right. After all, he'd been kind and patient. He deserved a wife who respected him enough to offer him the comfort of her body.

But whenever she imagined herself lying next to him with his hands on her skin the way Mr. Braxton had touched her, her stomach clenched until she felt ill. She went back into her room and closed the door. Her appetite had disappeared.

That night, she dreamed of lying in Cole's strong, gentle arms. Then he began tearing her bodice. Cole's face twisted and transformed into Mr. Braxton. She struggled to free herself as his hands pawed at her body, but his face changed again and he wore her husband's mask. His leather gloves felt cold and lifeless on her skin.

"Alicia."

She cried out, bolting upright and whirling toward the disconnected voice in the darkness.

"Are you all right?" The baron's voice cut through her fear, its soothing tones quieting her panic.

"Yes," she managed. Cold sweat drenched her nightgown.

"You were dreaming."

"Yes."

"You were begging me to stop."

She pressed the heels of her hands into her wet eyes.

"Do you still fear me so much?"

She had no reply.

Soundlessly, he left the room and closed the door firmly behind him. Alicia laid her head down and wept.

****

On the morning of her one month anniversary, the butler informed Alicia that a visitor by the name of Lady Edenburgh had come to call. Pleased that a neighbor had chosen to pay a visit, Alicia smoothed her hair and greeted her caller.

Lady Edenburgh met her with a warm smile. The lady was perhaps ten years her senior, with a lovely face and bright, lively eyes. She wore a tastefully simple, yet fashionable gown.

"Lady Amesbury," she said with a charming accent Alicia could not quite place. "I am so happy to make your acquaintance. When I learned that a lady had come to live here, so near my own home, I waited impatiently until after you'd been married a month so I could come welcome her."

"I'm so glad you did."

"I've been here for three years, yet I still sometimes feel as if I am a newcomer."

"You have such a lovely accent. Where are you from?"

Lady Edenburgh smiled. "I grew up in Ireland. My parents and tutors were all English, but when everyone else speaks with an Irish accent, one picks it up."

They chatted comfortably, and Lady Edenburgh filled her in on the latest gossip. She spoke briefly of her husband. "Unfortunately, a year after we were wed, he suffered an apoplexy and is a near invalid."

"Oh, how terrible for you both."

"We have learned to cope."

Emboldened by her guest's forthright manner, Alicia said, "Pray tell me, have you ever met my

182

husband?"

"No. Lord Amesbury has been either absent, or reclusive for as long as I can remember."

"Then he seldom attends any social functions?"

"None that I'm aware of."

Poor man. He kept himself shut away from the world. No wonder he was willing to go to such measures to find a wife. His alternative was to live his entire life in solitude.

CHAPTER 20

On the day of the ball, Monique arranged Alicia's hair with all the care of a sculptor. Alicia sat looking somberly in the mirror wishing she felt more excitement. Before events put her into mourning, she had anticipated a ball with eagerness. There was little she loved to do as much as dance, to feel completely carried away by the music. Tonight, however, a sense of foreboding dampened her enthusiasm.

Alicia worried that she and her husband would create a sensation when they arrived. She knew he seldom attended social functions.

She wondered if their every move would be discussed and analyzed. Some might look upon her with sympathy, others, with scorn. Perhaps they'd view him as a curiosity, or as the source of apprehension, ridicule, or fear.

By the time Monique slipped her gown over her head, Alicia was tempted to cry off.

"And this one, I think, would be perfect." Monique retrieved a pearl and diamond necklace from the jewelry case and held it up.

Alicia hesitated. She seldom removed her mother's locket, yet the baron might feel slighted if she failed to wear any of the family jewelry he'd so generously given her. She removed her locket, set it carefully in the jewelry case, and allowed Monique to fasten the pearls around her neck.

As she pulled on her gloves, Lord Amesbury knocked respectfully and entered at her bidding. She turned to face him, her dress making a slight rustle.

"You look exquisite, my darling. The dress is lovely, don't you agree?"

The dress had arrived the day before from Paris, a pale green silk with a darker green sash. The hemline pulled up in little flounces held with tiny green ribbons. The wide neckline showed off her smooth white shoulders. She almost felt beautiful.

"It's lovely, my lord."

"And the jewels are perfect." He drew closer. "You look like a queen."

"I think I will be afraid all night that I might lose them," she confessed.

"I hope you will enjoy yourself tonight, Alicia. Do not hurry back. I will see you at dinner tomorrow night."

Her eyes opened wide.

"I am not going with you, my darling. You are a rare beauty and you should not be seen with a frightening creature like me. Our neighbor, Lady Edenburgh, has agreed to attend with you."

Alicia nodded. She looked forward to spending more time with her nearest neighbor.

"And my cousin Cole has agreed to attend. He normally dislikes balls, he calls them marriage marts, but he has promised to watch over you this evening."

Alicia stared. "My lord—"

"I understand your feelings, but I want to make sure you are safe. Cole is the only man I'd trust to protect you as I would if I were present."

He kissed her cheek in that muffled way that had become familiar to her, and left before she could argue further.

Monique fussed over her several more minutes while Alicia fought the rising tremor that leapt to her throat at the mention of Cole's name. After Monique was satisfied that she appeared picture-perfect, Alicia picked up her reticule and left her room. Her husband's door was closed. She paused before it, but then moved on.

Lady Edenburgh's coach waited outside. The night had cooled and the trees glistened silver in the moonlight.

Alicia chatted happily with Lady Edenburgh and asked about the nearby residents. In her charming Irish accent, Lady Edenburgh gleefully repeated the local gossip.

Although the journey took nearly an hour, time passed quickly and they soon arrived at the duke's home.

When the major-domo announced her, an excited hush rippled through the crowd. Alicia keenly felt the eyes of everyone in attendance upon her, as if wondering about the bride of the crippled Baron Amesbury. Desiring to reflect well upon her husband, she tried to move gracefully as she entered the ballroom. Her gown and jewels, she knew, were perfect and she caught smiles of approval, and even one or two of envy.

The host and hostess greeted her warmly and she made her apologies for her husband. They did not seem surprised that he had chosen to remain behind. She turned and halted.

Cole stood within arm's reach, smugly handsome, dressed in impeccable blue superfine that showed his broad form to its full advantage. A sapphire the exact color of his eyes glittered from his snowy cravat.

His smile flashed, calmly stirring her into chaos with even greater efficiency than normal. Yet tonight she saw him in a new light. She knew deep hurt resided behind that confident smile, a hurt she wanted to help heal if she could. But somehow, his effortless control over her senses threw her into a state of irritation.

"My lord," she greeted him. She tried to keep her voice nonchalant. His handsome grin widened, and her knees weakened.

"Can't you agree to call me Cole just for tonight? Cousin?"

She raised her chin haughtily. "Very well, *Cousin Cole*, you scoundrel. I will be civil to you, for my husband's sake. I am sure you are somehow behind this. How you ever convinced him to allow this ridiculous scheme, I shall never know."

He awarded her his heart-stopping grin. "Would you believe it was his idea?"

She sniffed. "I suppose he isn't as intelligent as I thought. It's like asking the cat to guard the fish bowl."

He grinned. "An apt metaphor." Then he leaned closer, and her swirling senses spiraled higher. "I have been looking forward to spending this evening with you, Alicia." He chuckled softly at the look of alarm that must have come over her face. "Fear not, I promise I will be a perfect gentleman. Your gown is exquisite. It suits you perfectly. And the jewels are a nice complement."

"Thank you." She eyed his immaculate blue superfine and the stark white of his shirt and cravat against his tanned skin. "You look well. Dashing, as usual."

He grinned while something dangerous smoldered in the depths of his eyes. "Dance with me." It seemed a plea rather than a command. Against her better judgment, she allowed him to lead her to the dance floor.

Armed with an arsenal to keep him talking about safe subjects, she said, "I understand you spent much of your youth at sea?"

He nodded. "I left Cambridge and joined the British Navy when I was fourteen."

"I am surprised your family let you go away to

sea. Normally the eldest son is required to stay home, isn't he?"

"I often break with convention. I was angry, foolish, and craving excitement. I'm surprised my father approved. Perhaps he thought I'd do some growing up."

"Were you in many sea battles?

His face closed over. "Yes."

She paused, wondering if she should pursue this topic, but the desire to understand the man beneath the calm exterior urged her on. The dance pattern took them apart. When they were back together, she looked up at him. Very gently, she pressed, "Were you wounded?"

Tension radiated from his body. "Everyone is wounded at least once."

She suspected that he had been hurt in many ways. The ravages of war left their mark on many men. Some wore their scars on the outside where a mask must shield them, others wore their scars on the inside and masked them with a careful expression and a teasing manner.

His voice took on a lighthearted tone, but it sounded forced. "My brother Jared had a different idea. He signed on with a privateer. Fewer rules, better pay. Jared was promoted faster than I. He loved to lord it over me that my younger brother was ahead of me in rank, but since he wasn't in the Navy, I did not consider it a contest."

"Did you serve with my husband?"

"On different ships, of course, but we were in some of the same battles. I sold my commission after the war. My brother Jared is still at sea, as captain of his own ship." His face softened as he spoke of his brother, and his tension dissolved.

The dance set ended and he led her off the floor. They sat on a sofa between two large ferns and sipped drinks Cole snatched from a passing tray.

"Tell me of your brother," she urged. "Jared, is it?"

"I have three living brothers. Jared..." he let his breath out slowly as is trying to determine how much to divulge. "He's been living as a pirate for nearly three years. It's a role he's taken to rather well. Perhaps too well." He glanced at her. "I'm trusting you with this family secret."

She nodded to assure him she'd never breathe a word.

He grinned at some fond memory. "He's arrogant, incorrigible, and completely without honor."

"So, in other words, you are much alike," she interjected with a teasing smile.

He chuckled, his eyes glittering. "I see you know me well."

He began relating their antics as children. She easily pictured a younger Cole causing mayhem in his corner of the world with an adoring younger brother innocently participating in all of his exploits. With her gently probing questions, he told her of his school days and the pranks he and his classmates orchestrated. Alicia laughed until her cheeks hurt.

Putting her hands against her face, she cocked her head to the side. "What do you do when you are not frittering about the countryside, trying to tempt hapless relatives to cuckold their husbands?"

His easy laugh coaxed another smile out of her as well. "Seeing to the estate takes much time. In my free time, I ride and hunt. When I want something more vigorous, I box and fence. I am fond of horses and horse racing. I actually own several winners." He spent the next several minutes telling her about his horseflesh, races and hopes for the future. He related the loss of his newest horse, and the injury of the jockey.

As they talked, she felt her defenses fall. She

told him of her childhood and of her parents, her brother, her terrifying first season in London with the *beau monde* dowagers watching her critically.

"Alicia. And—Lord Amesbury, what are you doing here with her?"

Alicia looked up in surprise to see Catherine standing over them, virtually glittering from head to toe.

Cole shot her quizzical grin. "I was invited, I believe. And you?"

"Visiting my dear niece for her first ball. And you were supposed to come alone."

Cole smiled. "My cousin asked me to watch over his delightful wife, and I was only too happy to oblige. Lovely to see you again, Miss Sinclair. Good evening."

He stood and led Alicia away as she tried to stifle a smile. "That may be the first time anyone has ever dared cut Catherine Sinclair," she said when they were out of earshot.

"She is a shallow, vain, conniving woman. I have had my fill of that sort. They fail to hold my interest."

"Oh? And who would hold your interest?"

"Someone who's already rejected me soundly." He spoke wryly, but without rancor, and his smoldering gaze heated her cheeks.

The evening was a magical swirl of music, lights, dancing and Cole's beautiful blue eyes. When other men asked her to dance, he glared at them and only grudgingly stepped back to allow them to take her hand. Under his attentiveness and open looks of admiration, she blushed with pleasure and something else she did not dare identify. Light and giddy, she forgot everything but the brightness of his smile and the feel of his strong arms around her waist as they floated across the dance floor. After a mouth-watering dinner, there was more dancing.

Captain Hawthorne had come as Catherine's guest. His handsome face and dark eyes brought a smile to her lips as he greeted her with a polite bow and asked for a dance.

Alicia accepted. "I am happy to see a familiar face here, Captain Hawthorne," Alicia said as they danced. "You've come a goodly distance."

"You're looking well, Lady Amesbury," he replied.

She glanced at Catherine, who stood laughing in a circle of ardent admirers. "Are you and Miss Sinclair...?"

His dark eyes were shielded. "I'm not certain. I do not believe my lineage is impressive enough for her."

"Then she is blind. You are handsome, polite, and your father is a respected gentleman. Any girl should be grateful for your attentions."

He inclined his head in a bow. "You are very kind."

The dance ended and he thanked her for the honor. Cole appeared at her side, greeted Captain Hawthorne civilly, and took her hand again, sweeping her away.

A footman appeared with the message that Lady Edenburgh had fallen ill. The hostess had offered to let her remain for the night and had already put her to bed.

Alicia's bliss faded. "Oh, dear, nothing serious, I hope?"

The footman shook his head. "No. The doctor was not sent for, but she developed a dreadful headache."

Cole seemed to be amused by the whole thing.

"What?" Alicia demanded of him when the footman departed.

Cole shrugged. "It's possible her 'headache' is nothing more than a tryst with her lover."

"Cole Amesbury! What a thing to say."

He chuckled. "Her husband is sixty and an invalid. You can't expect a thirty-year old woman to live a life of celibacy, can you?"

She glared at him. "Are all men so depraved, or just you?"

He laughed. "Most are, I fear. However, I'd expect her to be a bit more discreet than to leave you to return home alone. Who knows? Maybe it is a mere headache." He turned pensive. "Nicholas would have my head if he found out I'd let you travel all that way alone. You had better let me escort you home."

"What? And risk that kind of scandal?"

"You're a married lady now, Lady Amesbury. The scandal dwindles once you are no longer husband-hunting."

"Still," she sputtered. "It would reflect poorly upon me. And him. He—"

"Would shoot me if harm came to you. He's as good a shot as I. And Aunt Livy likes him better. She'd never let me live in peace." He grinned.

Alicia smiled reluctantly. "Very well. I admit, I'm not overly fond of traveling alone at night."

His grin widened. "Someday, you'll say you'd love to spend an hour in my company."

A gentleman approached for a dance, and the dancing and music swept her away.

All too soon, the magic ended. Alicia's joy did not, however. She climbed in to Cole's coach still smiling at her charming escort. They talked and laughed while the coach made its way down the road. The swinging lamps played with the shadows. He lounged across from her, his long legs stretched out and she marveled again at his handsome face and the breadth of his shoulders.

Dancing for hours began to catch up with Alicia and she had to fight her fatigue. She removed her slippers and rubbed her feet.

"Here, let me," he said.

She only weakly protested as he massaged her sore feet. They looked tiny in comparison to his large, strong hands.

"Ohh," she moaned, "that feels wonderful."

With controlled strength, he coaxed the soreness out.

"Mmmm," she heard herself moan again.

"Stop that, you're making my imagination run wild."

"Hmmm?"

His eyes glittered darkly in the lamplight. "Never mind." He rubbed her feet until she felt both renewed and drowsy before his hands stilled. "Better?"

She smiled at him, her eyes half opened. "I think I could dance for a few more hours now. You have magical hands."

He opened his mouth, but then closed it firmly without speaking. The carriage rolled its way over the rutted road and they fell into a comfortable silence.

He moved to her side. His hands cupped her cheeks, his thumbs caressing her skin as ever so slowly, his head lowered toward hers. Her heart pounded in anticipation as his nearness, his touch, filled her senses.

A tiny smile touched one corner of his mouth an instant before he brushed her lips with his. Once. Twice. Then he settled in for a kiss. She was lost in the sweet warmth that permeated her body, vibrating every nerve, stirring her to acute alertness. He tasted mildly of sweet wine and cinnamon. She breathed deeply of his masculine scent while his surprisingly soft lips gently tugged at hers.

The only other man who had tried to kiss her

had been rough, brutal, and nothing like this. Only the slightest pressure of his large, strong hands on her face kept them anchored beyond the gentle contact of their lips. She knew she could escape at any time and he would not press her, but escape was not her wish. She wanted more.

He obliged her unspoken desire. His hands guided her head to a different angle, coaxing her lips to part. He deepened the kiss, his controlled passion coaxing her to follow, stirring her to greater heat.

She met him, hesitantly at first, but as desire stirred her blood, she let her hunger guide her in response. She felt the fabric of his superfine and his heart thudding under her hand. Instinctively, she slid one hand up his coat toward his head, speared his hair with her fingers and pulled his mouth more firmly upon hers. A strangled groan escaped him and he trembled with restraint. Sweet desire made her pulse gallop.

"My lord?" The coachman's voice broke through the darkness.

Cole closed the kiss and lifted his head. "What is it, Parker?" His voice sounded hoarse.

"Trouble."

He released her with a regretful, rueful smile, caressed her cheek, and then put his head out of the coach's window to converse with the driver, but the wind carried their voices away from her. Her senses spun with Cole's taste, his scent, his touch, the desires he stirred.

Cole pulled his head back inside, his expression grim. He drew in a breath, held it a moment, and then released it slowly.

"Forgive me, my lady, but I must ask you to move to this seat." He indicated the bench across from her.

After she complied, he knelt and lifted the cushion of the seat they had recently vacated to reveal a compartment filled with handguns. Cole deftly loaded them all and laid them out on the seat next to her in a neat row, all the handles facing the same direction.

Seeing guns in his hands left her cold. "What is it?"

"Highwaymen. Take off the pearls and give them to me."

At his commanding tone, she obeyed without question. After placing her jewels in a small cache hidden in one corner of the compartment, he blew out the lanterns and parted the curtains over the windows. Alicia craned her neck around his head to see riders approach from both the front and the rear of the carriage.

A voice called out, "Stop the coach and cooperate and no one will get hurt."

The coach stilled and the riders surrounded them. Alicia's heart pounded. Her breath sounded loud in the stillness.

Cole placed a hand over hers. "Courage," he whispered.

As her eyes adjusted to the darkness, she watched Cole soundlessly heft a gun in each hand and held them poised, his hands steady, his expression impassive. She could easily imagine him as a soldier; deadly, ruthlessly calm in the face of danger.

"We aren't carrying any money," Cole called out.

"Send out the lady."

They exchanged wide-eyed glances and then Cole frowned, clearly wondering why they would make such a demand. "Lie down," he mouthed.

Alicia sank to the floor and flattened herself.

"If it's ransom you wish, take me!" Cole shouted.

"We want the girl."

Alicia peered out from a crack between the door and the frame. In the bright moonlight, she could see that all of the highwaymen had guns pointed at the coach. One of the highwaymen, she presumed the one who had spoken, eased his mount closer.

"Send her out now, unless you wish for bloodshed!" the leader called.

She glanced up at Cole who had his guns trained carefully upon the highwaymen. An explosion erupted from beside her. With a gasp, she covered her ears and realized Cole had fired one of his guns. The leader let out a grunt and folded in his seat, but before he dropped from his saddle, Cole fired again, and another rider fell. Both lay motionless in crumpled heaps on the ground. With howls of fury, the highwaymen all opened fire.

The coach began moving again, and judging from the swaying, the horses were at a full run.

Alicia watched a hole appear in the doorframe, and then the wall behind her splintered. She flattened herself to the floor, her heart hammering against the floorboards. Cole dropped his discharged guns and picked up others, firing without pause as incoming balls tore their way through the walls of the coach and the seats. The acrid smell of gunpowder filled the air.

Cole dropped his guns next to Alicia in the small pile of firearms scattered on the floor and picked two more, watching out the narrow back window. He continued firing outside as the highwaymen pursued, their shots growing wider as they fell behind.

He looked down at her. In the semi-darkness, she could not see his expression, only the direction of his gaze. "Are you all right?"

She nodded mutely.

"Alicia?" A trace of panic colored his voice and she realized that he could not see her clearly enough to have seen her nod.

"Yes."

"A ball didn't strike you?"

"No."

Another gunshot from outside shredded the back curtain. Cole grunted and fired back both guns. He dropped them and picked up his last two, his eyes sweeping the road behind them. They rode in silence for several moments while Cole kept watch. Finally satisfied, he set down the guns and helped Alicia to her seat. He scooped her into his arms, crushing her against his hard, strong body, and let out a ragged breath. She felt him tremble as his iron control slipped.

As the danger passed, the reality of their peril caught up to Alicia and she shuddered, tears gathering. They might have been killed. If not for Cole's skills as a gunman, they surely would have been. Or she would now be in the hands of criminals.

Cole held her tightly, arms strong and soothing, all signs of the merciless gunman gone. He murmured words of comfort while she wept. She lay against him, wishing things could have been different between them. How right it felt to be encircled by his arms!

By the time they arrived in front of her husband's home, she had pulled herself together and dried her tears.

"You took a terrible risk, Cole."

"I'd die before I'd deliver you to unscrupulous men." His voice sounded tight, angry.

Predawn gray spread across the eastern sky and mist swirled above the ground. He helped her out, holding her hand for a moment longer than necessary. His eyes searched hers with an intensity that set her heart racing. Then his expression softened, and he brushed a kiss against her temple before turning away.

He looked up at the coachman. "Parker? Are you all right?"

The coachman sat hunched over. Cole swung up onto the seat and carefully eased the driver's body back, causing him to unbend. The man sucked in his breath as Cole probed his side and then swore softly.

"Come inside, Parker, we need to have that attended."

"Jest a scratch, milord."

Cole helped the man climb down while Alicia stood by feeling useless. As they mounted the front steps, she offered her arm to the coachman who obliged her, but leaned more heavily on Cole.

"I'm sorry," she said to them both.

The coachman managed a weak smile, revealing a gap in his teeth. "We wouldn't let the likes o' them 'ave ye, milady."

Servants swarmed around them as Cole explained. Mrs. Hodges waded in, shooing the rest away. "Come on then, let's have a look at you. Potter, send for the doctor." She led him away, leaving Cole and Alicia in the foyer.

In the dim lighting, Alicia saw a dark stain spreading on Cole's arm below a tiny hole in his sleeve. "You're hurt," she gasped in alarm.

"It's not bad."

"Mrs. Hodges!"

Alicia's frantic cry brought the woman running. "The driver will be all right. I've sent for the doctor—" she began and then stopped short. "You, too, my lord?"

"It's nothing."

"You men!" Mrs. Hodges sighed in exasperation. "Come into the kitchen where the light is better and let me have a look at you."

"I'm only grazed," Cole protested.

Her eyes flicked to Cole's. "My lord would have my head if he thought I hadn't seen to you properly."

Cole's mouth lifted in a crooked smile. "Very well."

They lit every lamp in the kitchen before Mrs. Hodges peeled off his cravat, frockcoat, and waistcoat. With his shirt unbuttoned, he pulled the neckline aside just enough to expose his wounded shoulder. Alicia set her teeth, unable to keep her eyes off the rounded, solid muscles of his chest and shoulder. His body had been beautifully sculpted. Even wounded, he was large, powerful, and oh, so wholly male.

The bullet had cut a path through the flesh of his upper arm below the shoulder. The wound still bled freely.

"It's not bad, my lady," Mrs. Hodges assured Alicia.

Alicia hoped she would never see a wound that the intrepid housekeeper would consider serious. This one made her shiver. While Alicia helped Mrs. Hodges clean the wound, Cole's eyes remained shielded.

The desire to offer him comfort beset her. "Does it hurt very badly?"

He shook his head but his teeth remained clenched.

Mrs. Hodges scoffed. "Asking a man if it hurts will never bring the truth. They think they have to be so manly. But really, they're just big children. I'm going to need fresh bandages. I'll be back momentarily." She swept out of the room.

Cole stirred. "I'm sure it must give you some sense of justice seeing me this way."

She stared at him, completely caught off-guard by his comment. "No. Of course not. How can you say that?"

The shields dropped, baring his self-recrimination. "Poetic justice, I suppose, since this is what I did to your twin."

Alicia sank into a kitchen chair next to him. She kept her voice soft, but spoke with fervor. "I take no

199

satisfaction seeing you hurt."

He continued as if he had not heard her. "If I develop a sickness and die, you can dance on my grave. Perhaps I should insist they cut off my arm first."

Truly alarmed, she leaned in. "No. I do not wish you to...." She could not even bring herself to say the word.

She wanted to hold him, comfort him, reassure him. Blood ran continually down his arm. She cleaned it again, wondering if a man as strong as he could actually die from such a minor wound as this.

She forced cheer into her voice. "This is only a scratch. You shouldn't sicken from this."

"It's no worse than I did to Armand," he said darkly.

Panic seized her at the thought of the possibility of Cole lying feverish and dying. "I'll have the doctor—"

Cole stood, his face wooden, and looked down at her, his chest rising and falling quickly as if he found breathing difficult. "Don't trouble yourself. My valet comes from Romany stock and has more medical knowledge than any English doctor I know. He'll attend me." He took the cloth from her hand and pressed it to his arm. With his other hand, he scooped up his discarded clothing and headed for the door.

"Cole."

He halted, his broad back still toward her.

"Thank you. For saving me. You are very courageous. I'm sorry you and the coachman got hurt."

He turned slowly. "I will never allow harm to come to you."

"I know. And I owe you an apology."

He stared.

"You've tried to help me many ways, the offer

you made to my uncle, paying his debts and sponsoring Hannah for a Season. That was most generous. And thoughtful. As was the offer to elope. And then you convinced your cousin to marry me and give me a place of safety. I never thanked you for your kindness. Instead, I've been rude and hateful to you. I'm sorry."

He watched her, his blue eyes carefully shuttered. "You lost your brother and your parents because of me."

"I had painted you as a monster, but I was wrong. And I had become so comfortable blaming you for all my troubles that it clouded my judgment."

He swallowed hard. "Alicia, I swear to you by all that's holy, if I could change the past, I would."

She teared up at the anguish in his face. "I know. After you told me about the events that led up to—" she choked, "the duel, I realized that you never meant to really harm him. Or me. For the first time, I see you clearly."

He grimaced. "You might not like me any better, then."

She laughed softly. "I like you better now that I'm not trying so hard to hate you. I truly am sorry for being so terrible to you." She rose up on tiptoe and pressed her lips to his cheek, resisting the urge to kiss those lips that so recently had devoured hers and reawaken the passion that had been between them only moments ago.

He stood with his eyes closed for a moment before turning to stride quickly away.

Desolate without him, Alicia resisted the urge to call him back. She realized kissing Cole in the carriage had been a catastrophic mistake. Guilt for betraying her husband ate through to her soul. She wept for the man she could never have and cursed herself for being so faithless.

CHAPTER 21

Cole glared at the canopy over his bed and watched the shadows slowly slip from the room as the sunrise sent thin rays between the draperies.

Stephens had cleaned his arm where the bullet had grazed him and applied several painful methods of insuring sickness would not set in. After Stephens sewed the wound and properly bandaged it, Cole sent him away with every intention of pacing the floor restlessly, but apparently Stephens had given him something to make him sleep. The wretch.

Painfully, he rose. He tried to dress without waking Stephens, but his sore arm prevented him from doing anything so independent and forced him to ring for help.

Stephens entered, looking disgustingly fresh and alert, and all too pleased with himself. He cleaned the wound again. "This will be fine, no need to worry." He wound a bandage around it.

"I need to shave and dress."

"You should stay abed and rest another day."

"Stop coddling me and help me dress," Cole snarled.

Stephens wisely kept silent, but continued to fix him with looks of remonstration.

"How is Parker?" Cole asked.

"Well enough. I looked in on him after I left you and cleaned off the manure the doctor put on the wound and dressed it properly." He shook his head. "I'm surprised people ever heal with the imbeciles the English have for doctors. Romany children know more about healing." He pushed on Cole's boots.

"I slept from dawn yesterday until dawn today. You drugged me," Cole accused.

Stephens grinned, his teeth a flash of white against his brown face. "You have to sleep sometime. I figured that was as good a time as any since you were wounded and all. And you had about a month's worth of sleep to catch up on."

Cole glared at him. "I'm going to make you taste all my drinks from now on."

"Yes, Your Majesty. Shall I taste all your meals, too?"

"Insolent cur."

Stephens grinned.

Cole cuffed him on the back of his head but Stephens took more exception to the fact that his hair had been mussed. He hastily smoothed it.

Outside, the air was brisk and clean, with a faint mist hanging about the trees. Dawn glimmered on the far edge of the world, but there would be enough light to find his way. He knew the grounds well enough to navigate in total darkness. The lamps were already lit in the stables as the grooms and stable lads went about their work.

Cole greeted the workers briefly before moving down the row of stalls. "I've neglected you of late, André," he said to his favorite horse. He offered an apple he'd pilfered from the kitchen. Talking soothingly to André, he tried to tack him up, but the pain in his arm forced him to accept aid from a vigilant stable lad.

Mist swirled around him like sleepy wraiths as horse and rider walked to the open field, but when Cole urged André to a gallop, darts of pain shot through his arm and he was forced to slow. While birds serenaded him with their morning chorus, Cole wended his way through the grounds and down the hollow leading to the woods. Wind whispered through the leaves.

As he thought back over the events of the highwaymen attack, Cole scrutinized each word, each act. Why did they demand Alicia? Normally they only desired money or jewels rather than prisoners. They seemed to know who it was that they had attacked, at least that a girl was in the carriage. More specifically, they'd wanted 'the girl,' as if they had been after her in particular. If they knew who they were stopping, he, as a viscount and son of an earl, clearly outranked the lesser title of baron's wife and should have been the object of their demands. Most people assumed that the higher the title, the more wealth they possessed. So why did the highwaymen not ask for him instead of her? Unless they were not simple highwaymen.

And prior to that, someone of shady character had come into town asking for Lord and Lady Amesbury. Right before her room caught on fire. Slow dread crept in.

For weeks, the nagging suspicion that her parents had not died in a mere accident had grown. And as he thought back on the duel, and the events preceding and following it, his instincts whispered of sinister forces at work. Perhaps it was time to do a little investigating.

And what to do now about Alicia?

He had two choices. He could leave and try to banish her from his thoughts, or he could try and coax her into liking him.

He grinned. If her kiss was any indication, she liked him at least at some level. And her words in the kitchen gave him hope.

But Alicia was not the kind of woman with whom a man could merely trifle. He knew the first day he met her that she would never consider a dalliance. Any man who would win her affection would have to be willing to offer her his heart first.

Offer her his heart.

He couldn't do that. And unless he did, she would never be his.

But he didn't love her.

Then why did his thoughts always spiral back to her? And why could he not sleep for the yearning of her?

****

"I need to go to London on business. Would you care to accompany me?"

Alicia looked up at the expressionless mask that concealed her husband's face. "London?"

"I know it isn't the Season, so there may not be as much to do as you would like, but between the theater, opera, and the modiste, we might be able to keep you busy. And I do have friends who live there at this unfashionable time of year and would welcome you. Someone is always sponsoring a rising musician or hosting a charity function."

Alicia laid down her pen on the writing desk and gave him her full attention, her letter to Elizabeth forgotten.

London. She hadn't been there in a year and a half. Living here with only her untouchable husband and the servants had left her feeling restless, caged. The ball should have solved that, but instead her thoughts centered on Cole whose easy laughter but tortured eyes tormented her constantly.

"I think I would like to go to London."

"Excellent. Tell Monique to pack your things. We'll leave at the end of the week."

Alicia spent the next several days in a flurry of excitement. Her enthusiasm even seemed to rub off on her quiet husband who seemed to have more energy than normal.

"The staff at my house in London have been informed of our arrival and should have the house in order by the time we arrive," he told her as they skirted the edges of the lake. Two swans glided silently by, leaving ripples in their wake. The lake mirrored a clear blue sky, darker in the reflection. Deep blue, like Cole's eyes.

With a start, she smothered any further thoughts of Cole Amesbury and fixed her mind upon her upcoming trip to London. She realized her husband was speaking, his soft, muffled voice outlining details of his Town home and of the servants' names and duties.

"I understand Cole returned to London last week. Perhaps he will agree to escort you to the diversions the Town offers when I am unable."

At the mention of Cole's name, her cheeks heated. "I'm sure he is quite busy."

The baron turned to her. "Did you not enjoy your time at the ball with him? He said you spent much of the evening together."

"Yes, of course I did. He was very attentive to me."

"I knew he would be."

"My lord." She hesitated. "Do you trust him that much?"

"Why? Was he not a gentleman?" he asked sharply.

Oh, heavens, she couldn't have her husband challenging Cole to a duel! "Yes, of course he was," she replied quickly, her face warming at the lie. "But are you sure he will remain such?"

With a slight chuckle in his voice, he said, "You are a temptation to any man, Alicia. I am sure that he is not immune to your charm. However, I trust he knows his place."

Alicia frowned at her husband's choice of words.

"And did he not protect you when the highwaymen attacked?"

"Yes. He was very brave." She paused. "A bullet grazed his arm."

"A minor wound that has healed completely." His voice sounded flat.

She took a breath. "I thought you were close. But you often speak of him in less than flattering tones."

"I love him like a brother. But he is whole. I am trapped inside this mask. I cannot help but envy him."

****

Their trip to London began at the same slow pace as their trip to their estate had been right after their wedding ceremony, with frequent stops for meals and stays overnight at the posting inns that dotted the roads. Monique saw to her every need with tender loyalty. The baron watched over her protectively, and their conversation grew more comfortable.

One morning, as she left the inn and climbed into the front carriage, she paused. Both footmen and the coachman carried guns.

She turned to her husband. "We are traveling heavily armed."

"I am taking no chances with your safety, My Lady."

"Because of the highwaymen attack?"

"I fear that may not have been an isolated incident." He handed her in and climbed slowly in to sit across from her. He laid his cane on the floor and wedged it to prevent it from rolling.

"Meaning, you think highwaymen are getting bolder, or that they were specifically after me?"

"I have not yet decided." He offered no more on the subject and steered the conversation to other matters.

The crowded streets of London caused them to wind slowly along their way. The working classes hurried along in the streets and the parks today, while the nobility were notably absent. Most left the

207

city for the summer months and would not return to Town until the Season began.

The baron's coach stopped in Pall Mall near a beautiful park in front of a house with a tastefully elegant façade.

"Home at last," Lord Amesbury muttered, his muffled voice betraying an uncharacteristic tone of irritability.

Her eyes moved to her husband. With shame, she realized that he was probably miserable always wearing his hood and mask.

Inside, the town home rivaled his country home in grandeur. With Grecian flavor, the entry boasted of sweeping staircases and marble floors that managed to be lavish without being ostentatious.

Her husband presented her to the staff and then she was led to her room. Peach silk papered the walls, and the furniture was white and gilded.

After a taking a bath and changing into her evening gown, Alicia felt much more refreshed. The servants seemed eager to please her and the meal was excellent, but eating alone invoked a deep loneliness. Normally, Lord Amesbury joined her as she finished dinner, but tonight he failed to appear. Perhaps the journey had aggravated old wounds.

As the sun set, she stepped out to the diminutive city gardens under a sky darkening with thunderclouds. A chill gust of air flowed over her. Deeply breathing, Alicia let her head fall back and closed her eyes. Moments later, the soft pattering of raindrops broke the stillness of the evening. Alicia remained still, reveling in the icy drops on her face.

Her thoughts inexplicably turned to Cole. She remembered the hurt in his eyes after he'd been shot defending her. Not from the pain of the bullet, but the thought she might be glad he had suffered the same wound he had inflicted on Armand. A few months ago, she might have felt a grim satisfaction at the poetic justice fate dealt him. Now that her feelings toward him had softened, seeing him wounded only grieved her.

She pressed her hands over her face. This would not do.

When the rain began to fall with more force, she went back inside. As she approached a liveried servant hovering nearby, he jumped to attention.

"My lady?"

"Where is Lord Amesbury?"

"Resting, my lady. He took his meal in his room and has not come out. Rather tired from the trip, I should think."

His valet, Jeffries, approached. "My lady? My lord sends his regrets. He is quite fatigued. He will not be joining you this evening."

Disappointed, she murmured, "Thank you, Jeffries."

Alicia mounted the stairs to the drawing room and sat by the windows, listening to the soothing cadence of the softly falling rain. Turning, her eyes fell upon a richly carved pianoforte.

Having been assured throughout her life that she had no talent for it, she seldom played unless no one listened. Still, playing soothed her and she was not above recognizing that her skill, if not her talent, had improved since she renewed her daily playing.

With the rain as accompaniment and with her thoughts circling, her fingers touched the keys. She played a minuet first and then a rhapsody. After running through easier pieces, she launched into more difficult pieces. They took all of her concentration and she completely immersed herself into the music.

Calmed, she began playing a slow sonata. Something about the sweet, sad feeling of the music again brought to mind thoughts of Cole. She relived his gentle, hungry kiss, the restraint he exercised when he could have easily overpowered her, the aching tenderness he stirred in her. She had progressed well into the third movement when she heard a soft sound behind her. Turning, a slight gasp escaped her lips. Her fingers fell away from the keys and she stood.

"I didn't know you played so well." Cole's voice washed over her, warming her face and spurring her heartbeat.

She clasped her hands together. "I don't."

"Trust me, that was truly great. I've never heard that piece played with such feeling, such...passion. Please, continue. I did not mean to interrupt."

He stood leaning lazily against the door frame with his arms folded, something forbidden smoldering in his blue eyes. Impeccably dressed as always, dark hair smoothed to a shine, he radiated confident sensuality. No lady should have to endure his presence unchaperoned.

The memory of his kiss and her traitorous desire to repeat it leapt into her thoughts, but guilt squashed them ruthlessly. She consciously released her clenched hands and placed them to her sides.

"Do you make a habit of walking into your cousin's home unannounced?" she asked irritably.

Unperturbed, he grinned, his eyes making a slow perusal of her body. "Only with the proper motivation."

She frowned at him and folded her arms. "May I ask the reason for your visit, sir?"

His maddeningly handsome grin only deepened. "Nicholas sent word that you had both come back into Town. I came to speak with him, but I think I'd rather spend the evening with you."

"He has already retired."

"Excellent. Then I have my wish." He crossed the room and sprawled in an armchair as if he belonged there. "How was your journey? Tedious?"

She sighed that he'd so blatantly taken a seat while leaving a lady standing. "Has anyone ever told you that you are impossible?"

"Frequently," came his cheerful and instant reply.

"And do you always flout the rules of etiquette this way?"

"Just often enough to be annoying."

When she did not soften, his tone turned slightly pleading. "Talk to me, Cousin. London has been dreadfully dull. Now that you are here, I know it will improve."

"Don't you have some poor, defenseless courtesan to harass?"

His contagious laughter drew a reluctant smile from her lips. Seeing him did much to assuage her concern over his gunshot wound, and her guilt that he had received it protecting her. She was sure that he had actually grown more handsome in the weeks since she'd last seen him. Torn between hope and fear that he might broach the subject of their actions during their last encounter, or try to repeat them, she sat near the window at a safe distance from him.

A knowing smile touched his expressive mouth. "Have you ever been to the opera?"

His sudden change in topic caught her off guard. "The opera? Yes, I attended twice when I was last in London."

"How did you find it?"

"Breathtaking. And I was glad that my mother insisted I learn Italian as well as French."

"Then you'll accompany me tomorrow night?"

"Don't you think that will create a scandal?"

"You should know by now, I've never cared much for the approval of others. However, I do not wish to tarnish your reputation. Aunt Livy has asked me to accompany her, both in the carriage and in the box. My uncle came into Town on business and she accompanied him." At her hesitation, he added, "Nicholas told me he would be unable to attend you as he ought during your stay due to his many business obligations. He was quite insistent that you not be neglected. You wouldn't want him to feel guilty for not attending to you after all he's done for you, would you?"

If his eyes hadn't twinkled so merrily, she might have been angry at his implication, but she found she could not resist his winning smile. Throwing up her hands in resignation, she said, "Very well, I accept. For his sake. And because I'd like to see your aunt and uncle again."

He inclined his head in a mocking bow. "I'm speechless at your enthusiasm."

A smile escaped in spite of her efforts.

"Ahh, there it is. The reason I rise every day. I was beginning to despair of earning one of those today. You have no idea what a beautiful smile you have, do you?"

Her smile dimmed. "I don't…."

"Of course you do. The problem is, no one has paid you enough compliments. I must have a word with your errant husband about the necessity of expressing praises to your beauty. Or perhaps I should take over that duty."

Alicia lowered her eyes.

His voice softened. "What troubles you this evening?"

She blinked. "Pardon?"

"You seemed a bit out of sorts. Nicholas not treating you well?"

"Of course he's treating me well," she snapped.

"Then what is it?" Though a teasing smile played around his lips, his eyes took on a curiously serious light.

How could she tell him that her treacherous thoughts often rested on him and that his frequent appearances only made it worse? He was not a man she wanted her mind to dwell upon.

"I'm a bit fatigued from the trip."

Cole quietly watched her, thoughtful, assessing. "I cause you distress."

She folded her arms, hoping he did not know the turmoil of her thoughts, and tried to formulate an appropriate reply. She failed.

"You still harbor resentment for me."

This caught her attention. His carefully impassive face almost fooled her, but something flickered in his eyes.

"No."

He leapt to his feet and moved to the window. The rain pattering on the panes and the distant rumble of thunder were the only sounds audible. She remained rooted in her seat, using every shred of self-control to refrain from going to him, putting her arms around him, comforting him, reassuring him.

She remained still. "I told you the last time we were together, I do not hate you. Nor do I resent you any longer."

Hope and despair mingled in his expression. With all the silence and grace of a cat, he slid into the seat next to her. His hand covered hers as his focus moved downward to her mouth. Her breath caught. His eyes darkened with desire and his thumb lightly caressed the back of her hand.

Dangerous.

She withdrew her hand and moved to a safer distance, when all she wanted was to throw herself into his arms and press her mouth against his. Quelling such inappropriate thoughts, she drew a steadying breath and laced her fingers in front of her.

A wry smile touched his lips.

"Forgive me, but I'm a bit tired from the trip."

"Then I bid you good night."

Both disappointed and relieved, she summoned a smile. "Thank you for calling. Shall I tell my husband that you wished to speak with him?"

"No, don't trouble yourself. I will meet him tomorrow."

He leaned in and quickly kissed her cheek before she could back away. His sardonic grin flashed and then he was gone.

She bit her lip to prevent herself from calling him back. His absence accentuated her loneliness.

CHAPTER 22

Cole fairly skipped to the foyer in the baron's town house. He knew he was foolish to feel such anticipation at seeing Alicia again, but he seemed powerless to stop himself. His harebrained scheme to save Alicia had done nothing to cure his yearning for her. She would think him unconscionable, but he would do whatever he must to crumble her resistance and earn a place in her arms.

It wouldn't be simple, but he could deal with Nicholas if Alicia decided she wanted to be freed from him. After all, Cole's only reason for bringing in Nicholas was to save her from her other prospects when all of Cole's attempts to save her honorably had failed. And since no love appeared to be forming within that relationship, there was no reason why he should not court her. He'd know soon enough exactly how to proceed.

He grinned. He couldn't remember the last time he had actively pursued a lady. Normally, he dodged them and their schemes. The role of predator was invigorating, and he had no doubt that it would prove a thrilling chase. The reward, when he succeeded, would be sweet. And he would succeed sooner or later.

As he waited in the foyer, he felt a sweet presence behind him. The vision that greeted him nearly brought him to his knees.

Had he ever thought her only pretty? This glorious being gliding down the stairs in an apricot and cream evening gown robbed him of his breath.

And when she smiled at him, he knew he'd never use the word 'beautiful' lightly again. Her lustrous hair shone rich honey brown and her skin glowed in flawless perfection. The haunting sorrow that had been her constant companion at their first several meetings had faded. She appeared to have found peace and healing.

"Alicia," he murmured when he found his voice. "I cannot begin to tell you how exquisitely beautiful you are."

Her brown and golden-flecked eyes shone, and the color at her cheeks deepened. He felt himself falling further. He made no attempt to save himself. He was hers. He could no longer deny it.

"Glorious," he whispered. "Breathtaking."

She laughed softly. "Thank you, but don't you think that's overdoing it a bit?"

"Absolutely not. I shall have to come up with better ways to compliment you on your beauty." He bent over her gloved hand and kissed it, wishing he could feel her skin against his lips instead of her gloves.

Aunt Livy arrived a moment later. "My dear, girl, how lovely to see you again!" She drew Alicia into a motherly embrace.

With obvious embarrassment and pleasure, Alicia returned the embrace and murmured her joy at seeing her again, and made to move away, but when Aunt Livy continued to hug her, she surrendered and leaned against her with her eyes closed, reveling in the touch that had obviously been long absent in her life. She must be missing her own mother a great deal.

He couldn't bring back her mother, any more than he could bring back his own, but he planned to shower her with all the affection she deserved, whether or not she knew she needed it.

When Aunt Livy released her, Alicia smiled

shyly and turned away to let the footman put on her wrap. "Where is Mr. Fitzpatrick ?"

"He hates the opera, but he sends his best."

"I hate the opera, too, but you make me go," Cole grumbled.

"That's because I can bully you better than I can bully my own husband." Aunt Livy winked at Cole as they entered the carriage.

They made small talk, Livy providing her usual charming, dry humor as she gossiped about mutual acquaintances. Then, she threw up her hands. "Oh, and I simply must introduce you to my niece Mary."

"Mary is here?" Cole asked with mingled delight and dread.

She nodded, sending her ostrich feathers bobbing furiously. "She will be simply mad about you, my dear."

"Another cousin?" Alicia asked, her eyes moving to Cole.

"My father has six brothers and his father had nine. There are Amesburys everywhere."

"Mary and Cole were kissing cousins, if I recall correctly," Livy said with a gleam.

Cole groaned. "Don't remind me."

"Kissing cousins?" Alicia echoed with a delighted smile.

"Please do not give her more ammunition to use against me, Aunt," Cole pled. "She already thinks I have no redeeming qualities."

"I caught them in the music room," Livy continued with cruel glee as if Cole were not merely a few feet away. "She is four years his senior, you know."

"She begged me to do it," Cole interjected. "She said she didn't want to appear foolish when her beau kissed her, so she wanted to learn how to do it first. What could I do but let her practice on me?" He winced when he realized he'd said too much.

"Oh, Cole, how shameful," Alicia scolded with mock severity, a smile curving at such a delicious tale.

Cole turned imploring eyes upon Aunt Livy. "Aunt, please, I'm trying to give her hope that I may not be a complete reprobate."

Livy only waved her folded fan in the air. "Too late, my dear. She knows you already."

"Did you teach her anything useful?" Alicia asked Cole with a daring smile.

"I—" Realizing he would never survive this gracefully, he snapped his mouth shut and glared at Aunt Livy. "I can see now that agreeing to ride with you was a dreadful mistake."

Both ladies laughed and Cole forced a straight face. Livy mopped her face with her handkerchief and began fanning herself. "Oh dear, it's a bit warm, isn't it?"

"I hadn't noticed," Alicia said.

After the carriage pulled up in front of the opera house, Cole escorted the ladies inside to his private balcony. Before the performance began, he felt the eyes of the *ton* in attendance upon them, whispering, speculating, but Alicia's eyes, dazzled by the theater and the excitement, remained thankfully unaware of the sensation she stirred simply by being an unknown lady at his side. Aunt Livy nodded with queenly grace, and Cole was glad he had invited her to keep Alicia's reputation pure.

"Oh, Mrs. Fitzpatrick, this is so grand."

"Please, my dear, call me Aunt Livy. After all, you are married to my nephew."

She started and then looked ashamed. "Oh, yes. Of course. My husband is a nephew of yours as well."

"Great nephew, actually. His father and Cole's father are a generation apart."

"First cousins once-removed, I believe it's called," Cole added.

The Marquis of Trimbull, an old friend of his father's, stopped by their box. "Amesbury, glad to see you back in Town." Lord Trimbull's gaze settled on Alicia, curious, assessing, but he turned to Aunt Livy. "Dear Olivia. It has been too long. You are lovely as ever."

Aunt Livy took out her fan and began to wave it furiously. "You are a silver-tongued rogue, Lucius," she replied with a disapproving frown, but Cole saw pleasure gleam in her eyes. "Lady Amesbury, may I present Lord Trimbull? My lord, Lady Amesbury is one of my many nieces by marriage."

The marquis extended his hand and she allowed him to take hers, poised and gracious, and fixed her eyes upon him, a genuinely warm smile curving her mouth.

"My lord."

Though his expression remained carefully schooled, his eyes unmistakably approved of Alicia as he bowed over her hand. "I'm delighted, my lady."

The marquis and Aunt Livy exchanged pleasantries and asked after each other's families before the gentleman moved on.

Cole managed to evade explanation to others who stopped by their box until the lights dimmed and the curtain rose. The music was well-done, and the costumes, set, and acting better than normal, but his eyes strayed to her so often that he finally gave up and simply watched her watch the performance. The performance enthralled her.

She enthralled him.

He was lost and happier than he'd ever been.

At intermission, Cole's cousin Mary, a buxom beauty, came to their box, and Aunt Livy, waving her fan frantically, introduced the ladies. Mary greeted Alicia cordially, calling her Cousin, and directed a smile toward Cole.

"My husband just left for his club, Cole. Perhaps

you will join him there?"

"I regret, Mary, that these two ladies would not forgive me if I abandoned them without seeing them safely home first."

Mary raised her eyebrows, but said nothing.

"Charleston, go fetch me some lemonade, there's a good lad," Aunt Livy said to her footman. He leaped to his feet and bounded away. She pressed a hand to her forehead, her fan flapping furiously, and a sheen appeared on her flushed face.

Mary leaned in. "Aunt Livy, are you unwell?"

"I am afraid I'm not feeling well. It seems terribly warm in here, but no one else appears to be suffering from the heat."

Cole half-rose. "Shall I escort you home, Aunt?"

She waved him away. "No, dear, don't trouble yourself." The footman reappeared with the lemonade, but it failed to refresh her.

Mary sent her footman for her carriage. "I will take you home, Aunt."

"Do you wish us to accompany you?" Cole offered.

Mary shook her head. "Not necessary, Cole. You and Alicia remain here and enjoy the performance. I will see to her." She turned to Alicia. "I hope to see more of you later, Cousin."

"I do, as well." Alicia cast a teasing, sideways glance at Cole.

He inwardly groaned. The stories Mary could tell about him made him shudder. If he ever hoped to redeem himself in Alicia's eyes, her association with his cousin Mary certainly would undermine his efforts.

"I hope you feel better, Aunt Livy," Alicia said as she took her hand.

"Nothing to fret about, my dear. Merely something I ate, no doubt."

After the performance ended, Cole guided Alicia

to the carriage. He knew riding in the carriage alone with her pushed the edge of propriety, and might cause tongues to wag. He had done it in the country, and had enjoyed it immensely, but looking back, realized how careless that had been. Although it had probably saved her life. Still, he never wanted it said that Alicia was anything less than a perfect lady. He'd spent most of his life sneering at convention and shrugging at the tales told about him, but he wanted no scandal to touch Alicia.

Inside the carriage, Cole forcibly kept his thoughts on neutral matters to avoid drawing her into his arms. His best defense was humor. He kept her laughing with the contents of his brother Jared's latest letter which outlined a harrowing flight during a visit to a tiny island. They'd encountered hungry natives who invited him and his crew to stay for dinner. As the main course. He also hinted at lovely native girls who offered themselves as his bride the night before the feast.

"Does he live a life of debauchery, then?"

"Undoubtedly. I think it's in our blood."

"You value a woman's virtue so little, then?" She looked away.

Cole softened his voice. "I have never robbed a woman of her virtue. The first virgin I make love to will be my wife. And it will be with her consent. Not only her consent—her desire."

She turned to him, astonishment clear in her expression. "Then you will marry someday?"

He laughed. "Of course. Don't look so surprised. We discussed this the time first time we met, remember? I must, sooner or later, produce an heir, which requires that I be married to his mother at the time."

"Then it will be a business match." She looked disenchanted.

"Good grief, I hope not. I am not so foolish as to

think that everyone marries for love as my parents did, but I hope to be at least fond of my wife." He watched her, falling further under her spell. "I entertain hopes that I might actually love my wife. Whoever she might be."

"I dreamed of marrying for love once," she murmured, her eyes far away.

He remained silent to allow her time to her thoughts, and only admired her. And desired her. And plotted how to make her dream come true. And his.

She hugged herself, staring out of the window. She spoke so softly, he had to lean forward to hear her. "Of course you should marry. Your family is counting on you."

Cole wasn't sure what to make of her words. She appeared sad, disappointed. In him? He wished he could truly divine her thoughts. She used to be easier to read, but with his emotions so strongly overshadowing his judgment, his perceptiveness regarding her had dimmed.

"My father's health is poor. Soon he will leave me with his title. Much is expected of an earl."

"You never speak of your father."

"He lives in Bath with my brother, Christian, and my sister, Rachel. We hope he will improve. Since my mother's death two years ago, his health has steadily declined. They were desperately in love. Some of his friends tried to convince him to take a mistress in the hopes that it would restore his vitality, but he refused."

"It is my understanding that many men keep mistresses. Even while still wed."

"That doesn't make it right, does it?"

Her golden eyes appeared luminous so near his face, and his eyes were drawn downward to her lips. It took all of his self control to not move nearer and capture them with his mouth.

"Then you would not do the same?" she asked.

He had to replay their conversation to remember what she meant. He forced levity into his voice. "Take a mistress? Absolutely not. If a lady were mad enough to marry me, the least I could do is be faithful to her."

A smile touched her lips. "You surprise me, Cole."

He swallowed at the sound of his name on her tongue and his voice was husky when he found it. "How so?"

"I thought you a man of loose principles and morals."

"Perhaps you were wrong about me," he whispered.

"Perhaps," she whispered back.

Her light fragrance taunted him, her lovely face tormented him and their conversation had taken an unexpected turn. This was getting too serious.

Turning on a flippant grin, he leaned back lazily and stretched out his legs. "You were right the first time, I am an unprincipled, incorrigible cad."

"Oh, good. Glad to hear I was right about you all along, then." Though she attempted to use levity, she sounded strained.

He admired the fine lines of her face, the soft ringlets brushing against her neck, the fullness of her ripe, soft lips. "Astonishing."

She blinked at him.

"Mesmerizing. Exquisite."

"Pardon?"

He grinned. "I am thinking up new words to describe your beauty. Remember, I promised to compliment you more often."

"Oh." A smile began at her mouth and found its way to her eyes. "Do you flirt this brazenly with everyone, or only married women?"

"I haven't earned the reputation of a shameless

philanderer by accident," he quipped.

She frowned. "Did I say incorrigible? I meant impossible."

"Thank you."

"You said earlier you have three brothers, but you've only mentioned Jared. Tell me of the others."

Cole grinned again at her obvious attempt to introduce a new topic. "Grant is younger than Jared. He's friends with some Bow Street Runners and often helps them on their more interesting cases. He also likes skulking about the streets going after the most dangerous criminals. He tracked a fleeing murderer all the way to Scotland."

"An odd pastime for the son of an earl," Alicia mused.

"Like the rest of us, he's always sneered at convention. But he came back from the war positively hardened. I can't decide if he's that dedicated to making London a safer place, or if he's trying to get himself killed. Maybe he just likes scrabbling in the streets with ruffians. I never understood Grant."

"Poor man. He must be protecting a wounded heart."

Cole uttered a sharp laugh. "You wouldn't say that if you met the lout."

"And the youngest?"

A surge of mingled protectiveness battled with old resentment. "Christian. The favorite. He, unlike the rest of us, plays the piano with admirable skill and he's one of the finest amateur painters I've ever seen. Women adore him, but he's a bit shy around them."

"How refreshing."

Cole ignored the barb. "He fences, boxes, and hunts with the best of them. He's also mad about the steeplechase. It has been the plan all along for him to become a clergyman, but he hasn't seemed to be in any hurry to do so. He frequently buries himself in his art. Still, he's young, only three and twenty. There's time to decide."

"You mentioned sisters?"

"Two, both older. Rachel is with Christian in Bath with my father. Margaret is here in Town. I hope to introduce you to her soon."

The carriage stopped in front of the house on Pall Mall and he saw her to the door. Formally, he bent over her hand and stepped back. He clenched his hands behind his back to avoid touching her. A soft light entered her eyes and she looked up at him with affection. Encouraged, he returned to the carriage grinning like the fool he knew he was.

****

"Lieutenant Amesbury, you ol' dog, what brings you here?"

Cole grinned and clasped the hand of his former shipmate, Charles Grady. "I heard you needed a good navigator. Something about guiding your bank through the murky waters of finance."

Grady laughed. "If I needed a good navigator, why have you come?"

"For a chap who couldn't add, I'm surprised they gave you a job in a bank," returned Cole.

"Come into my office, dolt, before I embarrass you publicly.

"That's Lord Dolt, to you," Cole corrected him with a wry smile.

"Oh, right, you're some kind of swell, eh? I know you were an officer and all, but you so seldom acted respectable."

"Not respectable. Just born under the right blanket."

A few bank employees smiled at their exchange as Grady led Cole to an office in the rear of the bank.

Grady closed the door and sat down at the desk. He folded his hands and eyed Cole searchingly.

"What brings you here, my friend?"

"I need a favor. And you're not going to like it."

"Do I ever?"

"I need to know if a large sum of money mysteriously appeared in Vivian Charleston's account a year and a half ago."

Grady frowned. "You're right. I don't like it."

"I'm not asking for you to reveal any sensitive information, or any specifics, I'm only looking for a possible motive."

"Are you in trouble?"

"No. But a friend is. I'm looking into the possible murder of her family."

"'Her family', huh? And now you're a Bow Street Runner?"

"No. I'm just trying to determine if my gut instincts on this are right before I take action."

Grady stroked his chin. "Your gut instincts got us out of a few scrapes on the ship. Think they're as reliable on land?"

"One can only hope." Cole waited while his former shipmate struggled between ethics and his desire to help a shipmate.

"You're doing this for a bit of muslin?"

"A lady."

"Ahh." A glint came into his eyes and he grinned. "Not as untouchable as we thought, eh?"

Cole mustered up his most fearsome scowl. "Are you going to help me or not?"

"All right, all right, I'll see what I can find. Wait here. Ah, my lord," he added as an afterthought.

Cole paced the office while Grady was gone. In the wee hours of the night as he wrestled with his conscience and the desire to simply throw Alicia over his shoulder and carry her off, he relived details of the encounter with Armand and their subsequent duel. Those urges danced with a suspicion that continued to nag him that something seemed terribly wrong with the duel, not only the incident itself, but everything that led up to it.

Then, only days after the duel, a carriage accident killed both of Alicia's parents as well as the coachman and footman while they traveled to London to be with their injured son. From the moment he first heard of the accident, it had seemed wrong. Too neat.

Then Armand had died of an opium addiction. Since opium was so addictive, no one would have questioned it. He could easily have been poisoned with no one the wiser.

Before Alicia married Nicholas, Robert had told Cole that she'd been bitten by a snake. A venomous snake, whose bite might have killed her. Someone who knew where she liked to walk could have placed it in her path.

Later, there had been a fire in her room; apparently a candle had fallen out of its holder. Had someone set the fire?

Then highwaymen attacked and only demanded Alicia. What highwaymen would rather have a woman than money or jewels, or a future earl for ransom?

Cole had given up on sleep and departed for London to solve the riddle.

If he failed, he'd enlist his brother Grant's help. Grant was as cynical and acerbic a man as Cole had ever known and preferred to keep a low profile, but Bow Street Runners, some of whom were his friends, often turned to him for aid with their most difficult cases. He was resourceful and intuitive and had never failed to learn the truth. Grant would certainly make asking for his help an unpleasant task, but Cole trusted him to ferret out the truth.

What Cole didn't understand was motivation. Her uncle would profit most by her father and brother's deaths. But why attack Alicia now, more than a year after the last murders, if that's what they were? Willard had already inherited. Then he had practically sold her and profited handsomely in the transaction. Even greed seemed a thin reason to kidnap her for ransom.

Unless he, or someone, else simply wanted her dead. Which would explain the snake and the fire in her room. And if her family were being systematically murdered, it also meant Alicia's younger sister, Hannah, could be in danger as well. But why?

Grady returned looking deadly serious. "The sum of two thousand pounds was deposited into her account on May fourteenth of last year. That's a bigger sum than ever appeared in her account prior. Does that mesh with your gut feelings?"

Cole nodded soberly. That would have been about a week after his duel with Armand. So Vivian was involved. She had set them up. But why?

"Amesbury?"

"Thanks, Grady, I appreciate it."

"She got married a few months ago. She is Lady Featherstone now."

"Featherstone? He's thrice her age."

Grady shrugged. "He's titled. Rich."

"I knew she was only a fortune hunter," Cole said with disgust.

"Aren't we all?"

They shook hands and Cole left with as many questions as he had answers. He dreaded seeing Vivian again, but he would do whatever he must to protect Alicia. This time, honor had little to do with it.

CHAPTER 23

Alicia seldom saw her husband during the day, but Cole was with her frequently. They went to the museums that interested her, and knowing her love for the gardens, he even arranged to take her to some of the more famous private gardens.

He was gallant, attentive, and charming. Through it all, her husband gave no indication that he thought her frequent outings with his cousin seemed odd or inappropriate, but Alicia began to worry that tongues were whispering of scandal, despite them always being accompanied by Aunt Livy, or Cousin Mary, or another appropriate chaperone.

One evening after sunset, Alicia had the rare opportunity to sit with her husband in the walled garden. She looked over at him, thinking that, as difficult as it was to discern Cole's thoughts given his practiced façade, determining her husband's was nearly impossible, even when he spoke. She tried to pay attention to his posture, his movements, but he always sat erect and still, giving little clue as to his mood.

She attempted again to picture his face. Dark, he'd said. Before he was burned, he might have been handsome, perhaps resembling his cousin. But she only could visualize Cole's face, not a variation of it.

"Will you trust me with your face, someday, my lord?"

He blew out his breath, and the cloth of his mask rippled. "Trust me, Alicia. You are not ready for this face. Seeing it would only drive you further from me." He arose and offered her his arm.

She took it, wondering if she imagined his tension.

"Alicia, when my business here is concluded, I will return to my country home."

She looked up at him, but when that proved futile, looked away again.

"I want you to stay here in London. Permanently."

Desperate, she gasped, "My lord, please no."

He turned to her and awaited an explanation for her outburst.

"I will be your wife in every way if I must, but please, do not cast me off."

A tiny voice inside her mind whispered that if her husband freed her, Cole might want her.

Yet, he probably did not want her for a wife, only for a dalliance. Even if he did wish to marry her, she did not dare, knowing she would grow to love him and that he would only break her heart with his unfaithfulness. She was already half in love with him now.

She must not harbor any hope of a marriage with Cole. And the only way she could receive a divorce from her husband would be if he accused her of adultery. Considering her frequent public appearances with Cole, such a claim would be easy to believe. But the scandal would ruin them all. Annulments were even more difficult to obtain, and she had no idea what the legalities for those involved.

Her only chance lay with her husband. Her current husband.

Lord Amesbury remained silent, and she imagined he carefully weighed whether he wished to continue this unprofitable marriage with his unwilling and undeserving wife.

Alarmed that he seemed so unmoved, she continued, "I'm sorry I have withheld myself from you for so long. You've been more than generous. You may have me now, if that is your wish."

"That is not truly your wish," he said sharply.

"I beg you, my lord. Do not set me aside."

"Why? You clearly do not desire to be with me. My very appearance makes you shudder."

She closed her eyes as the realization of how badly she hurt him sank in. She had treated him poorly. She'd indulged in selfishness far too long.

"Your appearance does not make me shudder. I'm much more comfortable with you. I enjoy your company. I can be a good wife. A true wife. In every way." Her words nearly choked her, but she held her head up and looked directly into the mask.

She tried to recall every act of kindness he'd ever shown her, every pleasant conversation, every soft spoken word. Her courage strengthened.

He was silent for so long that Alicia feared she was too late. "Very well." He held out his gloved hand.

She placed hers in it. He led her in the house and up the stairs.

Now? Alarm mounting, she stumbled beside him. Her courage fled. Fear coiled, tightened.

Inside her room, he locked the door and pulled the heavy drapes to block out what remained of the sunset. Her heart jumped into her throat as his dark, shadowed form approached.

His gloves rustled as he pulled them off and let them land with a soft thud on the floor. Next came his hood and mask. They too, hit the floor.

Involuntarily, she backed away from him as he advanced upon her. His uncovered face remained completely darkened. When the back of her legs found the bed, she stopped and forced herself to remain still, to breathe. She had asked for this. This was her price for a home and food. For safety.

He had proven himself a good man. Perhaps he would not frighten her or hurt her beyond her ability to withstand. Her breath rasped raggedly in the stillness of the room and she clamped her mouth closed to quiet it. He neared. His hands found her shoulders and he drew her toward him. A tiny sound of fear escaped her throat as she relived Lord Braxton's humiliating advances, his rough hands, his violence. She squeezed her eyes closed.

He made no further move. "You are not ready for this," he whispered.

"I—"

"Alicia," his bare hand found hers. It was surprisingly warm. "Your hands are icy and you are shaking."

She swallowed and felt tears run down her cheeks.

He drew in a long breath, held it, and let it out. "I ache for you, Alicia. I crave you. But I will not take you when you fear me this much. You must first trust me."

A bare hand touched her cheek, cupped it. Gentle lips pressed a kiss to her forehead. His mouth felt warm and soft, not cold and lifeless as she had feared. Then she heard him gather up his protective coverings and pull on his mask. He went out, leaving the door open. Light poured in through the doorway.

"Your coat milord?" one of the footmen asked from out in the hall.

"Yes, Sexton, thank you," came the baron's voice.

"Shall I call the carriage?"

"No, don't bother. I wish to walk."

She heard the front door open and close.

She drew a shaking breath. She had just attempted to save herself from ruin by offering him her body like a common whore, but without the courage to go through with the act. And in the process, she had again hurt her husband, a kind and patient gentleman. He would never want her now. He must despise her.

She despised herself.

****

Alicia took a carriage out to Hyde Park early enough in the morning to avoid the crowds. Her husband had already left for an appointment, so Alicia ordered the tamest mare hitched to the phaeton. The servants groused about wanting her to take the landau with a driver, but Alicia had grown weary of the smothering attention of the servants. She drove the phaeton herself, with only a footman in accompaniment, confident that she'd meet few people at this unfashionable time of day.

The morning proved bright and clear, and a chorus of birds serenaded her as she drove along the paths of the park. In the distance, she spotted two figures, one astride a magnificent white horse. She recognized the rider the same instant that she recognized the animal. Sunlight dappled Cole's figure astride his beautiful white horse, André, standing next to a carriage that she realized was the baron's. As she moved closer, she spotted her husband's cloaked form inside the carriage.

Cole spoke earnestly, his face solemn. They appeared deep in conversation, but when Cole noticed her, his face brightened. He said something to the baron and gestured toward her. The baron turned his masked face her direction. They both raised their hands in greeting.

Feeling strangely as though she'd been caught with rival suitors, she guided her carriage to them, and managed a smile. "I didn't realize your appointment was at the park with Cole," she said to her husband upon her arrival.

"I've already finished my first appointment, my

dear," the baron said softly. "I thought I'd enjoy the fresh air first before going to my next one. Meeting Cole here was a happy coincidence."

"Do you have time to accompany me to my club first? I have not had breakfast yet," Cole said to the baron.

"Nor I," the baron said, his voice hushed as if deeply troubled. "I accept."

Alicia realized that she had intruded and wondered what had her husband so troubled. Her behavior last night?

"Then I shall bid you both good morning." She inclined her head to them and snapped the reins.

After passing them, she glanced back to see that they had fallen into deep conversation again. Cole, his expression grave, dismounted, tied up his horse behind the baron's coach and got inside. The coach drove toward the park entrance.

Alicia frowned. Seeing them together came as a stark reminder that she might be coming between not only cousins, but close friends. She needed to stop seeing Cole. No good would come of this dual loyalty.

But the following afternoon, Cole bounded in, his smile lighting up the gloomy day, and she lost her resolve.

"You must save me," he exclaimed.

Unable to resist his smile, she patted the seat next to her.

He accepted her invitation and held out a printed piece of stationary. "I have been invited to the one hundredth birthday celebration for the grandfather of one my father's closest friends."

She paused. "A birthday celebration?"

"I think one hundred years of life is worth celebrating, don't you?"

She smiled. "It certainly is."

"I don't normally accept invitations to these

kinds of social affairs. They always end up being husband marts. But my father wrote me and specifically requested that I attend in his stead. Yet, if I attend, I become the target of every lady, widowed and unmarried, in Town. And there are a great many, even this unpopular time of year. Others have come into Town specifically for this celebration. It will be a crush as big as those during the Season. I daren't go unprotected. You have no idea how terrible it is to be so targeted. It's like being a fox, surrounded by hundreds of yelping hounds."

"It must be such a burden to be so handsome and charming," she said dryly.

He smiled wryly at her comment and then sobered. "I'm the heir to a powerful earl and stand to inherit a vast fortune, plus what I have built up with my own investments. They see only a title and a bottomless money vault when they look at me. Others only desire an empty affair. I've grown weary of those. No one knows, or cares, about the man I am underneath." His voice hushed. "Then again, perhaps they have it aright."

"You have much more to offer a lady than that."

"What do I have to offer, Alicia?" Vulnerability crept into his beautiful face.

She paused to choose her words. "Things you don't often show others. You hide your kindness and your honor behind a careless exterior. You are courageous and you have a deep sense of justice. You are truly caring, but you keep others at arm's length, seldom trusting them to see the man you really are."

His eyes searched hers, one corner of his mouth raising. "Your good opinion matters more to me than any other's." Moving slowly, he leaned toward her, desire clear in his face.

As badly as she wanted to taste his lips, she stood. "What do you plan to do regarding the birthday celebration?"

He looked as if he'd received a death sentence. "I wish I could avoid it. But for Father, I will attend." He glanced at her. "Perhaps if you also come, and remain at my side constantly, you might help stave off the harpies who will be there."

She laughed at the image of bejeweled ladies in ball gowns that were half-human and half-bird circling the ballroom floor with outstretched claws extended toward Cole and screeching, "Pick me, rich earl's son!"

"Does that mean you will rescue me?" He smiled at her hopefully, and with a twinkle in his eye.

How could she refuse that charming smile? It reached inside her and drew out a nod. "Yes. I will rescue you. Far be it for me to ever abandon someone in need. Besides, you're family. I vow to protect you from the harpies."

His relief was like a ray of sunlight spearing a storm cloud. He pressed her hand to his lips. "I am in your debt. Mary and Charles will come for you in their carriage, and I will eagerly await you there. The birthday celebration is Tuesday next."

She smiled. "I'll be ready."

"I can hardly wait." There was a bounce to his step when he left.

After dinner, the baron joined her with a challenge to play backgammon.

Alicia moistened her lips as they set up the game pieces. "My lord, with your permission, I've been invited to attend a birthday celebration. If you have no objection, I'd like to accept."

"You need not ask my permission, Alicia. I shan't attend, but there's no reason why you shouldn't."

Wanting to be perfectly forthright, she added, "Cole asked me to be there. Something about helping protect him from the ladies who are always pursuing him."

He lifted his head and she felt his heavy gaze even without through the mask. "I see."

"Mary and Charles are to pick me up in their carriage. I'll only see Cole at the party."

He leaned back and steepled his fingers. "What exactly are your feelings regarding Cole?"

She blinked and looked away. "I find him arrogant and annoying. But he can be diverting. Charming, at times. I can see why Mary and Aunt Livy are fond of him."

"Is that all?"

She faltered. "My lord, I have not betrayed you, nor do I plan to, with Cole or any other. I won't go if you wish me to—"

"Go."

"You...you don't mind?"

"You may do as you please." He rose and left the room. She looked down at their unfinished game and wondered how she'd become so selfish.

****

The evening of the birthday celebration, Alicia asked Monique to do something special with her hair. As a result, a cascade of ringlets showered down the back of her head, lightly brushing her shoulders. She dressed in a silk gown and donned a tastefully simple strand of pearls.

The baron appeared in the doorway and said in an even voice. "I hope you have a nice time."

She looked at him sharply, but he turned and left.

Perhaps after their last failed attempt at intimacy, he did plan on going through with a divorce, despite the irrevocable scandal, and simply had no interest in her activities now that he had decided to cast her off.

Guilt shot through her. She couldn't blame him. She was using him and giving nothing in return except a good reason to throw her out on the streets. Perhaps he had found consolation in the arms of a mistress. The image disturbed her more than it assuaged her guilt.

She pressed a hand over her face. When had it all become so tangled?

A footman knocked at the door and informed her that Mary and Charles's coach had arrived. Without any joy, she rose and descended the stairs to the waiting coach, however Charles and Mary's lively conversation kept her entertained and they became a merry group.

Charles and Mary introduced Alicia to the host and hostess, and their surprisingly bright-eyed centurion. The crowd was full, though not the crush it would have been during the London Season. Still, for an off-season gathering, a goodly number of well-wishers had arrived.

Cole sidled up to her the moment she'd been introduced and had finished greeting the host and hostess.

"Dearest cousin. You look magnificent. My sister Margaret is here. I'll introduce you. Come."

Eyes watched Alicia next to Cole. Some nodded, others whispered. Gazes, openly admiring, fixed upon Cole.

She glanced at him from beneath her lashes. Only a fool would not stare at him in admiration. Broad, striking, exuding strength and masculinity, as well as a sensuality she had never felt from another man, his very presence taunted a lady's sensibilities. He misunderstood his appeal. He assumed as a wealthy viscount and heir to an earldom, he was the target of any member of the *ton*, or any fortune hunter. He did not seem to understand that no woman alive could look upon him without desiring him.

Pride swelled within her as she realized that, of

all those women, many of them beautiful, he had chosen to be with her. As they walked together through the crush, he gave no outward indication that he even saw any of the ladies clustered in their finery hoping to catch his eye.

Pity she could no more attain him than they.

Guiltily, she swallowed. Her husband should be claiming her thoughts, not his errant cousin who so blithely escorted her in his stead. But her husband had practically washed his hands of her.

Cole led her through the crowd to an imposing lady with sleek, sable hair the same color as his.

"Alicia, may I present my sister, Lady Hennessey. Margaret, this is Alicia, Nicholas's new wife."

The intimidating woman turned to her. "Alicia, I'm very happy to finally meet you. Nicholas has told me so much about you." A smile began in her mouth and finally reached her eyes, casting off the earlier imperiousness.

Margaret glanced back at Cole and something unspoken passed between them, reminding Alicia of the way she and Armand often communicated with a mere glance. Others used to comment on their finely tuned intuitive ability to converse in avenues beyond normal comprehension. A sharp pain shot through her heart. How she missed him!

Cole touched her arm. "Alicia?"

Alicia blinked and focused on Cole's face, realizing her expression must have betrayed her thoughts. She forced a smile and turned to Cole's sister. "I'm very pleased to meet you, my lady."

Cole excused them from his sister with only a glance and placed his hand under her elbow, guiding her away from the crush. "What is it? You're pale."

She shrank from his touch and averted her gaze. "Nothing."

"Do you wish to leave?"

"Ahh, the infamous Viscount Amesbury." A booming voice drew their attention to an older gentleman who peered at them through a monocle.

Cole glanced at Alicia, worry creasing his face, but replied dutifully to the gentleman. "Lord Hamilton."

Alicia, grateful for the interruption, quietly excused herself to gather her wits before Cole even had the opportunity to introduce her. She felt his eyes follow her as she wound her way through the crowd to a seat.

Cole had suffered enough. If she revealed how deeply she still felt Armand's loss, she would hurt him again. She remembered the tormented expression she witnessed in him every time the subject arose, and knew he did not need her condemning behavior adding to it. She took a breath and released it slowly.

As the music began, the hostess arrived with a young man with dark auburn hair. "Lady Amesbury, please allow me to introduce Sir Reginald Orr."

Alicia and the gentleman exchanged greetings and very proper pleasantries. Then he asked her for a dance.

In spite of her aching heart, Alicia managed a smile and accepted his arm. He was pleasant, if a touch arrogant. The dance had barely ended when another gentleman was presented to her and he too, asked for a dance. Her mood lightened as she danced and conversed with her partners.

Cole arrived for a dance, begging for rescue from the harpies. She smiled up into his beautiful eyes, forgetting everything but the feel of dancing in his arms. The warmth of his hands, the glint in his eyes that alternated between playful and dangerous, the potent sensuality of his nearness, all combined into a force she could not easily deny. He awoke every nerve in her body.

He bowed and stepped back as another arrived to claim a dance. Each partner varied in age, temperament and talkativeness, but danced reasonably well. All lacked Cole's athletic grace, his stirring masculinity, his potent gaze, his expressive mouth. None possessed eyes as beautiful, a face as perfectly sculpted, shoulders as broad. No one had his quick wit, his ready smile, his manner of treating her as though she were the only woman in the room.

She had to purge him from her thoughts somehow. Such thoughts would only lead to heartache. And betrayal.

Remembering his plea to be saved from the ladies of the *ton*, she scanned the crush and finally found him in a circle of older gentlemen. He stood in urbane boredom, blatantly ignoring the ladies who did indeed seem to circle like great predatory birds awaiting his departure from his haven of male companionship.

One of the gentlemen said something to Cole and he nodded. The group moved toward an exit together. Cole paused, his eyes scanning the room until they fell upon her. His brilliant smile flashed and he mimed billiards. She smiled and nodded to show she understood. That would be a safe, if temporary, reprieve from the harpies. With a sheepish shrug, he left with the men to the obvious disappointment of the ladies watching him.

One of Alicia's partners tactfully pointed out that she had a piece of lace at her hem that appeared to be dragging. She thanked him for the dance, and the observation, and retreated to the withdrawing room where a willing maid quickly stitched the lace back into place. Alicia smoothed her hair in the mirror and took a moment to make sure no other trimmings had come undone. A group of ladies came in, chattering like a gaggle of geese.

"Don't worry, Josephine, he won't spend all

night in the billiards room," a petite, plump brunette said.

"I will secure him this Season, just you watch. He always chooses a widow, something about not wanting to infringe upon a gentleman's wife," a redhead who must have been Josephine explained to another, much younger young lady.

The younger lady looked sorrowful. "Oh. So he wouldn't agree to a liaison with me because I'm married, then?"

"Oh, no. Besides, you're much too young, Violet," the plump brunette informed her with a knowing tone. "Lord Amesbury prefers ladies with more experience, and therefore skill."

A fourth giggled. "I'd be tempted to slip too much opium in my husband's drink, if the result might be a romance with *him*."

"But we must agree to still be friends no matter who he chooses."

There were murmurs of affirmative all around while Alicia's heart sank. Standing frozen, for fear of drawing attention to herself, Alicia prayed they would leave soon. She did not want to know details of Cole's debauchery.

"The problem is, he seems to be besotted by that country miss," Josephine said. "Whenever he's in public, he's with her."

"Who is she?" asked another.

"No one of consequence."

"No, not his usual type. She seems rather, well, too innocent for his taste, if you know what I mean," added the brunette. "And too young."

"I heard she's married, so he's either breaking his earlier vow, or it's an innocent friendship."

"Innocent? *Our* viscount?" They laughed raucously.

Alicia forced her hands to relax when her nails dug into her palms. How dare they speak about Cole in such a manner! What did they know about his type? Clearly none of them knew him. Cole was right; women only saw a conquest when they looked at him.

"Well, you've had a romance with him, so it's my turn," the redhead informed them with an imperious wave. "And I will do whatever it takes to lure him to my bed. As long as we can keep any ideas of marriage out of his head, we'll have him for a few more years."

"He'll have to marry sooner or later. After all, he'll be an earl, and he has an obligation to his family line."

"I'm sure a mere marriage won't stop him from his dalliances."

"I'm not so sure. He's a difficult man to predict. But what a lover." She heaved a lusty sigh.

"Well, we all know he never pursues the debutantes, so perhaps he'll choose a widow for a wife. Why not one of us?"

The plump brunette's eyes fell upon Alicia and her expression turned frosty. The chattering fell away and all eyes rested upon her. Their hostility rippled through the room.

Josephine sneered. "Oh. The latest favorite." Sarcasm dripped from her words.

"Enjoy him while you can, dearie. He won't be yours much longer," warned the redhead.

Alicia squelched her instinctive desire to make a hasty exit. Her clear duty, and her privilege, lay in protecting Cole from such shallow, vicious women.

She raised her chin. "If any of you possessed any depth of character, you'd know there is much more to Lord Amesbury than his looks or his fortune. I doubt very much any of you possess the intelligence, or the grace to see the man inside." She smiled victoriously at their amazed expressions. "Excuse me." She swept past them.

Donna Hatch

Cole had returned from his billiards game when Alicia came out of the withdrawing room. His smile, genuine and affectionate, lit up his face as he wound his way through the crowd to her. His gaze focused, his graceful, athletic stride purposeful, he completely ignored the ladies who followed him hungrily with their eyes.

When he reached her side, he raised her hand to his lips. "I've been looking for you. They've announced dinner." He wound her hand through his arm and pressed his hand against it with a slight squeeze. "Are you enjoying yourself?"

"Very much. Have you evaded the harpies so far?"

He grinned. "The night is still young. I will need your continued protection, if you can drag yourself away from your many new admirers."

As they approached the table, Alicia saw that she had been placed several places away from Cole. He gave her a secretive smile and moved to his place. As she moved to her place setting, a young lady tilted her head condescendingly. Someone introduced her as Miss Stockton.

Miss Stockton said, "Lady Amesbury. Ah, yes. You are married to that horrible cripple who never shows his face. How terrible it must be for you." Her expression of triumph underscored her mocking pity.

Alicia raised her chin. "On the contrary."

Miss Stockton shivered dramatically. "I'd rather remain unmarried than have a beast for a husband."

"Lord Amesbury is a kind and devoted husband, and I'll thank you not to speak ill of him." The hypocrisy of her words twisted in her stomach.

Guiltily, she glanced at Cole who gave no indication he had heard the exchange. Then his eyes flicked her way briefly.

Even though she and Cole were not paramours in the complete sense, they were playing a

244

dangerous game that would only lead to disaster. And, if the ladies in the withdrawing room were correct, she would only become one in a long line of illicit lovers should she succumb to his advances.

After dinner, the host made a toast to his grandfather and they all raised their glasses to a man who had reached his one hundredth birthday. The guest of honor gave them all a toothless grin, and in halting tones, thanked them for their friendship.

Later, as the lights burned low, and the strains of a waltz began, dancers sought out lovers and drew closer. Others left together in search of a more intimate setting. Cole drew her to the dance floor. She hesitated, but went with him.

"What is it, love?" he murmured, his warm breath stirring the tendrils next to her ear.

She shivered. "Please don't call me that," she pled weakly.

"Why?"

"Because you don't mean it."

He eased her closer, his beautiful smile brightening his already handsome face. "Do you want me to mean it?"

"No."

"Why not?"

She steadied her breathing. "You should know."

Cole's intoxicating, male scent permeated her senses. His light touch was fire through her silk gown, awakening an undeniable ache for him. His smile deepened further and his eyes darkened with a longing that exceeded hers. The potency of his desire made hers even more acute.

No. Not him.

"Please." She sounded plaintive, childlike to her own ears.

"Please, what, Alicia?" He asked in low, provocative tones.

A deep quiver began in the bottom of her stomach. "Please don't look at me like that."

"I don't think I could stop myself if I tried," he murmured close to her ear. His breath warmed her cheek and neck, and only succeeded in deepening her desire.

Several ladies circled purposefully, and Alicia realized that Cole needed to find a wife, if only to protect him from the lecherous women who had targeted him. And he was right, he needed an heir. Then why did he attempt an affair with a married lady instead of seeking a wife?

"And then what? Add my name to your rather long list?"

He pulled back enough to study her features. "What list?"

"The one that includes Josephine and Violet."

A puzzled frown creased his brow and he pursed his lips. "Josephine Winchester?"

"I don't know her surname, but she was a tall lady with red hair."

Cole's frown deepened. "That sounds like her. What list?"

"The one of all your past paramours. I heard them in the withdrawing room, discussing you and that you prefer widows and how you chose a new lover every Season."

Looking deadly serious, he led her from the dance floor without waiting for the end of the dance. He took her out of the ballroom and began to open doors until he found an empty room. He drew her inside, closed the door, and turned to her.

The look he fixed upon her left her with the urge to squirm. He shook his head slowly. "Alicia. I had hoped you knew me by now."

"I thought I did, but..." she trailed off helplessly.

"Remember the harpies? You clearly met them. I have a reputation, that's true, but believe me when I say that it is grossly exaggerated. I did have an affair with a widow last year, but she decided to go live with her sister in Scotland, and we parted ways. But I was very discreet, and I would be surprised if anyone knows about it. There have been few other love interests. Not Josephine Winchester or anyone named Violet, whoever she may be."

Alicia looked hopefully up at him. She wanted to believe him, but the things they said about him seemed too much in line with his character. His charm, his magnetism, all exuded dangerous sensuality, which made believing him a heartless philanderer all too easy.

He sighed. "And a few months ago, I was at a house party. I went to my room to discover a beautiful widow, with whom I have been acquainted for years, in my bed. I'm only human, Alicia. She offered enthusiastically and I accepted—"

"Please," Alicia cut in. "I do not want to hear the sordid details. I know that you frequently engage in lechery and—"

"Only if you listen to rumor," he said with an angry tinge to his voice.

She opened her mouth and then closed it. "You truly don't?"

His blue eyes found hers and he actually looked embarrassed. "You wouldn't believe how many ladies have tried to seduce me. I suspect that, regardless of the outcome, they tell their friends they were successful, as if it's some kind of accomplishment. According to rumor, others I have never touched boast of an affair, and of my...er...skill." Decidedly uncomfortable, he cleared his throat.

Harpies. They were using him even worse than she thought. "I'm sorry. I should have known better than to listen to such vicious gossip."

"I cannot even look at another woman now. I only want you."

Before she realized what was happening, or had time to be afraid, he gathered her into his powerful arms. His lips found hers and gently, skillfully kissed her mouth, sending tingles throughout her body. He crushed her against him and drew deeper kisses from her until she completely melted into his arms. There was no fear, only sweet, velvet pleasure and white-hot need.

His lips moved from hers down to her throat where he kissed a tingling trail of flame, and then slowly worked up to her lips again. He deepened the kiss and she completely succumbed to his will. Burning desire rose up inside of her. She arched her back and strained against him. His hands caressed her quivering body, drawing out a soft moan. His lips moved over her face, her eyes, her cheeks, her temples. They returned to her lips again.

This time, her hunger matched his. Their ragged breathing became one. His taste, his scent, the warmth and power of his body flooded her senses. Kissing her passionately until her head spun, he slowly laid her down on a nearby divan. As his mouth moved downward and he slipped her gown off one shoulder, a glimmer of conscience broke through.

"We mustn't," she whispered hoarsely.

"Don't be afraid." His mouth engulfed hers. Bright need flamed her body as he drew progressively hungrier kisses from her. There was no fear, only a driving ache for more.

Again, the conscience broke through.

"Cole, please, we cannot do this."

With a ragged groan, he raised his head, his lips swollen and moist from their kissing. His darkened eyes revealed passion she had never dreamed.

"Please, stop." She hoped her voice sounded more determined than she felt.

His voice was achingly gentle. "I won't hurt you."

"This is wrong."

"How can it be wrong? I love you, Alicia, and I know you have feelings for me." Desperation appeared in those blue eyes but he touched her face with unsurpassed tenderness, gliding a finger across her cheek and then brushing the pad of his thumb over her lower lip.

He loved her?

Tears came to her eyes. "I am married, Cole."

"I know," he whispered.

"Please, don't make this more difficult than it already is. You know this is wrong. I belong to another, who—"

"—Whose very presence makes you shrink in terror." A bitter edge lanced his voice. "You would be faithful to him rather than be with me, but you won't honor your marriage vow to him and be with him as his wife."

She pushed him away and sat up, still giddy from the force of his passion and her own that so quickly rose to meet it. Shame and confusion jumbled against each other.

"You ask me to be unfaithful to my husband. You would betray your childhood friend. Your kin."

He opened his mouth and then clamped it shut, with no excuse to offer. He took several steadying breaths. "Alicia, if you weren't married to Nicholas, would you—"

Her confusion transformed into anger. "I was just beginning to think you actually possessed some scruples, Cole Amesbury, or perhaps even—heaven forbid—a heart." She made an inarticulate sound of derision. "I should have known. I don't know why I let myself continuously be fooled by your deceptively pleasing face. Everything those women said about you is probably true. And any man who'd purposely shoot another man obviously has no heart."

His breath caught loudly in the silence. He

stared at her as if she'd slapped him and the color slowly drained from his face. Outside, she heard voices and footsteps approaching, but they passed by the room.

She shouldn't have said that. She truly didn't mean it. In her frustration, she had lashed out at him unfairly, hurting him, but it was too late to take it back. And if it drove him away, she would deserve it.

Besides, if this were his true character, even if she had married him, he would never be faithful. No man who would seduce his own cousin's wife had the moral fiber to stay true to his own vows. And such a man would only break her heart.

Cole turned away and rubbed his hand over his face before returning his gaze to her. "So that's it?" The pain in his expression nearly crushed her.

Unable to speak, she lowered her eyes.

He pressed the heels of his hands into his eyes. After another deep breath, he stood and held out a hand. She let him pull her to her feet. He squared his shoulders, opened the door, and peered out. When he was satisfied that no one would see them leave the room, he stepped through the doorway.

"Tell Mary and Charles I took a hackney to White's." His stalked away.

Oh, how badly it hurt to know she'd wounded him!

Yet, perhaps it was better this way. Without him always so near, she may learn to love her husband, or at least truly be a wife to him, and then he wouldn't abandon her. And Cole would be free to find a wife who would overlook his many indiscretions and give him his heir.

She waited until she composed herself and then went to find Mary and Charles. Mary was dancing. Charles leaned against a column nursing a drink.

Charles held a hand out. "Dance with me,

Cousin Alicia, I beg you."

She nodded numbly, unable to form words enough to refuse, and let him lead her out to the floor.

As they followed the dance pattern, he looked at her in concern. "Are you unwell?"

She managed a wan smile. "I believe I'm tired."

"Shall we go?"

Alicia nodded. "Yes, thank you. Cole left already, I believe. He said something about going to his club."

He nodded. "He hates these things. I'm surprised he came at all tonight."

"I believe it was under duress from his father."

"Ah. That explains it."

Mary arrived then. After a startled look at Alicia, she turned to her husband. "I have grown rather weary and wish to return home, if you have no objection."

Alicia smiled in gratitude for her perceptiveness.

Charles nodded. "I promised to meet a few friends at Brooks, but I'll take you ladies home first."

They fetched their wraps, thanked the hostess, and climbed into the carriage. Mary chatted happily, and Alicia was grateful no one required her to make a contribution to the conversation. She stared out the window, reliving the passion of Cole's kiss, cursing her own unfaithful heart, wishing for things best left unsaid.

The carriage pulled up in front of her husband's London home. In the moonlight, it loomed ahead like a cursed fortress. Her home. Her prison.

After preparing for bed, she paced the room, sleep lost from her.

How could she be so drawn to a man like Cole? He was a rake who trifled with other men's wives, even his own cousin's. He gambled. He dueled. He was probably the most skillful liar in London. There was nothing to recommend him.

Except his astonishing good looks. And his charm. And his ability to coax a smile and even a laugh from her when she needed it most.

Trivial things. In time, these would fade and leave only the ugly truth of his soul.

But he had saved her from a terrible marriage by convincing his cousin, a good and honorable man, to marry her and give her a life of comfort. From their first meeting, Cole always treated her with compassion and gentleness. In spite of the fact that he was a sought after bachelor who clearly had his choice of beautiful and wealthy ladies, he remained by her side, escorting her anywhere she wished to go.

And without hesitation, he protected her from the highwaymen at great personal risk; an act of valor she knew had little to do with his devotion to his cousin. And more, he was a man of great feeling, tormented by ghosts of the past, and desperate to find redemption.

So who was the real Cole? The good, honorable gentleman? Or the unconscionable rake?

He was right about one thing; she refused to cuckold a husband with whom she had yet to share her bed.

She was the real monster.

CHAPTER 24

After passing one of the most miserable nights of his life, Cole stood in the receiving room of a fashionable home in London, his stomach clenching as he gazed upon whom he once believed the most beautiful lady in all of London.

Vivian's smile, so provocative a year and a half ago, now looked only vulgar. "If it isn't the brave defender of my honor."

"Did you know he died?" he demanded angrily.

Her smile never dimmed. "Pity." She moved toward him with the languid movements of a predatory feline.

He stiffened. "I came to ask you a question."

Her eyes focused on his mouth and her voice dropped to a purr. "The answer is yes. My husband has been most inattentive and I've been dreadfully lonely. You look absolutely divine. Better than candy. Come upstairs."

Cole stared at her in amazement.

Mistaking his reaction, she smiled. "Don't worry, darling, the servants can be trusted to keep my secrets."

He turned cold at the thought of ever being attracted to this woman. What a fool he had been. "Who put you up to it?"

Her smile turned vapid. "Cole, darling, whatever do you mean?"

"The rivalry between Armand Palmer and me. The duel. Who was behind it?"

Ah. A crack in her composure. She recovered

quickly and slid her hands up his chest and around his neck, gazing up into his eyes in that familiar way that used to make him feel invincible. Today it made him feel nauseated.

"What makes you think anyone would put me up to anything?" She smiled seductively.

"Don't trifle with me, Vivian. I'm not in the mood for your foolish games. I need answers."

Vivian's smiled faded. "I don't know what you mean."

"Someone is trying to kill everyone in the Palmer family, starting with the heir. And clever enough to make it not look like murder."

Her gaze turned cold and she removed her hands. "I think you'd better leave. Now."

Shaking in fury, Cole advanced upon her. "I will leave when you tell me what I need to know."

She stepped back with true fear in her eyes. He backed her against a wall and placed a hand on the wall on either side of her shoulders, trapping her. Her breath quickened and her eyes darted over his face in an attempt to discover his intentions.

Leaning in close, he whispered, "If you cooperate with me, I will not reveal your involvement in the murder of an innocent man. He had a twin sister, did you know? She is most distressed by his death. She was left to the mercy of a greedy uncle."

Some of the fear left her eyes and her voice took on a careless tone. "And I should care about this chit?"

Cole leaned in until his mouth was a fraction of an inch from hers and noted with satisfaction that she drew in her breath. "How discreet are your servants? Enough that they would never investigate your screams because they'd assume them to be sounds of passion?"

Vivian's eyes widened.

Cole stepped closer until his whole body pressed

against those curves he once found so appealing, and glared at his opponent. "Did you know, dearest Vivian, that I learned many useful things in the war? Wringing information from a prisoner was one of them."

"You'd never hurt a lady," she said uncertainly.

Cole didn't bother pointing out that she hardly fit the profile of a true lady. "Female prisoners are especially vulnerable to questioning. There are so many more ways to hurt them." With his lie falling easily from his mouth, he grabbed her wrists and pulled them up over her head, shackling them in both of his, leaving the other to caress her neck purposefully. "Give me a reason to not hurt you."

She gasped. If Vivian truly ever knew him, she would never believe him capable of causing harm to a woman, despite his deadly tone and expression. Thankfully, she believed his empty threat.

Pale and trembling, she swallowed. "What...what do you want to know?"

"Who paid you to coerce us into a duel?"

She shook her head once, her breathing ragged. "I don't know his name."

Cole put his hand around her throat, not squeezing, but resting it there to make sure she understood the warning. Her eyes dilated in terror and Cole felt like a beast threatening a woman in this manner, but he remained focused.

"I don't, I swear! He handed me a hundred quid and promised me a fortune if I'd help him humiliate Armand."

"And you decided the best humiliation was for us to duel?"

"He told me to do it. Said you were the best shot in London and to make sure you dueled."

Cole's practiced shields kept his gaze steady when he wanted to cringe. He needed her to believe he was the worst kind of scoundrel, capable of anything. "You asked me to meet you at the park that afternoon. You wanted me to 'catch' you together."

"It seemed the best way. You won't tell my husband, will you? He has such a terrible temper." Tears shimmered in her eyes and Cole began to believe she actually understood her peril rather than using tears as just another feminine ploy.

"That depends. How can I contact this man who paid you?"

"I don't know. We met outside the opera house and he handed me the money after the duel. I never saw him again."

Swearing, he pushed away from Vivian's body and paced.

Vivian visibly relaxed now that he had released her, but still watched his with wary eyes. "I vow, that's all I know."

He swung back to her. "Describe him."

She flinched as if she expected him to hit her. "Very ordinary-looking, like an attorney. Middle-aged, balding, gold rimmed glasses. His suit was not a gentleman's cut."

That could describe half the bourgeois in London. Cole reined in his frustration and lowered his voice to a deadly tone. "I will say nothing about your involvement to your husband...yet. If I discover that you've lied to me, or withheld any information that could help me, I'll be back. To inform your husband, ruin your reputation, and," he grinned wickedly, "have my own kind of revenge on you."

She paled further and clutched at the wall. "I've told you all I know."

With all the ruthlessness of a pirate, Cole traced his finger down the side of her face. "I actually hope you'll prove to be a liar. I truly want to make you suffer."

White with fear, she merely stared at him.

Cole bowed with exaggerated formality and left. Outside, he swore again as he climbed into his curricle. His tiger fixed him with a wide, toothy grin, not the least intimidated by Cole's mood. Cole winked at the boy before taking the ribbons. Grateful she hadn't called his bluff, but fuming that he still had not learned enough, he drove through the streets of London.

At least he knew his duel with Armand had indeed been arranged. But he still did not know if Vivian's employer believed Cole would kill Armand instead of, as she said, merely humiliate him. Nor did he know if the murderer went back and finished the job later, making it look as though Armand had died of an opium addiction.

Cole arrived in front of the town house the Palmer family rented during their stay in London, handed the ribbons to his tiger, and climbed out.

A footman opened the door.

Cole swept off his hat. "Good afternoon, my good man. Were you here when the Palmer family let this house two Seasons ago?"

The footman eyed him suspiciously. "No, sir."

"It's very important that I speak with someone who was here then. Please?" He painted on his most disarming smile so many found irresistible and handed him his calling card.

He read the name, eyed his attire, and appeared to consider.

Cole reached into his pocket and passed some coin to him. "I'd be most grateful."

The footman glanced around as if to determine there were no witnesses and snatched the money. After tucking it away, he opened the door to admit Cole and showed him into a small front parlor tastefully decorated in restful blue. "Wait here, my lord."

He disappeared, and Cole waited for several

minutes. Noise from the streets as people passed mingled with voices within the house. He stood looking at a surprisingly well done watercolor. He smiled as he recognized the style and felt his grin widen as he read the artist's signature. Christian Amesbury. His youngest brother. The pup had developed remarkable skill the last few years. Perhaps he wasn't meant for the church, after all. He turned at the sound of footsteps.

A vaguely familiar-looking older man approached slowly. He walked slightly stooped as if his rheumatism had been acting up. "I am Forrester, the head butler. You wished to speak with me, my lord?"

"Yes, thank you. I am sure your many duties require much of your time."

"Yes, my lord."

"Were you here when this house was let by the Palmers two Seasons past?"

"Yes, I was, my lord. The mister and missus were here, with their son and daughter, and a cousin, I think it was. Delightful family. The daughter was here for her first Season. Quite successful, as I understand. They left after the Season, but the young gentlemen remained." His face clouded. "The son died later that summer."

"Yes, Armand was shot. But only in the arm."

"Yes. Odd, that. The wound did not look life-threatening; more a graze, if I recall correctly. But then he developed fever. The doctor bled him and did everything he could, but his arm sickened and had to be amputated. Tragic thing to happen to anyone, but especially one so young. Then I heard he died only a few months later."

"Did there appear to be anything odd about his illness?"

The furrow returned. "He seemed to be recovering, and then took a rather sudden turn. But that can sometimes happen. I hear that tiny bugs we can't see can cause mysterious fevers."

"The sickness in his arm was sudden, then? He seemed to be well at first?"

"Yes, my lord."

Cole carefully composed his next question. "Did he have many visitors?"

"Perhaps two or three. His family was on the way here to visit him, but never arrived."

"Would you remember the faces of any of his visitors?"

"I'm sorry, my lord. Not from two Seasons ago."

Cole nodded. "I understand. How may I contact the former head housekeeper?"

"She passed on, sir, only days after the young gentlemen went home. Took a nasty fall."

Now that was peculiar news. Had she been eliminated because she knew too much? A nasty fall seemed too convenient. The housekeeper could have been a witness. Or she might have been an accomplice, paid by Vivian's employer and then silenced.

"You've been most helpful." Cole passed him several coins. "Thank you for your time."

The butler bowed. "Thank you, my lord."

Cole stepped out and frowned up at the rain. Why did it always seem to rain on him? He fumed while his curricle made its perilous way through the crowed streets toward Pall Mall.

Cole knew little about poisons, but he was fairly certain any number of them could have caused an infection and fever. Or imitated an opium overdose. Cole was tempted to go back to Alicia's family home and ask if anyone saw anything the night Armand died. Opium overdose was not uncommon, but in light of everything else, Cole had no doubt that Armand had been cleverly murdered.

With a chill, Cole realized Robert had been there

both when the duel took place and when Armand took ill. What he did not know was whether Robert had been present when Armand died.

The uncle, Willard Palmer, might have killed him, hoping to eliminate his brother's heir so that he would inherit the family estate and lands after causing his brother's untimely death. He would be a much more likely suspect. But why go after Alicia now? Their money problems were over now that Alicia had married Nicholas.

The rain stopped by the time Cole arrived at Nicholas's house.

"She's in the garden, sir," the footman informed him as he took his hat.

Cole strode through the house to the rear, squared his shoulders, and followed the garden path that led to Alicia. Unaware of his approach, she gazed at something near the horizon. She sat silhouetted by the setting sun, her hair burnished by the light, a halo surrounding her slender body. Cole ached at the sight of her.

He still couldn't believe that he had actually told her he loved her. Stupid. He should have held his tongue.

She hated him. Despite her earlier words of forgiveness, underneath it all, she still harbored a hatred she would not easily release. Her words after he kissed her at the birthday celebration had been proof.

He had shot her brother. It did not matter that he had been a pawn in someone else's game and that his actions had not actually caused Armand's death. Her brother was dead, and Cole had pulled the trigger. She would view anything else as a moot point. And he still did not have any evidence to prove that there was another, larger, more ominous plot at work.

And worse, she believed him unprincipled. She

may never trust him.

Nicholas's valet, Jeffries, nodded at Cole as he walked with controlled casualness near the house. Cole nodded in return, relieved to see his directive to keep Alicia under watch at all times was being studiously honored. Since the highwaymen attack, the staff had been most cooperative about guarding her.

As he neared, her head turned toward him, and he felt his smile rise as he beheld her gentle beauty, but her body tensed as she awaited him. That hurt.

He excelled in games of chance with good reason. Keeping his expression pleasant, without any sign of his inner turmoil, he forced lightness into his voice.

"Cousin Alicia. How are you this fine afternoon, love?"

"Good afternoon." Her tone was civil but aloof. Chilly.

He bent over her hand and released it, the picture of perfect propriety.

When she raised her eyes, he noticed the dark circles beneath them betraying a sleepless night. He had expected that, but the anguish in them stopped his heart.

He folded his hands behind his back before he did something foolish. He dragged in a shaking breath and tried to order his thoughts.

A servant approached. "My lady, this just arrived."

Alicia paled at the sight of the black-trimmed stationery that signified an announcement of death. She took the envelope and began to sway. Alarmed, Cole steadied her and guided her to a stone bench. Had the killer gone after Alicia's sister? With shaking hands, she tore the seal. And gasped.

"What is it?" he asked.

"Uncle Willard is dead."

Cole blinked. "Willard?"

"They found him on the highway. Apparently he was set upon by thieves. His purse and watch were gone and his horse was taken."

Another Palmer dead. Without a doubt someone was systematically eliminating the entire family. But for what purpose?

Cole hailed Phillips and had him summon Alicia's maid.

"Poor Robert," Alicia moaned. "He still grieves for Armand. And now his father is gone. Oh, Cole, he and Hannah will need me. I must go to them."

But what if Robert was the killer? Alicia could be in danger if she returned.

Cole rubbed his hands over his face. "Of course."

"But the baron has gone on business and won't be back for several more days."

"Have your abigail pack your things. We leave first thing in the morning."

She nodded, not questioning his use of the word 'we.'

Cole made sure she was steady and in the care of her competent, sympathetic maid before telling his own valet, Stephens, to pack for him as well.

He went to White's to meet his brother Grant, who'd agreed to see him. Inside the club, he found Grant sitting in a comfortable armchair in the shadows. He looked as if he sat lost in thought and nursing a drink, but a covert alertness told Cole that Grant listened to every conversation around him and saw everyone who entered. Grant possessed the uncanny abilities of a chameleon. He could blend in with even the roughest thugs in London's streets one moment, and consort with royalty the next. Of course, he seemed to prefer the thugs over the royalty. As the black sheep of the family, Grant delighted in not only snubbing polite company, but grappling in the streets with thieves and murderers.

Cole pulled up a chair and sat. "Grant."

"Cole." Grant's eyes glittered in the firelight. People often remarked that Grant looked the least like the Amesbury brothers, but Cole thought he bore a vague resemblance to Jared. All four brothers had the same build, but Grant's eyes were steely gray, while the other brothers' eyes were shades of blue. Grant's hair was darker, as if reflecting his dark soul. He looked the most hardened with a long, ragged scar that ran the length of his face. He'd come home from the war with it, and had never offered an explanation. He'd always possessed a rather cutting sense of humor, but he'd returned home more caustic, and more closed up.

"Mind telling me why you summoned me here?" Grant growled.

"I need your help."

Grant's expression did not change, but he raised one brow slightly and spoke in dry tones. "How quaint. The eldest asking his younger brother for help. Why don't you ask Jared?"

"He's indisposed. And I need your particular skills."

"I see." Grant sounded bored, but his eyes lit.

Cole paused. "I want you to keep this confidential."

"Of course." Grant waved impatiently.

Cole took a deep breath and plunged in. He described the events as they had unfolded, beginning with the duel and ending with the death of Willard Palmer. Grant listened without interrupting, his expression never changing.

When Cole finished speaking, Grant nodded absently. "You're right. This is part of a grander scheme. I need to question her, see if there are any other incidents she may believe were unconnected at the time."

Cole paused. "Ah, I don't want her to know yet.

263

Either that she's in danger, or that I've contacted anyone."

Grant looked disgusted. "You're in love with her."

Cole sighed and braced himself for the sarcastic comment he knew Grant's cynical mind was formulating. "I am."

Grant made an inarticulate noise of revulsion, but instead of the insult Cole expected, he asked, "Exactly how involved are you with her?"

Now that was a question. Cole hesitated, but knew that if he withheld any information, his brother would unravel it on his own anyway, which would create further complications. Cole answered truthfully, not leaving out any pertinent information. Surprisingly, there was no judgmental frown in Grant's face, only an absorption of facts.

A rare smile touched one side of his mouth. "You are in a corner."

Cole let out his breath slowly. "That's putting it mildly."

"I'll begin immediately. Meanwhile, question her discreetly, and keep your eyes open for anyone who might wish the family harm. We have no motives and no suspects, yet." His eyes glittered at the thought of the hunt.

Cole almost shivered at the feral glint in Grant's eye. "I'll send word if I find anything else."

Grant asked more background questions regarding her parents, nodded, and left without preamble. Cole returned home to dash off a few quick notes and made the necessary arrangements. After spending the night pacing and agonizing over decisions he had to make, he made sure the groom hitched his favorite horse, André, to the baron's coach. The servants loaded Alicia's trunks while she waited in the foyer, dressed in traveling clothes.

Soulful eyes greeted him. "I posted a message to

my husband but he will not have even received it yet. I don't know what business he had that could not be conducted in London. I thought business is what brought us here." She clenched together her hands.

"I'm here for you, Alicia," he said gently.

She glanced at the servants, but they waited at a discreet distance and would not overhear her words. "And may I be assured that you will behave as a gentleman?"

Her words, though certainly valid, stung. He drew himself up. "I give you my word."

She nodded wearily.

Keeping his word proved easier than he'd feared as they traveled together over the next few days on the way back to Alicia's former home.

Stephens and Monique rode with them in the same coach which left Cole little opportunity to break his promise. Stephens worked his Romany charm with Monique. They flirted and laughed most of the way, leaving Alicia to stare out of the window and Cole to watch her with growing hunger.

Late one evening after dinner, they sat in a sitting room of an inn. The quaint inn felt warm and restful, but the tension in the room mounted. Cole gave up trying to read after he realized he had been staring at the same page for an hour, and turned his attention to Alicia.

Her head bent over her embroidery, her expression serene except for the tiny frown of concentration at her brow, yet she remained unusually quiet.

"Alicia, what troubles you?"

She looked up at him in surprise. "I apologize if I have been poor company."

He waited.

She lowered her hands and rested her needlework on her lap. "I'm concerned about Robert.

And troubled about Uncle Willard's death. And I...I wish Lord Amesbury could have come with us."

Cole leaned back in his chair, stretching out his legs in front of him. "Do you always speak of him as Lord Amesbury, or the baron? Have you never called him by his given name? Even in private?"

Alicia flushed. "No, I suppose not. I never think of him that way."

"Are you so unhappy with him then?"

She glanced at him sharply and looked away. "No, of course not. I have been content. Why do you continue to ask me that?" Her voice sharpened.

"I only want to see you happy, Alicia." Cole braced himself for the tirade he knew would follow— he should not ask such personal questions, he is a reprobate for trying to steal his cousin's wife, he is without honor—and she would be right on all accounts.

Instead, her voice quieted. "He spends little time at home. And now when I need him, he's away." She stopped as if she had revealed more than she thought prudent.

"He would have been here for you if he had known," Cole suggested as kindly as he could, wishing he could just be rid of Nicholas.

"I'm not so sure."

"You don't doubt him, do you?"

"I'm not certain of anything."

When the silence deepened, Cole pressed. "What else ails you?"

She drew a breath. "I feel guilty for harboring such unkind feelings for Uncle Willard."

Exasperated, he said, "Alicia, the man practically sold you to the highest bidder."

"He had few options. Some men simply discard unwanted relations, but he took Hannah and me in."

Outside, lightning flashed, followed by the slow rumble of distant thunder. A moment later, the pattering of raindrops fell against the window. She stared unseeing out the darkened window before speaking again.

"And now, Robert has no other family. His mother died years ago. His sister died as a child. He and Hannah were never close. Armand is gone. Now, his father. He is completely alone."

"He has you," Cole said softly.

She turned to look at him as if she had forgotten he was there and her lips curved in a brave, mirthless smile. "He doesn't. Not anymore." She arose, her needlework forgotten. "I believe I shall go to bed. Good night."

He forced himself to remain still. Not gather her up into his arms and kiss her. Not scoop her up and carry her to his room. "Good night."

CHAPTER 25

They pulled up in front of the Palmer manor house. Alicia regarded the structure with mingled dread and affection. Her whole life had been spent here. Joys and sorrows she had experienced here threatened to overwhelm her. As if sensing her rising emotions, Cole reached out and took her hand. He gave it a comforting squeeze. To her surprise, it helped.

As she and Cole alit from the carriage, a butler Alicia had never seen before opened the door and a plump, motherly woman greeted them. The estate still appeared slightly understaffed, but at least it was functional. Every surface gleamed under constant care now.

"Good day, Lady Amesbury. I'm Mrs. Dobbs, the head housekeeper.

Alicia introduced Cole as Lord Amesbury, her husband's cousin. She also introduced Stephens whose teeth flashed against his darkly handsome face, and Monique, whose eyes flitted over the bare interior with a hint of condescension after the much finer baron's home.

"Your rooms are prepared," Mrs. Dobbs said. She directed footmen as to where to place the trunks.

Hannah flew to her and broke down in Alicia's arms. "Lissie!"

"Good heavens, Hannah. Are you ill?"

Hannah's letters had not reflected her poor health, and seeing her sister thusly was a shock. The pallor of her skin approached gray, and her golden hair had lost all of its former luster. Her eyes looked dull and lifeless and her body felt gaunt.

"Oh, it's been simply terrible without you," Hannah sniffed. "And Robert..."

"Where is he? Is he home?" When Hannah could not speak, Alicia glanced at the housekeeper.

"Mr. Palmer is still abed, my lady."

Alarm began in Alicia's stomach. "Is he unwell, then?"

"He's been deep in his cups," said Hannah. "Worse than ever. He keeps mumbling something about his family being taken from him as punishment for all his past misdeeds."

"Oh, poor Robert. I will see to him at once."

Hannah nodded. "I knew you'd make it all right now that you're here."

Alicia never failed to be both touched and overwhelmed by Hannah's trust in her to resolve every problem. "Why don't you go lie down, Hannah? I'll see to Robert."

Alicia knocked at the door of Robert's room. There was no answer, of course. She opened the door to find a shapeless heap on the bed, reeking of spirits. She threw open the draperies and let the sun shine in.

"Wake up, Robert. It's tea time."

An incoherent mumble replied.

"Robert, I have made a very long journey, and I expect a civil greeting. Get up, or I will be forced to take drastic measures."

The mumble turned into a grumble.

"I shall go and change out of my traveling clothes, and then I will return. If you are not awake by then, you will regret it."

"Hmmmphmm."

Alicia went to her old room, and with Monique's aid, changed into an afternoon gown and re-styled her hair. Overcome by nostalgia, Alicia picked up and set down every object within the room while Monique unpacked her things. Though the last year and a half since she lost first Armand and then her parents had been a difficult, lonely time, there were so many other memories here. On the wall by the window were tiny marks that *Maman* had made, measuring Alicia's height as she grew. The window seat, worn and faded, reminded her of rainy days spent reading, or learning embroidery, or simply dreaming. Several books, carefully dusted, remained sitting on the bookshelf.

She picked one up and opened it to find a tiny sprig of violets pressed into the pages; a token of young love her first ever suitor had given her. The top drawer of the desk held the secret compartment where she had hidden many childish treasures over the years.

Her first impulse was to call Cole and share it with him, but that would not be appropriate; respectable ladies never invited gentlemen into their boudoirs. The gentleman she should be inviting to her room was her husband, and for completely different reasons.

What a stubborn fool she had been. Cole had offered to elope with her, and looking back, she realized that she should have accepted. Though the social ramifications would certainly have been unpleasant, as the eldest son of an earl, he might have been able to deflect much of the criticism. Now that she knew him, she knew he surely would have tried to shield her from the difficulties. Her hatred of him had been entirely misplaced. If she'd married him, she would be with him. As his wife. In every way.

Instead, she was married to a man whose face she'd never seen, who, in many ways, remained a stranger. A man she had never tried to accept, but who was good to her. There were things she admired about him, others she loved about him. He was intelligent, kind and patient, and possessed the heart of a poet. She'd never met such a gentle soul. He valued her as a person and never indicated he thought of women as annoyances, or even commodities. And, more importantly, she truly believed he was not only fond of her, but would be faithful to her because he was a man capable of forbearance.

Unlike Cole. Despite his assurances to the contrary, she did not delude herself into believing that Cole's life of debauchery would magically transform into one of fidelity after he wed. Her heart could never survive such betrayal by a man she loved.

For a number of reasons, it would be best to nurture her feelings for her husband and avoid developing any sort of feelings for Cole.

Too late.

Frowning, she went back into Robert's room. As expected, the lump in his bed had not moved. Alicia firmly grabbed the blankets and threw them back revealing Robert sprawled in bed, naked from the waist up. She glared at him. His snoring never broke rhythm. She took the pitcher from the washbasin and carefully poured it over his head and torso.

He came up swearing and sputtering. When he recognized his assailant, he glowered at her, his wet hair dripping into his eyes. "Confound it, woman, are you trying to drown me or give me my death of cold?" Rubbing a hand over his stubbled face, he staggered out of bed.

Despite his state of undress, Alicia kept her gaze fixed unflinchingly on his face.

"Well done," came a lazy, deep voice from behind her. "You've managed to wake the dead, I see." Cole leaned against the doorframe, dangerous and handsome.

Robert glared at them both. "What are you doing here, Amesbury?"

"I escorted your cousin to your death bed, as it were." Cole's grin spread slowly over his face. "Come Alicia, let's give the man some privacy now that he is back among the living."

"Have you a valet yet?" Alicia asked Robert.

Robert's glare deepened. "No. I am having difficulty persuading anyone to come work for me. Respected gentlemen's gentlemen seem to think we are a disreputable lot, what with forcing our family members to marry masked monsters to save ourselves from debtor's prison." He muttered another curse and pushed his wet hair out of his eyes.

"No matter. I shall send mine in to aid you with bathing and shaving," Cole said.

When Robert began to protest, Alicia added, "You certainly look as if you've been dead and buried. And you smell the part as well. Let his valet work his magic on you. I shall expect you for dinner, since you are obviously not going to be able to join us for tea." She eyed him in disapproval.

"Vindictive wench," Robert grumbled.

Alicia smiled sweetly at him and left the room. She, Hannah, and Cole enjoyed sandwiches and cakes with their tea and chatted about nonsensical things. Hannah looked dreadful. She even appeared to be losing her hair. Alarm took root and grew quickly. Perhaps she should bring Hannah home with her. But would her fear of the baron hinder a recovery?

Hannah went to lie down again in the hopes of taming a headache. After Hannah left, Alicia gave in to the desire to confide in Cole about a suspicion that had begun to take grow.

"Poor Hannah. I've never seen her so ill. And I

also fear for Robert."

His eyes flicked to her in interest, but his expression revealed nothing of his thoughts. "That he'll drink himself to death?"

"That, too. But I fear that Armand's death was not coincidental. Please don't discount my words for the ravings of an overactive imagination, or a hysterical female, but I can't help but wonder if someone has arranged all these 'accidents' that have beset my family."

Cole's expression never flickered. "What do you suspect?"

"Armand's wound was superficial. You said when you visited him, you were informed that his injury was not life-threatening, no worse than the one you received from the highwaymen. Yet, he grew very ill, so badly that his arm had to be amputated as the sickness spread. And I know that even small wounds can sicken and become ultimately fatal, but it seems too coincidental when I consider the rest. Then he developed that addiction as a necessity to help him deal with the pain. What's odd is that he was trying to cut back and eventually quit. So when I found him..." she struggled a moment before she continued, "it was such a shock..." she had to stop again. "And we must consider the accident that took my parents."

She rose and began to pace. "The carriage was relatively new and yet, the tongue broke, which caused the driver to lose control. We went off the road where the highway runs along the side of a hill. I watched as we traveled here, and that only happens in one place, and for only a few miles. But that happened to be where the carriage broke. No one survived, except me, and I was unconscious for days. I might have been left for dead."

Cole watched her attentively but his face remained inscrutable.

"There's more. I hadn't thought it significant until now, but my mother had a bad fall when she was out riding only a few weeks before your duel with Armand. She was an excellent rider and had not fallen in years. The cause appeared to be a worn strap to her saddle, but I am beginning to suspect that it was cut cleverly enough to not appear deliberate."

Cole's eyes widened.

"And a few months ago before I married the baron, a poisonous snake lay in my path where I always walk. It bit me. The gamekeeper told me later that kind of snake is normally afraid of people. Also, it usually stays deeper in the forest. There is some bracken in the stand of trees where I was walking, but it seems odd that an adder had come so close to the formal gardens. And you may not know this, but my bed caught on fire only weeks after I married the baron."

"I did know," he said in a strangled voice.

"Then there was that odd highwayman attack. And now my Uncle Willard is dead. Doesn't that all strike you as remarkably strange? Beyond coincidental?"

His expression grim, he nodded. "Quite suspicious."

"Then you believe me?"

He paused and carefully wiped his fingers on a napkin. "Yes. I had already come to the same conclusion. Hearing of your mother's riding mishap, and the details of the carriage accident, only confirms it. Nicholas and I have spoken and his servants have all been keeping you under guard."

"I have no idea who would want to kill any of us, much less all of us, or why. A magistrate would likely try to place the blame on someone within the family. Which leaves few obvious suspects. Robert. Hannah. Or me."

"I think we can safely eliminate you." Amusement touched his mouth. "And no one in their right mind would believe it of Hannah."

She gasped. "You can't believe Robert is responsible."

"You said he was the most likely suspect."

Frowning, Alicia continued to pace. "Yes, but I've known Robert all my life, and he has never shown any signs of violent behavior. He doesn't even have a bad temper. Besides, what possible motive would he have?"

"I can't explain why anyone would want you or your mother dead, but Robert might have wanted to eliminate your father and brother so he could eventually inherit their lands. His father squandered all the money on dubious business investments and excessive gambling once before. Perhaps now that the debts have been cleared, Robert feared there might be nothing left for him to inherit except for another mountain of debt if he waited for his father to die of old age."

"An investigator might have the same suspicions. That's why I don't want to go to one of them."

"I already have," Cole said.

She stared at him, her heart stalling. "What?"

"My duel with Armand was arranged. Vivian, the woman we dueled over, confessed someone paid her to coerce us into dueling. And Armand's consequent death was too sudden. He was murdered. Clearly, Willard's death is too coincidental to be a mere robbery gone bad. Someone is trying to kill everyone in your family. We need help uncovering the plot before it's too late. You or Hannah might be next."

Anger flared through her. "You went to a Bow Street Runner?"

"Not a Runner, but someone I trust to learn the

truth. He will give this his full attention."

She stared at him, her fury mounting. "You have no right to interfere with family matters!"

"I am involved. Someone manipulated me. I was the one who pulled the trigger that made Armand's death too conveniently arranged."

Alicia flinched at an image of a deadly calm Cole firing a pistol at her twin, watching him crumple, blood spewing from his arm. "You still have no right to go to the authorities without my knowledge." Her voice rose in both pitch and volume.

"I have every right!" Uncharacteristic anger gave volume to his words and he leaped to his feet. "If someone is murdering everyone in your family, then you might be the next target. The killer already tried more than once. I have a responsibility toward you and I'm not going to let someone murder you."

A responsibility? That's all she was to him? That explained much. His kindness, his protectiveness, stemmed not from his feelings for her, but a result of feeling responsible for the sister of a man he'd dueled. She shouldn't be surprised. He'd said as much when he'd proposed to her before she married Nicholas.

His words at the ball had been a lie. A means to seduce her.

Tears sprang to her eyes. "I'm not your responsibility. Now that I am married, that burden has passed from you to my husband. He should be here looking after me, not you. If he cared, he would be."

His legs devoured the space between them and he grabbed her by the shoulders, his face only inches away from her. "If you gave him reason to care, he might!"

Alicia's hand flew of its own will and the resounding slap echoed in the room. Stunned by her own action, she felt the blood drain out of her face.

Cole blinked at her in astonishment. He pressed his lips into a thin white line as the red mark on his cheek became more visible every second. His face hardened into granite.

Alicia put her hand to her mouth. "Oh, Cole, I'm—"

"Don't." He shoved her away and left the room. Seconds later, the front door slammed.

Alicia went to the window and watched him sprint athletically around the side of the house.

"How long have you been in love with him?"

Alicia whirled around to see Robert leaning against the doorway. Bathed, shaven and dressed as impeccably as Cole, thanks to Stephens's care, Robert appeared clear-eyed and sober, but the grief he bore weighed upon him. Losing Armand and his father in less than two years must be difficult to bear. Alicia understood all too well.

Alicia sighed. "What gave you that ridiculous notion?"

"Only lovers fight like that."

"I am *not* his lover!"

"Perhaps not in body, but you are in love with him." His head nodded toward the window.

Alicia glanced over her shoulder to see Cole, astride his favorite white horse, André, galloping away from the house. She turned back to Robert. "I am not. I could never love that...that..." At his look of sympathy, she gritted, "Be silent, you fool." She brushed past him, stormed up the stairs without aplomb, and slammed her door.

****

Dinner was a silent affair. Cole ate dutifully, barely tasting the fare and trying to ignore the hollowness in a place food would never touch. He glanced at Alicia. Her posture rigid, her eyes downcast, she merely pushed her food around her plate. He couldn't believe she'd slapped him. He never would have believed it of her. Her hatred must run deep. He was fast losing hope that she'd ever forgive him, much less care for him.

Robert drank more than he ate, but he still seemed to notice his guests' lack of enthusiasm over dinner. "Cook's meal not to your liking, cousin? My lord?"

Alicia raised her head. "It's fine."

"It's very good," Cole said.

Alicia rallied. "I'm sure it tastes better when your palate hasn't been numbed by strong drinks, Robbie." Forced levity colored Alicia's voice.

Wearing a half-smile, Robert saluted her with a glass of wine. "My Lord Amesbury, after dinner, can I interest you in a game of chess? The billiards table, among other things, was seized months ago, I'm afraid."

Robert's frankness and unabashed admission at his period of poverty surprised Cole.

"My man of business tells me I need to make a few more prudent investments before I start refurnishing or redecorating the place. I feel like I live in a monastery with such Spartan furnishings. Despite the baron's best efforts, Father didn't leave me with much..." His voice trailed off and stark grief crossed his features. He emptied his wine glass.

"I enjoy chess," Cole replied easily. At least, he hoped it sounded easy.

After dinner, they sat down together across the chess board. Alicia flitted about the room before finally settling down in a chair by the window.

"It's raining," she commented dully.

Dobbs knocked and delivered a missive to Alicia.

"Thank you, Dobbs." She frowned at the seal on the envelope. "It's from Lord Amesbury. Ah, I mean, my husband. Nicholas."

She had probably added the last for his benefit, due to his comment about her never using her husband's Christian name. She broke the seal and opened the letter.

"He's coming. He apologized for his absence but he will arrive shortly. That was thoughtful." Her voice betrayed her lack of enthusiasm.

Cole nodded slowly. Robert watched him curiously, an eyebrow raising and his eyes flicked between Cole and Alicia as if awaiting reactions.

Keeping his face devoid of expression, Cole said, "Then I will take my leave as soon as he arrives."

Alicia straightened. "You're leaving?"

"As you said. It is for your husband to look after you. Not me. I will remain to watch over you until he can take over that duty. I have responsibilities elsewhere."

And if the person who wanted the Palmers dead thought they were only guarded by a few elderly servants and a cripple who couldn't even sit a horse, then all the better. The murderer would attempt to strike when he perceived them most vulnerable. Cole would remain hidden and could protect them better. He'd sent a letter by express courier to Grant, telling him of the events Alicia had revealed. Perhaps it would help with the investigation.

"Check." Robert grinned at him.

Cole snatched his thoughts back to the game. He countered and tried to clear his mind, but his whole body thrummed with awareness. Alicia remained tantalizingly close and yet, more out of reach than ever. She resumed her pacing, the firelight and shadows playing hide and seek with her soft, womanly contours.

"Check."

Blast! Focus, Amesbury.

He countered again. Alicia carefully folded the letter and rewrapped it in the envelope.

"Checkmate."

With a sound of disgust, Cole pushed away from

the table. "Forgive me for not providing much sport. You played very well, Robert. And now, I believe I will retire."

They said their good nights and he headed upstairs, weary deep in his soul. He felt her presence behind him in the hallway.

"Cole."

He froze. Alicia's voice, gentle, full of regret, nearly undid him. She did not speak until she came within arm's reach. He folded his hands together behind his back and looked down at her lovely, guileless face. With childlike vulnerability, her eyes probed his.

"I'm sorry. My action was uncalled for. I can't believe I slapped you. Please accept my apology."

"Apology accepted," he replied more abruptly than he meant.

She winced and moistened her lips. "You were right about everything. I shouldn't have lashed out at you. And I'm sorry for becoming angry that you went to an investigator. I feared if we brought in an outsider, that he might implicate Robert. Cole, I know he didn't do it. It's not possible."

He looked down at her pleading face and gentled his voice. "I don't believe he's guilty of murder, either. Or even capable of it. And trust me, I said as much."

Relief sweetened her face and she touched his arm. He swallowed hard and clenched his hands.

"Thank you. I'm sorry. I seem to be continually trying to find sinister motives for your actions. I see now that it was only out of a sense of duty that you've been helping me. I am grateful." Her voice sounded oddly choked.

Duty. That may have spurred his initial interest in Alicia, but did not even begin to touch his motives now. Best if that's how she saw it, despite his earlier blunder at confessing he loved her.

No doubt she thought he used the words merely in his attempt to seduce her.

"I'm happy to be of service to you. Good night, Alicia."

"Good night, Cole."

Inside his room, he waved away Stephens and sat by the fireplace, wondering if there would always be so much left unspoken between them. Or if he would ever be free to tell her the burning desires of his heart. First, he had to keep her safe. He paced, casting about for ideas, solutions, turning them over and discarding them.

Then he plotted how he might lure the killer to strike again. This time, Cole would be ready. With his own kind of justice.

CHAPTER 26

"The Baron's coach is here," Dobbs announced as she entered the drawing room. "I've prepared the bedroom that you requested."

At the head housekeeper's words, Alicia stood to go greet the baron. Nicholas. She needed to think of him as Nicholas.

But his arrival meant Cole would leave now.

Heavy of heart, she followed Dobbs downstairs to greet her husband. The baron's valet, Jeffries, barked commands while others swarmed in the entryway. When the baron entered, they stopped and gaped, as unnerved by him as she'd been at first. Jeffries frowned at the servants and took a step toward the baron. Whether he did this out of protectiveness for his masked employer, or as a show that his master was not a man to fear, she could not decide.

Jeffries nodded to her. "Milady." He drew himself up importantly and turned to the baron. "You're room is prepared, my lord, and your things will be situated to your satisfaction."

"Thank you, Jeffries."

Alicia arranged her mouth into a smile as the dark, masked figure turned toward her.

"Alicia, my darling. You have become even more beautiful since I last saw you."

His soft, muffled voice evoked an unexpected warmth within her. Awkwardly, she moved to him but then hesitated. "It was kind of you to come, my lord."

"I came the moment I knew of your loss," he said in that familiar muffled voice.

"You did?"

She could hear the smile underneath his mask. "I did. I'm your husband. I should be at your side in times such as these."

Touched, Alicia could barely utter, "Thank you."

She saw to it that her husband had settled comfortably in the room next to hers. Somehow, it seemed right to put him in Armand's old room.

"The trip has tired me, my darling. I believe I shall rest before dinner." The baron—Nicholas, she corrected herself—sat heavily on his chair inside his room and allowed Jeffries to remove his boots.

Alicia left his room. As she passed Cole's open door, she saw his valet carefully packing everything into a trunk.

"Is he leaving so soon, Stephens?" she asked the valet, pausing at the doorway.

"I'm afraid so, my lady," he replied soberly. "He has his reasons."

Alicia nodded, heaviness settling over her. What a tangled mess. She wanted both men in her life, and yet refused to allow either one of them to love her. She hovered in the doorway, while Stephens packed Cole's clothing. "You are fond of him."

Stephens' mouth curved upward in a lopsided smile, brightening his already striking Romany features. "Aye. I've known him a long time. We served on the same ship. He saved my life more than once."

"It's more than that."

He nodded. "He's a good man. A good friend. One of the few who looked past my half-Romany breeding. After we came home, he offered me a position and was patient while I learned it." He looked as though he wanted to say more and chewed his lip in indecision, his handsome, dark face pensive. "There is much more to him than people see."

She nodded, heaviness deepening. "You're right. They see a scandalous libertine, but he is much more than that."

"Aye, he is."

Alicia wondered how much of her relationship with his master Stephens knew. Probably much. "Take care of him."

"Count on it, my lady."

After donning her bonnet, she went to walk in the gardens. The summer was waning and soon autumn would arrive. She greeted the gardener bending over his 'lovelies' and admired the flowers still in bloom. She made her usual circuit, passing, without a qualm, the place where the adder had bitten her, and completed the circle back to the house.

Cole, astride his white horse, cantered toward the stables. From her viewpoint in the gardens, Alicia imagined him as a knight of old riding his destrier, with a sword strapped to his hip and chain mail under his tunic, her favor tied around his arm, returning from slaying enemies or another noble quest.

He dismounted and led his horse toward the stables. He glanced her way, did a double-take and halted. As if he fought some inner battle, he stood motionless. Then he moved toward her, looking wholly, dangerously male, but his face was solemn, and his blue eyes were shielded.

Alicia moistened her lips. "Stephens tells me you're leaving now."

He nodded, his body stiff and guarded.

"It's already late afternoon," she protested with rising alarm. "You won't be able to go very far today."

"There are plenty of inns along the way where I

can lodge."

"You could stay here tonight. Begin your trip back in the morning, or in a few days. You haven't even seen your cousin."

"We spoke at length out near the highway." His smile saddened, and she caught a glimpse of the hurt inside him. "It will be better this way. Without me reopening old wounds, perhaps you can begin a real marriage with your husband." He quickly kissed her cheek and left without giving her an opportunity to reply.

She remained motionless in an attempt to sort out her thoughts. She failed, and fled back to the house out of fear of missing his departure.

While Cole's servants loaded his things into the coach, Alicia hovered in the foyer and tried to think of something to say, but nothing seemed appropriate. Or proper. Or honorable.

When he came downstairs, his eyes softened and his lazy grin reappeared. Still, underneath it, that hint of inner pain remained. Or was it resentment?

"You've come to see me off, have you? How thoughtful."

"I...I wanted to thank you for escorting me here. And for—" she choked on her words, "—for all you've done to help me. Us."

He kissed her hand without lingering. "I'm your humble servant, my lady. Goodbye." He abruptly turned to the coach.

Suddenly desperate to detain him, she cried out. "Cole."

With one foot on the step, he turned back, eyed her thoughtfully, and returned. He stood close enough that she could smell his masculine scent, feel his warmth. His expression was perfectly inscrutable, but she felt the tension radiating off his body. He waited while she struggled with her torn desires, the words she wished she could express.

"Please don't leave like this."

"Like what, Alicia?" His voice was toneless.

"Angry. Hurt."

He traced her cheek with ungloved, gentle fingers. Without speaking, he turned and walked out of her life. She watched the carriage pull away, unable to shake the gloom that settled over her.

Robert slung an arm around her shoulders. "You're pitiable."

"Be silent, you fool," she snapped, throwing off his arm and walking purposefully away. She should look in on Hannah. She had been abed for three days and complained of a constant headache. Even for her, she seemed unusually ill.

Then perhaps she should go speak with cook about dinner. After all, now that her husband was here, her loyalty and attention should be to him. What was Nicholas's favorite dish? He never said. And he never ate with her, so she had no way of knowing. She could have asked. She should have cared enough to ask him a great many things. They often had pheasant for dinner, perhaps because he favored it. She would go ask Cook to prepare pheasant.

She dried her eyes and peeped in Hannah's room. Her sister slept, her breath rattling a little, but she looked peaceful.

A well-rested Nicholas appeared to be in high spirits as he spoke to Robert and Alicia during dinner. He had taken his meal in private as was his custom but had joined them for conversation while they dined.

"How thoughtful of you to have Cook prepare my favorite dishes, Alicia," he said with a smile in his voice. Then he turned to Robert. "I'm grateful for your hospitality, Mr. Palmer."

Robert looked startled, as if he hadn't yet grown comfortable with the baron's thoughtful ways.

"You're quite welcome here, my lord." He turned an affectionate smile on Alicia. "Thank you for letting my cousin come. I would have remained in drunken oblivion if she hadn't."

It was partially true. Out of respect for her sensibilities, he only drank himself into a stupor late at night instead of all day long.

Alicia raised her chin. "I excel at waking up drunk men with cold pitchers of water."

Robert actually shook off his grief enough to laugh mildly. It was the first time she'd heard him laugh since she'd arrived. It occurred to her that Cole had made it easy for her to laugh, when she'd found it difficult to do so. There was such good in him. Protected behind a façade of a careless, reprehensible rake, and his annoying habit of tempting her to betray her husband, there was a better Cole, a man of honor and decency. He evoked strength and tenderness in her. He made her want to stop running away from her difficulties and face them. Guiltily, she glanced at Lord Amesbury. Her husband. Nicholas. She needed to face her duties regarding him. Be his.

Robert bid them good night. She heard his footfalls up the stairs and hoped he wouldn't drink himself into unconsciousness the moment he was alone.

Nicholas' voice broke the ensuing silence. "Come sit with me, my love."

Alicia followed him into the study and did not resist when he took her hand in his glove. "Tell me what has you so distracted."

"I am concerned about Robert and Hannah." She related her fears that someone had killed her parents, brother, and now uncle. "Cole contacted an investigator, without my knowledge, I might add, and I fear Robert will be their prime suspect. He has already suffered so much; I don't want him to endure anything more. And I worry that Robert will be the murderer's next victim. Or Hannah." The thought of sweet, gentle Hannah, helpless in the face of violence awoke something akin to panic.

"Or you," Nicholas said grimly. "After the highwaymen incident, I suspected your life was in danger and alerted my servants. I did not speak of it to you because I did not wish to alarm you, but all my servants have been watching over you. My coachman in particular is an excellent shot. We will protect you and your sister and cousin, my love, do not fear. As far as the investigator Cole mentioned, he probably only went to his brother, Grant. I am sure Grant will expend his efforts in the right direction."

His assurance comforted her, oddly enough, despite his imposing appearance, and her anxieties faded. As his hand held hers, she felt a desire to touch his skin instead of the coldly impersonal glove.

"I admire you for your devotion to your cousin, Alicia."

She shrugged. "We've been dear friends since our childhood. He and Armand were inseparable. I always felt jealous when Robert came to spend the summers with us because then I was no longer the center of Armand's world. They tried to lose me frequently, but more often, they allowed me to tag along since I was difficult to pry away from my twin. Eventually, they accepted that I would always be there. Just the three of us. Hannah was so much younger, that I'm afraid we quite ignored her. And now, she and Robert are all the family I have."

"You have other family now, Alicia."

She looked up at him in surprise and then realized that he meant himself. "Of course, my lord."

"Will you stay with me, Alicia?"

She hesitated, uncertain of his meaning.

"I know that you did not marry me by choice,

but rather out of a need to help your family. I should do the honorable thing and release you, but I find that I am reluctant to let you go." His voice quieted. "If you desire, I will annul our marriage and you can return to London this Season and search for a husband of your choice. I realize that the last time I offered to let you stay in London while I returned to my country home, you thought I planned to drag you through a divorce or throw you out on the streets."

Guiltily, Alicia twisted her wedding band.

"I'm offended that you would think me so heartless. You may stay in my London house and you will want for nothing. I will continue to care for you financially until you find another." He paused. "I will, if you wish it. But that's not what I desire. So now I ask you; will you stay with me, or do you ask me to give you up?"

Tears sprang to her eyes. She didn't bother to point out that an annulment was nearly impossible. Perhaps he had connections she did not know, but not even the most important connections would make a clean annulment. Anything would be messy, public, and scandalous. But she said nothing. None of those things mattered. The man behind the mask was not a monster. He was a warm and caring man with the needs of any man. And like a true gentleman, he was giving her a way out. He had treated her with kindness and more tenderness than any other man.

Except Cole.

But Cole had his motives. Nicholas had none, only a hope that his wife would develop affection for him. And be his wife in every way.

She did have affection for him, she realized. It was not pity, or duty, or guilt. She truly cared for him. A deep desire to soothe his hurts, offer him the solace of her body crept over her.

"Oh, Nicholas, of course I will stay with you. You

are the finest man I know."

His breathing became ragged beneath his mask.

She had to fist her hand to avoid ripping it off his face. How she longed to see emotion in his eyes, the shape of his smile. She could overlook his scars to the man underneath. Couldn't she?

"That is the first time you have ever called me by my given name," he said in a hushed voice.

She flushed. She had treated him badly and purposefully kept him at a distance.

He reached for her, but his hand paused mid-air. "May I…hold you, my love?"

Alicia paused, swallowed, and then leaned in toward him. He gathered her close, wrapping his arms around her and pulling her against his chest. Solid. Strong. There was nothing weak or crippled about the way he held her.

The housekeeper, Mrs. Dobbs, came in quietly, checked the windows, banked the fire, and left without disturbing them. Sounds of her checking doors and windows before returning upstairs echoed in the empty halls.

"Oh, my love, how I've longed to hold you," he whispered, his arms tightening.

His kiss on her cheek, still covered with cloth, warmed her further. When he released her, a foreign longing to be back in his arms crept over her.

"Perhaps we should retire." His voice sounded tight, yet resigned.

If she continued this insane game of caring for two men, she would end up hurting herself and certainly Nicholas. Cole, she wasn't so sure about. He did seem to care. He had even said that he loved her. But that had been in a moment of passion. Probably just part of his seduction repertoire. There were times, though, when she thought he might care.

She gave herself a mental shake. Cole's feelings

did not matter. She had to stop thinking about Cole. She was with Nicholas. Her husband. Her mind needed to be here with him. As she looked up at the featureless face without a drop of dread, she came to her decision.

At her door, he pressed a kiss to her face, and began to turn away, but she placed her hand on his arm. "Nicholas."

He froze. Even his breath seemed to still.

"Come inside."

He turned slowly. She would have given anything to see his expression. "Are you sure?" he whispered.

"I'm sure. You have given me more time than I deserve. I need to be your wife. In every way."

He still waited, as if watching her carefully. "I don't want you to regret this."

"I can't imagine that I will. You are a good man. I trust you. I'm ready." And she would hate the person she would become if she postponed this any longer.

He nodded and motioned her to precede him through the door. Inside her bedroom, he blew out all of the candles and placed a chair in front of the fireplace until the room was so dark Alicia knew she would never see his features clearly.

Nervously, she waited, uncertain of what to do. But when he came to her and enfolded her into his embrace, her fears quieted and she leaned against him.

He pulled off his gloves and touched her face with his bare hands. They were warm and gentle. "If I hurt you, or frighten you in any way, tell me and I'll slow down. If you need me to, I will stop."

She nodded. Her heart swelled with tenderness for him. Supremely gentle, and surprisingly passionate, he touched her and kissed her until she was never more certain of anything in her life but that she wanted him. And wanted to be his wife in every way.

As she lay in his arms after they'd became truly husband and wife, she knew she had made the right choice.

CHAPTER 27

Alicia woke to the sound of shouting voices. Sleepily, she sat up. Pale, predawn light seeped in between the heavy draperies over the window. Her cheeks heated as she remembered the delicious sensations to which her husband had introduced her last night. Smiling, feeling whole, she simply was unable to muster a terrible amount of alarm for the noise outside her room. As the volume increased and the footsteps thundered through the halls, Alicia threw back her covers, feeling obligated to at least pretend an interest in the commotion. She pulled on a peignoir, ran her fingers through her unbound hair and opened the door to a barrage of different voices.

"Bring the doctor, now!"

"Phillips has already gone for him."

"Don't move him."

"Bring a pillow to place under his head. And bring a blanket."

Alicia peered over the banister to the open foyer below. The servants huddled over a motionless form on the floor.

"Move back, give him some air," Nicholas ordered in a commanding voice. His cloaked form bent over the person on the floor, running his gloved hands over the body's arms, rib cage and then over the legs. Nicholas leaned in closer, and when his head moved, the face of the injured person came into view. Robert lay pale and unmoving at the foot of the stairs.

With her heart in her throat, Alicia flew

downstairs to him. "Robert!"

Nicholas continued his gentle probing. "He's breathing and he has a pulse. I'm just making sure nothing's broken before we move him." With a growl, he finally tore the glove off his right hand and felt along the back of Robert's neck with care.

"I don't think anything's broken. Let's carry him to the nearest couch." He replaced his glove.

The men lifted Robert, careful to not jostle him as they carried him to the sofa in the parlor. A maid placed a pillow behind his head and a blanket over his body. Another built up the fire. Robert lay unconscious.

Alicia took his hand, but it remained limp and cold. She realized that someone, probably Monique, had placed a blanket around her to ward off the chill of the early morning.

Clutching the blanket, she turned to Nicholas. "What happened?"

He drew her into another room and pressed her hands in between his gloves, making her long to pull off his gloves and feel the warmth of his flesh against hers. "One of the servants found him at the bottom of the stairs. He appears to have fallen down them."

"Couldn't he have simply passed out from too much drink where they found him?"

He shook his cowled head. "The way he was laying suggested he had fallen down at least several steps. And he's bruising more than a simple fall would cause."

The doctor arrived and they were ushered out. Alicia paced outside the door. She did not know if she could bear to lose Robert, too. He'd been her childhood friend. The thought of losing him frightened her more than she'd imagined. And his friendship with Armand seemed one of her last connections with her lost twin. She heard the soft murmur of voices but did not heed them until a glove rested on her arm.

Lifting her head, she looked up at Nicholas's dark form. The mask did not unnerve her as it once had. It only made her want to prove to him that he could trust her with his face someday. She had been timid about touching his skin last night, since he clearly wanted to hide his scars. She also hesitated out of fear of what she might encounter. But her hands had touched a smooth, rippled scar on his back that she knew was owed to a severe burn. It rekindled sympathy for what he must have suffered, especially if his whole body had been likewise damaged.

"Come with me, my love," he urged, his voice gentle.

He slid an arm around her back and led her upstairs where he simply held her. With his warm, strong body against her, encircling her, she leaned into him, thoughts of last night's beauty returning; his tenderness, his patience, his reassurances, his careful yet passionate loving. She had never dreamed the depth of emotional and spiritual intimacy that could result from such a union.

How wrong she had been about him. Simply because she had imagined a monster behind his mask and cloak, she had feared him. Unnecessarily. His face might be unsightly, but the soul trapped inside the scarred body was beautiful. She wished she'd seen it sooner. What a selfish fool she'd been to have withheld her love from this dear man who so desperately needed love!

As he placed a glass of water into her hand and rang for Monique to help her dress, all the while whispering reassurances, she realized that she loved him, and had for weeks. No man had ever touched the tender place inside her heart he had found. No man possessed his patience, his gentleness, his poetic soul. She opened her mouth to tell him, but Monique came in with fruit, buttered bread, and hot chocolate.

"Most distressing, *madame*. Fear not, your cousin will be well. Here, I've laid out your morning gown and now I shall draw a bath." She paused, glancing at Nicholas and then at Alicia while a knowing smile began to form. "Shall I return later, *madame*?"

"No, Monique, see to her now." Nicholas squeezed Alicia's arm reassuringly. "I'll let you know as soon as the doctor informs me of his condition." He brushed that familiar, masked kiss to her temple and Alicia had to resist the desire to tear the cloth away from his face. Even covered, his kiss seemed more intimate this morning than it had ever before. As he turned to go, she clung to his hand, halting him.

He turned back to her and brought her hand to his lips, but they were separated from her skin by the cloth of his mask. How she longed to see the tender expression she knew must be there. With another brief squeeze, he withdrew his hand and left the room.

Despite her concern over Robert, she found her thoughts dwelling on Nicholas and the new feeling of wholeness that infused her soul.

Monique smiled at her. "Lord Amesbury is a good man, *madame*, despite his intimidating appearance. I know it isn't my place to say, but I rejoice that you have found happiness with him."

Realizing that she had been smiling and humming as she bathed, Alicia felt a blush creep clear down to her toes. "It is that obvious?"

Monique poured lavender water over her hair, carefully washing and rinsing it. "A woman who has been loved well glows, *madame*."

Alicia sighed and stood up to accept the towel. "I

regret that I feared him for so long."

"It takes a heart to see what the eyes cannot."

Alicia silently mulled that over. "It takes a heart to see what the eyes cannot," she repeated slowly. "You are a very wise woman despite your age, Monique."

The maid smiled serenely while she dressed Alicia and worked on her hair. Alicia indulged in sweet memories of a husband with gentle hands and a whole body.

Mrs. Dobbs came in. "The doctor has completed his examination and is leaving."

Alicia rose unsteadily. "How bad is it?"

The housekeeper shook her head. "I have not been advised of his condition."

Alicia forced herself to remain composed as she descended the stairs. She arrived in time to see Nicholas bid the doctor good bye. "Nicholas?"

He turned to her. "He's awake. You can see him as soon as the servants have moved him up to his room."

After much fussing, they got Robert settled comfortably in his bed and then Alicia was allowed to go in. Robert sat propped against the pillows on the sofa.

At Alicia's entrance, he grinned, despite his pallor. He looked like he'd been brawling. "Stop fretting, Lissie, I'm all right. Try and convince your stubborn husband that I can get out of bed now. He's worse than a nursemaid."

"Hush, you fool, you've had a bad fall."

"Hah! I didn't fall, I was pushed."

"What?" Truly alarmed, Alicia sat on the bed beside him and took his hand.

"I know I was. I was going downstairs. I thought I saw a shadow but it was pretty dark—"

"—and you were inebriated—"

"—and I felt a push on my back and the next

thing I knew, I was falling." He scowled. "I wasn't *that* foxed."

"Are you sure you didn't just miss your step?"

"I've been up and down these stairs hundreds of times. I have never fallen down them before. And after I landed on the floor at the bottom of the stairs, I saw someone coming down after me."

"Perhaps it was one of the servants."

"No, but a servant scared him away before he got near enough to finish me off. Before I passed out, I heard a voice muttering something about breaking my neck if the fall didn't do it."

Chills ran down her spine.

"And it would have if you hadn't been so drunk," Nicholas added as he thumped in. "The doctor said your body was relaxed enough to take the fall. Sober, it probably would have killed you."

"I never thought I'd say that I am glad you'd been drinking." Alicia tightened her grip on her cousin's hand.

He looked at her through a blackened eye. "Armand always said I had a thick head."

Alicia fought a sudden wave of dread as tears sprang to her eyes. "I can't lose you, too, Robbie. You and Hannah are all I have left."

Robert pulled her into a rough embrace. "I'm sorry, Lissie. I have let you down in many ways."

Dobbs came in with a tray, tutting and clucking as she settled the tray on Robert's lap. She returned a moment later with a tray for Alicia. "I thought you'd like to take your meal with him, my lady."

"Thank you, that was thoughtful." She had eaten breakfast so half-heartedly that she now ate with a ravenous appetite.

"May I bring you a tray too, my lord, or would you prefer to eat in your room as usual?"

"My room, if you please," Nicholas replied. An odd quality to his voice raised Alicia's eyes but he arose without further comment. There seemed to be an uncharacteristic heaviness to his step as he left the room and thumped down the hall.

"He's a good man, Lissie. He treats you well."

"Yes. Much more than I imagined." She hoped he didn't notice the slow blush that developed at the memory of how well Nicholas had treated her last night. "Has he told you we suspect someone is trying to kill everyone in our family?"

Robert stilled, considered. "No, but I can see how you drew that conclusion."

Alicia related all that she knew about the deaths of her family and her suspicions.

Robert dragged his fingers through his hair. "That explains it rather well."

"Nicholas said he'd hire more help to stand guard. He's developing a plan."

"Alicia, I want you to go home with your husband."

"No. I am not leaving you here alone."

"I won't risk you being hurt in this madman's attempt to kill me."

"He wants both of us dead." She thought of Hannah, lying so ill in the next room. "Probably all of us.

"He could have killed you when the carriage overturned. You aren't a target."

"I was hurt badly enough that he might have mistaken me for dead. We are safer if we stay together. Besides, some highwaymen tried to stop us but they didn't want anything except me. And remember the adder bite? Then there was fire in my room only weeks ago."

Robert began to swear and then caught himself as Alicia frowned at him. "Devil take it, Lissie, you might be killed."

"Then let's all leave. Perhaps we will be safer far from here. London. Or France. Nicholas said he'd take me in the spring. Maybe we could go now. Surely the killer won't follow us there."

Robert silently considered her words. "Let's forget for a moment that I hate the idea of running away like a frightened child. Running will only prolong it. We need to stay here, somehow draw him out, and end this."

Dread filled Alicia's heart. "Do not offer yourself as bait for a trap."

"I'll speak with your husband and we'll come up with something. You trust him, don't you?"

Alicia was surprised that she could answer without any hesitation or reservation. "Yes. I do trust him. Completely."

"Then trust us. We'll come through this, all of us. Alive." He leaned back wearily and closed his swollen eyes.

Alicia rose. "I'll let you rest."

"I wish Amesbury were still here," Robert said quietly. "He's the best shot I've ever seen. We'd be safer with him and his guns here with us."

Alicia frowned. Her very new, very tender feelings for her husband might not flow as freely if Cole were here clouding her judgment.

"My lady, you have visitors," said a footman from the doorway. "They are waiting for you in the parlor."

"Thank you." Alicia left Robert to rest.

She looked in on Hannah who lay propped on her pillows, gray and listless. "Has the doctor been in to check on you?"

Hannah nodded. "He gave me an elixir."

Concern grew into alarm, but there appeared to be nothing she could do for her sister. She remembered her visitors, and closed the door quietly. Hoping at least one of her visitors was Elizabeth, who might have somehow learned she was here, Alicia hurried to the parlor. Before she reached it, she heard Catherine's unmistakable, throaty laugh mingled with a man's voice that sounded familiar, but Alicia could not identify it. Steeling herself against the inevitable, Alicia put on what she hoped was a gracious smile and entered the parlor.

Catherine Sinclair, in all her glory, sat upon the new parlor sofa next to Captain Hawthorne.

"Captain Hawthorne, Miss Sinclair, what a pleasant surprise."

Catherine's gaze flicked over Alicia's gown, probably noting every wrinkle despite the elegant cut and fabric.

Captain Hawthorne rose and bowed over her hand. "I hope we haven't called at a bad time, Lady Amesbury."

"Not at all, Captain Hawthorne. We did have some excitement this morning, though. My cousin Robert took a bad fall down the stairs."

"Good gracious!" Catherine sounded truly concerned.

"Oh? Nothing broken, I hope?" asked Captain Hawthorne.

"No."

Catherine fanned herself dramatically. "Thank the powers that be."

They struggled through a few minutes of awkward and insincere conversation, Alicia wondering why they had come at all. She searched for a subject of interest. Fortunately, Catherine filled in the silence.

"And how is dear Hannah?"

Alicia cringed at the false tone of her voice. "She's taken ill, I'm afraid."

Catherine clucked. "Poor dear. She's rather frail, isn't she?"

"She is delicate."

"Have you heard Captain Hawthorne is about to

receive another promotion? He's so brave. And he has such a great head for business that he's tripled the family fortune with his investments. Isn't that right?"

"Something like that." Captain Hawthorn's dark eyes remained unreadable.

Alicia had never been so tempted in her life to snort like Cole's Aunt Olivia. Catherine probably wasn't even interested in Captain Hawthorne until she discovered he had money, the little fortune hunter! Where he had gotten it, she couldn't imagine. Soldiers did not make a great deal of money, unless they plundered spoils of war. Although, he did come from a respectable family.

In any case, Catherine did not deserve him. Captain Hawthorne had always been a polite, attractive man, and had much to offer anyone with the sense to see it, although his serious dark eyes tended to change into brooding.

An image of a laughing Cole came into her mind, a direct contrast to Captain Hawthorne. Cole was a confirmed flirt, but he made her laugh, something she hadn't done much until she met him. Guiltily, she redirected her thoughts. She was married to a good man and she had just realized today that she loved him. Thoughts of Cole would only confuse her.

Alicia drew a breath. "Elizabeth Hancock told me in her last letter that your father passed on several weeks ago, Captain Hawthorne. Please allow me to offer my condolences."

"Thank you, Lady Amesbury."

"With losing first your mother and then your father, you have suffered many losses over the last few years," she added.

His dark eyes held hers. "As have you."

Alicia nodded silently.

"You look surprisingly well, I must say," Catherine said to Alicia. "I'd thought you'd be gaunt and sickly after months of marriage to a monster."

Anger rose up and nearly choked her. "My husband is no monster. And I'll thank you to cease making disparaging remarks about him."

Taken aback, Catherine blinked. "Well." She glanced at Captain Hawthorne. "Well. It takes all kinds, I suppose."

Captain Hawthorne arose, his dark eyes enegmatic. "Lady Amesbury, you have been very gracious. I hope to see you again."

Alicia saw them out, wishing Elizabeth had come instead. Perhaps she should go and pay her a call. She wondered if Nicholas would want to accompany her. She went upstairs and found him inside his room, standing by a window, leaning on his cane.

At her approach, he turned. He stood stiffly, as if angry or upset. Was he annoyed at her intrusion?

"Am I disturbing you?" she asked hesitantly.

"Not at all. Come in." He sounded tired. He indicated a nearby chair and waited until she sat before he took a seat opposite her.

"I'd like to pay a visit to Elizabeth Hancock. She has been my dearest friend for many years and I'd love for you to become acquainted with her."

He was silent for so long, she began to doubt the wisdom of extending the invitation. She slipped back into formal speech, not wishing to displease him and break the newly formed bond between them. "My lord?"

Still he remained silent. Alicia twisted her hands in her lap. The clock on the mantle ticked noisily in the quiet room.

"So I am 'My lord' now again and not Nicholas?"

When her fingers began to hurt, she unclenched them and consciously smoothed her skirt. "I didn't mean that."

"You regret our union last night."

Aghast, she stared at his faceless head. "No."

Before she could elaborate, he hurried on tersely. "I do not wish to frighten your friend with my horrible appearance. Go."

She nodded, fighting disappointment. This was the man who had no comment when she spent so much time with his cousin, and who even encouraged her to do so. He'd become distant again, despite the beauty of last night.

"But take at least three servants with you," he cautioned. "I will make sure they are armed. I do not want our killer to strike while you are helpless. Or better yet, perhaps I will accompany you as part of your guard."

She stilled. "Why?"

"Because I am not a complete invalid. I can still shoot a gun!" Uncharacteristic anger laced his words.

Confusion and hurt swirled around her heart. "I know you aren't an invalid. Why are you angry? What did I do?"

He let out his breath and turned his masked face away. "I am not angry at you, Alicia. I see things that aren't there and then I'm foolishly surprised when I do not find them."

She blinked. "I do not understand."

He leaned forward and put his arms on his thighs, his head bowed. "You don't consider me a part of your life. I was foolish to believe that, even after last night, you would actually have feelings for me."

"But I do. That's why I wanted you to come with me to call upon Elizabeth."

"But I'm not a part of your life. Not really."

She started to reach for him, but stopped. "Of course you are."

"Then why did you tell Robert that he and Hannah are all you have?"

Screams and shouting came from the corridors, interrupting their exchange. "The East Wing is on fire!"

Alicia jumped to her feet and ran out to the hall, Nicholas right behind her. On the way, she found Monique.

"Monique, please go sit with Hannah. She'll be frightened."

The maid's eyes were wide with fear. "*Mais oui.*" She disappeared into Hannah's room.

The faint, but unmistakable smell of smoke assailed Alicia's nose as she ran to join the servants forming a bucket brigade. Alicia passed more buckets than she could count as the servants battled the fire. It hadn't spread to the main house yet.

"What are you doing out of bed?" she snapped at Robert who stood further up in line.

"Saving my house!" he shouted back.

"Daft fool," she muttered.

Nicholas stood in line as well, barking orders like an admiral and passing buckets with the dexterity of a whole man. He may be scarred, but was certainly no invalid.

Alicia's back ached and her arms throbbed, but still she passed an endless row of buckets. The acrid smell of smoke stung her eyes and made her cough. The efforts of the group prevented the fire from spreading, but it seemed they worked for hours before they extinguished the blaze.

"That's done it!" Someone called.

Alicia set down her bucket and pressed her hands to the small of her back. The brigade dissolved, some milling around as if unable to determine what to do next. Others drew to the house to view the destruction. Great plumes of black smoke billowed high in the sky as the sunset spread its golden glow over the land.

Weary and aching, Alicia followed her husband

and cousin to survey the damage. Ash and charred timber lay in confusing rubble. Fortunately, the structural integrity of the house had only been destroyed on the far end of the wing.

"Seal off the wing until repairs can be completed." Robert voice betrayed his emotion.

Alicia picked her way on the muddy ground among the smoking wreckage, amazed at the loss she felt. A nearby tree she and Armand had climbed as children now stood charred and lifeless. She didn't even have that to remind her of her twin now.

A blackened corner of a gilded picture frame that once framed a portrait of an ancestor stuck out of the rubble. She picked it up but it was hot and she dropped it. It crumbled into dust when it hit the ground. Others like it that had once lined the hallway of the wing could not be found; probably buried in the rubble, a lost link to her family. She had lived here all her life. And now so much was gone.

Robert moved past, looking as bereft as she felt. One eye in his battered face had swollen nearly shut, and he was smudged with soot, but the grief in his face brought tears to her eyes. Alicia wished she had something to offer as consolation.

She wandered down what was left of the smoke-darkened hallway. The closer she drew to the main house, the less damage she saw. Alicia went into *Maman*'s room. Everything would need to be washed to remove the soot and ash, but most of it could be saved. The satinwood vanity stood in its usual place. Alicia remembered watching *Maman* as she prepared for a ball or a dinner party, a smile of anticipation on her gentle, lovely face while her maid arranged her glorious blond hair.

Alicia ran a hand over the wood, dusting off the ash. She pulled open a drawer and found several letters bound by a ribbon. Further back lay a small book. *Maman's* journal. Alicia had known of the existence of both of the letters and the journal, and had attempted to read them after *Maman's* death, but doing so only aggravated her pain. Perhaps now they'd be of comfort.

"The loss isn't catastrophic," Nicholas said from the doorway.

"No."

The servants made exclamations of horror now that the danger had passed as they worked to seal off the gaping hole from the elements.

"What is that you are holding?" Nicholas asked.

"My mother's journal and some letters."

He said nothing. Looking up at him, she wondered if she'd ever really know this enigmatic man. She touched his arm briefly as she passed him and went into her room. Refreshed from her bath and a change of clothing, Alicia went to check on Hannah.

Monique sat by her bed. She arose silently at Alicia's entrance and motioned her out the door. In the hall, they conferred in whispers.

"She grows worse, *madame*. Her breathing is not good. I think we should call the doctor again."

Alarmed, Alicia went inside and tiptoed to the bed. Hannah had turned a deathly gray. Her chest indented as she drew in a rattling breath as if it required great effort.

Alicia immediately sent for a doctor. Then, when she couldn't find Nicholas, she went in search of him. One of the servants said they thought they'd seen him near the burned wing. She steeled herself against the sight of such stark destruction, and the loss it would undoubtedly kindle, and made herself return there. Heavy, oiled cloth had been nailed over the charred opening, flapping ominously in the darkness.

Nicholas appeared behind her. She looked back

and felt her expression soften. Strange how his appearance no longer frightened her, but had the opposite effect now. He pulled her toward him slowly, as if giving her time to escape if she wished. When she went to him willingly, he folded her into him. She wrapped her arms around him, leaning against his chest.

"I'm afraid for Hannah," Alicia said. "I've never seen her so ill."

"Did you send for the doctor?"

"Yes."

They waited, unwilling to move from each other's arms, and stared at the destruction.

"It can be rebuilt, Alicia."

"I know. But it seems so ..."

"As if a part of you has been lost."

She nodded.

"We're very fortunate no one was hurt."

She nodded again and snuggled against his chest. His arms tightened around her and he rested his chin on top of her head.

"One of the maids went into a guest room to clean at the far end of the wing, and found the fire. It had already spread through two rooms. If she hadn't discovered it, the fire would have reached the main part of the house tonight after everyone was abed."

She lifted her head. "Someone started it."

"In light of everything else that has happened, we would be foolish to assume otherwise." Footsteps crunched outside and Nicholas tensed. "Who's there?"

"Collins, sir."

Nicholas relaxed. "All is well?"

"Yes, my lord."

"Robert set up a guard to patrol the grounds," he told Alicia. "Collins, Smith and Barnett are keeping guard tonight. My valet, Jeffries, volunteered but he's a lousy shot." His head tilted down toward, tenderness softening his voice. "I will keep you safe, my love, do not fear."

"I don't deserve you. I have hurt you many times, Nicholas, and I am so sorry. I do care for you." It suddenly became difficult to use the word love. After all, he hadn't said it to her. Would he mock her?

No. Nothing about her husband was spiteful or mocking.

She looked at him unflinchingly, longing to see his expression, his eyes. "Nicholas. I don't know if you return the sentiment, and given my behavior most of our marriage, I certainly don't deserve it, but I want you to know that I love you."

He expelled his breath and his words came out strangled. "I can't tell you how I've longed to hear those words. I believed I would remain unloved all the rest of my life."

She tightened he arms around him, and burrowed into his chest, still amazed at how natural, how right, he felt. As if she'd always been meant to be there.

He held her, breathing raggedly. When he spoke again, emotion laced his voice. "I love you, Alicia. I loved you the moment I saw you."

Warmth and peace flowed through her and she closed her eyes, reveling in the knowledge that he loved her, and in the feeling of his arms around her. If only they didn't continue to have that barrier between them. She lifted her head. "Will you ever trust me enough to take off that mask?"

He hesitated, his body tensing. He let his breath out slowly. "I don't think either of us are ready for that."

She laid her head against his shoulder again. "I shall look at you with my heart and see the man underneath your scars. When you're ready. You gave me time. I shall give you the same. Perhaps, someday, when you trust me enough, you will."

His arms tightened, but he made no reply. "Come. Let's go back where it's warm and wait for the doctor."

In the parlor in front of a roaring fire, Alicia sat and opened the letters. Words of love, not eloquent, but full of sincerity, flowed from the pages as she read the missives written between her parents when their love was new. Others had been written when they were apart as her father made trips to London for business, still loving, still tender, now more confident.

Smiling, Alicia picked up the diary. *Maman's* neat, elegant writing painted pictures in her mind. This volume began with meeting a handsome young man. Cautious, philosophical, with dark serious eyes, he stole her heart the first evening they danced together. Over the course of a year, they courted, and wrote letters, until he finally asked her father for her hand.

Alicia read of their happy years together, her deep sorrow at burying a baby only a few months old. The next several entries were filled with despair. Then she recorded her joy at learning she was increasing again. Later she recorded giving birth to twins.

A passage recorded her discovery that before their marriage, he had kept a mistress who had borne a son, but that he had given her up when he decided to marry.

"I should not feel such dismay at this discovery. After all, keeping a mistress before marrying is not terribly uncommon. Many men keep their mistresses even after marriage. He has sworn that he has not even looked at another woman since he fell in love with me, but I can't help but fear he compares me to her, or wishes he were still with her. I question if his

heart is true."

How well she understood those fears! She'd had them many times regarding Cole. A few pages later, she wrote; "*Through my sorrow, I cannot help but wonder about the woman who claimed him for so long. Was she devastated when he told her he must give her up? What of his son?*"

Later, Alicia read an entry expressing her joy at expecting another baby.

Robert staggered in carrying a bottle and slouched into a chair.

Alicia frowned at him. "Robert. If you ever loved me, stop drinking."

He stared at her blearily. "I just buried my father. My best friend is dead. Someone is trying to kill me. It will probably take whatever is left of my money to repair the damage to the house that is all I have of an inheritance. I am a reputed lout and no lady would ever consider an alliance with me. Tell me why I should have to face this sober."

"Because I need you. And Hannah needs you."

Startled, he gaped at her. With deliberate movements, he got up and set the bottle on a sideboard table. "Forgive me, Lissie. I have been very selfish." He leaned down and kissed her cheek and then threw himself back into his chair to stare moodily into the fire and drag his fingers through his hair.

Alicia stared at him in astonishment, and wondered if he were in earnest. He had never acted thusly before. Robert made no further move to drink, only remained silently brooding. She puzzled over his behavior a moment and then returned to her mother's journal.

The next entries were of trivial things, but then in a shaking hand, *Maman* told of a miscarriage. Alicia remembered her mother's heartbreak at losing her unborn child, but reading about her anguish brought tears to Alicia's eyes. Much later, *Maman* recorded; *"After searching my soul, I realized that my beloved husband's actions long ago does not affect us now. He is a good man, and the qualities I admired in him when I fell in love with him still exist. His love is true, and always has been. I have learned to forgive his past."*

Alicia raised her eyes to her mother's portrait. How she wished she could have spoken to *Maman* whose guiding influence might have helped her find forgiveness for Cole sooner. She would not have—

No. She was happy with her husband. He was a good man and she loved him. With any luck, she'd never see Cole again.

The doctor arrived then and Alicia showed him to Hannah's room. When he reappeared, he looked apologetic. "I've done everything I can. I'll return in two days to check on her."

With heavy heart, Alicia nodded. The smell of the sickroom only reminded Alicia of Armand's illness that set in after he'd been shot. Alicia swallowed her rising fear. Hannah could not even open her eyes but her fingers curled around Alicia's. She stayed next to Hannah's bed until far into the night. Alicia's head shot up in alarm when the door opened.

Nicholas and Monique came in. "Come rest, my love. Monique will stay with her."

"I will watch over her, *madame*, never fear," Monique said.

Alicia argued, reluctant to leave Hannah's side, but they insisted. At her door, Nicholas took her into his arms. She turned to him, seeking solace. He scooped her up, carried her to bed and loved her sweetly and with all the passion of a whole man.

In the quiet moments, she snuggled up to him, listened to his heart beat and inhaled his masculine scent, amazed by the power of that union, and by the tenderness she felt for her husband.

"I love you, Alicia." His whisper caressed her.

"I love you, Nicholas."

Content, and at peace, she drifted off to sleep cradled in his arms.

But it was of Cole she dreamed.

CHAPTER 28

Cole shifted positions to relieve cramping muscles. He did not dare pace about. If the killer watched the house, movement might alert him to the trap. Cole should have taken his post inside the house sooner and not let any distraction keep him from protecting Alicia, Hannah, and Robert. Once he eliminated the threat, he planned to pursue leisure and pleasure to his heart's content, but now was not the time.

With Nicholas's grand arrival, and Cole making a show of leaving, the killer would believe them defenseless. A crippled man who could not sit a horse and few servants would not be enough to dissuade him from striking again.

That the killer would strike again soon, Cole had no doubt. He cursed himself for his carelessness. Within the week, the killer had gotten inside the house, pushed Robert down the stairs and later started a fire. Bold. Hopefully, carelessness would follow.

But who would be his next target?

Cole glanced toward the door where his brother, Grant, sat, alert and ready. Grant had arrived quietly after sunset. He had a suspect, but no concrete proof. Grant sat utterly still.

Cole peered into the next room where his valet, Stephens, kept a quiet vigil. The darkness prevented him from seeing the other man, but he knew Stephens would be attentive. The coachman kept watch from the far end of the house by the wing that had been burned. Every two hours, they whistled to each other and to those keeping watch outside to ensure each remained safe.

The sound of a door creaking upstairs sent Cole to his feet. Tensed, he stood motionless, listening, waiting. It might be someone getting up to use the necessary. Alicia's room remained out of view, but he wanted more than anything to be inside it with her now instead of waiting in a cold room with a gun in his hand.

A door closed softly. All Cole's senses strained. Grant arose silently, his gun at the ready.

A muffled scream spurred them both to a run.

Cole raced up the stairs, taking two or three at a time, with Grant only a pace behind him. Stephens's footfalls trailed Grant. When they reached the hall, they paused to listen. The sounds of a scuffle came from Alicia's bedroom. With cold fear turning his blood to ice, Cole dashed to her room, his pistol primed and ready. Inside the doorway, he crouched down and scanned the darkened area. He crept forward with Grant and Stephens flanking him. Heavy breathing and a soft whimper nearby drew his eye. Two shadows lay on the bed; one prone, the other straddling.

A feminine voice let out a strangled cry.

The thought of what the killer might be doing to Alicia flooded him with terror. And rage.

Cole launched his body at the upright figure, knocking him off the bed. They both landed heavily on the floor. The killer let out a grunt of surprise. Alicia gasped and began coughing. Cole landed a punch on what felt like a jaw. A sickening crunch rewarded his efforts. He began swinging his fists, using his ears more than his eyes to guide him. The other man fought back with surprising strength. Someone lit a taper and Cole blinked in the sudden light at the man crouched in front of him.

"Hawthorne." So Grant had been right.

An ugly smile darkened Captain Hawthorne's bloodied face. "Amesbury. You are supposed to have gone home."

"Sorry to disappoint you, old boy," Cole shot back.

Hawthorne threw a fist. Cole dodged it, then lunged. His hours spent at fisticuffs had not been for naught. Fueled by anger, he pounded Hawthorne until he collapsed, senseless, his face a hardly discernable mass.

Alicia's coughing turned into weeping. She lay curled up in a ball.

"Alicia?" He moved to her.

At the sound of his voice, she lifted her head and said hoarsely, "C-Cole? You're here?"

He pulled her into his arms and began rocking her. "Alicia, my love, did he hurt you?"

Crying so hard that she could not speak, she only burrowed into his chest while his alarm spiraled. He held her while fury and helplessness battled for power.

"Alicia, what happened? Did he—? Did he—?" He could not bring himself to say the word.

"He was choking me," she sobbed, her voice raspy. "Couldn't breathe. Thought he would crush my throat."

"Then he didn't...force himself on you?"

"No."

Cole nearly wept in relief. But the monster would pay for trying to strangle her.

From behind him, Grant's voice thundered, "Look out!"

Cole flung Alicia down onto the bed with his body as two simultaneous gunshots roared through the night. Searing pain exploded in his back. It transported him to Trafalgar, to the middle of a sea battle. He sank into utter darkness.

****

Alicia watched in mute horror as Cole stiffened, his face twisted in pain, and then collapsed on her. A male's voice moaned, drawing her gaze away from Cole. Captain Hawthorne, badly battered, dropped the smoking handgun he'd been pointing in her direction, and crumpled into a heap.

A man Alicia had never seen stood by the door holding a gun aimed at Hawthorne. A tendril of smoke curled out of the barrel of his pistol. The stranger lowered his arm and tucked away his gun. Behind the stranger, Stephens stared with ashen face.

For a brief moment, stunned silence fell over the room. Then it erupted into sound and movement. Cole lay motionless.

"Please, no," Alicia gasped.

The stranger sprang forward and bent over Cole. "He's still breathing."

She touched Cole to assure herself he did indeed still live. He breathed. He had a pulse. But the color drained out of his face. On his back, a spreading red stain soaked his clothing.

From somewhere in the crowd, she heard Robert and another voice she didn't recognize calling out commands. Alicia cradled Cole's head in her hands and carefully pulled her legs out from under his limp body. She snatched a pillow and slid it under his head. Voices became a jumbled cacophony, creating a buzz that made thinking difficult.

"Everyone out! Now!" Her voice sounded strangled to her own ears.

Men picked up Hawthorne's unconscious—or was he dead?—body and removed it. Robert ordered Hawthorne placed in the bedroom down the hall. Other male voices reverberated outside the door, but she returned her attention to Cole on the bed.

"Don't you die. Don't you dare die." With

shaking fingers, she ran her hands over his hair. "Cole!"

He did not respond. Kneeling beside him, she tried to roll him on his side so she could reach the buttons of his waistcoat. He was a large man, and completely limp, moving him proved a greater challenge than she had supposed.

"Here." Another pair of arms turned Cole.

She looked up into a pair of steely gray eyes set in hard, yet handsome features. A thin scar ran raggedly down the right side of his face from eye to lip. Black wavy hair, longer than fashionable, framed his face. He was the man who shot Captain Hawthorne at the same instant that Captain Hawthorne had shot Cole. At the time, she'd assumed him to be someone who'd been helping guard the house, but he seemed too commanding to be merely hired help. He bore an imposing mien. He wore simple clothing in subdued colors, completely without adornment.

Alicia stared. "Who—?"

"I'm Grant Amesbury."

She saw the family resemblance to Cole immediately; they had an identical build and the same well formed mouth, but where Cole was masculinely beautiful, this man had harsher features, making him appear stern and unyielding. His silver-gray eyes were unnervingly hard. Whether the hardness arose from years of war, or his recent pastime dealing with criminals, she did not know. She only knew she never, ever wanted to cross this dangerous, determined man. If she'd had to guess, she would have assumed this was Jared, the pirate.

Grant's gaze passed over her briefly, his steely eyes grim before turning his attention to his brother lying still and pale in bed.

Stephens appeared. "My lady. He would trust

me over a doctor."

She nodded. Cole had said something like that the last time he had been wounded for her sake.

The three of them turned Cole and stripped off his stained waistcoat and shirt. In her concern, Alicia did not even flinch at his state of undress. The amount of blood gushing unimpeded from Cole's back left Alicia sick with worry.

Grant stepped back and waited silently at the foot of the bed while Stephens examined Cole. The bullet had gone in at an angle in his back from his waist up to his left shoulder and exited below his shoulder blade. Stephens pressed his lips into a white line, his face set and grim. Coles' blood continued to bubble out, soaking Alicia's nightgown and the bed. Stephens cleaned Cole's wounds and pressed a cloth over them. Grant remained perfectly detached, watching without the slightest sign of emotion.

"Press here firmly," Stephens instructed, placing her fingers over the lower wound.

He did likewise on the upper wound. He called for aid, and Jeffries arrived, looking ill at the amount of blood on the linens. Stephens gave specific instructions of a salve he needed, and exactly where to find it. Jeffries left unsteadily as though he might faint at any moment.

When Jeffries returned, Stephens applied the salve to the wounds. "Grandmother's special blend," he quipped in an attempt to appear optimistic.

They applied thick bandages using torn cloth. Grant wordlessly helped them lift Cole so the bandages could be wrapped and secured.

Terrible, ugly scars marred Cole's muscular back. Alicia recognized the new pink scar high on his arm from the highwaymen's attack when he protected her. Another above his other shoulder blade looked much older.

She reached out and traced the scar. "He was shot here, too?"

Stephens nodded soberly. "In the war."

She traced large scar on his side. "And this?"

"A pirate's cutlass."

Other scars were even more alarming. All along the left side of his back were white, wrinkled scars that looked as if his flesh had been melted.

"Was he burned too?"

"Fire on ships are a more common occurrence than people realize."

Alicia marveled that Cole had survived at all. She glanced at Grant to see if he would reveal a hint of any emotion. He didn't. He was handsome in a terrible, ruthless sort of way. He would have made a great model for a statue of the Greek god of war. Grant stood like a soldier at attention, looking as if he cared nothing at all about Cole's well being. How could anyone be so cold and unconcerned about his own brother?

Stephens pressed his lips pressed together. "I think he was trying to get himself killed to rid himself of his guilt. He got so reckless after the war."

"Guilt for what?" Her voice cracked. She cleared her voice and swallowed, but her throat pained her so badly, she wished she hadn't.

Grant broke his silence. "Living. Hundreds around him died. He lived."

Grant spoke sharply, accusingly, but the bleakness in his eyes revealed Grant Amesbury wasn't as unfeeling as she'd first supposed. He shared his brother's anguish, but hid it beneath an impenetrable armor.

When Stephens finished, he attempted a smile. "He'll be all right, my lady. He's survived much worse."

She nodded, hoping Cole's faith in his valet had been well-placed. "I pray you're right."

Alicia looked down and realized, belatedly, that she wore nothing but a nightgown and had been thusly immodest in the presence of several men. At the moment, it was so bloodstained that she probably looked more ghoulish than indecent. Then it occurred to her that she hadn't seen Nicholas since the attack.

"Have you seen my husband, Stephens?"

Stephens paused, his brow wrinkling slightly. "I haven't seen him, my lady. I was downstairs keeping watch."

Panic seized her. "What if Captain Hawthorne took him prisoner, or killed him before he came after me?"

"He went for the constable," Grant said.

Her fear quieted. "Oh. I didn't see him leave." She realized with a healthy dose of guilt, that she'd been so concerned over Cole, she'd given no thought for Nicholas.

Alicia rang for Mrs. Dobbs. When the housekeeper arrived, looking strained and upset, Alicia requested clean bed linens and the assistance of a footman. As Stephens gathered up his things and moved them to a bedside table, Mrs. Dobbs returned with the linens. Jeffries, trailed behind. Grant, Stephens and Jeffries lifted Cole while Alicia and Mrs. Dobbs pulled off the soiled bed linens and replaced them with clean ones.

When they had Cole resettled and lying on his stomach, Alicia said, "He'll be all right." She tried to sound assuring, but instead sounded forlorn.

Grant's face was an impenetrable fortress. Phillips looked frightened. Stephens nodded bravely, but his eyes betrayed his concern.

She drew a breath. "Is Captain Hawthorne dead?"

"No," Stephens replied, "but I doubt he'll live through the night."

"If he dies, it'll save me the trouble of dragging him to the nearest Magistrate. I'd like to plunge a knife in his heart to make sure," Grant said savagely.

Alicia shivered at the fierceness in his tone and the murderous look in his cold, gray eyes. It was a pity he hadn't acted an instant sooner than he did, thus saving Cole from Hawthorne's bullet. It occurred to her that Grant must be berating himself for the same thing.

She touched him lightly on the sleeve. "I'm sure you did all you could have."

Grant stiffened and pulled away. He turned to Stephens. "Notify me immediately if Hawthorne rallies. I want answers."

"Of course," Stephens replied.

Alicia wanted answers, too; why Hawthorne attacked her, and if he had indeed arranged the death of the rest of her family. If he died, she might never know. What possible motive he had, she could not imagine. They'd been acquaintances since childhood and she could not remember any sort of altercation.

She stilled. Her father's illegitimate son. Could he be Captain Hawthorne? There was no strong resemblance. Although they both had dark eyes that Alicia had mused bore a resemblance to her father's. But that still did not explain why he'd seek to destroy them. No illegitimate son could inherit, so that removed any motivation she could imagine.

Phillips and Stephens left the room. With a silent prayer, Alicia coaxed water between Cole's lips and brushed his hair back from his pallid face. His lashes lay close to his cheeks. Alicia despaired of ever seeing the deep sapphire of his eyes.

He must not die. He must not.

"I don't believe Hawthorne acted alone."

Alicia tore her eyes away from Cole and focused

on Grant. She'd forgotten he was there. He stood utterly still, his face immovable, his mouth pressed into a line. Only that brief flicker of pain in his eyes a moment ago hinted that he did possess some humanity. Deep, deep inside.

Grant continued speaking. "Hawthorne's had many accomplices, most of which he later killed to cover his trail. But there's someone within the house who's been aiding him."

She turned cold at the thought. "Any suspects?"

"Not yet. I'll question the servants."

She nodded numbly and turned back to Cole.

Grant left as silently as a wraith but she heard him conferring in whispers to someone in the hall.

Stephens returned. "I'll stay with him. You'd best look in on your sister. I think she's being slowly poisoned."

Alicia drew back in horror.

"I gave her some herbs that should help. Your abigail is with her now."

With a small cry of alarm, Alicia fled the room for Hannah's. Hannah, lying in her bed, opened her eyes at Alicia's arrival.

"How are you, dearest?" Alicia asked.

"Is it true? Mr. Hawthorne tried to kill you?"

Alicia nodded.

Tears formed in Hannah's eyes. "I almost lost you tonight."

Alicia stroked her hair. "I'm all right. He won't hurt any of us again."

"Why would Mr. Hawthorne want to hurt us? We've known him forever. I thought our families were friends."

"I'm not sure, dearest. But I hope he'll tell us. And who his accomplice is."

Monique spoke from the corner. "He has an accomplice, *madame*?"

"Cole Amesbury's brother, Grant, thinks so. It

makes sense. Captain Hawthorne couldn't have slipped into the house often enough to administer poison. It could be anyone. Monique, don't let anyone near her. And don't give her anything to eat or drink that the others don't consume. This may not be over."

Monique nodded, looking terrified.

"I'm going to go check on Cole. I'll return shortly."

"*Madame*, take a moment to change," Monique advised.

Surprised, Alicia looked down. Only then did she remember that she wore only a badly bloodied nightgown. "My clothes are in the room where Cole is."

"Take something of mine," Hannah said.

With Monique's help, Alicia undressed and took a quick sponge bath to remove the blood that had soaked through her nightgown. Monique made an exclamation when she saw Alicia's neck. Alicia turned to the glass.

Ugly, black and purple bruises ringed her throat. The horror of the night's events washed over her anew. She relived her paralyzing terror, the feel of his fingers around her throat, squeezing. Silent sobs shook her body and she pressed her hand over her mouth.

"Lissie?" Hannah called weakly from the bed.

Alicia pulled herself together. "I'm all right." She dried her eyes and drank some water, wincing in pain with the effort of swallowing with a battered throat.

She returned to her bathing. After donning one of Hannah's gowns, she added a spencer with a high neck to help cover the bruising. She had to arrange the neckline carefully, cautious of her sore and swollen throat. Monique quickly brushed her hair and twisted it into a simple knot.

Refreshed, Alicia leaned over Hannah.

Hannah opened her eyes. Tears slid silently down her cheeks. "I can't get over the thought that he tried to kill you."

"All is well, now. You just get better." Alicia kissed her brow and went back to Cole's room.

She halted in the doorway. In a chair drawn up to the bed, Grant sat hunched over, bracing his arms on his thighs, and talking softly to an unconscious Cole. Alicia paused, unwilling to disturb him.

"—and I know we seldom saw eye to eye. You and Jared were always inseparable. But deuce take, it Cole, you're the heir. Think of the family line. Father won't be around much longer and the rest of us are too disreputable to marry and have children. Except Christian. He's probably too pure to think of touching a woman." His head sunk lower and his voice dropped to a whisper. "First Jason, then Mama, then Tanner." He let out a weighted sigh. "I can't lose you too, Cole. I couldn't bear it."

Tears slid down Alicia's cheeks. She moved to Grant, longing to comfort Cole's hurting brother.

He straightened at her approach. As if donning a mask, his expression turned impassive, with no trace of the grief-stricken brother a moment ago.

She knelt at his feet and touched his arm. "He'll be all right."

Stone-faced, he stood and spoke gruffly. "I'll finish questioning the servants." He strode from the room.

Cole's moaning brought Alicia to his side. She touched his cheek. As she'd feared, he had developed a fever. She bathed his face with cold water and pressed a cup to his lips.

Monique brought her a tray of food. "How is he, *madame*?"

"Feverish. Who's with Hannah?"

"Robert, *madame*."

"Find Stephens for me."

"I'm here, my lady," the Romany valet replied from the door. "I knew he'd develop a fever. We must bathe him in cool water."

Using cold water and soft cloths, Stephens helped her bathe Cole's quivering flesh. When they had cooled his skin, Stephens nodded. "That's all we can do for now. I will care for him, my lady. Go rest."

"Is Lord Amesbury home, yet?"

"Yes, he arrived while you were with Hannah. I'm sure he'll come to you soon," Stephens assured her smoothly.

A knock sounded and Mrs. Dobbs came in, her eyes lined and shadowed. "How is he?"

Touched by the woman's apparent concern, Alicia shook her head. "No change."

"Captain Hawthorne is awake."

Alicia nodded and went to the room where Hawthorne lay. Stephens followed her in. Hawthorne's ashen face turned upon her, his dark eyes, so much like her father's, flicked to her. She shook her head at her own blindness. How had she missed the resemblance?

His eyes narrowed, glittering with hate, his malevolence palpable. She forced herself to not shrink away from him and instead looked back unflinchingly.

Stephens retrieved a gun from his belt and toyed with it. Grant entered, his grim presence filling the room. He withdrew his pistol and cocked it. What harm they thought a dying man could offer, Alicia couldn't guess. Stephens glowered at Hawthorne, no doubt wishing he could thrash the man for assaulting his master and friend. A third person entered. Alicia drew a breath of relief as Nicholas's familiar form approached, leaning more heavily than normal on his cane. He came to her at once, and briefly rested his hand on her shoulder. Robert came in and stood next to Nicholas.

Alicia fixed her gaze upon the man in the bed. The memory of Captain Hawthorne's hands at her throat made her shiver.

Grant stood over Hawthorne, his face grim and drawn. "Why?"

Hawthorne's mouth twisted into a cruel smile. "Would it be too blasé to say Revenge?"

Alicia sank into a chair near the bed. "What wrong have I done you? What has anyone in my family done to you?"

"Your father used my mother, sired me, and then cast us off like trash. All for a 'proper lady'. The man who later married her—John Hawthorne— never let her forget that he took her despite her fallen state and claimed her son as his. All my life, I thought my father hated me. That I disappointed him. All those beatings..." His voice faded, his face twisted in pain and hatred. "It was only upon my mother's deathbed a year and a half ago that I learned the truth; my real father had rejected us."

Alicia's heart felt leaden. "I didn't know until yesterday after the fire. I found my mother's journal. She never knew the name of my father's mistress or her son."

"Her name was Ruth Scarlett. She both loved and cursed your father until the day she died." Hawthorne coughed and blood seeped out of his mouth.

Alicia leaped up to help but he waved her away and wiped his lips with the back of his hand. Alicia sank back against the chair weakly, heaviness weighing upon her soul. "If we had only known..."

"What would you have done? Tried to form a relationship with your bastard half-brother? Protected us from the man who called himself my father? I think not." Another wave of coughing left him spent. His lips developed a bluish tint.

Robert leaned forward. "So her death prompted you to kill us all?"

He dipped his chin once, his breathing became labored.

Grant wasn't finished. "You paid someone to kill Mrs. Palmer, but she was only mildly injured. Then you hired Vivian Charleston to arrange for Armand to duel."

"Vivian was so easily persuaded."

"Did you poison Armand's opium?"

Hawthorne's eyes took on an unholy glint. "Of course. *After* I arranged for the dressings to be tainted so his arm would sicken and have to be amputated. I enjoyed watching him suffer through that."

Alicia wrapped her arms around herself. Captain Hawthorne, the handsome man with the serious dark eyes, her unknown half-brother, had destroyed Armand. All the time that she blamed Cole, hated Cole, he was an innocent pawn in this madman's deadly game.

"And the carriage?" Grant pressed.

"I had it sabotaged to fall apart and the coachman drugged so he would not be able to save them. And I personally walked among the wreckage and killed the survivors." Hawthorne's eyes turned to Alicia, filled with cold hatred. "I had thought you dead already. I should have made sure and broken your neck. Like I did your mother's when I found her still living."

Alicia pressed a hand over her mouth and squeezed her eyes closed. Hearing the depth of this man's hatred and his capacity for violence left her ill. How could he have coldly wrapped his hands around *Maman's* neck and taken her life? She remembered too clearly the feel of his hands around her throat, choking her until she had no breath.

Nicholas squeezed her shoulder. She drew a

shuddering breath and ordered herself to not fall apart.

Warming to the idea of horrifying them with his actions, Hawthorne continued. "Your father—my father—was supposed to have been the last to die. I wanted him to lose everything and everyone that he loved. I wanted him to suffer. He wasn't supposed to have been in that carriage. Hannah was." Another coughing fit brought up more blood and halted his confession.

Alicia nodded numbly. "Father had planned on taking care of some urgent business first and then joining us late that night at the inn where we planned to spend the night. At the last minute, he decided to go with us instead. Hannah had been too ill and remained behind."

"Did you tamper with Willard Palmer's investments when he inherited?" Grant demanded.

"I made sure all of them failed. It was so satisfying to watch you all suffer through debt and poverty. Then you married and saved them." He turned a poisonous glare upon Alicia.

"Then your adopted father died and you learned he'd changed his will and left you cut off. Didn't want any of his money to go to his wife's by-blow," Grant taunted.

Hawthorne's face twisted in anger and pain.

"So you decided to finish us all off in revenge," Robert said in disbelief. "Including my father."

"My dear," he sneered, "sweet half-sisters..." his voice trailed off. His breathing turned into wheezing.

"You put the snake in the garden where I always walked. And you had highwaymen attack me," Alicia accused.

"And I set your bed curtains on fire." Blood came out of both sides of his mouth. "I am only sorry I did not avenge her fully...." But Hawthorne lacked the strength to continue. He drew a rattling breath and then was still.

Alicia left the room and began to wander the halls, cold down to her soul. A moment later, she realized Grant and Nicholas strode on either side of her. She reached for Nicholas, finding strength in the touch of his large, gloved hand. She turned to Grant.

"You knew."

"I did. But I lacked concrete proof. That's why I came here. We needed to catch him."

"And now your brother—"

"Lies dying because I thought to trap the killer." His narrowed eyes, clenched jaw, and the flat tones in his voice betrayed his protected emotion.

"It was the only way to catch him, Grant, don't blame yourself." Nicholas's voice sounded oddly hollow, as if he shared the blame he sought to dissuade Grant of bearing.

When Robert joined them, he looked broken.

"Mr. Palmer, a word?" Grant had a way of making a polite request sound like a command.

Robert turned toward him bleakly. "Of course."

"Many of your staff are new, correct?" Grant began.

"Yes.

"Anyone from the Hawthorne household?"

"Yes. The stable master and..." Robert paled, "Mrs. Dobbs, the head housekeeper."

"Find her," Grant barked.

They scattered. With her heart in her throat, Alicia ran immediately to Hannah's room. Hannah blearily opened her eyes and Monique looked up from her sewing. The room appeared peaceful.

"Have you seen Mrs. Dobbs?" Alicia panted.

Monique blinked. "She looked in a moment ago."

A woman's scream sent a bolt of fear through her. She followed the sound to Cole's room.

She ran in through the open doorway to see

Grant grappling with Mrs. Dobbs. Cole lay unmoving on the bed, a pillow over his face. With a cry, Alicia leaped forward and threw the pillow away. Cole still breathed, shallow and uneven, but he was alive.

Nicholas picked up the pillow from where it landed on the floor at his feet, and turned toward Grant and Mrs. Dobbs. Grant subdued her and wrenched her hands behind her back. He clapped on her wrists a pair of small shackles. Once he had her restrained, Grant pushed her into a chair. He stood over her like an avenging angel, looking positively murderous.

"Why?" he snarled.

"My mistress should have had him. She loved him. And he loved her. But he married a simpering fool. And he cast off my dear mistress."

Alicia stared at her in horror.

"Did you push Robert down the stairs?" Grant demanded.

"After I realized he wouldn't drink himself to death."

"And you've been poisoning Hannah," Alicia said.

Mrs. Dobbs broke into sobs. "My poor, poor mistress. How I loved her."

Aghast, Alicia stared at her while the valets-turned-guards hauled her out. Cole began to thrash and moan as fever ravaged his body. Alicia went to his side, laid her head on the bed next to his shoulder and wept.

She wept for a woman who was discarded for another because of her caste. She wept for a battered child, a half-brother, who grew up in fear. She wept for the loss of her twin brother. For her parents. For Cole's grief and suffering.

And she wept for the futile realization that she loved Cole.

CHAPTER 29

Alicia began a sleepless vigil. Fearing to leave Cole's side, she remained with him throughout the day and all that night. When she wasn't bathing his shivering, feverish body, she tried to coax water, or Stephens' tea down Cole's throat. All the while, she talked to him softly, caressing his face, stroking his hair. He roused occasionally, but never stayed awake long.

Only when Nicholas gently but firmly ordered her to rest did she retire to an empty bedroom. Without undressing, she collapsed on the bed. After a few hours of dreamless sleep, she awoke. Outside, darkness still enshrouded the land. She immediately went to check on her sister.

Alicia touched her hand. "Hannah?"

Hannah opened her eyes and turned her hand over to squeeze Alicia's. "I'm all right, Lissie." She smiled and drifted into a healthy sleep, her breathing slow and even.

Alicia left Hannah's room for Cole's. She stopped short inside the room. Grant stood at the foot of the bed, his face grave. Next to him sat a man who might have been Cole's twin, but where Cole had always been immaculate, this man looked like he'd been through a battle. He wore black breeches and boots, and a green waistcoat, but no frockcoat. The top button of his shirt had been undone and his cravat hung in disarray. His dark hair, longer than Cole's, was tousled. A cloak had been hastily discarded on the chair.

"Have you notified the rest of the family?" the stranger asked Grant in a hushed voice.

Grant nodded. Then his eyes flicked to Alicia.

She came in all the way, eyeing the stranger who had turned at her arrival. The disheveled look-alike watched her with vibrant aquamarine eyes laced with concern.

She moistened dry lips. "Christian? Or Jared?"

He glanced at Grant and stood. "I'm Jared. I came as soon as I received Grant's message."

Jared. The pirate. His face, so like Cole's, was lined with worry, and the shadowed eyes revealed his sleepless nights. For a criminal, he seemed surprisingly humane. She'd expected a pirate to look harsher.

"You must be Alicia," Jared said with a gentle smile.

She nodded, astonished at the show of humanity in a pirate.

"I apologize if my arrival disturbed you," he added.

"Not at all," she stammered, unnerved by the resemblance.

Jared had Cole's athletic build and the same expertly chiseled features. Yet he appeared more rugged, as if his life aboard the sea had hardened him beyond his years.

Alicia nodded toward Cole. "How is he?"

Jared glanced at Stephens who stood in the shadows, his concern resurfacing.

Stephens shook his head. "The fever is worse. We must submerge him in a tepid bath and gradually add cold water. It'll bring the fever down better than wet cloths."

It sounded dreadful, but she had grown to trust Stephens. "I'll have the slipper tub brought in."

"I'll see to it." Jared scooped up his cloak and left. She heard him shouting orders.

"I must take my leave," Grant said. "The constable took Dobbs to the local Magistrate. I'll deal with Vivian Charleston in London." Grant paused. "Take care of my brother." It sounded more like an order than a request.

Alicia nodded, knowing his gruffness concealed a human heart. "Of course I will."

His forehead creased into a frown as he briefly regarded her. Muttering, he shook his head and left.

A moment later, Stephens also slipped out. Alone with Cole, she ran her fingers down his broad, strong back, now bandaged where the bullet had torn through him.

"I love you, Alicia," he murmured.

Heaven help her, she loved him too.

She leaned down and put her arms around him, inhaling his scent, feeling the roughness of his whiskers. She caressed his cheek and stroked his hair. Stretching out beside him on the bed, she closed her eyes and wrapped her arms around him, her body snuggled against him the way she had curled up by Nicholas those two magical nights.

Repulsed by her own traitorous heart, she leaped up. How could she love two men so deeply?

The bath arrived and she numbly rendered whatever aid she could. It took Jared, Stephens, and Jeffries to lift Cole from the bed and place him in the bath. When they added the water, he thrashed. With the men holding him down, they gradually added more chilled water. It took the strength of all the men to hold Cole down as he ranted and struggled.

Alicia wept and prayed.

From his anguished cries, Alicia knew he relived the war, the horror of the battles, the young men and boys who died all around him. He called out for Alicia, warning her, begging her forgiveness, confessing his love for her. He agonized over his role in Armand's death. He cried for a brother who had died as a child. And for his mother. He suffered through lost battles. Lost lives. Lost loved ones.

While Cole thrashed, water splashed over the edge and drenched everyone. By the time Cole's skin cooled, they were exhausted and soaked. By tacit agreement, no one spoke of Cole's delirium.

Jared's wet clothing stuck to his tall, muscular form so like Cole's. He met her gaze with a frank stare of his own, his eyes betraying his concern. His expression softened. "Go change into something dry. We'll get him out of his wet clothes."

Alicia nodded. She took a change of clothes with her and went into the room in which she'd slept but she had to ring for Monique to help her out of her gown and stays. After she changed, Alicia stood by the window. The sun shone and few puffy clouds graced the sky. Her eyes absently followed the garden pathways. Gloom settled over her. If Cole died, she didn't know what she'd do.

Monique moved about the room quietly, setting things in order, and then left her alone with her thoughts.

Nicholas came to her, leaning so heavily on the cane that Alicia wondered if his leg pained him more than normal.

She managed a tired smile. "I thought you were sleeping."

Nicholas shook his cowled head. "I can't sleep."

"Perhaps we should still send for a doctor."

"Trust me when I say Cole thinks they are all incompetent. He'd have my head if I let one near him." He sounded oddly hoarse.

Alicia went to Nicholas and wrapped her arms around his waist. He hesitated. Then his arms encircled her. She leaned against him, but he stood stiffly, his arms barely holding her.

She pulled away and looked up into the mask. "Are you fearful for Cole?"

Nicholas took his time answering. "We must prepare ourselves for the worst."

She pushed away. "No. He'll recover. You can't lose hope."

Stephens poked his head in through the open doorway. "My lady, I—" when he saw Nicholas, he frowned. His eyes darted between Alicia and Nicholas. "Forgive me for interrupting. I'm out of herbs. I must go to the apothecary. I will return as quickly as I am able."

Alicia nodded. "Of course."

Nicholas sank into the nearest chair. He hunched over and pressed his hands into his eye sockets. "What am I to do without him?"

Tears sprang to her eyes. She'd known her husband and Cole were close, but his stark loss tore at her heart.

And she shared the sentiment, for entirely different reasons.

"Sleep, Nicholas," she said. "I'll notify you of any new developments."

Nicholas nodded but made no move. She took him by the hand, pulled him to his feet, and guided him toward the bed. As he dropped across the bed, still fully clothed, she closed the door quietly and went back into Cole's room.

He lay so utterly still that a bolt of alarm shot through her. She put her hand on his back and felt it rise and fall as he breathed.

She sat back in relief. Fatigued, she curled up in the chair next to Cole and closed her eyes to rest them for a moment.

She woke to Cole thrashing. She sprang to his side and touched his face. His fever had returned. Outside, dusk gathered.

Nicholas entered. "How is he?"

"If Stephens is back, you'd better get him."

Nicholas came nearer, took off a glove and

touched Cole's forehead. He swore under his breath and strode from the room. In the hallway, he called for Stephens in a loud voice.

Odd. Nicholas had walked quickly, without even carrying his cane. And the timbre of his voice sounded different. He must be concerned, indeed.

Cole moaned.

She stroked his hair, leaned in and kissed his cheek, deeply inhaling his familiar scent. A scent so like Nicholas's.

How could that be? Unless....

Her focus moved to his back, to the terrible scars that marred its sculpted muscles on one side. With a barely conceived suspicion, she traced the burn scars that were every bit as severe as Nicholas's. She'd been shy about touching much of Nicholas's skin at night, partly out of fear of what she'd find, and partly out of respect for his privacy, since he clearly wanted to hide his deformities. She'd always assumed Nicholas had been burned all over his face and body, but since she'd never seen him without his mask or clothing, she did not know for sure. But she had touched his back.

Now, as she ran her hands along the rippled scars resembling melted flesh, she was sure. Cole's scars were exactly like Nicholas's.

The burns were the same.

Her heart gave a lurch. The men who bore them must be the same, as well.

Nicholas was Cole.

She leaped to her feet and curled her hands into fists. She wanted to weep, scream, rail against the world. She nearly laughed with relief that she no longer loved two men. She was tempted to slap him soundly for deceiving her.

How could she have not noticed sooner? They had the same masculine scent. They kissed with the same gentleness and passion. They'd both been burned in a fire while serving in the Navy. What other clues had she missed?

She almost smacked her own forehead. Nicholas Amesbury. Cole Amesbury.

But wait, that wasn't possible. She'd seen Cole and Nicholas side by side many times. A moment ago, for example, and many other times since Cole had been shot. In London, she saw them together in the park. Surely there were other times.

Alicia froze. A moment ago, Nicholas walked steadily without a cane and his voice sounded different. Earlier that day, he'd limped strangely and he'd held her differently. He was different.

With growing certainty, she knew that the man in the mask was not the man she'd grown to love. Someone else wore Nicholas's mask just now. Cole's mask. But why? Who? Jared? Grant?

All three brothers had the same build. They could have all been trading places, taking turns wearing the Nicholas disguise.

Surely not Grant. He seemed incapable of any of Nicholas's gentleness. But Jared? Possibly. She'd only spoken with him for a few moments, so it was difficult to judge, but he had shown instances of gentleness that had surprised her.

She pressed her hand over her eyes. It was too awful to contemplate. Had they been switching places only since Cole had been shot, or had it happened several times?

Another horrifying thought occurred to her. Had it been Cole she'd loved at night, or Jared? Or both?

No. Somehow, trading places in her bed seemed too unbelievable. It had been Cole each night. Hadn't it?

Nicholas was Cole. How could she have been so blind? How could she not have noticed?

He'd deceived her.

Had he laughed at her all those times she had

shrank from his frightening form as Nicholas? Had he mocked her when he tried, as Cole, to seduce her?

He'd lied to her.

All those times they had spoken, what had been truth? What had been fabrication to further his masquerade? What had possessed him to do it?

He'd frightened her.

She had been so terrified marrying a stranger, a man in a mask which supposedly concealed a scarred, disfigured face and body. She recalled her crippling fear each time she thought of being intimate with the masked baron. All of that had been for naught. A ruse.

Was their marriage a ruse, too? Was it even legal?

Cole's laughing blue eyes and self-deprecating grin settled before her face. He had told her that he felt a responsibility toward her. Had he married her to save her from marriage to Colonel Westin? Had he married her because he wanted her? Or because he felt he owed Armand?

Duty or love?

She sank down in the chair and hugged herself. Whatever his original motivation, he loved her now. Of that she had no doubt. Nor did she doubt that she loved him, both as the confident, roguish Cole, and as the thoughtful, gentle philosopher Nicholas.

But could she forgive him? Could she trust him to not break her heart? Or lie to her? He'd worn a mask. She wondered in what other ways he had deceived her. What else about him did she not know?

Through the window, she saw a rider gallop to the house. Alicia recognized Stephens on horseback. She squared her shoulders. Cole needed her now.

Stephens took command with confidence. Jeffries, Nicholas' valet, assisted.

Nicholas's valet. She wanted to scream.

Stephens cleaned out the infection and poured

distilled spirits over it. Cole moaned and beads of sweat formed on his skin. Tears stung Alicia's eyes. Through her anger and confusion, seeing him suffer caused her pain. Stephens applied a sweet-smelling poultice of several herbs, and bandaged the wounds with clean bandages.

Alicia sat back and looked him in the eye. "I hope this helps my husband."

The men froze. Jeffries ducked his head.

Stephens sighed wearily and nodded. "I knew you'd figure it out before he was ready to tell you."

"What's his real name?"

"Nicholas Richard Amesbury the Third. He has been called Cole since he was a child. I suspect few outside of his family even know that's not his Christian name."

Alicia was silent. She should have figured that one out. "And the titles? The baron is one of his father's secondary titles?"

He nodded. "I believe there are seven or eight family titles. This one's not common knowledge, I suppose."

"If he survives this, I'm going to make him miserable."

The corner of the valet's mouth lifted in ghost of a smile. "I hope that means you're planning on staying with him."

She turned to Jeffries. "Who were you before you became his valet?"

He managed a sick-looking smile. "A footman. When he said he needed two valets, I thought he was mad. Then when he swore me to secrecy and told me his plan, I knew he was."

"Who's been wearing the mask since Cole was shot? Jared?"

Stephens nodded wearily.

"How many other times have they traded places?"

"Twice, that I'm aware of; in London and now here."

"Stay with Cole, Stephens. Jeffries, please ask Jared to meet me in the parlor. And tell him to leave behind the mask and cane."

Looking supremely uncomfortable, the valets obeyed. Alicia went into the parlor and glared at the fire popping in the grate. She did not have to wait long.

Jared arrived, sleepy-eyed, rumpled and unshaven. If she hadn't been so angry with him, she might have found him adorable. He looked so exhausted that she felt a pang of remorse for having him awakened.

He held up his hands in surrender. "Don't shoot."

"I'm not holding a gun, you scoundrel, but I would like to throw something at you."

"Get in line," he muttered.

"Why didn't you tell me?"

He stared at her as if she'd sprouted a horn. "It isn't my secret to tell."

"What if Cole had died?" her voice rose to a shrill note.

"Then I'd tell you, of course. I certainly wouldn't carry on the charade. Tempting as it is." A rakish glint entered his eyes and one corner of his mouth lifted in such a perfect imitation of Cole that her heart gave a lurch.

Alicia sat down weakly and ignored his innuendo. "So you donned the disguise the moment you arrived here?"

"Yes." He threw himself down into a chair and stretched out his legs as she'd seen Cole do on so many occasions.

"And in London, when I saw you together in the park?"

"That was by accident."

She folded her arms over her chest and glared. "You put on a mask by accident?"

He smiled. "No. You saw me by accident. I wear the Nicholas costume to move freely about London. There were certain reasons I could not let my presence in London be known."

"I imagine there's a price on your head, what with being a pirate and all," she said dryly.

"I have enemies on both sides of the law. I've been using the baron's disguise in London the entire time you and Cole were here. And a few times before."

"Not..." she was fearful to ask. "Not ever with me?"

"No." Gravely serious, he moved to join her on the settee. "Alicia." He waited until she made eye contact with him. Anxiously, his blue-green eyes looked into hers. Next to Cole, he was the most handsome man she'd ever beheld.

She sighed, her heart softening. "I'm listening."

"His reasons are his own, but I can tell you he did not do it to hurt you. Or embarrass you."

"He's done both," she snapped indignantly. Without another word, she left the room. Her traitorous feet took her to Cole's side.

She sat next to him and began stroking his hair. Her thoughts swirled, some forging a coherent line, others spinning off unconnected. All those nights filled with guilt for rejecting her husband. Desiring Cole. The loneliness. The despair. If only he had told her.

But up until a few weeks ago, she would have rejected him, just as she had when he'd asked her to marry him.

She pulled herself together. In spite of the deception, she knew him well enough to draw her own conclusions. He had worn the mask to marry her, to protect her from Colonel Westin and save her family. She pressed her hands to her head. All that time, she'd thought Cole was a callous philanderer, trying to steal his cousin's wife, and that Nicholas wanted to cast her off.

He'd seemed different as Nicholas. It was possible Cole used his charming, practiced unconcern to protect the hurting man underneath. Only when he'd worn the mask, did he feel safe enough to show the man inside.

She smiled wryly. Perhaps he used his handsome face as a mask as much as he used the dark cloth.

Robert brought Alicia a tray of dinner and remained to eat with her. They sat in comfortable silence.

She struggled to swallow her food past her sore and battered throat.

"Did you know, too, Robbie?"

"Know what, Lissie?"

"That my husband, Nicholas, and Cole are the same man."

Robert let out an ungentlemanly expletive. "Are you sure?"

Alicia glanced over at the man lying on his stomach in bed. Despite her earlier hurt and anger, tenderness overcame her. "A woman knows her husband." She felt a smile tug at the corner of her mouth. "And his valets—both of them—confessed when I confronted them."

Robert shook his head. "But I've seen Nicholas since Cole was shot—Oooh. Someone else in the mask? Grant? No, Jared."

Alicia stabbed her chicken viciously. "Jared."

"Bastard sons trying to eliminate an entire family, murderous housekeepers, rakes disguised as scarred cripples and getting married, brothers switching places, what next?"

"I would appreciate some predictable joy."

343

"Nicholas. Cole. I should have seen that. At least you don't have to decide where your loyalties lie. You clearly loved them both."

She rubbed her eyes. "I did. And I suffered for it."

"Are you angry at him for lying to you?"

"Yes!" With her eyes fixed upon Cole's motionless form, she heaved a mighty sigh, releasing the last of her frustration, and shook her head. "Not any more. But I look forward to needling him about it for years to come."

But could she trust him?

After checking on Hannah, who was eating and looking noticeably better, she returned to Cole. He remained unconscious all evening, but his fever came down. She lay next to him, trying to offer him comfort with the warmth of her body, and finally fell into an exhausted slumber.

She awoke slowly, aware first that a large, masculine arm was wrapped around her, pulling her in closer. Then she realized that the rhythm of Cole's breathing had changed. His eyes were open and focused.

Her relief left her weak.

"Good morning." She touched his forehead. The fever had left him.

A tiny smile appeared in the corner of his mouth.

"How do you feel?"

He moistened his lips. "Like a man who wishes he had a whole body."

"To love your wife?"

The smile faded. He closed his eyes. "Do you hate me?"

She caressed his face. "I was hurt. Angry. But no, I do not hate you." Putting a light-hearted tone in her voice, she added. "It's fortunate you were unconscious or I might have done you bodily harm."

344

He did not smile. "I married you because I wanted you for my wife. I hated deceiving you." He coughed, and then winced. "You know my secret, now. And still you stayed with me," he said in wonder.

"Of course I did. I'm your wife."

"Is Hawthorne dead?"

"Yes. But, he made a full confession." Alicia related all she had learned about Hawthorne and his mother while Cole listened without expression.

Cole touched her face. "I nearly died when I thought he had hurt you."

"You were there to protect me just as you have been since we met."

A haunted expression flitted over his face. "I tried to do the right thing for you, Alicia, but I don't know if I have."

She tried to bring levity into her voice. "Of course you have. And now I no longer have to be torn between loving Nicholas, my gentle, thoughtful husband, or Cole, the reprehensible scoundrel who could always make me laugh."

Despite her effort to coax a smile from him, he remained grave. "I couldn't stand the thought of you wed to another man, especially someone like that boorish colonel. But you refused when I asked you to marry me. I just didn't know what else to do."

She swallowed, but her throat was still so battered and bruised that it caused pain. "Did you ever mock me behind my back?"

He blinked. "Mock you? Of course not, why would I?"

"Because I was afraid of you in that mask as the baron, but I was tempted by you as Cole."

"I hated deceiving you. But I couldn't tell you until I was sure you no longer hated me."

She sighed. "I was so stubborn."

"You are wonderful, and beautiful, and I'm

fortunate, indeed, you are even speaking to me."

"You and Jared must have shared a laugh over me seeing you together," she groused, still feeling petulant.

"Jared was enchanted. He threatened to steal you away if I don't treat you well. And truly, Alicia, I never laughed at you."

"And if I'd asked for an annulment?"

He stared straight ahead and let his breath out slowly. "I don't know. Since I married you in such a deceitful way—wearing a mask, and pretending to be another—the marriage could have been declared invalid. It still wouldn't have been a clean process, but it could have been done. If you'd wanted it badly enough. But even if I had, I would have pursued you as Cole until you agreed to marry me. Again. I could never truly let you go."

"Then our marriage is legal?" she asked.

"Yes. I stood next to you in front of vicar, used my full name, and spoke my vows, as did you. It is legal, unless you decide to contest it." He watched her.

"I have no intentions of contesting it, Cole."

As if a terrible burden had been lifted, he drew a deep breath. With his eyes closed, he raised her hand to his lips, kissed it and held it against his cheek. He was silent for so long, she thought he had fallen asleep again. "I hope you will love me someday. As I love you."

She touched his face. "I already do."

His hand tightened on hers. How she loved this man! If only she could truly trust him.

"But I fear it," she whispered.

"Fear what?"

"Loving you. Wondering how soon you'll break my heart. Whose bed you will be in."

He opened his eyes and in the depths of the blue hurt mingled with astonishment. "Alicia, I haven't gone near another woman in months. Not since before I married you."

"Why?"

He looked her in the eyes, and, despite his weakened state, spoke with emotion. "Because, for one thing, I spoke truthfully when I said I don't fully deserve my reputation. Remember the harpies? But more importantly, I have no desire to go near another woman. I want only you. And I want to be worthy of you. I love you. And I will be faithful to you all of my days. I vow it." His eyes pled for understanding.

She remembered the words *Maman* had recorded in her journal about forgiving her husband's past. They gave her the courage to believe Cole now. Her heart assured her he spoke sincerely. Tears formed in her eyes, and the swelling in her heart left no room for doubt.

With a gentle hand, he caressed her face and then he kissed her, tenderly, hungrily.

Mindful of his injury, Alicia snuggled against him and held him until he went back to sleep; a healthy sleep, undisturbed by fever or delirium.

She kissed his brow and tightened her arms around him. She had hoped her husband would one day show her his face when he trusted her, but she never dreamed that it would reveal the other man she loved. Her beloved husband. Cole.

Marveling at the contentment that soaked through her, she held on to Cole—Nicholas—and thanked her Maker for the gift of him, and the healing he brought to her wounded heart. And the fulfillment of her dreams.

CHAPTER 30

"So it appears I'll be landlocked for the next few months," Jared said with obvious reluctance.

Alicia walked beside Cole, her fingers twined in his, as they skirted the lake in the Amesbury family estate. Alicia looked up at Jared striding next to her husband, looking more like Cole's twin than his younger brother by fourteen months. Jared pulled at his cravat as if unaccustomed to it.

"Isn't that rather dangerous for you to walk about openly in England?" Alicia asked.

Jared's penetrating gaze swept over her. He and Cole shared the ability to make one think keeping one's thoughts private would be impossible. "Yes, but on land, I'm simply Jared Amesbury, second son of the fifth Earl Tarrington. I never use my real name when I'm at sea. I hated to besmirch the family name while I played pirate." He quirked a self-depreciating grin and looked so much like Cole that Alicia blinked.

Cole snorted. "Could've done better than a stupid name like Black Jack."

"It was all I could come up with in a pinch," Jared said easily with a shrug.

"So no more donning a Nicholas disguise when you come on land?" she teased with a smile.

A glint that exceeded Cole's in wickedness glimmered in his eye. "Too bad we couldn't play the part beyond a brotherly embrace."

Alicia put her hand over her mouth to stifle a laugh at his brazen suggestion.

Cole punched him in the arm. "Watch it, *little* brother, I can still thrash you," he growled, but an affectionate light shone in his face.

Jared grinned in reply. "To answer your question, Sister-in-law, I will wear the disguise whenever I go into London, at least for a while, but in the small town where I've let the house for the summer, no one should know my face. Besides, I've cut my hair, shaved my beard, and with these ridiculously uncomfortable clothes—" he gestured to his finely tailored suit "—I doubt any former foes, or victims, would recognize me as Black Jack. My first mate hardly knows me now." He pulled again at his cravat until it became quite rumpled.

The first flowers of spring dotted the lawn by the lake. After Cole had sufficiently healed, they had settled a whole and well Hannah in a reputable school for girls where she blissfully made new friends. After seeing to it that repairs on Robert's manor house were underway, they returned home and enjoyed a magical Christmas together. Then she and Cole had spent the rest of the winter and spring in the happiest months of Alicia's life.

This morning, Jared had come for a visit on his way to a country house he would use for the summer. Alicia drew a deep breath, perfectly happy, perfectly at peace. She looked up at her husband, gratified to see him fully recovered. Every time she thought of how close she had come to losing him, she could barely hold back the tears. She squeezed his hand. He released her hand so he could put an arm around her.

Jared shot them a look of reproach. "Perhaps I should leave you two alone?"

"Would you mind?" Cole grinned wolfishly and Alicia blushed.

"When the staff gets the house prepared, I'd love to have you both visit," Jared said. "That is, if you can refrain from indulging in these sickening displays of affection."

Alicia smiled. How easily she smiled these days! A light heart did that to a person. "We would be happy to visit. That is, if the doctor approves."

She touched her stomach and felt the hint of roundness that had recently begun to develop there. Cole placed his hand on her abdomen, infusing her with warmth, and looked at her with such tenderness that tears pricked her eyes.

Self-consciously, she glanced at Jared and then blinked at the unexpected wistfulness in his expression as he watched them share such an intimate moment.

Jared looked away and cleared his throat, tugging at his poor, abused cravat again. Then he brought a careless tone to his voice. "I can't picture you as a father, Cole. That seems to defy reason."

Cole chuckled. "I agree. Alicia deserves your pity for her having me as the father of her children."

"You deserve my pity just for being stuck with this lout," he whispered to Alicia. "Do you wish to escape? With me? The house I've let is quite fine. You even have the correct name, so no one will ever be the wiser."

"It might be hard for her to ignore the knife sticking out of your heart, you blackguard," Cole warned.

Alicia glanced at her husband. She sighed blissfully. Her husband. Cole. "I can see your atrocious manners must be a family failing, Husband. He's as incorrigible as you were."

"I, at least, was trying to steal my own wife, not my brother's."

"But you led me to believe that you were trying to steal your cousin's wife," she reminded him.

"See? He's a cad," Jared interjected. "You deserve someone better. Someone honest."

Alicia raised her brows. "A pirate is more honest?"

He puffed out his chest. "I'm an honest pirate."

Cole choked and Alicia patted him in consolation. "Poor dear. With this family, it's a wonder you've turned out as well as you have."

Cole and Jared exchanged a look. "She hasn't met Christian, yet," they said simultaneously, then burst out into laughter.

Cole shook his head. "Not until she's firmly in love with me. It will be several more years before I risk that encounter."

"Why?" Alicia wanted to know. "From everything you've told me about him, he's perfectly respectable."

"Not merely perfectly respectable. *Perfect*," Cole replied mournfully.

"The perfectly perfect Christian," Jared added in a sing-song voice as if they'd said that phrase repeatedly, and probably at poor Christian's expense.

"The youngest. Mother's favorite," Cole explained. "He always does and says everything exactly as he ought. If he wasn't so humble and likeable, I'd hate him."

"I plotted to kill him once," Jared offered cheerfully.

Alicia gasped. "You didn't!"

Jared blinked as if surprised she'd oppose such a thing. "I didn't carry out my plan. Mother found out." He let out a slow breath as if he'd been the one who nearly lost his life.

"Oh, dear, what have I gotten myself into?" Alicia fanned herself dramatically.

Cole swept her into his arms and kissed her soundly. "A lifetime of happiness, my dear."

"It certainly won't be dull," she agreed.

Rudely ignoring Jared, Cole kissed Alicia again.

This time his lips lingered. She sighed and leaned against him, counting herself fortunate indeed, and vowed again to love him for all eternity. Then, immersed in his scent, his warmth, his kiss, she thought of nothing at all.

A word about the author...

Donna has had a passion for writing since the age of 8 when she wrote her first short story. During her sophomore year in high school, she wrote her first full-length novel, a science fiction romance. She wrote her second novel during her senior year, a fantasy romance. Needless to say, English and Creative Writing were always her favorite subjects. In between caring for six children, (7 counting her husband) she manages to carve out time to indulge in her writing obsession, with varying degrees of success, although she writes most often late at night instead of sleeping. A native of Arizona, she is currently a member of Desert Rose RWA where she serves as the chapter secretary, and is a member of Beau Monde, a Regency Chapter of RWA. She is the winner of two RWA Chapter contests and has finaled in several others. And yes, all of her heroes are patterned after her husband of 20 years, who continues to prove that there really is a happily ever after.

Visit Donna at www.donnahatch.net

Made in the USA
Columbia, SC
29 July 2019